FURTHER ADVENTURES OF ELLI & OVI

An account of the brothers' brave mission to tackle the mysterious and elusive Taxman with the help of family and friends (both old and new)

P P Leonard

CONTENTS

Cover Art by: Gill Gill Illustration

This story is a sort of 'spin-off' from *The Fictionary* in that it takes us off on a diversion into the prehistoric world of the cavemen brothers Elli and Ovi. It does not form part of the main narrative of The Fictionary, so in that sense is an 'optional extra' for readers who enjoyed their escapades with the many exotic 'colourful' creatures who became their companions.

If you liked Al the Mythological Creature as well as Hopi and Wishi the nevasaurus cousins, then I have good news, Dear Reader, they are back centre stage in this adventure. There are plenty of new characters for you to meet too, including my personal favourites Oxo the Great Poltroon and the white winged-slipper birds who always operate in the same pairs for a very good reason.

I dedicate this book to Laurel and Hardy who were very much the 'model' for Elli and Ovi, in particular the comic genius that was Stan Laurel who for me was quite simply the funniest person of the twentieth century. Long may his many gifts to us be remembered and enjoyed!

Chapter One

Taxing times

'Right! I'll give it another try,' said Ovi, putting on his fiercest 'let's-do-this' face and clearing his throat. '*Ahem!* Excuse me, kind sir; I wonder if I could interest you in some of this *honey* of mine in return for one of those lovely, ripe bananas of yours?'

'No-no-*no-ooo!* Not "*honey*"*!*' Elli's patience was clearly wearing thin. 'How many more times! It is *not* "honey"! Neither is it "sunny" *nor* "bunny"—oh, and it is most definitely *not* "funny"!' He held a couple of flat round pebbles up close to Ovi's nose. 'One last time; please listen carefully. This is "*money*" "mo–ney" —Gottit?'

Elli and Ovi were down by the wadi, where they often went to have a good '*splash*' after the rain. They were seated cross-legged and facing each other. Elli had a bunch of bananas in front of him and Ovi had a couple of melons – one chock-full of nice big juicy maggots. Between them was a pile of circular disc-shaped pebbles.

'Right … gotcha … ' said Ovi doing his utmost to sound interested. 'I'll remember next time promise … "mo–ney".'

'Yes, that's right "money".'

'Not pebbles?'

'No, *not* pebbles!' Elli's eyes rolled upward with frustration. '"Mo–ney" … money-money-*money!*'

'Not small wheels?'

'No, of course they're not small wheels you poltroon! Wheels are never completely round; you know they always have to have a flat edge to stop them rolling away; and anyway— '

'*Rumble—grrr-rrr … rumble!*'

The ground suddenly shook causing the melons to wobble and the pebbles to rattle. Elli gave Ovi a 'what-was-that?' look to which Ovi replied with a 'don't-ask-me' glance followed by a 'I-think-it-might-have-been-my-belly-Elli-I-*am*-feeling-rather-peckish-you-know' expression.

'Aaa-anyway,' said Elli returning to his theme. 'Let's try this again shall we? I'm determined to get you to understand my new idea; I need you to grasp the basic concept of "money" – of how it works as a means of exchange … *Ahem!* … Right, now you've got a couple of melons and I've got a bunch of bananas … right?'

'Right.'

'And I want one of your melons … right?'

'Right.'

'And you want one of my bananas … right?'

'Right.'

'Right. Now listen carefully. This is the important bit.'

Ovi frowned the most serious 'I've-got-this-honest-I-do!' frown he could muster.

'I'll give you *three* of these … ' Elli held up three 'money-pebbles', 'for *one* of your melons which, in turn, will enable you to give me one back for a banana.'

Ovi looked hard at Elli. Then he looked down and equally hard at his melons, before across and even harder at Elli's bananas; and then, finally, long and extremely hard at the "money" being offered.

'You give me three pebbles for a melon?'

Elli nodded.

'And I give you one pebble back for a banana?'

'Exactly.'

'*Rumble—rumble—grrr-rrr … rumble-drumble!*'

Elli glanced up and tutted at the loud rumbling that was distracting them, then returned his attention to Ovi and nodded.

'Now you're getting it; that's how money works. It's a means of exchange. Don't you see?'

Ovi suddenly burst into a broad smile.

'You know something Elli. I think I actually *do* see what you're getting at.'

'At last! *hoo-ooo-ray-yyy!*'

'But I have a better idea.'

'What's that?'

'Why don't you just give me three bananas for one of my melons—four if you want the one with maggots?'

'*No-no-no!*' cried Elli, frantically waving the pebbles in front of Ovi's nose. 'You've missed the point entirely! Now, listen carefully— '

'I'll take that!'

Elli and Ovi had become so engrossed in money matters, they'd failed to spot a stocky man with a mane of jet-black hair sticking up in stark erratic spikes coming rapidly towards them. They'd also not noticed that something very big had blocked out the sun and drenched them completely in shadow. The man strode very purposefully with the attitude that nothing – repeat *nothing* – was going to get in his way. The moment he'd rounded the corner in the wadi and spotted the two brothers he'd zeroed in on them and started to run. The '*snatch'* itself was swift and painless. One moment the brothers had a bunch of bananas, two melons and a pile of pebbles; next they had half a bunch, half a pile and melon singular – minus maggots.

'*Oy!*' shouted Ovi, '*Give me back my melon!*'

'Who in swamp-fume-blazes do you think you are?' cried Elli. 'And what do you think you're doing?'

'I'm the Taxman,' called the stranger over his shoulder, 'and I'm collecting my tax that's due.'

The shadow passed leaving Elli and Ovi blinking and looking blankly at each other in the bright daylight. Continuing to blink, they looked back towards the figure and saw that he'd completely disappeared taking his shadow-maker with him.

'Where did he go?' said Ovi after a long pause.

'It looked like he was heading toward our cave,' replied Elli.

All of a sudden, a great big penny dropped!

The two brothers ran as fast as they could to catch the Taxman before he could reach their cave, but by the time they arrived they were too late; he'd been and gone. Ovi's wife was standing motionless, staring wide-eyed with disbelief at the fire pit, her finger poised in mid nag-wag and her mouth still open wide in astonishment. Elli's wife too was frozen with shock, holding a hyena leg and staring blankly at the point where the Taxman had disappeared. Stiff as a tree trunk, she'd toppled to one side and was leaning at a precarious angle against the cave wall.

'What's – *puff* – just – *puff* – happened?' cried Elli, gasping for breath after his hasty climb up the mountainside.

'Has someone – *puff-puff* – called – *puff* – "Taxman" – *puff* – been here?'

Ovi's wife, still in a daze, nodded slowly.

'We're too – *puff* – late Ovi!' shouted Elli over his shoulder. 'He – *puff-puff* – beat us to it!'

A loud '*Whe-eee-eee-eee-eze!*' sounded in reply. Just then, a red-faced-and-completely-out-of-breath Ovi staggered into view, gesturing with his hands that Elli was welcome to continue proceedings without him.

'What exactly – *puff* – did this "Taxman" take?' asked Elli, looking frantically about the cave's entrance.

Without moving a jot and still leaning at an angle, his wife answered, her voice unfamiliarly soft with a faraway dreamlike quality.

'He took the biggest of the hyenas and the best bits of the rest.'

'You mean – *wheeze* – we're low on – *wheeze* – hyena?' blurted Ovi, finally managing some speech.

'He also took the thingummy,' mumbled Ovi's wife, referring to the water vessel the brothers had returned with the year before from their quest to find God's lunchbox which they hadn't gotten around to giving a name to.

'*And*, he took the hottest part of the fire,' added Elli's.

'You mean – *puff* – we're low on – *wheeze* – fire?'

'Anything else?' Panic-stricken, Elli rushed over to his precious pile of inventor bric-a-brac and began rummaging furiously. 'Did he take anything else – anything important?'

The wives looked at each other and shrugged their shoulders.

'What about the rest of our food supplies?' blurted Ovi, suddenly regaining his breath and matching his brother's panic. 'Did he touch our store of maggots?'

'Oh yes, the maggots … ' The wives both nodded. 'He took those.'

'*Great-Sun-in-the-Sky!*' Ovi fell to his knees, his face racked with tortuous pain. 'Does this-this-this *Taxman* know no mercy!'

'Everything seems to be all right here.' Elli re-emerged from his pile of inventions looking relieved and proudly carrying his "bow" and half-finished "wheel". 'It's all there. Nothing taken as far as I can— '

There was a loud '*clatter*' and Elli's prototype "wall" collapsed. His look of relief turned to one of despondency as he realised the main base stones had been removed. Putting down his "bow" and "wheel", Elli went over to his wife, grabbed her shoulders and gently stood her up straight.

'Are you sure he didn't take anything else dearest wife?'

She shook her head.

'There's nothing missing of any importance or value?'

Again, she shook her head; then she shuffled off back into the cave for a much-needed lie down. Suddenly she paused and turned to look back at Elli and Ovi.

'What is it dearest?'

'There *was* something else; I almost forgot.'

'What?' said the brothers in unison.

'He took Granddad.'

'Remind me – *burp* – dear,' belched Gusto. 'What exactly are we – *pf-pf-fff-fart* – doing up here?'

'Well darling,' said Zatt. 'You know I want to try putting some 'cloud' in my dainties to see if it will make them lighter?'

'Right – *belch* – gotcha! Great idea, by the way – *burble* – babe. Should make 'em nice n' tasty too, 'specially if you use those – *p-p—ppp-fff-art* – chewy-looking extra fluffy white ones.'

'And you may recall dearest, that we couldn't reach them from below no matter how high you managed to throw the kids.'

'Oh yeah! – *pf-pf-fff-fart* – You're right! I forgot that was why we were – *belch* – flinging them out of the tallest tree in the jungle. *Ha ha ha!* Boy, that was – *burp-belch* – fun! Oh boy … *Ha-aaa ha ha ha!*'

'Aaa-anyway, my darling; that's why we're here—*ooo look!* Here come some nice tasty-looking white ones now!'

Elli's twin sister Zatt and her husband Gusto were standing on the edge of an extremely high cliff on the other side of the mountain from Elli and Ovi's cave which overlooked the jungle far below where the Treetop Tribe lived. They were so high up they were well above the clouds and able to look directly down on the fluffy delicate-looking little darlings as they flitted past below.

'*Aaa-aaa-all* righty! – *burp* – they're the finger-lickin' yummy-scrummy little fellas all right! Tell me my beautiful babelicious box-of-tricks; how're we – *belp* –gonna catch 'em?'

'We're going to use these.'

Zatt proudly produced two leather bundles. She handed one to Gusto and indicated he should copy her as she un-bundled hers and spread it out on the ground. Gusto duly did the same, and in barely a jiffy the platform at the top of the cliff with its bottomless-looking sheer drop had two leather sheets spread out upon it each made of several animal hides stitched together with good sturdy leather straps tied to all four corners.

'Right dearest, that's that,' said Zatt, standing back to admire their work. 'Our "cloud-catchers" are ready!'

'Oh boy, oh boy, oh boy – "*cloud-catchers*"*!* We've got – *burp* – "cloud-catchers"! I can't – *pf-pf-pf-fff-fart-belp* – wait! What happens now?'

'Well my darling, you take hold of a pair of straps in each hand like this … ' Zatt bent down, grabbed her straps then stood up again. Gusto eagerly copied her and in much-less-than-a-jiffy they were standing side-by-side on the cliff edge with their leather "cloud-catchers" to their rear.

'Oh boy, oh boy; what – *belch* – now?'

'We jump—aiming for those little fellows. Hopefully, some of their yummy fluff will get caught in the catcher as we pass through.'

'Did you just – *burp* – say we – *belch* – "jump"?'

'*Grrr-rrr-rumble—rumble-drumble!*'

'Was that you dearest?'

'*Er* – Nope! At least I – *belch* – don't think it was me. It could, of course, have been my— '

'*Shh-hhh-hhh!*'

'*Rumble—gr-rrr-rrr-rumble-drumble!*'

Zatt span round to scour the mountainside surrounding them, but there was nothing to be seen that could account for the sudden tremors they'd just felt.

'Did you hear that dearest?'

'Yep – *burp* – sure did!'

Zatt looked once more, but still couldn't see anything that might have made such an ominous noise. Shrugging her shoulders, she turned back to face Gusto and smiled.

'*Right!* Ready to go cloud-catching?'

'Why the heck – *burp* – not?'

'Well, then … let's go *Gusto-ooo-ooo-ooo-ooo!*'

Zatt leapt from the ledge and plummeted towards the clouds, her catcher billowing out behind parachute-style. Gusto paused for the briefest of moments in order to glance at his wife with loving admiration … then leapt after her.

'You sure are where it's – *belch* – at *Za-aaa-aaa-aaa-att!*'

The instant they were both in the air with their animal hides stretched taut behind them the entire mountainside became smothered in shadow.

'*I'll take that!*'

Just as Zatt was about to reach her target cloud a pair of hands appeared from behind a protruding bluff and grabbed hold of her leather straps. With lightning-quick reactions she partly-managed to fend off the snatch, but only after two of her straps had been taken. Struggling to recover with her two remaining straps, she looked up to check on Gusto and saw the hands readying themselves for their second snatch.

'*Gusto! Look Out!*'

'What's up – *belch* – babe?'

'*And … I'll take that!*'

Distracted by Zatt's cry, Gusto reacted a tad too late and the hands succeeded in grabbing all four of his straps.

'Grab hold of the sheet dearest! For goodness sake grab something—*anything* – *quick!*'

'He took *Granddad!*' exclaimed The Great Ug; his face staring wide-eyed in consternation and disbelief.

'Yes, Oh Great Ug,' Elli nodded vigorously, 'I'm afraid so. We don't know where— '

'As well as all our maggots,' said Ovi leaning across in front of Elli.

The Great Ug lowered his head in disbelief. In the background several of his wives giggled*. Elli and Ovi, along with their wives and children, were standing in a destitute cluster in what was left of the Palace (the huge tree nest at the top of the tallest tree in the jungle and home of The Great Ug, leader of the Treetop Tribe).

(In case your memory is of a similar ilk to mine, Dear Reader, I think it might a good idea for me to remind you that The Great Ug and Granddad had been close buddies as young men and were standing beside each other when they were struck by lightning. Granddad had spoken in rhyme ever since and The Great Ug's hair had been left in five permanent shiny spikes around his face, giving him the appearance of "a real star"!)

Elli and Ovi's families had had to leave their cave and make the trek to the jungle because the Taxman had left them with very little food, and they weren't able to cook what meagre morsels were left because when Elli's "wall" had collapsed, the rocks had tumbled into the fire pit putting out the few remaining remnants of their fire. Their journey to the Palace had then been made all the more difficult by the fact that the Taxman had taken most of the tree creeper network used for jungle transportation. Then, when they'd arrived at the Palace, they were in for an even bigger shock because much of the luscious green foliage that had previously made it comfortable had been snatched, leaving just bare twigs and stalks plus the odd straggler of a leaf – which tickled (*hence the sporadic giggling).

'Ahoy-yyy everyone!' The shrill-but-distant sound of a woman's shriek made everybody jump. *'Look out belo-ooo-ow!'*

Everyone did as they were told and looked out—below.

'No-no-no, you poltroons! Look up! Look up!'

Everybody dutifully obeyed and there – coming at them fast – was Zatt. She was dangling from her "cloud-catcher" and struggling with her two remaining leather straps to control her descent. A little above her – but coming down even faster – was Gusto. He was holding onto the corners of his catcher with just his fingers, teeth and toes.

'*Clear for landing!*' she cried.

Just then, one of Zatt's straps snagged on a spiky bough causing her to swirl round it like a poltroon with one of its legs stuck in its nest. On her third circuit she became entangled with Gusto and the two of them twirled round and round the bough until they came to rest in a bundle with one of his feet jammed up against her chin and her arms knotted round his neck.

'Hello Sis,' said Elli once Zatt and Gusto had finally untangled themselves and joined the assembly in the Palace. 'What sort of experiment was that?'

'We were trying to get some cloud samples for me to try in my dainties, but without sufficient strapping it's really hard to control those cloud-catchers.'

'Well, why didn't you put more strapping on?' suggested Ovi attempting to be helpful.

'We did have more strapping on you poltroon!' Zatt rounded on Ovi. 'You don't really think we would jump off an extremely high mountain without the correct strapping, do you?'

Ovi started to 'yes'-nod, then thought better of it and started to 'no'-shake, then thought again … and got completely confused.

'We'd just taken off,' continued Zatt, 'when this man I'd never seen before reached out from behind a rock yelling '*I'll take that!*'. Before I knew it, he'd grabbed half of my straps and all of Gusto's. Oh, and there was this dark shad— '

'Hhh-Mum-nnn! Hhh-Mum-nnn!' One of Zatt's children suddenly appeared. He was painted bright blue and had a yellow stick up each nostril. 'Hhh-mum. Hhh-you'll hhh-nevhhher hhh-guess hhh-what hhh-just nnn-happhhhen-nnn-ed hhh-Mum-nnn.'

'What have I told you? Take your sticks out when you're speaking.'

'Hhh-sorry hhh-Mum-nnn.' The lad removed the sticks and, much to everyone's surprise (apart from Zatt, of course), each one had a large green ant on the end. 'A strange man just came to your laboratory Mum and took loads of stuff. He said it was "due max" or—wait a minute, was it "tox"?'

'It wasn't "*TAX*" by any chance, was it?' asked Elli, sounding suspicious.

'"Tax"? *Yeah* Uncle Elli, it was "tax"! How did you know that?'

'Never you mind.' Elli assumed the air of a master sleuth gathering clues at the scene of a crime, and began pacing up and down with his hands clasped behind his back. 'I am merely examining the evidence as it presents itself. Please go on. What precisely did he take from your mother's laboratory, this man collecting his so-called … "tax"?'

'He's taken your tyrannosaurus turds Mum, the ones covered with green mould. He said he liked the colour.'

'*Blast!*' exclaimed Zatt before muttering to herself. 'How am I supposed to perfect my 'anti-fart dainty' recipe? That green mould took ages to cultivate.'

'Anything else?' said Elli, pretending to smoke one of Zatt's cigarettes and narrowing his eyes.

'Yeah, loads Uncle Elli. All of Mum's bladders of dog puke are gone and most of her poltroon eggs too, except for the ones we'd taken the spikes off for— '

'Not my poltroon eggs too!' cried Zatt in anguish. 'They're irreplaceable. Everybody knows poltroons only lay eggs when they really, really have to. Anything else?'

'Nah, nothing important, just the baby tyrannosauruses.'

'What *all* of them? Even the one with big ears?'

'Yup.'

Zatt span round to glare at Gusto and fix him with one of her fiercest 'this-is-serious' stares.

'It looks like this-this *robber* has taken most of the stuff in our laboratory and wiped out my *entire* experimentation programme. What are you going to do about it?'

Gusto tutted an exaggerated '*tut*', raised his eyebrows expressively and put his hand to his mouth to politely cover a mild burp; he then started to shuffle from foot to foot, looking decidedly uncomfortable.

'Well?'

Gusto was saved by his son who suddenly remembered something.

'Oh, I forgot Mum; he almost took your last sheet of paper, but I managed to hide it from him just in time … '

He produced a flattish brown blob of irregular shape from behind his back and held it out to his mother.

'Well done son.' Zatt took the brown blank blotch and stared at it with a forlorn smile as if it were a tiny ray of hope in an otherwise bleak world.

'Well, well, well.' Elli-the-sleuth resumed his pacing. 'It would seem he has taken quite a "tax-haul"—this *robber!* Not only has he robbed us in our cave, taking nearly all of our food and cooking equipment *as well as* Granddad, he's also robbed you folks here in the jungle, taking most of the creepers and foliage, as well as a lot of Zatt's experimentation—*er,* stuff.'

'How do you know it's the same man?' asked Zatt, emerging from her gloom and beginning to apply her scientific mind to the situation.

'Oh, it's the same man all right Sis. And what's more I even know his name.'

'You do?'

'Yes – he calls himself ... *the "Taxman"!*'

'*A-aaa-ahem!*' The Great Ug had heard enough. He coughed a loud magisterial cough and lifted his hand for silence. The Palace duly fell completely quiet (apart from the occasional giggle).

'My friends; it is clear to me that this-this despicable *fiend*, this so-called "Taxman" or whoever he is ... ' He paused and looked questioningly around the assembly as if to say 'Does-anyone-actually-*know*-who-he-is?' In return, all he could see in reply was a sea of wide-eyed 'don't-ask-me-I've-got-no-idea-who-he-is-or-where-he-came-from' looks and shrugs. 'Well, whoever he is, he has *got* to be *stopped!* Why, this devilish villain has even had the audacity to take one of my wives, or so I believe ... ' He looked questioningly at his Head Wife who nodded. 'Which one?' he muttered through the side of his mouth. 'Og,' she hissed. 'Who?' he asked. She smiled politely at the gathering then shouted in his ear.

'*OG!*'

'Ah yes, Og. My poor Og! My poor darling Og! My poor, poor, *poor* sweet Og. Og-Og-Og! *Gone-Gone-Gone!* And Granddad too. Both taken! Both gone! Both whisked away from us and snatched into this so-called Taxman's fiendish clutches ... along with loads of other important stuff ... far too much for me to remember!'

'Oh-oh– I know! I know! I have an idea!' exclaimed Zatt, excitedly brandishing her remaining sheet of dirty brown paper. 'Why don't we make … a "list"?'

The Great Ug gave a questioning look at Elli who in turn passed it on to Gusto who then batted it over to Ovi before they all looked back at Zatt and spoke in unison.

'A "what"?'

'A "list".' Zatt waved the rather putrid and very pongy brown 'sheet'. 'We can use this last piece of my paper to make a list. Look I'll show you … ' Zatt took out a stick of dried out poltroon poo and began to scribble. 'We know he's taken;

… moul–dy … ty–ran–no … saur–us … turds

… blad–ders … of … dog–puke

… ba–by ty–ran–no … saur–uses

… a–wife–called … Og

… Grand–dad— '

'Oh, I see what you're doing,' blurted Ovi. 'Don't forget the melons!'

'Right … mel— '

'Oh, *and* all the maggots!' continued Ovi undaunted by his sister's sharp 'slow-down' glare.

'Right … mag— '

'Oh, *and* that—oh, what was it now – "moany?" "manky?"'

'You mean "Money"!' exclaimed Elli. 'He's right Sis. Don't forget my money. It was the very first thing this Taxman chappie took actually.'

'Right … "mo … ney" … ' Zatt stopped scribbling and looked up with a quizzical expression. 'What's that exactly?'

'It's something I'm still working on; I've not quite perfected it yet.' Elli warmed to his favourite subject – his 'inventions' – with a cocky wobble of his head. 'It's actually a means of excha— '

'G-G-G-ROO-OWW-WWW-LLLL!!!'

A monstrous reptilian head the size of squadron of poltroons in side-flight suddenly punched its way through the tree's branches and burst into the Palace making everyone scream with fear and run about in panic, desperately trying to hide. The giant head was a murky dark brown in colour with blue and green splotches. It had large yellowy-green eyes with a tiny horn sticking out behind each one and an enormous mouth with multiple layers of gnosh-gnashing teeth. Rather unusually for such a fierce-looking gargantuan monster it also had long floppy furry ears rather like a modern-day Basset Hound except they were each the size of an ornamental lawn – and they were cocked-up like a dog's when it's trying to listen.

'Sorry about the 'growl; I *do* apologise,' boomed a rich velvety voice which had the distinct reverberant roar of a giant reptilian monster whilst, at the same time, sounded surprisingly educated and polite. 'I accidentally trod on a large tyrannosaurus as I approached your lovely big tree and it – rather foolishly I hasten to add – attempted to nibble one of my lower appendages. *Ahem!* I wonder if you could possibly help me. I'm looking for two cave-dwellers called Elli and Ovi or failing that their sister who I believe goes by the name of Zatt.'

'*HOPI!*' exclaimed Elli and Ovi in unison, jointly peeping out from beneath the branch they'd dived under.

'*Why are you here?*' shouted Ovi.

'Well, well, well, what a fortuitous stroke of good luck! If it isn't Elli and Ovi, the very humans I'm looking for.'

Hopi's face burst into a broad grin, fully exposing his formidable dentitional arsenal. There were teeth in his mouth for every possible eventuality: flesh-ripping and bone-crushing, of course; but also; gnoshing, gnashing and gnarling, and even gristle-grinding. The act of smiling made his teeth '*jangle*' together with a noise that was similar to the sound made by heavy metal medieval weaponry; all of which caused much of the Palace's remaining foliage to shake and tremble with untrammelled fear … and the giggling to almost cease.

'That's funny,' said Ovi to Elli as they broke cover to greet their old friend. 'I thought his head was bigger than that. What do you think?'

Elli didn't say anything, but he did narrow his eyes to study Hopi's head as he clambered over another branch.

'Oh, what a relief!' said Hopi. 'I'm so pleased to find you at last!'

While the two brothers were making their way forward, Hopi's smile waned then disappeared; his huge reptilian eyes filled with tears and his large floppy ears drooped.

'Why, whatever's the matter Hopi?' said Ovi with concern. 'Are you all right?'

'Something terrible has happened in the Ancient Jungle Ovi. We need your help; and, I'm afraid to report, it is a matter of some considerable urgency.'

'Oh dear, I'm so sorry to hear that,' replied Elli as he dropped down onto a convenient bough immediately in front of Hopi's face. 'What exactly is the prob— '

'*OW!*'

Elli jumped with fright at the sudden shriek that had issued forth from beneath his feet. Looking down, he realised he'd just trodden on The Great Ug's face. He was peering up from the sparse foliage, busily re-straightening the points of his hair spikes.

'*Um* – before we proceed any further Hopi, do you mind if we introduce you to some of the others?'

'Of course not my dear chap.' Hopi sniffed and, with a big effort, managed to force a polite smile; he even got his ears to perk back up. 'My apologies for not introducing myself properly to begin with.'

'Right you are then. *Erm* – Hopi, this is The Great Ug, the leader of the Treetop Tribe whose home this is; it's called "The Palace".' Elli looked down and tried to coax The Great Ug out of his hiding place. The old man looked back up at him and shook his star-shaped head vigorously in a 'not-on-your-nelly' kind of way.

'It's all right Oh Great Ug. This is Hopi the nevasaurus. He's – *um* – he's a very, *very* good friend of ours who we met last year. Don't you remember? We told you all about him.'

'It is an honour and a pleasure to meet you Oh Great Ug. I've heard a lot about you.' Hopi looked admiringly around the large tree top and nodded appreciatively. '*Mmm-mmm-mmm* … nice Palace you have here.'

Following an earnest 'please-don't-be-rude' look from Elli, The Great Ug reluctantly rose to his feet and stood before his giant reptilian visitor.

'Any friend of Elli and Ovi's is a friend of the Treetop Tribe and welcome here anytime. We are pleased to meet you Hopinevas-russ … Hopisaurus-ness … Hopinesaur— '

'"Hopi" will do just fine Your Great Ug-ness.'

'Oh right, "Hopi" it is then. I'd like to introduce my wives if I may.'

'Oh, yes indeed Great Ug. T'would be an absolute delight and truly a pleasure.'

'Ladies? Ladies?' The Great Ug waved his arms, urging his wives to stand up. 'Come now ladies, present yourselves to – *um* – to Mister Hopi.'

Hopi smiled politely, once more jangling his awesome array of teeth. This prompted lots of delicate-but-decidedly-firm little 'No's' from the surrounding tangle of twigs and foliage, forcing The Great Ug to re-double his cajoling. 'Come now my dears, don't be shy. Mister Nevasaurus here has come a long way in order to pay us a visit. You wouldn't want him to think us rude now, would you?'

Slowly but surely, one-by-one, The Great Ug's wives started to '*pop*' out of the foliage like sprouting shoots. As they popped up, each one said 'Hello Hopi' in a cute tribal-leader's-wifey kind of a way.

'Hello Hopi.'

'Hello Hopi.'

'Hello Hopi.'

'*Hello Hopi!*' boomed a much louder voice from one of the upper branches where she'd been hiding. It was Zatt.

With all eyes looking at her, she grabbed hold of one of the creepers the Taxman had left behind and swung dramatically down to land on the bough beside Elli and Ovi, right in front of Hopi and beside The Great Ug.

'Allow me to introduce myself.' She planted her feet firmly on the branch and placed her clenched fists upon her hips (one still clutching her "list"). 'I'm Zatt!'

'*Hello Hopi big buddy!*' Another deeper and much more phlegmatic voice boomed out on high; making all present look up once again. This time it was Gusto. He too grabbed a creeper and – determined to match his wife's dramatic entrance – he too let fly. Unfortunately, he missed the all-important bough and flew right past the gathering to plummet out of sight. 'I'm Gustooo-ooo-ooo-ooo-ooo-ooo-ooo'

A fleeting flicker of amusement flicked across Hopi's face but, being a well-mannered enormous reptile, he quickly resumed his polite poise.

'Ah, the-one-and-only-Zatt; we meet at last! I have heard a lot about you from your brothers. We really ought to compare notes on therapeutic potions sometime. You never know, I may have some interesting concoctions for you to try.'

'I'd … I'd really like that Hopi.' Zatt was clearly warming to the erudite-and-seemingly-quite-knowledgeable gigantic reptiloid.

Just then a loud *'BU-UUU-UUU-URP!'* sounded and Gusto reappeared, poking his head 'Hopi-style' up through the scantily-foliaged branches. His burp was so loud the humans present had to bang their ears to get them working again. Hopi took advantage of the pause that Gusto's 'entrance' had created to address the gathering.

'My friends—incidentally, I very much hope I may call you all "friends"?' Everybody nodded vigorously to indicate his-or-her ready and willing compliance with the fearsome reptile's request. 'My friends, I'm afraid we come to you in our hour of dire need. We have journeyed far from the Ancient Jungle which used to be our happy home because we need your help with a very serious problem that has befallen us. We don't like to impose or be a burden to you, but we— '

'"We"?' interrupted Ovi frowning. 'You keep saying "we" Hopi. Is Wishi with you?'

'Oi'm hoire oill roight!' A shrill little voice – not dissimilar to the whine of a poltroon's mating cry – came from somewhere nearby, causing Ovi and Elli to scratch their heads in confusion.

'Ois thoit yoi Woishoi?' said Ovi adopting a nevasaurus accent.

'Yois Oivoi; oit's moi.'

'Boit Woishoi, yoi … yoi soind soi doiffoirount!'

Hopi gave a little cough.

'Kindly move aside Ovi.'

As Ovi stepped aside one of Hopi's giant front claws emerged from out of the foliage. Then, slowly, with all present holding their collective baited breath, the talons parted to reveal a tiny Wishi about the size of a poltroon.

'Wishi? Is that you?' asked a stunned Elli.

Wishi nodded in reply before lowering his head with embarrassment.

'My dear, dear friend … ' Ovi momentarily forgot to speak in a nevasaurus accent as he dived forward to give his old pal a hug. 'Wh-wh-whatever has happened to you?'

Ovi's hug moved Wishi, making his tail wag and his floppy ears flap up and down alternately. The poignant scene brought a tear to many an eye in the Palace, and caused Gusto to emit a long rather emotional belch.

'Ak … hem!'

As well as causing the Palace to shake, Hopi's polite cough re-commanded everybody's attention and all present looked on doubly-attentively as he turned to formally address The Great Ug.

'I think perhaps I should explain what has brought us here, Your Great Ugness, and why we need your help.'

The Great Ug twiddled three of his five-pointed-star hair-appendages and adopted his most stately pose with his best foot forward and his hand tucked in behind his beard.

'You may be assured my dear Mister Hopi that you are amongst friends here, friends who will do whatever they can to help you with whatever it is that you are in need of help with.'

'That is, indeed, most generous and gracious of you, Oh Great Ug,' replied Hopi. 'Wishi and I have come here today to seek— '

'I feel it pertinent to mention however,' continued The Great Ug, clearly beginning to warm to his newfound status as 'Host-a-Hopi'. 'That whilst you are indeed amongst friends here Mister Nevasaurus, you are not amongst quite as *many* friends as there would have been a few days ago before that blasted fiend the Taxman paid us a visit.'

'A—HAAA-AAA-AAA!' Hopi's sudden ear-splitting roar took everyone by surprise, forcing a few timid souls to 're-disappear' back into the foliage fast. *'So, that-that-that … MAN has been here too!'*

'You mean— ' began Elli.

'Yes, Elli … ' Seeing the effect of his roar, Hopi lowered his vocal volume to a range more comfortable for human ears. 'We too have had a visit from this so-called "Taxman"; indeed, *that* is the very reason why Wishi and I are here. We desperately need your help to track him down and persuade him to give us back that which he has taken.'

'Whoit hois hoi toikoin froim yoi Woishoi?' asked Ovi.

'Hoi's toikoin hoilf oiv Hoipoi's hointoing broith; oind oill oiv moine.'

'Goidnoiss. *Oill* oiv oit?'

'Yois ... oind yoi coin soi whoit oits doing toi moi. Oi coin't coitch oinoithoing whoich moins Oi coint oit oinoithoing whoich moins Oi'm goittoing smoilloir boiy thoi doiy. Oit's thoi soime foir Hoipoi boit hoi's woistoing oiwoiy moire sloiwloiy.'

'Excuse me.' It was Zatt who interrupted. 'Any chance of a translation?'

'I do apologise my dear Zatt,' said Hopi. 'You'll have to excuse my cousin; he has a rather strong nevasaurus accent. He was just explaining that our entanglement with the Taxman has been an unmitigated disaster for us. Not content with taking *half* of my hunting breath rendering me half the nevasaurus I used to be, he then helped himself to *all* of Wishi's breath and … well, you can see for yourself the unfortunate result.'

Everyone present looked from Wishi to Hopi then back to Wishi again. They then started exchanging expressions like 'I-don't-see-that-smaller-one-lasting-much-longer' and 'poor-little-nevasaurus-shame-he-can't-catch-any-food'.

'Tell us how we can help you Hopi.' said Elli.

'Wishi and I are reasonably confident we can go after this-this *ruinous* "Taxman" chappioso and track the blighter down; but when it comes to persuading him to give us our hunting breath back—well, we think that is wholly different matter, one best tackled by a fellow human … '

His left eye looked at Elli.

'a smart intelligent creative and resourceful human … '

His right eye looked at Ovi.

'or perhaps an intrepid full-bodied go-getter of a human; and we thought who better than our old friends Elli and— '

'Woi doin't knoiw oinoiy oithoir hoimoins oipoirt froim yoi twoi!'

'*Ahem*, yes, thank you Wishi!' Hopi looked awkward. 'Would you please consider helping us Elli? Ovi? … we are desperate to get our hunting breath back!'

Before Elli or Ovi could say anything, Zatt stepped forward.

'*Ah-hhh!* The famous "nevasaurus breath" we've all heard so much about.' She strode up to Hopi's glinting wall of razor-sharp dentition and sniffed, then she walked over to the 'dinky' Wishi, bent forward and sniffed again. 'Speaking purely as an experimentrix-deluxe, I am quite keen to sample this so-called "hunting breath" for myself. You never know, I might even find a use for it in some of my dainties.'

'Boi moi guoist,' Wishi smiled and inhaled deeply.

Elli and Ovi shared looks of alarm.

'*Er* – Zatt. I'm not sure this is such a good— '

'Aw, don't be so silly Elli! You heard for yourself that Wishi's breath has been stolen. I don't suppose there's much left for me to sample, is there Wishi?' Wishi glanced up at Hopi then shook his head with a firm 'no'-shake. 'Go on then Wishi, give me all you've got!'

Zatt closed her eyes, placed her face directly in front of Wishi's and opened her mouth wide. Wishi glanced again at Hopi who gave a discrete nod, then he breathed out as hard he could. The blast of hot air filled Zatt's cheeks and blew her hair out in a streamer behind, but she didn't flinch. After it stopped, with her hair still sticking out, she licked her lips – then licked them again.

'Mmm – quite a curious taste that,' she proclaimed after a long pause. 'Very sweet. Reminds me of a potion I once made; I called it "cola"—turned out to be great for cleaning.'

'Yoi're moist koind.' Wishi blushed and looked coy.

'Wishi? Why are your horns turning round?'

'*Er* – Zatt?' Hopi intervened on behalf of his cousin. 'That's how a nevasaurus blushes.'

'Oh, I see.'

Zatt patted Wishi kindly on his head – making his horns turn even faster. She then strode back to Hopi and squared up to him with her hands upon her hips.

'How about you, big boy? Any chance of a quick blast of the real thing? Just a little itsy-bitsy soupçon of the half-strength version?'

'*Uh-oh!*' exclaimed a panic-stricken Ovi. '*No Sis! Don't—* '

'*You really don't want to do that Zatt!*' Elli sprang forward waving for her to stop, but his warning was lost in a great '*WHOOO-OOO-OOOSH*' as Hopi – in his usual keen eagerness to oblige – started sucking in air.

Zatt clapped her hands and looked round excitedly at the gathering who were all staring wide-eyed with fear and horror, then she turned back to face Hopi.

'I don't understand it Hopi; why are they all so afraid of— ' Hopi let out his breath; and the last thing Zatt registered before losing consciousness was the faint sound of her own voice saying ' —you—*ooo-wwweee-eee-eerrr-r-r-r-r-r-r-r—*'

Chapter Two

The Tax-Taker-Backer-Gang

It took a whole day for everyone to recover from Hopi's hunting breath (with the notable exception of Gusto who wasn't affected at all and was actually quite keen to try it again).

Once people were feeling better, The Great Ug held a Grand Feast in honour of the Treetop Tribe's esteemed visitors, the Nevasaurus cousins. He proudly opened proceedings by unveiling a colossal mountain of food. The spread was so huge, even Ovi was daunted by it. Had "boats" been invented, The Great Ug and his wives would have certainly pushed one out. The feast was truly magnificent with: bounteous bunches of bananas, bloated bladders galore, a heap of cooked baby-bison and hyena a-plenty, plus a selection of Zatt's dainties; all of which went down a storm with the two nevasauruses (by the time the feast was over Wishi was back up to half the size of Hopi). Eventually, the last banana bunch was stripped to its stalk, the bloated bladders were all empty and there were no more baby-bison to munch or pick clean; even the hyena legs had all been consumed, along with every single one of Zatt's dainties. The Great Ug patiently waited for everyone to 'settle' (which meant rolling over onto their back with an overstuffed bulging belly, groaning) before addressing the gathering.

'Well, everybody,' he said, loosening the leather straps on his animal hide. 'I hope you all enjoyed your gnosh! I don't know about you but I'm so gnoshed-up I feel ready to burst like a full water bladder dropped on a pointed stick!' A chorus of giggly laughter was followed by a loud burp from Gusto. The Great Ug's happy expression then soured; his smile waned and all five of his shiny star points began to droop. 'I'm afraid my fellow Tree Toppers, we now need to turn our attention to some "less happy" matters. I invite you all to join me in deliberating upon how we are going to help our friends Hopi and Wishi here to get back their hunting breath. In addition, and more generally, we need to decide what in swamp-fume-blazes we are going to do about this blasted menace the Taxman!'

Elli and Zatt both stood up to speak, but while they were clearing their throats in preparation to say something, Gusto beat them to it.

'*BO—WAA-AAA-ARR-RRP!*—pardon. Well, I for one say– *belch* – that we go after this – *belp* – Taxman and – *burp* – take our stuff back!'

'Whoa-whoa there big fella,' said Elli. 'Let's not be too hasty! We don't know this Taxman; we have no idea what he might be capable of.'

'Elli is right dearest,' added Zatt, 'all the reports we have of him mention a terrible dark shadow that precedes each of his snatches; we saw that for ourselves—remember?'

'Good point Sis!' Elli shared a look of concern with his twin. 'If he can command shadows, who knows what else he might be able to control—the sun perhaps or-or even the sea!'

Just then, Ovi stood up to address the gathering. He'd been lying on his back, contentedly patting his swollen belly when, suddenly, in mid-pat, an idea had occurred to him.

'Gusto is right; we *do* need to get back our stuff, but Elli and Zatt are also right; we don't know nearly enough about this Taxman chap; he might be really, really dangerous. So, I say, if we do go after him, we need to do so safely; and I've heard it said many times that the best place for safety is in—oh, what are they called, those whatchamacallit-thingies— '

'Caves?' suggested Elli.

'No, not "caves"; you know, those things where there's supposed to be safety—oh, what *are* they called?'

'Deep holes?' ventured Hopi.

'No-no-no, not "deep holes". Oh, you know the things I mean—"eight, nine, ten, ele—"'

'Oh, "*numbers*"*!*' cried Zatt. 'You mean "numbers"!'

'Yes, that's it! Thanks Sis. "Numbers"! They're the fellas I mean. Eleventy-twelvety-seven, onety-doublety-nine, nonety-dozen and so forth—them chaps!'

'Do you know something Ovi,' said Elli. 'I think for once you're right. What you're saying is; if we're going to go after this Taxman and bring our stuff back safely, we need to form a "gang".'

Everybody (apart from Elli and Zatt) looked nonplussed and started mouthing 'gang?' while sharing puzzled expressions.

'When you say "gang"?' said Ovi looking and sounding confused. 'What do you mean exactly?'

'Well, a "gang" is when a group of us do something together with a shared purpose,' explained Elli.

'What, like when you and me – the two off us – went off on our quest to find— '

'Don't be daft Ovi!' exclaimed Zatt. 'Two individuals on their own doesn't make a "gang"! You need more members than that! Anyway, it won't just be you two; there'll be four of us.'

'You mean— ' said Elli.

'Yes, you can count me and Gusto in too!'

'*Oh boy, Oh boy!* I'm in a "gang"!'

'*Erm* – actually Sis,' said Elli. 'Technically speaking, I'm not sure whether four constitutes a "gang". We'll need way more than that if we're going to succeed in tracking this Taxman down *and* persuade him to give all our stuff back.'

'*Ak-hem*, aren't you forgetting something?' Hopi was looking intently down at Elli with both eyes. 'I'll be with you!'

'Moi tooi!' added Wishi with one eye staring firmly at Elli and the other rotating for emphasis.

Elli looked up at Wishi and Hopi then back down to Zatt, Gusto and Ovi.

'Yup, it looks as though we've got ourselves a "gang"!'

The crowd erupted.

'*Yay! We've got a "gang"! We've got a "gang"!*' '*Now there's a chance we might get our "tax" back!*'

'*Wait a moment! Wait a moment!*' Elli waved his arms for silence. 'A proper gang has to have a proper name and I've just had a brilliant idea what we can call ours. How about … ' He picked up his bow and plucked it for dramatic effect. 'The "Tax-Taker-Backer-Gang"?'

There was a pause while everyone mouthed 'The Tax-Taker-Backer-Gang' to themselves; then they all cheered and started chanting wildly as one voice.

'*Hooray for the Tax-Taker-Backer-Gang! Hooray for the Tax-Taker-Backer-Gang! It's starting to look like we're going to be getting at least a modicum of our "tax" back which is a blessed relief after all this uncertainty! Hooray for the Tax-Taker-Backer-Gang!'*

The entire Palace was a-buzz with excitement as the notion took root of the "Tax-Taker-Backer-Gang" hunting down the Taxman and getting all the "tax" back that he'd taken. The Great Ug and his wives clapped their hands and started dancing Treetop jigs to the rhythm of the chanting. Elli and Ovi's wives joined in as well as all the children, and even the nevasauruses could be heard amongst the '*whooping*' and '*whoo-hoo-ing*'.

Eventually, the last jig was jigged, the 'whooping' died out and the Palace grew quiet. Realising the party had run its course, The Great Ug and his wives retired to the far end of the Palace, taking with them Elli and Ovi's families as well as Zatt's children.

All of sudden the members of the newly-formed Tax-Taker-Backer-Gang found themselves alone together for the first time. They huddled in front of Hopi's head so they could talk quietly without disturbing the others.

'Well, well, well,' said Elli forcing a jolly smile. 'Here we all are then – the "Tax-Taker-Back-Gang" – a *proper* gang with a *proper* name about to embark upon a *proper* mission.'

Zatt suddenly looked gravely serious.

'And, what exactly is our "mission" Elli? We don't *really* know what we're looking for, or *even* where to start looking for it!'

'Good point,' muttered Gusto nodding sombrely. 'Boy that's – *belch* – a real bummer—*BO-WAA-ARP-bur-rrr-rapple-pfffazzz-za-aaa-rrp-p-p... belp!* Sorry Dearest.'

Zatt gave Gusto a 'look' before resuming what she was saying and lowering her voice to avoid being overheard.

'The more I think about it, the more dangerous our mission is looking. For example, what *was* making that deep, menacing rumbling sound we all heard before each of us was "taxed" and what *did* create that dark ... ominous ... shadow?'

While they pondered the seriousness of what Zatt had just said, an eerie silence filled the treetops. The night cries of nestling poltroons ceased and even the depleted foliage of the Palace stopped rustling. After a long pause she spoke again, this time in a hushed and muted whisper.

'Then there is the most vexing question of all … who exactly is this-this-this "Taxman"?'

At the mention of the name "Taxman" the unnervingly creepy silence grew even quieter.

'I agree with you Zatt, that is indeed the most puzzling of our many questions,' said Hopi doing his best to match her hushed tones. 'In all my many years as a well-travelled denizen of the Ancient Jungle, I don't think I have *ever* before come across a human calling himself the "Taxman".'

'Moi noithoir,' hissed Wishi, shaking his head in agreement.

'All of which leads me to think … ' Hopi leaned forward conspiratorially, ' … he might not be … "of … this … world".'

'Moi … tooi,' added Wishi, nodding in agreement.

'And, *that* makes me wonder; if he is indeed not of this world … ' by now Hopi's voice was reduced to a barely audible murmur, ' … what other world might he possibly hail from?'

Hopi looked at Wishi with both eyes; and Wishi rotated each of his sombrely to indicate that he should continue.

'Well, after much contemplation of all the different "other worlds" there are "out there" so-to-speak, I've concluded there is only one possible – one feasible – "other world" that this Taxman could be from … ' He paused to look each of his fellow gang members in the eye. As he did so the entire jungle – both treetop and below – anxiously held its collective breath. Then Hopi continued. 'The only possible "other world" that this Taxman could feasibly have come from … is … '

Somewhere nearby, a solitary poltroon could be heard falling out of its nest and hitting the ground with a short sharp high-pitched *'squeak'* follow by several grumbly grunts. Hopi paused and waited patiently for the poltroon's noises to cease before continuing.

'The only possible "other world" that this Taxman could feasibly have come from … is … '

The poltroon made a loud yawning sound which ended in another grumble, then fell silent; allowing Hopi to attempt his sentence once more.

'The only possible "other world" that this Taxman could feasibly have come from … is … '

The poltroon grumbled again, then made a '*ba-doing!*' sound like a bedspring being sprung, then fell silent. They all listened intently for more noises from the poltroon, sharing 'will-it-make-any-more-do-you-think?' glances. Content that it had finally settled, Hopi tried again.

'The only possible "other world" that this Taxman could feasibly have come from … is … '

The poltroon suddenly made a loud and protracted wheezing sound rather like a saw sawing wood—followed by a short sharp raspberry.

'*Oy, you!*' shouted an exasperated Ovi. 'Will you please *shut up!* We've got some really good suspense going here.'

'Sorry,' came a tiny high-pitched voice from somewhere nearby.

'Thank you Ovi,' said Hopi. 'Now, as I was saying, the only possible "other world" that this Taxman could feasibly have come from is … ' he paused out of habit, but Wishi gave him a swift 'get-on-with-it' kick ' … *the mythical world!*'

All three siblings exchanged glances and silently mouthed "the mythical word" in astonishment. Gusto tried to join in but he only got as far as the "th" in "mythical" before belching.

Hopi continued.

'And you know my friends, if it is the *mythical* world we're dealing with, there's only one creature, and one creature alone, who can help us … '

Hopi's eyes fixed firmly on Elli and Ovi.

'Y-y-you d-d-don't mean?' stammered Elli.

'D-d-does he mean h-h-who I th-th-think he means?' Ovi's stomach involuntarily let out a '*rumble'* to rival one of Gusto's best.

Hopi's eyes narrowed and swivelled to Wishi.

'*You* know who I mean, don't you Wishi?'

'Yois, Oi doi.'

All eyes turned to Wishi.

'Oil.'

'Who?' Zatt sounded more than a little confused. 'Who's "Oil"?'

'He means Aloysius Meredith Plantagenet Fortesque-Smyth Fitz ... *Dragon!*' declared Elli.

Hopi nodded in concurment, as did Wishi; and as indeed did Ovi.

'Who?' Zatt was still none the wiser.

'You remember "Al" Sis!' exclaimed Elli. 'We told you about him. Al, the mythological creature who led us to Hopi and Wishi by flying us to the Ancient Jungle.' He turned to Hopi. 'You mean, if we're to stand any chance of catching up with this Taxman and getting some of our precious stuff back— '

'*And* Granddad,' interjected Ovi.

'Yes, and Granddad ... we need to— '

'*And* all our maggots,' inter-further-jected Ovi.

'Yes, *and* all our maggots.'

Elli glanced at Ovi, challenging him to interject again and forcing Ovi to suddenly take a keen interest in his toes.

'Are you saying Hopi,' hissed Elli, 'that if we're going to stand any chance of getting our stuff back, we *first* need to find Al?'

'Yes, that's entirely correct young Elli,' Hopi nodded.

'Oixoictloi,' said Wishi, also nodding.

'And what's more,' continued Hopi. 'Wishi and I think we know where we can find Oil—I mean, Al.'

Chapter Three

River crossing for beginners

The following morning, with the help of The Great Ug's wives, the newly-formed gang quickly completed preparations for their expedition in search of the Taxman. Several brace of baby-bison were baked in lava pits, fresh bunches of bananas were picked (closely supervised by Ovi), Zatt filled several bundles with her dainties and half a wadi-pool was used to fill up water bladders. By midday they were ready to depart.

So it was that the Tax-Taker-Backer-Gang set forth on their quest to find the Taxman to retrieve all the "tax" that had once been theirs. Each human gang member had a selection of provisions on their back while the nevasauruses were laden with assorted bundles, bunches and bladders all tied to their ample frames by creepers. In addition, they each carried in their giant talons as many baby-bison as they could manage.

Hopi led the way with Wishi following. It had been decided that the humans would take turns riding on their heads; Elli was the first on Hopi's with Zatt on Wishi's.

The nevasauruses' footfalls were so heavy and made the ground judder so violently, they caused poltroons to topple out of their nests. Because of this, Ovi and Gusto followed a couple of trees behind to avoid being hit by one of the unfortunate creatures.

Despite the falling-poltroon hazard, the gang made good progress and by late afternoon they'd left the jungle home of the Treetop Tribe far behind. Ovi's belly was just starting to make its presence felt, and the day's sun was getting close to its daily collision with the distant horizon, when all of a sudden, they came to an abrupt halt.

There before them, stretching as far as they could see in either direction and completely blocking their path, was a broad expanse of flowing water. Without hesitation, Hopi strode out into the fast-moving current in an attempt to cross it and, after a few strides, his head disappeared below the surface taking Elli with it.

The others all looked on with curiosity, watching the bubbles where he'd disappeared dwindle to a trickle before stopping completely.

After a very long pause, Ovi broke the silence.

'Is it safe for them to stay under the water like that?'

'Dunno?' said Zatt. 'I've never tried it. But then I've never seen so much water in one place before. The most I've seen was when Gusto— '

Zatt was cut short by a huge '*SHWHO-OOO-OSH!*' as Hopi's head suddenly shot to the surface. As the spray cleared, Elli became visible; he was seated exactly as before except that his face was now bright blue.

'*Wow!*' cried Zatt, clapping her hands excitedly. '*I bet that was fun!*'

Elli simply stared wide-eyed at his sister then opened his mouth wide to draw in a deep breath. Hopi did the same and the sudden rush of air was so strong a nearby oak-willow-hornbeam-fir tree leaned over and a poltroon fell out. It wasn't until he'd taken several gasps that Elli was finally able to speak.

'It is very, *very* wet under that water Sis.' He bent forward to shout into Hopi's ear. '*Where's it all coming from Hopi, and what's it for?*'

'Do you know something Elli, I'm not entirely certain. I've heard mention "on the grapevine" so-to-speak that it's called a "rover" or "river" or something like that. I expect it is mainly for drinking purposes, though I can imagine one could have some rather pleasant amusement upon it if one wanted to.'

'A "rover" or "river" eh? Well, well, well, who'd-a-thought?' said Elli. '*So, how are we going to get across it Hopi?*'

'Yeah. Good question,' added Zatt. '*Come on Hopi; you must have some idea how we can— *'

'*WHOO-HOO-WUP! HOOT! HOOT! WUP-DI-WHOOP! HOOT, HOOT, HOO-WUP!!!*'

At that moment, a giant-coney-furnut-redwood-larch-spruce-pine-monkey-puzzle tree floated past heavily laden with ripe coney-furnuts plus a whole Hoot of monkeys jumping about on it, '*hooting*'. This distracted everyone's attention and left the entire Tax-Taker-Backer-Gang staring blankly at the passing tree completely lost in thought. Eventually, long after the '*hooting*' tree was out of sight and could no longer be heard, Hopi snapped from his trance.

'*Aa-aaa-ak—hem!* I think Wishi and I will go off and see if we can find a crossing point. We can cover much more ground on our own; so, I suggest the rest of you say here. Whilst we're gone, why don't you go over to that nice quiet inlet over there. You never know, you top-notch thinkers of the first order might come up with a clever idea for getting across this – *um* – this "river"-thingummy.'

Elli and the others agreed with Hopi's suggestion and, as soon as the nevasauruses had disappeared, they made their way over to the nearby creek for some serious creative thought.

To aid his thinking, Gusto grabbed a handful of Zatt's dainties (his favourite ones with extra poltroon excretions) and waded out into the creek where he could wiggle his toes in the water and watch them changing colour. With Gusto gone, the three siblings moved over to the bank of the creek and readied themselves for some serious thinking: Elli assumed his best 'thinking' pose seated with his right elbow on his left knee and his chin perched on his fist; Zatt adopted her contemplation pose with her head looking up and her fists firmly planted on her hips; and Ovi did what he always did whenever a spot of serious thinking was called for … he grabbed a banana.

Ovi was just finishing off his first mouthful of banana and was about to enjoy a nice big swallow, when he thought he spotted something move in the creek behind Gusto. He paused pre-swallow and stared. Whatever it was had just moved again, there was no mistaking it. He opened his eyes wide and stared intently—swallow now completely forgotten. The surface of the creek's still water suddenly broke in two places about half a tyrannosaurus apart and two enormous yellow-green eyes with streaks of black and silver protruded above the ripples. As Ovi looked on, the eyes blinked and focussed very firmly on Gusto. They then continued to rise steadily out of the water, bringing with them the top of a distinctly reptilian-looking head. This was all happening to the rear of Gusto who was busily wiggling his toes and tucking into his dainties, relishing each and every 'sour-sweet-pickled-putrid-rich-n'tasty-n'acrid' mouthful.

Ovi suddenly remembered his swallow and gulped his banana down. Avoiding any sudden movements, he slowly and very carefully sidled over to Elli and nudged him in the ribs which had the effect of tickling him and making him jump into the air with a loud squeal of a giggle.

'*Shhh!*' hissed Ovi, pointing pointedly at Gusto. '*Look!*'

Elli looked.

By now the whole of the creature's head was visible. It was about half the size of Hopi's, but nowhere near as nice and friendly. Before either brother could say or do anything, the huge reptile (which incidentally, Dear Reader, was an ancestor of both the crocodile and the alligator – a crocogator) opened its jaws wide and moved very purposefully toward an oblivious Gusto.

Deciding it was time to warn his sister, Elli tugged at Zatt's arm. Annoyed at being disturbed mid-think, she gave him one of her most withering 'go-away-can't-you-see-I'm-busy' scowls; but then, upon seeing Elli's anxious face, she followed his gaze and saw her husband's plight. Still blissfully unaware of what was happening, Gusto was now framed by the crocogator's open mouth with its monstrously sharp teeth. The huge array of gnosh-gnarling-gnoshers was oozing drool all about him and the crocogator itself had a clear expression of glee as it anticipated the prospects of munching its lunch.

'*GUSTO-OOO!!!*' It was Zatt who finally sounded the alarm, causing Gusto to look up in mid-dainty-bite and see the look of horror on his wife's face. '*LOOK OUT!*'

The shock of realising he was in big trouble caused Gusto to drop the rest of his dainty. At the same time, his belly started a '*gurgle*' that quickly became a '*rumble*' then even more quickly escalated into a full-blown '*roar*'.

The resulting cacophony of sound from Gusto's innards was so loud, the crocogator attempted to peep round either side of its gaping mandibles to see what the noise was.

At that precise moment, a giganto-enormamentally-immense fart erupted from Gusto's rear. This wasn't one of his usual very large farts; this was a fart of truly momentous and absolutely ginormous proportions – and it was also very, *very* powerful. The force of the expelled gas against the back of the crocogator's palate was so great it actually propelled Gusto forward at quite some speed in an upright position across the creek, out of the water and up to the top of the bank where he skidded to a halt right beside Zatt, Elli and Ovi – still standing up. As soon as he came to a halt, he looked round and saw for the first time his erstwhile nemesis.

The crocogator was frozen in the same position where it had ingested Gusto's 'emission' of highly noxious gas directly down into its gizzard. They all watched with a mix of curiosity and amazement as its mouth turned a putrid and rancid green with streaks of yucky yellow and bile blue. The poor creature then slowly closed its mouth and sank into the water looking very sickly indeed. Eventually, just its wide staring eyes were visible; they blinked twice, turned bright green with bloodshot streaks, went cross-eyed and disappeared beneath the surface. Although now out of sight, they could still hear its grumbles and groans reverberating in the depths of the creek. Elli tried to say something but was interrupted by a prolonged underwater retch. The creek then filled with pungent slimy green bubbles that burst to release a puff of acrid yellow-green smoke. As they watched, the trail of bubbles zig-zagged its way crookedly out into the river then slowly wended its way downstream accompanied by a string of underwater grumbles and groans. The grumbling could still be heard long after the bubbles disappeared from view punctuated by woozy hiccoughs and the odd extended burp.

(You may be interested to know, Dear Reader, that after it had recovered from its encounter with Gusto this crocogator went on to be the very one who, after making its way to the sea, was the first to meet and marry an allidile. The pair fell deeply in love and quickly produced many healthy offspring which were actually the world's first ever generation of pure alli-croco-gator-diles who would eventually, of course, many millennia later evolve into the adorable cuddly beasts we all love, admire and cherish today.)

'*We've done it!*' cried a triumphant Zatt as Hopi finally returned carrying a much-diminished Wishi in his talons. 'We've worked out a way to cross the river!'

'Really? How wonderful. Now, that's what I call top quality thinking,' replied Hopi. 'We knew they wouldn't let us down, didn't we Wishi?'

'Woi coirtoitloi doid.'

'The secret is to add extra bison puke and well-rotted poltroon poo to my dainty recipe; look, see for yourselves … '

She pointing over to the creek where Ovi and Elli were holding their noses while busily feeding Gusto some dainties that were so 'pungent' they gave off a green gas with orange sparks.

'*Watch this!*'

Just then, Gusto gave a 'thumbs up' sign to say he was ready. He then pointed pointedly with his pointing finger at the opposite bank of the fast-moving river. As Hopi, Wishi and Zatt looked on, Ovi climbed on Gusto's back and Elli scrambled back up the bank still holding his nose. Without further ado, Gusto gave a little wave and crouched forward. His belly then gave a deep rumble and at this signal both he and Ovi started pointing pointedly towards the opposite shore. Then, with an almighty '*Fff-blahhh … whoooooosh!*' that blew several poltroons out of nearby trees, Gusto released his pent-up fart.

It worked a treat. Elli and Zatt started clapping while jumping up and down with excitement, and the two nevasauruses clacked their talons, as Gusto and Ovi – fingers pointing forward – shot out across the water with a churning wake of white water behind them. Within moments they were out in the middle of the river where the water was fast-flowing and rather rough with waves as high as a poltroon stretching its neck after a bad night's sleep. All of a sudden Gusto's fart ran out and the two brave Tax-Taker-Backers – fingers still pointing – sank beneath the waves.

Elli and Zatt stopped in mid-jump and Hopi and Wishi paused in mid-clack.

'What ratio of bison puke are you using to poltroon poo?' asked Hopi after a few more moments had elapsed.

Wishi looked up at Hopi in disbelief.

'About equal measure actually,' replied Zatt, warming to the prospect of a meaningful chat about potions with a fellow concoction-aficionado. 'Why? Do you think it needs more?

Maybe I'm using the wrong puke or the wrong poo. What do you— '

'*Er* – excuse me,' interrupted Elli.

'Yois. Moi toi,' added an indignant Wishi.

Zatt span round and gave her brother an emphatic 'What-is-it-now?-Can't-you-see-I'm-discussing-something-important?' look which Elli chose to ignore.

'*Si-iii-is!* I don't think we should leave Gusto and Ovi under the water so long. Don't forget, only the other day I— '

'Foir goidnoiss' soik Hoipoi, goi oind goit thoim!'

Wishi kicked his cousin on a secret little spot near a nevasuarus's ankle that only fellow nevasaurus's knew about … and it really hurt.

'*Aaaooowww!!!*' cried Hopi, hopping on one leg. '*Ahem!* Will you please excuse me Zatt? I think our friends here might be correct in their assertion that the sensible thing to do at this particular juncture would be to go and retrieve our fellow Tax-Taker-Backer-Gang members from this raging torrent of a "river" before any harm might come to them. I shan't be a moment.'

The Tax-Taker-Backer-Gang hurriedly set about perfecting ways to cross the "river" that was preventing them from making any progress in their mission.

Hopi and Zatt worked together on improving the fart-propulsion recipe for her dainties while Elli, Ovi, Wishi and Gusto experimented with river-crossing techniques such as: digging a hole in the water, walking backwards, walking upside-down, walking backward *and* upside down, jumping off long over-hanging boughs head-up, jumping off long over-hanging boughs head-down and trying to float on a poltroon nest (which is made from pointy sharp sticks and stones).

Eventually, on the third day, both 'teams' made the all-important breakthroughs they so desperately needed. Zatt and Hopi developed a dainty that not only fart-propelled Gusto quite some considerable distance, it also actually tasted quite good. (It turned out the trick was to add a soupçon of a specific grey mould that only grows between a poltroon's toes after they've eaten fish.) At the same time, Elli finally hit upon the secret to underwater travel … taking a deep breath before going under. The 'breath-holding' technique was crucial for the nevasauruses because there was no way Gusto could carry Hopi who, even in his diminished state, was still the size of a large tyrannosaurus. Instead, all Hopi had to do was lift Wishi above his head and take a deep breath.

Thus it was that late in the afternoon of the fourth day into their mission, Gusto completed the last journey across the river, bringing the final of the Tax-Taker-Backer-Gang's fart-lift-loads safely ashore. As he glided deftly and safely to a halt and put down his load – a brace of baby bison, two bunches of bananas and a water bladder – the gang began to congratulate themselves with a round of applause.

'I must say, my fellow Tax-Taker-Backers,' said a very wet Hopi, clacking his talons, 'How fortunate we are to have amongst our number such broad-shouldered brawn as well as brilliant bright brains.'

'Goid oild Goistoi!' chirruped Wishi who was getting distinctly tinier by the day.

'Yes, well done Gusto,' said Ovi, peeling a well-earned banana. 'Who'd have thought farts could be so useful. You live and learn eh?'

'Yes indeed, very well done Gusto,' added Elli. 'When it comes to gas-propulsion, you really are a fartico-supremioso par excellence! I do believe there is nothing in this world stronger than your farts and that's true in – *um* – well, in more ways than one actually! Tell you what Gusto, when we get back, I think I might work with Zatt on her dainties to see if we can – *er* – you know tone down the – *um* – well, to be honest tone the "smell" down a bit. They are a tad – *um* – well – *er* – "over-ripe" if you don't mind me saying— '

'FAH-WHOOSH-PAH-LOMP!'

A huge shadow suddenly swept over them, blocking out all daylight; and the sound of gigantic flapping leathery wings filled the air.

'*I say down there! What on earth is emitting that foul, dreadful and thoroughly obnoxious smell?*' boomed a thick dark treacly voice that was so frightening even Hopi ducked under a nearby tree top.

The shadow-darkness passed and daylight momentarily returned, but before anyone could breathe a sigh of relief—

'FAH-WHOOSH-WHO-OOO-OSH-PAH-LOMP!'

—it was back.

'Hoi! You down there! What do you think you're doing, polluting the place like that? You can even smell it halfway up God's Crown where I was trying to enjoy a pleasant commune with Nature, don'cha know!'

Yet another '*Fah-whoosh-pah-lomp*' sounded and an enormous creature landed on the open area beside the water's edge where the Tax-Taker-Backers had piled their supplies.

'Fff-hhhex-fff-kkkyyyuse – *burp* – fff-mmm-hhheee,' came a muffled cry from beneath the huge beast.

'*Oops! Terribly sorry young thing,*' said the creature apologetically as it shuffled to one side to allow Gusto to extricate himself.

'*Al?* Is that you?' Elli peered out from behind Ovi. 'What a coincidence you finding us like this; we were actually trying to find you!'

Chapter Four

Flying lessons for beginners

'*Oh, I am most certainly no stranger to our Mister Taxman …* ' Al paused in order to gnaw on a baby bison. Whilst he chewed and chomped, he kept his piercing yellow and black snakc-like eyes narrowly open so he could glance at the various members of the Tax-Taker-Backer-Gang, sizing each of them up and paying particular attention to Hopi. '*I know him – and his "ways" – very well indee-eee-eed, don'cha know!*'

They were seated in a circle by the riverbank. Hopi and Al were opposite each other, Elli and Zatt were to one side, with Ovi, Wishi and Gusto to the other. The daylight was fading fast and the jungle was quiet apart from with the sound of the odd poltroon missing its nest.

'Does that mean he's a monst—I mean – *er* – mythological beast like your good self Al?' asked Elli.

Al paused in mid-chomp and fixed his stare upon Elli.

'*The Taxman? A magnificent mythological beast like me?*' Al extended his neck toward Elli, shimmering his bright green and gold frills as he did so and baring his impressive array of glintingly sharp teeth. Elli started to tremble, at which point Hopi gave a gentle cough to remind Al he was there. (I should perhaps point out, Dear Reader, that under normal circumstances Hopi would have been roughly twice as big as Al, but now in these far-from-normal times they were about the same size.) Al raised his head to look Hopi directly in the eye before lowering his frills and contracting his neck to resume a more affable pose. '*He most certainly is* NOT *a mythological creature; and most definitely* IS *human. If anything, he's too human … "extra human" you might say or perhaps even … "super-human"!*'

'So, you've met him before, have you Al?' said Elli.

'*Met him? Of course, I've met him young thing. Who hasn't? You have to be very lucky in this world* NOT *to come across the Taxman, don'cha know! I'm surprised you cave and treetop-dwellers haven't met him earlier. Tell me, what has he taken from you?*'

'Well, let me see,' said Elli. 'There's so much, it's difficult to know where to begin … '

There was a short pause, then they all spoke at once.

'Granddad!'

'Tree – *belp* – creepers!'

'The foundations of my wall!'

'Moi noivoirsoirois broith!'

'Og!'

'The foliage at the Palace!'

'Moany—I mean, money!'

'Melons *and* maggots!'

'Half of my— '

'*EXCUSE ME!*' Zatt's exclamation was so loud it distracted a squadron of passing poltroons, causing them to crash into each other and fall to the ground still in formation but facing backwards with their beaks up in the air. "I think you are all forgetting that we actually made a "list"!'

She stood up, walked over to Al and with a flourish produced her slightly smelly blob of brown paper.

'There you go Al; it's *all* there!'

Al took the "list" in his talons, sniffed it and pulled a 'yuk'-face. He then proceeded to scrutinise it carefully for a few moments, turning it round in circles and making little 'ooohhh' or 'mmm I see-eee' noises sometimes with a curt 'tut' or a curl of his lip. When he'd finished, he handed it back to Zatt, snorted in a haughty dismissive manner … and scoffed.

'*That certainly is quite an impressive collection of items; however, I'm afraid it is but nothing – a mere trifle – compared to what he's taken from me, don'cha know.*'

'What do you mean "that's nothing"?' protested Ovi. 'That's a *lot* that is!'

'*Yeah big buddy!*' Gusto was in – *burp* – dignant. 'And we're gonna – *belch* – get it *aaa-aaa-lll* back – you betcha!'

'That's why we've formed our gang, The Tax-Taker-Backer-Gang,' added Elli.

Al gave another snooty and rather dismissive snort then looked upward. As he did so his lips began to quiver. The last of the daylight was fading fast and the sky was rapidly filling with twinkling stars. Something on Al's face also twinkled. Zatt spotted it first and signalled to the others to take a look. As they all watched tears started flowing down his cheeks and began dripping on the ground with tiny delicate little '*plops*'.

An awkward silence gripped the gang members and several 'what-shall-we-do-now?' glances were exchanged until Hopi eventually spoke.

'Well, well, well; what a long day this day has been; exceptionally long and extremely fatiguing. I think we would all gain much benefit from some somnolent respite and then perhaps we could return to such weighty matters in the morn— '

'*Yes-yes old thing, you are, of course, absolutely right. Let's get some much-needed sleep.*' Al lowered his neck, furled his wings and curled up in a tight ball which muffled his voice. '*And tomorrow I shall take you somewhere special, somewhere very special indeed, don'cha know.*'

'*Righty ho, you Tax-Taker-Backers!*' Al flicked a whole bunch of bananas up in the air and caught it in his mouth. '*Are you good to go?*'

It was the following morning. The Tax-Taker-Backer-Gang had slept like a clutch of baby poltroons beside their nests (poltroons can't actually sleep *inside* their nests; they are far too prickly). While they were still yawning, Al popped another bunch of bananas in his mouth and moved out into the centre of the clearing where he beckoned Hopi and Wishi to join him.

'*I suggest that I take the heavier pair aloft,*' Al nodded at Ovi and Gusto, '*and you Hopi take Elli and Zatt on your head. You and I can carry some of the supplies in our talons while we're airborne which means all our little friend Wishi here need do is follow behind, bringing up the rear so-to-speak. What do you think old thing?*'

Hopi frowned a perplexed frown, looked down at his cousin Wishi and then back at Al.

'I – *er* – I don't quite follow you Al. You appear to be suggesting that we nevasauruses can – *um* – well, can *fly* in which case I'm afraid I must relieve you of your unfortunate misapprehension and— '

'*But of course, you can fly you daft old thing! You're a nevasaurus, aren't you?*'

Again, Hopi looked down at Wishi by his side and they both shrugged. Al eyed the two nevasauruses closely and as he did so the frills in his neck fluttered.

'*I used to know your grandfather, Mighty Nevasaurus, don'cha know.*'

'What, old sprightly-and-brightly, feisty-and-fighty, quite-rightly Mighty himself,' said an incredulous Hopi. 'Really?'

'Whoit wois hoi loike?' chirped Wishi excitedly from down below.

'*Oh, he and I were great pals!*' Al stood up to his full height and un-furled his enormous wings. '*We often went off flying together, don'cha know. Why we even went to the far side of God's Crown once and saw the Land of Smoke and Fire.*'

By now, Hopi and Wishi were quite agitated; clacking their talons, twirling their horns and flapping their ears up and down. They'd never met their grandfather Mighty Nevasaurus, but they'd heard many stories about him. Al saw the effect tales of old Mighty were having on his two grandsons and smiled.

'*And, then there was the time we decided to follow the sun and found ourselves flying over the very edge of the Known World to a very strange place indeed … a place known to the ancient ones as "The Mystical Horizon".*'

Hopi and Wishi were now so enthralled and excited by Al's tales they were jumping into the air.

'Is it true that Mighty could go for eons without sleep?' said Hopi eager to hear more.

Al nodded. Wishi was so thrilled, he leapt up off the ground – clacking his talons in excitement – and hovered next to Hopi's ear, whispering intently into it.

'Oh yes-yes, thank you Wishi; I'd completely forgotten about that,' said Hopi, becoming highly animated. 'Is it true that he once got trapped by a huge horde of monster-nasty-sauruses and he dealt with them, all of them, with just one solitary blast of his nevasaurus hunting breath?'

Wishi continued to hover by Hopi's ear, eagerly awaiting Al's reply. Down on the ground, the others suddenly noticed this and – as one – they all spotted that he did indeed have wings; they were all a-blur like a modern-day humming bird.

'*Um – Hopi!*' cried Eli and Zatt in unison, pointing.

Hopi turned, saw his cousin hovering in the air right beside his head and did a double-take.

'Goodness gracious Wishi! Whatever *are* you doing?'

Wishi looked back at Hopi, then down to the ground – before he too did a double-take.

'*Oi'm floiyoing!*'

As soon as he realised what he was doing, Wishi lost the ability to do it and fell to the ground.

'Hoi doid Oi moinoige thoit?'

Al looked nonchalantly at his talons in a rather self-congratulatory self-satisfied manner.

'*Rather proves my point, don'cha think?*'

A strange expression came over Hopi's face which none of the others – not even Wishi – had seen before. As they looked on, he stood up straight and placed his hind legs firmly apart as if bracing himself for something. A creaky-leathery-crinkly noise could then be heard coming from behind him followed by the distinct sound of something unfolding. Suddenly, two great dark brown wings covered with yellow blotches extended outwards either side of his body. Similar-but-quieter sounds could then be heard from Hopi's feet; the others all looked down and saw that Wishi had done the same.

'*Very good old thing,*' said Al. '*Now why don't you try them out? Go on, give them a flap.*'

Hopi's wings made a lighter '*Fah-whoosh-pa-pa-dah-lommopp!*' sound than Al's heavy '*Fah-whoosh-pah-lomp!*', but the effect was exactly the same. As the two nevasauruses took to the air for a couple of practice circuits everyone looked on with eager anticipation at the prospect of really making some progress in their quest to seek out and hunt down the Taxman. Everyone that was apart from Ovi who went very quiet and – unseen by the others – suddenly looked a little pale.

Chapter Five

The Blue Moon

'*Wow! Will ya* – burp – *take a look at that little buddy!*' shouted Gusto, leaning forward so that Ovi could hear him. '*Have you ever* – belch – *seen anything like it?*'

'*No, never!*' Ovi called back over his shoulder. '*Great, isn't it?*'

Ovi was seated in front of Gusto as they rode on Al's neck; their backs stacked high with supplies. Gusto was sitting up straight and enjoying the view, but Ovi was bent forward holding on as tightly as possible. Further along the neck ahead of Ovi a pair of Al's frills were gently oscillating and constantly changing colour in time with the '*Fah-whoosh-pah-lomp!*' of his beating wings. Flying alongside Al a few tyrannosaurus lengths away was Hopi with Elli and Zatt seated side-by-side on his head, both fully laden with provisions and each holding on tight to one of his horns. Not far behind Hopi and Al, bringing up the rear, was Wishi flying solo.

'*Who'da thought trees could look so* – burp – *small?*'

'*Indeed-indeed … or so* – um – *so green!*'

'*"Green" little buddy? Don't you mean* – burp – *"brown"? I think they look more* – belch – *brown than green without their leaves, don't you?*'

'Er – *yes, of course! Did I say "green"? I meant to say "br—*'

'*Wow! Take a look at* – burp – *THAT!*'

'Um – *which particular "that" are you referring to Gusto?*'

'*Why, that long blue "that" there, of course – hiccough – little buddy!*'

'*Oh, that long blue "that"! Of course, yes! Gosh, isn't that "that" something? What a "that" that "that" is! In fact, that "that" is what I call a real "that"!*'

'*Right on, little buddy! That "that" sure is* – burp – *where it's at! I've never seen anything that long before* – belch – *have you, little buddy?*'

'Nope! You're right there, Gusto! That "that" there has to be the longest "that" there has ever been; no doubt about that!'

'I mean, it looks like it stretches right up to those – belch – *huge mountains up ahead!'*

'What mount—I mean, does it?—I mean, It sure does, doesn't it?'

'Ovi?'

'Yes, Gusto?'

'You've gotta – burp – *open your eyes little buddy!'*

Ovi tried to open his eyes, but they were having none of it; however, by concentrating really hard on one eye at a time he managed to persuade each of them to half open. With both eyes bravely peeping out between his semi-closed eyelids, he then forced himself to look down. There, far below was the Ancient Jungle spread out beneath him; and cutting through the dense dark browny-green foliage like a snake slithering through grass was a meandering blue line – the "river". It twinkled in the bright sunshine and in places was partly hidden in wisps of fine mist. He followed the river's line forward and sure enough as Gusto had said it led straight for a huge mountain range that was rapidly looming larger and larger in front of them.

Just at that moment, Al leaned his elongated neck over to Hopi so that the two giant flying beasts could exchange a few words.

'That's God's Crown dead ahead Hopi. We're about to dive down and for a while we'll be weaving in amongst its peaks. It can get bit dicey in places, don'cha know! I need you to keep close and stay tight on my tail; understood?'

'Message received and understood! Ready whenever you are Al!'

'Now, remember Hopi old thing, this is very important! Whenever I zig, you zig; and when I zag, you zag. Do you catch my drift? If you were to zag when I was zigging, for example ... well, things could get a bit tricky, don'cha know.'

'Roger that Al, wilco,' replied Hopi. *'You zig, I zig; you zag, I zag!'*

'Right, we're going in!' Al called back to his passengers. *'Hold on extra tight now you two!'* ... and then he dived.

'Zii-iii-iig,' murmured Ovi in a tiny high-pitched voice. He gave a nervous double-twitch and leaned over to one side. He followed this with several more nervous twitches and jerkily switched his lean to the other side before adding in the same squeaky voice, 'Zaa-aaa-aag.'

His face was as white as the snow-capped mountains surrounding them and his hair was sticking out from his head in spikes all stiff with shock. He was still in the same position with his arms clenched tight and his legs spread in an arc, except he was no longer on Al's neck but plonked on a large rock propped up by a banana bunch.

It had now been several minutes since they'd landed upon a rocky platform somewhere high up amongst the snow-covered peaks of God's Crown. Everywhere they looked, there were white pinnacles. Above them were endless white peaks and below them were yet more white crests and ridges. Indeed, the only thing in their vicinity that was not white and shaped like a mountaintop was the huge waterfall cascading down the side of the mountain directly in front of them which was also the largest of all the peaks by far. The constant rushing-gushing-swish-swoosh-swishing noise of the waterfall was almost deafening, forcing them to raise their voices in order to be heard.

'*For goodness' sake Ovi,*' cried Elli, shaking his brother. '*Snap out of it, will you! You're safe now. The flight is over!*'

'Zii-iii-iii-iig.'

'*OVI!*' Zatt strolled over and shouted directly into his face. '*You're not flying now. You're on a nice solid mountain. We need you to snap out of it and get with the plot!*'

'Zaa-aaa-aaa-aag.'

She turned and shouted into Elli's ear.

'*Gusto gets like this sometimes. It happens when I put too much tyrannosaurus poo in my dainties and he's been hanging upside down for several days, dangling over a pit of hungry anaconda-python-constrictors. Let me handle this.*'

She squared up in front of Ovi, then without warning slapped him across the face very hard several times. Each slap caused his face to wobble, his eyes to rotate in circles and his teeth to jangle. She then leaned forward and stared deep into Ovi's eyes before stepping back and allowing her treatment to take effect.

Ovi blinked once, twice, three times; then blurted in an even higher and squeakier voice than before, 'Zig-Zag! Zig-Zag! *ZIG-ZA-AAA-AG!*' Slowly, his hair spikes disappeared, his legs straightened and his arms relaxed. He then blinked several times, licked his lips and looked around him like someone waking from a very deep sleep.

'Well, well, well – *yawn* – that was a nice rest. I'm so hungry I could eat a tyrannosaurus on a stick – *yawn, yawn* – What's for breakfast?'

'*So, why have you brought us here Al?*' shouted Elli, attempting to attract Al's attention. '*Al? Can you hear me?*'

'*Yeah, Al! Why are we here?*' Zatt called up at Al through cupped hands, straining to get her voice to reach his perch high above their heads.

Ovi's reaction upon waking from his trance had reminded the Tax-Taker-Backer-Gang they were hungry, so they'd decided to take a short break in order to eat a quick snack. Hopi and Wishi had shared a brace of baby-bison between them; Gusto had rummaged and found a particularly acrid and chewy dainty while Elli and Zatt had joined Ovi in partaking of a couple of bananas each. Al was the only one who'd refrained from eating. Instead, he'd flown away from the others and came to rest on a pinnacle where he sat motionless rather like a carved statue of a mythological creature on a plinth, staring earnestly at the waterfall.

'*I say Al!*' cried Hopi; his deep rich voice reverberating over the constant noise of the waterfall. '*We're all nicely refreshed and fully replete now; and we're ready to resume our journey to* – er – *well, to wherever it is you're taking us!*'

Al finally stirred and slowly turned to look down upon the assorted individuals and creatures that comprised the Tax-Taker-Backer-Gang. Then, with a mighty '*Fah-whoosh-pah-lomp*', he took off and, in a long smooth glide, completed a full circuit of the rocky platform where the gang were waiting before landing expertly on a boulder right in front of them. He then carefully eyed each member of the gang one-by-one, leaving Hopi till last.

'*Hopi, old thing?*'

'Yes, Al?'

'How many moons ago do you remember?'

'Well Al, I may not remember as far back as you, but— '

'How many Hopi? How many moons ago do you remember … precisely?'

Hopi looked down at Wishi and both nevasauruses shrugged their shoulders.

'Well, we've not exactly been counting Al. I'm not entirely sure I follow what it is you— '

'The answer is six Hopi.'

'Six?'

'Soix?'

'Yes, that is correct, six. The yellow one we can still see today. The black one we still cannot see today … ' Al was forced to pause because his voice had become tremulous with emotion. *' … and four others.'*

'I'm afraid I'm still not quite following the general gist of your line of thought Al,' said Hopi adopting a gentle coaxing tone because he'd spotted that Al's lips had once again started to quiver. *'Are you saying there were once more moons than there are today?'*

By now Al was feeling so emotional he could no longer speak. Instead, he nodded a 'yes'-nod, looked up to the sky … then … after a long pause … he howled.

(Mythological creatures very rarely howl which is perhaps the reason why when they do, they make the most of it. Al's howl was so loud it could be heard the length and breadth of the Known World. The Great Ug over in the Palace heard it as did most of his wives. At first, they thought it was the Return of the Great Poltroon, but then they reasoned even he wouldn't be that stupid. As it happens, many poltroons heard it too; indeed, a lot of them mistook it for a mating call and tried to spruce themselves up. Interestingly, far out at sea, creatures in the ocean's deepest depths heard it, causing many to stick their heads out of the water for the very first time in their curiosity, thereby beginning a habit that persists to this very day, particularly in a certain loch in Scotland.)

Up amongst the peaks of God's Crown, Al's howl was so loud; it triggered both an avalanche and a landslide. If Hopi hadn't thought fast and outstretched his wings to envelope and protect the rest of the Tax-Taker-Backer-Gang, the torrent of ice, snow and rocks that assailed them might have caused a few problems.

Once his howl was complete, a forlorn Al was then able to recover sufficient composure to tell the others his tale.

'*It used to be something really special when you saw all six moons a-go. I used to—* '

'*I see!*' Hopi clacked his talons excitedly. '*Ha ha! You meant "a-go" as in "go-go" or "get up and go"; not "ago" as in –* um *– you know … last year, or something … sorry.*'

Al's withering 'how-dare-you-interrupt-me!' stare had its desired effect and made Hopi mumble to a halt.

'*Ah, such happy times we used to have when the world was young!*' Al began to warm to his soliloquy. '*The moons made the Music of the Spheres and we mythological creatures used to dance the night away to their tunes. The Red Moon would sometimes join with the green and silver ones and the three of them would spin ever so fast. The effect was startling and "magical" I tell you … such colours! … such joy!*'

He leaned forward purposefully and singled out Zatt.

'*You may be interested to know that is how rainbows came about.*'

Zatt looked at Elli and raised an inquisitorial eyebrow, but before Elli could respond, Al was off again.

'*And then there was the best, most marvellous, moon of them all … my favourite moon, and not just me incidentally; all of us mythological creatures were as one on this … the Blue Moon! Ahh-hhh, the nights we used to have together. We'd dance! We'd sing! We'd hullabaloo and coo … and all of it in the most wonderful shade of blue … the most perfect, most exquisite, blue of all blues …* '

Al tailed off and fell silent. His eyes closed, his neck began to extend and his head gently swayed to-and-fro as if he were listening to music. The others looked on in wonder as his frills started to glow with ever-changing luminescent colours that moved in waves from behind his ears down either side of his neck. His skin also began changing colour in waves; all colours at first – rich colours, fast colours – but all the time constantly moving toward blue. The display culminated in the rich dark blue of the sky before dawn tinged with something none of them had ever seen – the deepest of ocean blues.

Hopi and the others simply stared at Al, transfixed by his display; but then, after a while, they began to shuffle and feel awkward. They were just starting to exchange 'shall-we-disturb-him?' glances when his eyes snapped open and his fierce blue face returned to their midst with bright yellow eyes glaring wide, frills ablaze in scarlet-red and teeth fully bared!

'*And* that *was when the Taxman came!*'

It took Elli and Ovi quite a while to untangle themselves after their frantic attempts to hide behind each other in order to escape Al's fierce display. During the resultant 'intermission', Al slowly returned to his normal colour and composure; and, by the time they finally managed to free Ovi's head from Elli's bow, he was ready to begin telling them the story of the Taxman and the six moons …

'*It happened a long, long ago, on the occasion of the longest night of the epoch don'cha know, when the sun decided to take a well-earned rest and the moons were given plenty of time to indulge themselves in a spot of merry-making.*

'The evening had started well with a game of "hide-and-seek-behind-a-peak". Each round involved a single moon and just one of us mythological creatures. The moon would hide up behind one of the peaks and the creature whose turn it was would then shout out guesses like "Behind the peak shaped like claw!" or "Next peak to the left!"

'*As soon as the creature guessed the right location, the moon would shoot up into the sky and shimmer. All the moons would take part apart from the Black Moon. The best moon at hiding was always the Blue Moon, don'cha know; and I'll not allow due modesty to prevent me from telling that it was yours truly who was the best at finding—* '

'Er – *sorry to interrupt,*' interrupted Zatt, '*but, are you absolutely certain there actually* was *a "black" moon?*'

Al did a rather gangly double-take which is a bit of risky thing for a mythological creature with an extendable neck to do.

'I mean, I can imagine it's a bit hard to see at night … what with it being – um – *black and all that … sorry.'*

It was Zatt's turn to be withered by Al's 'how-dare-you-interrupt-me-when-I'm-in-full-flow' stare.

'As I was saying,' resumed Al, *'After "hide-and-seek-behind-a-peak" we then played "spot the Black Moon"— '*

Al stared pointedly at Zatt, who looked down at the ground in a manner which could well have been described as 'sheepish' had sheep existed then.

'All six moons would shuffle themselves helter-skelter; oh, it was so exciting; until no-one could tell which moon was which. Then, suddenly, they would come to a halt in a row of three with – and this was the crux of the game – three others remaining hidden out of sight behind. One of the hidden moons would always be the black one and we had to guess which of the others he was hiding behind.

'It was during the third round of the game that the Taxman struck. The moons had come to a halt in a row, blue-yellow-green, and we all agreed that the Black Moon was behind the yellow. It was my great uncle, the Cockatrice, doing the calling that night. He flew up high and cried at the top of his voice "Yellow!" but only the Red Moon emerged from behind the Blue. Beside the Red was a gap two moons in size. We all stared and stared waiting for the Silver Moon to appear … but it never did. Eventually, a number of us cried "Where's our Silver Moon gone?" And that was when HE *appeared!'*

'Who?' interrupted an excited Gusto with a burp. *'The Silver Moon?'*

'No, not the Silver Moon you poltroon! Your ears must need cleaning young thing. The Taxman, of course—or the "Tax-Tax-Tax-Tax-Taxman" as he might better be known!'

While Gusto took his turn to wither in the glow of Al's 'how-dare-you-interrupt-me' glare, he let out an extremely protracted fart which sounded like the extended wheeze of a poltroon snoring and which took an age to taper off with several false endings. After several corresponding false starts, Al finally resumed his tale.

'We were still crying "Where's our Silver Moon gone?" when, suddenly, we heard a chilling cry … "I took it!" *It was*

him, the Taxman, and he was standing on top of a mountain to our rear on the other side of God's Crown.

'*We all turned and there he was silhouetted against the stars; a shadowy sinister human-shaped figure with sharp spiky hair all smothered in darkness and oozing murk. I was utterly astonished when I realised he had human form. I mean, all the humans I'd ever met up till that point could only say "Ug".*

'*"It was tax that was long overdue!" he called out, taunting us. I can still hear his ice-cold voice as it filled the darkness. "You can regard that as your first instalment. I'll need three more of them moons before I'm through."*

Al shivered as he recalled the events of long ago. Hopi was about to say something to console him, but Al held up a talon and gave him an 'I'm-fine-thanks' look.

'*You can perhaps imagine how we felt. We were filled with utter, utter despair. I've never known such despair, before or since. I mean, we had been playing with the moons for as long as we could remember. To be without the Silver Moon was unthinkable, unimaginable even. My mother was inconsolable with grief, don'cha know, and two of my aunts fretted so much they lost their feathers don'cha know.*

'*But then, the following epoch, at the very next longest night things got even worse … the Red Moon failed to appear. And then, the following epoch, the Green Moon went missing. I tell you one thing about our Taxman; he is very true to his word.*

'*Anyway, it was after the disappearance of the Green Moon that I decided it was time to take action, so I—* '

'Um – *can I interrupt you there please Al?*'

Al give Zatt yet another of his 'how-dare-you-interrupt-me' glares, but this time she ignored it and pressed on.

'*I think I know where this is going. You decided to hide your favourite moon, the Blue Moon, from the Taxman in order to prevent him from taking it; and I bet you hid it behind that waterfall over there. You did, didn't you? I'm right, aren't I? And, I bet it's still there to this day. I'm right again, aren't I? That's why you've brought us here; that's why this place is "somewhere special"; because this is where the Blue Moon is hidden.*'

Al's deflated look and slight nod were tantamount to a 'yes'; at which point Ovi exploded.

'*Why did you have to say that Zatt? You've gone and spoilt his blummin' story now! I was really into that; it was good story-telling! The suspense was proper gripping and-and-and wicked, yeah? And now you've gone and given the blummin' ending away!*'

It didn't take long for the gang to get ready. While they were checking that their provisions were all securely tied, Elli sidled over to Ovi and spoke to him quietly.

'Are you going to be all right flying again?'

'I'll be fine, as long as I hold on tight,' said Ovi with a reassuring smile. 'Whatever happens up there I will *never* loosen my grip; you can be sure of that.'

In their by-now-familiar formation of Elli and Zatt on Hopi, Ovi and Gusto on Al, with Wishi bringing up the rear, they once more took to the air for the short hop over to the adjacent mountain, the biggest in God's Crown, and its humongously huge waterfall.

Following Al's lead, they passed across the front of the cascade as they headed for the far side. The roar of the gushing torrent was so loud Elli, Zatt and Gusto had to cover their ears. Only Ovi left his ears uncovered, preferring instead to hold on tight. Upon reaching the other side, Al glanced back at Hopi who in turn looked over his shoulder at Wishi who nodded he was ready, at which point all three flying creatures banked to the left and dived. Half way down the edge of the waterfall there was an opening created by a natural crevasse in the mountainside. It had been completely invisible from the front but now as they drew near, they could see there was a narrow gap between the falls and the solid rock; it also quickly became obvious that the only way through it would be for the three flying creatures to tilt sideways with one wing up and the other down.

'*Brace yourselves everyone!*' shouted Al over his shoulder. '*All passengers hold on extra tight—we're going in!*' With that he dropped his left wing, lifted the right one up high and swooped.

The '*WHOO-OOO-OOSH!*' of the crashing water crescendoed as they burst through the gap, completely drowning out any cries they may have been emitting, but once they were through, the acoustics behind the falls were such that it became mere background noise and the Tax-Taker-Backer's wild shrieks suddenly leapt to the fore of the soundscape.

Barely had Ovi's '*Aaaaahhhhh!*' and Gusto's '*Ooo* – burp – *oohhhhh!*' tapered off, when they were supplanted by Elli and Zatt's combined '*Wwwooowww-www-eee-eee!*' and Hopi's '*Gooooodnesssss!*', immediately followed by Wishi's shrill-if-diminished '*Yaaa-hoo-ooo!*' These sounds were soon followed by a second 'Aaaaahhhhh!' 'Ooo – *burp* – oohhhhh!' and 'Wee-eee-eee!' because the main feature of the acoustics behind the giant waterfall was a haunting and relentless echo … echo … echo.

The gang now found themselves in a very strange place the likes of which none had ever experienced before. The cavern behind the great waterfall was vast and bathed in the pale bluey-green light coming through what was now a solid wall of water. Far to the rear of the cavern and well away from the wild outer torrent, was a second 'inner' waterfall that was smaller and much 'tamer'. Instead of being a fearsome and impenetrable mass of churning white water, this was a smooth sheet of ever-shifting luminescent hues – sometimes green, sometimes blue – with fine delicate sparkles of yellow red and gold. It was much quieter than its noisy neighbour, making a faint '*tinkety-trickly-tinkle*' noise. Half way up the inner waterfall was a large outcrop of rock that divided it in two and was the obvious place to land. As they approached, they could see the outcrop had two levels. Al headed for the higher platform, a natural 'perch' immediately beside the gently falling sheet of water, while Hopi and Wishi landed on the lower one a bit further away.

As soon as they were settled, Elli and Zatt dismounted from Hopi's head, but Ovi and Gusto remained seated on Al's neck with Ovi still holding on tight, as was now his habit.

'*So, here we are my friends; welcome one and all to this – my secret special place"!*' Al's words were then repeated. 'my secret special place … my secret special place … my secret special place'

'Thank you very much, Your Al-ness, for bringing us here to this wonderful and, indeed, very "special" place,' said Hopi, adopting the role of gang-spokes-nevasaurus. 'It truly is an honour for us to be here. Never before have I, nor indeed any of our kind, had such an honour bestowed upon us; and it is with great humility that I, on behalf of the entire Tax-Taker-Back— '

'If I may Hopi?' Zatt interrupted him gently but firmly. 'Al, we've come an awfully long way, we've been travelling for days now and I for one am feeling rather tired. Can we please see this Blue Moon of yours—*like, right now?*'

'Yes ... *Please!*' added Elli whose eager cry echoed round the vast cavernous space. 'Please ... Please ... Please'

'*Oh, that's the easy part don'cha know young humans.*' Al smiled a 'you're-all-in-for-a-real-treat-now' smile. '*It's on the other side of this beautiful and serene "inner wall of water". All you need to do is poke your head through like this ...* '

Al extended his mythological neck upward to its full height and then, with a flourish, thrust it downward through the glistening sheet of water ... and then he froze.

The gang members continued watching him, eager with anticipation; Elli and Zatt even began to rub their hands gleefully in excitement. Ovi, however, looked more anxious than excited as he stared along Al's extended neck, waiting to see what would happen next. But nothing did happen; Al remained stubbornly motionless as well as totally headless.

'Um – *Al!*' Hopi called out eventually. '*Al old thing. Is everything all right and as it should be?*' There was no response; only the echoes of 'should be ... should be ... should be'.

'*Is everything all right with the Blue Moon Al?*' cried Zatt at the top of her voice, but again there was no reply; so she called up to Ovi instead.

'*Check that he's all right, will you Ovi? Put your head through the water and see what's happening.*'

'*Are you mad!*' exclaimed Ovi. '*What if the water has sliced his head clean off? That might hurt, that might!*'

'*OVI-III!*' Zatt stamped her foot. '*JUST DO IT, WILL YOU!*'

'*Ovi!*' Elli stepped forward and adopted a gentler tone. '*I'm sure that water isn't strong enough to cause you any harm. Why don't you test it first with a banana?*'

Reluctantly, Ovi shuffled his way along Al's neck until he was almost touching the water. He then reached back to his provisions, plucked a banana and, after a moment's hesitation, thrust it in the water. He held it there for a moment, then pulled it back out—intact. He held it up triumphantly for the others to see before eating it. Then he shuffled a little closer to the waterfall, braced himself and pushed his head through—then he too instantly froze.

Down below, Zatt looked with exasperation at Gusto, who was still seated on Al's neck and who, in turn, shrugged his shoulders with a loud belch that echoed profusely before it faded.

'*Can you please go and see what's happening Love?*' she cried in desperation; and her cry was repeated. 'Love … Love … Love'

Gusto nodded and was just about to shuffle forward along Al's extended neck when suddenly two things happened almost simultaneously. Firstly, Ovi's voice could be heard on the other side of the water shouting '*There's nothing here! There's nothing here!*' followed immediately by an earth-trembling, gut-wrenching cry.

'*IT'S GONE!!!*'

Both Ovi's and Al's heads suddenly reappeared.

'*It's gone! Gone, I say! Gone! Gone! Gone!*' Al's shrill hysterical cries filled the entire cavern. '*My beloved Blue Moon! It isn't there!*' His wings unfurled to their fullest extent and with a tremendous '*FAH-WHOOSH-PAH-LOMP!*' he flew off into the vast open space wailing '*Oh, woe! Oh, woe! My moon! My moon! My lovely Blue Moon! Where are you?*' with Ovi and Gusto desperately trying to hold on.

As the others looked on helplessly, Al headed up high into the far-off upper recesses of the vast cavern. Then, just as he was about to disappear into the shadows, he turned and headed back down, diving almost vertically. As he shot towards them, the others could clearly see Ovi desperately peering out from behind his flaring frills, eyes wide with terror.

'*Do something Hopi!*' shrieked Zatt.

'What do you suggest?' asked Hopi, looking highly perplexed as Al swooped past.

'*My moon! My moon! My blue, Blue Moon! Oh, where – oh, woe! My lovely Blue Moon!*'

They all stared in horror as Al plunged down into the dark depths far below; then, once again, just as he was about to disappear into the murk, he executed a tight turn and headed back up.

'*Fa-whoosh-pah-lomp-pah-lomp—fa-aaa … who-ooo-ooosh!!!*'

As he raced past them this time, they saw Ovi leaning forward over Al's frills and speaking into Al's ear in an attempt to calm him down; all the while, just about managing to stay on board—as, indeed, was Gusto.

'*Just do something Hopi; do something to make him stop!*' cried Elli.

Hopi suddenly had an idea. He waited for Al to turn and commence his next circuit then launched himself off the platform and hovered waiting to join him in his downward plunge. As Al drew near, Hopi half-furled his wings and dived. The two giant flying creatures then plummeted downwards together, zooming through the vast cavernous space side-by-side and close enough to exchange a few words.

'*I can see you're* – um – *well, more than a tad upset about all this Al, and understandably so, of course. I want you to know that we're all just as concerned as you are, honest we are. But we're* – um – *well, we're trying to assess the situation rationally old thing—you know, trying to work things out so-to-speak. Do you have any idea where this* – er – *this Blue Moon of yours might have gotten to?*'

'*Woe is my moon, my lovely Blue Moon! Oh, woe; oh, woe; oh, where is my lovely Blue Moon?*'

As Al flew upwards to commence another circuit, Hopi broke away in order to report back to Elli, Zatt and Wishi.

'It's no use chaps. We'll just have to wait till he calms down.'

'*"Wait till he calms down"? Are you mad!*' Zatt was pulling at her hair and sounding more than a little hysterical. '*If we wait much longer, we might never see Gusto or Ovi again!*'

'*LOOK!*' cried Elli. '*He's coming around for another pass! Go on Hopi; give it another go!*'

'*Coime oin Hoipoi. Oi'll hoilp yoi!*'

Hopi glanced down at Wishi and nodded.

'Right Wishi, get ready to fly-yyy-yyy … ' He looked back at Al and steeled himself. ' … *NOW!*'

Hopi and Wishi timed it perfectly and managed to catch Al just as he was approaching the low point of his circuit and readying himself for yet another climb.

'*Hello again Al old chap. We—that is Wishi here and I,* ha ha ha *we were* – um – *wondering if you'd had a chance to sort of mull things over since you were last* – um – *round this way so-to-speak? We* – um – '

'*My moon! My moon! Oh, woe is my lovely Blue Moon!*'

Hopi pressed on.

'*Gosh, it must be jolly tiring doing all these circuits. Maybe if you were to* – er – *land kind-of-thing we could perhaps, y'know, old chap, mull things over together-type-thing?*'

'*Where, oh where, is my moon; my lovely Blue Moon?*'

Al gave a double '*fah-whoosh-pah-lomp!*' of his wings and left the two nevasauruses behind; but then, just as Hopi and Wishi were about to return to the platform, he hesitated, swerved and tilted (causing Ovi and Gusto to dangle loose from his neck) then swooped back to where they were hovering.

'*I'm sure those traitors the Taur brothers are behind this!*' he growled through bared teeth.

'*The two who, old thing?*'

'*Whoi?*'

'*The Taur brothers, Cen and Mino; or failing that their mother, GG Mystery, though no-one has seen her for epochs.*'

With that, Al '*fah-whoosh-pah-lomp*'-ed once more and set off on his biggest circuit yet, still repeating his by-now-familiar refrain of '*My moon! My moon! My lovely Blue Moon!*'

'I think we need a bit more information than that before we return to Elli and Zatt; don't you agree Wishi?'

Wishi nodded vigorously.

'Oind woi noid toi coinsoirve oir oinoirgoiy. Woi coin't koip floiyoing oip oind doiwn loike thoit. Hoivoiroing oin moid-oir ois foir moire oicoinoimoicoil.'

They didn't have long to wait. Al was getting good at doing dramatic circuits of the vast cavern and very quickly he was back at the point where the two nevasaurus cousins had remained hovering.

'*We* – um – *we were just wondering whether you might be able to give us some idea of where to find these* – er – *these "Taur brothers" of yours; or their mother indeed. You know old thing, point us in the right direction so-to-speak.*'

"You'll find Cen up-up-up, high-high-high—high-as-the-sky; and Mino down-down-down, low-low-low—down-low-below, don'cha know . . . high and low . . . high and low . . . a bit like meee-eee . . . *weee-eee-eee!*"

Al was about to commence yet another circuit when the cavern suddenly went dark. Everyone turned to look towards the outer waterfall and they all saw a huge shadow, almost as big as the falls themselves, glide slowly past outside. In shape it was undoubtedly spherical, but its colour was more difficult to gauge through the opaqueness of the cascade ... though "blue" would have been a good guess.

'*My moon? My Blue Moon? Is that you, my lovely?*'

Al did two massive '*fah-whoosh-pah-lomp*'s in quick succession in order to pick up speed; but this wasn't in order to complete another a circuit; instead, he was heading straight for the outer wall of water.

'*STOP HIM, HOPI!*' screamed Zatt.

'*For goodness' sake, do something, Hopi!*' cried Elli.

Hopi started '*fah-whoosh-pa-pa-dah-lommopp*'-ing with all his might and darted after Al with an urgency rarely seen in a flying nevasaurus. Try as he might, however, he was unable to overcome the as-yet-un-discovered-Law-of-Physics which states unequivocally and empirically beyond doubt that a '*fah-whoosh-pah-lomp*' is always, and in any circumstances, much faster and far more powerful than a '*fah-whoosh-pa-pa-dah-lommopp*'.

Just then, with a final '*My moon! My moon! My lovely Blue Moon!*' Al flew headlong into the plunging torrent of water … and disappeared … taking Ovi and Gusto with him.

As soon as Al disappeared, Hopi realised he too was in danger of hitting the waterfall and began frantically back-'*fah-whoosh-pa-pa-dah-lommopp*'-ing not realising that an even more fundamental as-yet-un-discovered-Law-of-Physics was coming into play; the law which states that any, and/or all, frantic '*fah-whoosh-pa-pa-dah-lommopp*'-ing will create a powerful tail-wind vortex that can, and will, pull any, and/or all, following nevasauruses forward faster than they themselves can actually '*fah-whoosh-pa-pa-dah-lommopp*'.

As a result, Wishi – who had become sucked into Hopi's slipstream – was now going faster than he, or indeed any other nevasaurus, had ever flown before. The instant Hopi doubled-back away from the pounding crashing waterfall, Wishi picked up a slingshot effect … and was catapulted toward it.

'*PULL UP, WISHI! PULL UP!*' cried Hopi as he realised what was happening.

'*Oim troi-oing!*' The tiniest of voices was almost lost in the roar of the outer cascade. '*Oi thoink Oil'll—*'

… then he, too, was gone—sucked into the raging torrent.

Chapter Six

Ups and downs

'For goodness' sake, pull yourself together and try to calm down. All this hair-pulling, and gnashing of teeth, and tugging of toes and wailing like a poltroon having a bath isn't going to bring the others back; and it most certainly isn't going to get us out of this-this-this blasted *hole!*'

Zatt was doing everything she could think of to hold things together in their suddenly-rather-serious situation, but Elli was inconsolable and sobbing uncontrollably.

'*HOPI!*' she looked up, desperately seeking some help. '*Ho-ooo-pee-eee!*'

Hopi was perched on the upper platform that Al had used earlier. He'd been there ever since Wishi's disappearance, squatting on the high rock and completely motionless with his head through the inner waterfall.

'*Come down here Hopi ple-eee-ase; we need you!*'

Hopi's head reappeared sodden from the curtain of water. It was impossible to detect if there were any tears on his face, but his ears were all floppy and his horns were drooping.

'*I need your help Hopi; we must find a way to calm Elli down! He's got himself a bit over-excited.*'

Elli suddenly stopped wailing.

'"Over-excited"? You think I'm "a bit over-excited"? For goodness' sake Sis, we've just about lost anything we had of any real value and nearly *everything* we hold dear. Even before we set out on our "mission" we'd already lost; Granddad, most of your experimentation kit including the straps to your cloud-catchers, half the creepers and vines in the jungle, a whole year's supply of maggots and the base stones to my "wall"; but *now*, as if all that wasn't enough, we've also gone and lost Ovi, Gusto *and* Wishi too! Don't you think all that is sufficient reason to get—oh, I don't know just a little … a smidgeon … a tad … a teensy-weensy bit … *"excited"!?*'

'If you couch our predicament in those terms Elli,' said Hopi as he landed beside the two siblings and folded his wings, 'there is indeed some justification for a modicum of pessimism; on that I do concur. Furthermore, I admit that our mission to redress the disequilibrious inequalities brought about by the nefarious activities of this Taxman chap has suffered a slight setback and could be going a bit better, but I do think— '

'"*Suffered a slight setback, and could be going a bit better*"?' Elli stared firstly at Hopi and then at Zatt … before losing it completely. '*Ha-aaa ha ha ha!* – "Suffered a slight setback" – *ha ha ha!* – "and could be" – *Ha-aaa-ha-ha-ha!* – "going a bit better"?'

'Please calm down Elli;' said Zatt, 'getting hysterical doesn't help.'

'OK, OK, I'll try to calm down. Tell you what Sis; let's assess how well our little "quest" is going, shall we?'

'Elli, please don't— '

'Let's see now … oh yes; half the Tax-Taker-Backer-Gang has been swept away in that-that-that *water monster* over there, including your own husband and our dear brother, for goodness' sake—yes, I suppose that *could* be regarded as a "slight setback" … '

'Elli, this is fu— '

'What else? Oh yes, we're lost somewhere in the world's biggest mountain range, stranded inside a gigantic monster-sized cave with no easy way out; and on top of that we've only got half a baby-bison and half a bunch of bananas left between us!' He scoffed the most heavily sardonic scoff he could muster. '"Could be going a bit better"? *PAH!*'

Zatt attempted to say something but couldn't, her lip was quivering too much. An awkward silence then ensued, broken eventually by Hopi giving a gentle cough.

'*Ahem* – if I may?'

'What is it Hopi?' Elli glanced up at his old friend.

'I wonder if now might be an appropriate moment for us to consider the – *um* – the intelligence that Wishi and I were able to extract from our erstwhile companion prior to his – *er* – well, his rather rushed and "overly-hasty", if I may say so, departure.'

'Please tell me why it is Hopi,' Zatt clenched her fists, planted them firmly on her hips and glared at the still-dripping nevasaurus, 'that you are able to use the most beautiful of words, but I have absolutely no idea what you're trying to say?'

Hopi's eyes rotated in opposite directions and his floppy ears wiggled awkwardly with embarrassment.

'I'm so sorry my dear Zatt; kindly allow me to elucidate one more time … *ahem!* I was speculating whether this might be an apt juncture for us to contemplate the verbal utterances Wishi and I were able to exhort from our ex-companion immediately prior to his expeditious exit and distil some valuable information that we can utilise in our efforts to— '

Shaking her head vigorously, Zatt held up her hand.

'*Wait a moment Hopi!* Are you trying to tell us that Al told you something before he left?'

'Yes.'

'Well, why can't you just—*oof!*'

Elli gave Zatt a 'leave-this-to-me' nudge in the ribs, temporarily winding her.

'What exactly did Al say Hopi?'

'Well, first he said "I'm sure those traitors, the two Taur brothers, are behind this"; to which we – that is Wishi and I – replied "Whoi?" and "Who?"; to which he in turn replied "The Taur brothers, Cen and Mino, or failing that their mother, GG Mystery, though no-one has seen her for epochs." Then we – that's Wishi and I again, in case you were wondering – asked where we might find these "Taur brothers"; to which he then replied … ' Hopi took a deep breath.

' … "You'll find Cen up-up-up, high-high-high—high-as-the-sky; and Mino down-down-down, low-low-low—down-low-below, don'cha know . . . high and low . . . high and low . . . a bit like meee-eee . . . *weee-eee-eee!*"'

Hopi had just used a special talent that all nevasauruses had but they seldom used; namely an ability to mimic others perfectly. The effect was uncanny; it was as if Al himself had personally re-joined them. While he was speaking, both Elli and Zatt looked frantically about, trying to see where Al's voice was coming from before they realised it was actually Hopi talking.

'So,' said Elli. 'Let me see if I've got this right Hopi. What you're saying is if we are to stand any chance of getting this-this 'wreck' of a quest back "on track" so-to-speak, we have to start by making a simple choice. Do we head upwards and try to find this – *um* – "Cen Taur" chap, or do we head downwards in search of his brother—what was his name? "Mino"?'

Meanwhile, far up above the highest peak of God's Crown and continuing to ascend ever-higher, Ovi and Gusto were doing their best to hold on to Al's neck.

Like the others, they too had spotted the giant orb-shaped shadow pass by outside the waterfall and they'd also shouted for Al to stop when they'd realised he was heading straight for the humungous and fearsome cascade. But their cries had been completely extinguished the instant they'd hit the wall of water. Luckily, just before impact they'd both remembered to take in a deep, deep breath. In spite of this, by the time they'd emerged on the other side of the waterfall, Ovi's face had turned bright blue and Gusto's was a dark purple tinged with yellow which looked most unhealthy even for someone with his body-chemistry.

While they were still catching their breath, they had looked around and realised they were right at the bottom of the gigantic waterfall which towered far, far up high above them; and, moreover, there had been no sign of a moon anywhere to be seen.

Despite coughing, spluttering and struggling for breath himself, Al had immediately set off in search of the Blue Moon with some frantic '*Fah-whoosh-pah-lomp*'-ing, whilst at the same time resuming his cry of '*My moon! My moon! Oh, woe is my lovely Blue Moon!*'

It had taken Ovi and Gusto a bit longer to recover from being pummelled by the raging torrent and, by the time either was able to speak again, the mountain peaks were already far below … and receding fast. As soon as Gusto got his voice back, he had to shout as loud as he could in order to be heard above the loud '*Fah-whoosh-pah-lomp*'-ing and Al's plaintive wails.

'*Tell him to take us down, will you little buddy! I don't think I can* – burp – *hold on much longer!*'

'OK I'll try!' shouted Ovi over his shoulder. *'I'll do my best!'*

Ovi stretched forward as far as he could, but Al's ears were much farther away from him than Gusto's were to his rear.

'Al! ... Al! ... Al!' he cried, but to no avail.

'My moon! My moon! Come back to me; oh, my lovely Blue Moon!'

'I can't see any moon, Al! I think it must have gone back down in between the mountains. Don't you think it would be a good idea to go down now Al?'

'Oh, woe; oh, where is my lovely Blue Moo-ooo-oon?'

Ovi turned and shouted back to Gusto.

'It's no use, he can't hear me!'

'You've got to – burp – *go further forward little buddy!'*

To move any further forward Ovi needed to clear a row of Al's neck frills which kept opening and closing like a fish's gills. He could only do this by lifting himself up on his knees and clambering over the row of scarlet spikes one leg at a time. He waited for Al to complete a '*Fah-whoosh-pah-lomp*' and duly lifted his torso away from the safety of Al's neck. Unfortunately, the '*Fah-whoosh-pah-lomp*' was actually the first of a double wingbeat and the sudden jolt of the second caught Ovi off guard. In an instant he slipped and, in another instant, he lost his grip.

Luckily, Gusto managed to grab one of the creepers round Ovi's provisions and haul him back on board before he tumbled away into open sky. They were now both holding on to Al's neck—*just*; but where Gusto was still in his original position, Ovi was on the underside and struggling to hold on.

At that very moment, the creeper that Gusto had grabbed came undone and all of Ovi's provisions; baby-bison, bunches of bananas, water bladders and dainties were released to fall away free. They all rapidly disappeared apart from one baby-bison which somehow got tangled with Gusto's provisions. Dangling by one of its back legs, it started to bang repeatedly against the side of Gusto's head. Gusto reached round to rid himself of the pesky little cooked creature, but as he did so Al '*Fah-whoosh-pah-lomp*'-ed once more, causing him to slip.

'Uh–oh! *I say, little buddy?'*

'What is it Gusto?'

'I think I could – burp *– do with some help here. I— '*

'Fah-whoosh-pah-lomp!'

'I'll be with you in a moment Gusto! I just need to get back round where I was and— '

Ovi happened to glance downwards while he was struggling to get his leg back round Al's neck and he actually caught a fleeting glimpse of Gusto plummeting out of sight. He thought he heard a faint voice say *'Blasted –* burp *– baby-bison!'* but he couldn't be certain; he was too busy going into shock.

'*HE-EE* – belp – *EE-EEE* – belch-burp – *EEE-EE-E* – hiccough – *EEE-EELP!*'

Gusto's rational mind such as it was (learnt mostly from Zatt it has to be said) told him that shouting '*He-eee-elp!*' at the top of his voice was in all likelihood not going to achieve very much what with there being no-one around to hear him scream, but that wasn't going to stop him from giving it a jolly good try. It was, therefore, luck of the very highest order that as he uttered his wailing cry, he passed within auditory range of Wishi who was hovering just above the biggest peak in the whole of God's Crown (the mountain with the waterfall), wondering where everyone was.

Like Al before him, Wishi had been swallowed by the raging torrent and tumbled almost as far as the very bottom of the great falls before he'd managed to extricate himself from the water's grip. Also like Al, he'd barely managed to escape before the mighty cascade pounded onto the giant rocks at its base with a ferocious '*crash*', a deafening '*boom*' and a rapacious '*roar*'. *Un*-like Al, however, Wishi's wings weren't waterproof which meant he'd had to do a few circuits well away from the spray of the roaring waters in order to dry them off before he could set about trying to find the others. He'd just ascended the complete height of the waterfall and cleared the mountain's highest peak when the sky had suddenly filled with plummeting objects many of which looked familiar. He scrutinised them as they flew past and realised they were the gang's supplies. At that moment, he heard Gusto's cry ('*HE-EE* – belp – *EE-EEE* – belch-burp – *EEE-EE-E* – hiccough – *EEE-EELP!*' was how it actually sounded to Wishi's ears) and saw his fellow gang member plummet past fast. Without hesitation, he furled his wings and dived.

'Hoild oin Goistoi, oim coimoing!'

'Hey – burp – *Wishi! I need your* – belch – *help little buddy!'*

'Hoilloi Goistoi! Noice toi soi yoi oigoin! Whoire's Oil oind Oivoi?'

'They're still – belch – *going up, but never mind them little buddy, what about* – burp – *me?'*

'Yoire toi hoivoiy foir moi toi coirroiy Goistoi, boit yoi're oilroight foir noiw—yoi've stoill goit oi loing woiy toi foill. Oi'm soire woi coin thoink oif soimthoing boifoire yoi goi 'sploitt.'*!'*

'Well, actually – burp – *I've been falling for quite a bit now and had* – belch – *some time to think; and I think* – burp – *I have an idea!'*

'Thoit's groit! Whoit ois oit?'

'I think if I eat enough of – belch – *Zatt's dainties* – burp – *I might just be able to cushion my fall with a* – burp – *giant fart!'*

'Whoit oi woindoirfoill oidoia! Oih, yoi oire soi cloivoir Goistoi! Oit moist boi loivoing woith Zoitt thoit— '

'Er – *we need to move pretty* – burp – *fast little buddy!'*

A mountain peak had just shot by, forcing Gusto to cut Wishi short; there was a real sense of urgency in his manner and his voice sounded uncharacteristically tense. Picking up on this, Wishi put on his best 'don't-worry-I'm-determined-to-treat-this-situation-with-the-seriousness-it-deserves' look followed rapidly by 'now-how-can-I-help?'.

'See all these – burp – *falling supplies?'*

Wishi nodded.

'I need you to gather up as many of Zatt's dainties as you can find and – belch – *bring them to me. You* – burp – *got that little buddy?'*

Wishi nodded and set about his allotted task like a—well, a nevasaurus on a mission; and before long he returned to Gusto with his talons full of the curious-looking foul-smelling yellow-brown-puke-green-blue-gold-and-slimy balls. By now, Gusto was well below the top-most peaks and starting to 'mix it' with cliffs, bluffs and assorted jagged rocky outcrops all of which were rushing past. He grabbed as many of the putrid gooey-glutinous objects as he could and started gobbling fast. Realising a lot was at stake, Wishi dutifully waited patiently for Gusto to get well and truly stuck in before asking a question that was bothering him.

'*Whoit oiboit Oivoi Goistoi? Doi yoi thoink hoi's oilroight?*'

Gusto paused in mid-chomp to allow a particularly loud belch do its thing. He then smiled; the dainties were beginning to have the desired effect.

'*Oh, Ovi's in much more serious trouble* – burp-grumble-belch – *than I am little buddy!*' He popped another dainty in his mouth and then continued to speak while chewing. 'Mmm-*you* mmm-*should* – belch – mmm-*go and do* – burp-grumble-belp – *what* mmm-*you can* mmm-*for* – burp – *him!*'

'*Boit Oi coin't floiy ois foist – oir ois hoigh – ois Oil!*' protested Wishi. '*Oi'll noivoir coitch hoim oip!*'

'Buu-uu-urple – grumble-di-belch – *burr-rrr-rrr-RRR-UP!!!*'

Gusto's belly suddenly began expanding rapidly. He looked down and then back up at Wishi with a smile and a wink.

'*Right* – burp – *little buddy; that's me taken care of* – belch-growl-hiccough – *Now, go* – belp – *help Ovi!*'

'Hold on tight; gotta hold on tight.' Ovi kept chanting his mantra with his eyes firmly closed. He had decided the best way not to be frightened of the rapidly growing distance between his body and everything beneath him was not to look down. 'Hold on tight; gotta hold on tight.'

'*Oivoi!*'

'Hold on tight; gotta— ' Ovi paused and strained to listen. From somewhere beneath him, almost lost against the sound of Al's beating wings and the constant rush of air, he was sure he'd just heard the faintest of voices … and it sounded familiar.

'*Oivoi!*'

There it was again; a little less faint that time.

'*Is that you Wishi?*'

'*Yois, oit's moi!*'

Ovi opened one of his eyes and chanced a downward peep. Far, far below, between a green patch to one side and a blue patch to the other, was a ripple of white shapes rather like the white water in the middle of the river they'd crossed earlier. As he looked, he realised the ripples were in fact the now-distant mountain peaks of God's Crown, and like everything else they were moving away from him fast. But, there immediately below, he could also clearly make out something that wasn't moving away; it was a tiny black speck that was actually getting closer ... and what's more, it was distinctly Wishi-shaped.

'Yoi've goit toi loit goi Oivoi! Yoi're goittoing doingoiroisloiy hoigh!'

'I can't let go Wishi! It's too far to fall. That kind of fall will almost certainly hurt, and hurt a lot!'

'Doin't woirroiy Oivoi. Oi'll soive yoi. Joist loit goi!'

'Do you promise you'll save me Wishi?'

'Yois! Noiw ploise loit goi!'

Just then, Al cried yet another of his '*My moon! My moon! My lovely Blue Moon!*' cries and followed it by emitting another one of his primitive mythological extended howls. This time, however, he was so far above the world only Ovi and Wishi could hear it. The sound caused Ovi to look upwards ... and he gasped in shock at what he could see.

He was no longer heading *for* the sky; he was *in* it! All around him the light bright happy blue of daylight was rapidly giving way to the deep dark and actually-rather-menacing black of the night. He looked at the stars. He had never seen them so big and so shiny ... and so *near!* It was at this point that Ovi's head started to spin and go giddy like it did when he was on the riverbed waiting for Hopi to come and collect him. His grip on Al's neck momentarily loosened but, before he could tighten it again, Al did another double '*Fah-whoosh-pah-lomp*'.

It actually came as a relief to Ovi to finally be falling free. He'd been holding on to Al's neck for such a long time, his arms and legs had seized-up in a 'hold-on-for-dear-life' position. As he fell away, he heard yet another of Al's forlorn cries of '*My moon! My moon! Oh, where is my lovely Blue Moo-oo-oon?*' followed by one last-but-very-faint '*Fah-whoosh-pah-lomp*' before he disappeared completely out of sight ... into the very heavens.

Ovi hadn't fallen far before Wishi was by his side, accompanying him on his descent.

'Hello Wishi old friend! Boy am I glad to see you!'

'Hoilloi Oivoi! Goid toi soi yoi toi. Oi've boin voiroiy woirroid oiboit yoi. Oi thoight Oi'd loist yoi, boit Oi coime oicroiss Goistoi oin hois woiy doiwn oind hoi— '

'Um – *do you think we could possibly catch up on news a bit later Wishi?*' Ovi interrupted Wishi as politely as he could, not wishing to upset his old friend and only hope in terms of surviving his hurtle to the ground. '*Did you or did you not say something about saving me if I let go?*'

'Yois, thoit's roight. Oit wois Goistoi whoi soid Oi shoild— '

'Sorry to interrupt Wishi, I don't mean to be rude or anything, but do you think we could do a bit less "chatting" and – um – *a bit more "saving"?'*

'Oif coirse, Oivoi! Soilloi moi! Oi wois goittoing oi boit coirroid oiwoiy woith oill thois oixcoitmoint. Hoire woi goi … '

Wishi flew round underneath Ovi, grabbed hold of his back in his talons then turned him over and began back-flapping his wings as fast as he could in order to slow their ascent. Now that he was facing the mountains that he was rapidly hurtling toward, Ovi was filled with a surge of mixed feelings. On the one hand, he was relieved to be heading back towards them a bit like someone looking forward to a reunion with old friends; on the other, he was bit alarmed at the rapidity of their approach.

'Er – *Wishi!*' he shouted back over his shoulder.

'Grrr-rrr-rr-*y-y-yois?*' Wishi growled and grunted through gritted teeth as he re-doubled his efforts to tug Ovi upwards.

'*I* – um – *I have no wish to discourage you Wishi—far from it heaven forbid; but I* – um – *I'm afraid I don't think this is working!*'

Wishi let Ovi go and returned to his earlier position, nose-diving beside his friend's head. He then looked down at the rapidly approaching peaks and saw for himself how much closer they were.

'Oi hoive oin oidoia Oivoi! Woit hoire—Oi'll boi ois quoick ois Oi coin!'

With a '*FIZZ—FOZZLE … FUZZ—FA-ZURR-RR-RRLE … FA—ZUPP-UPP-UP … UP … P … P … P-p-p-p … … p*' Gusto's fart finally gave out and he dropped the final few feet to the ground, landing to one side of a small clearing at the bottom of a deep narrow canyon. The instant he landed, a large shadow filled the clearing and Wishi soared low over his head with Ovi in his talons. He let Ovi drop then, with an extra-strong '*Fah-whoosh-pa-pa-dah-lommopp*', banked hard left and shot back up to avoid hitting the wall of the canyon.

As soon as he was on the ground, Ovi started rolling in the dust and rubbing it all over his body. Spotting a boulder nearby, he dashed over and began kissing it.

'Oh, joy of joys, *land at la-aaa-ast!* Land, land, land … at last, at last, *at last!*' He tried to pick up the boulder for a full-on hug but it was too heavy. Instead, he knelt down, flung his arm around it and caressed it fondly. 'We are a pair you and I. We're meant to be together and never parted. I'm never *ever* going to leave you *ever* again! I promise!'

'*Hey, Ovi* – burp – *little buddy!*' Gusto picked himself up and started waving at his fellow gang member across the clearing. '*What a* – burp – *coincidence both of us landing at the same time and* – belch – *the same place like this?*'

'*Gusto!*' Ovi leapt to his feet and waved back.

They were both so relieved to see the other, they ran towards each other with their arms out-stretched for a hug. However, just then, Wishi came in to land with a double '*Fah-whoosh-pa-pa-dah-lommopp!*' that was so powerful it filled the canyon with a dense cloud of billowing dust which temporarily blinded them and forced them to stop running.

Once the dust had cleared, they rubbed their eyes in disbelief. There, standing on his hind legs exactly half-way between them, was a greatly-enlarged Wishi.

Ovi and Gustio stared open-mouthed in astonishment at their fellow gang member and joint rescuer. He was considerably bigger than he'd been at any time since the start of the mission.

'How did you get so big Wishi?' asked Ovi.

'Oi wois loickoiy! Oi foind oi boig boinch oiv boiboiy boisoin foilloing through thoi skoiy oind Oi goibbled thoim oip oin oine boig goilp!'

While Wishi was speaking, Ovi and Gusto resumed their run towards each other with their arms outstretched, only now their intention was a full-on 'group-hug'.

'Hey – *puff* – Gusto!' cried Ovi as he ran. 'How in swamp-fume-blazes – *puff* – did you manage to – *puff-puff* – get down safely?'

Gusto was about to reply, when suddenly—

'*Ba-doing!*'

—a baby-bison landed on his head.

He froze, lurched jerkily to one side and toppled over face down. Ovi paused for a moment in surprise then, with a loud splutter, burst into guffaws of laughter.

'*Ha Ha Ha!* Gusto, that was *so* funny! You look like— '

'*Ba-doing!*'

He was cut off as a baby-bison hit him on the head.

'*Ow!*' Ovi rubbed his head and gave a little 'what-was-that?' look up to the sky before he also wobbled and fell over to one side. (What Gusto and Ovi didn't know, of course, was that Gusto's earlier massive 'landing-cushioning' fart had not only slowed his decent, it had also created a vortex of billowing air within the confines of the deep canyon they had fallen into which had then gone on to propel all their falling Tax-Taker-Backer-Gang provisions back up into the air. The baby-bisons, banana bunches, bladders and what was left of the dainties had then bounced and re-bounced, bounded and re-bounded, from rock face to pinnacle to bluff to overhang – rather like lotto balls in lottery machine.)

Wishi, meanwhile, looked from Ovi to Gusto then back to Ovi in astonishment.

'Goidnoiss. Whoit oi coioincoidoince! Whoit oire thoi choincois oif twoi boiboiy boisoin foilloing oit oif thoi skoiy loike— '

'*Ba-doing!*'

A third baby-bison fell out of nowhere to hit him square between the horns. Being made of more sturdy stuff (especially after having recently eaten a whole brace of the little cooked beasts), he didn't fall down. Instead, he looked up with a 'whoit-oin-bloizois-wois-thoit?' expression on his face. And the moment he did so—

'*Splatt-squelch!*'

—a full water bladder hit him right between the eyes.

There's not actually that much difference between a '*ba-doing!*' and a '*splatt-squelch!*' when it comes to being hit on the head and sure enough the effect of the '*splatt-squelch!*' on Wishi was identical to the earlier '*ba-doings!*' on Elli and Gusto as he too lurched jerkily to one side … and fell forward face down into the dust.

The stunned gang members needed a moment to recover from being battered by their provisions; but eventually, all three stirred and picked themselves up, each one wobbly and groggy from their blows.

'Well, I must say,' Ovi had to shake his head and bang his temple to stop his eyes from rolling, ' … that was a bit unlucky. I hope there are no more of those heading for— '

A distant sound gave him cause to pause.

'*Ba-doing!*'

All three looked up.

'*Ba-doing!*'

There it was again. This time, Wishi spotted what was making the sound and pointed.

'*Loik! Thoire!*'

Bouncing from canyon wall to canyon wall with ever-louder resounding '*ba-doings!*' was a solitary baby-bison. Ovi recognised it instantly; it was the biggest one they'd packed and was intended to be a celebratory treat for when they successfully completed their mission.

'*It's the "Special Bison"!*' he cried. '*Remember?*'

Gusto and Wishi nodded. Then all three proceeded to watch like tennis spectators as the flying cooked beast '*ba-doing!*'-ed its way relentlessly toward them.

'*Ba-doing! … Ba-doing! … Ba-doing!*'

It did a final '*ba-doing!*' on a pinnacle of rock a little way off to their left then shot over their heads into a big clump of green foliage immediately behind Wishi.

'*Phoiw!*' said Wishi, making a 'thoit-wois-cloise' face and clacking his talons with relief. 'Oi'm gloid thoit doidn't hoit oinoiy oif ous. Oif oit hoid, oit— '

'*OOOWWW!*' A loud and intensely fierce growl suddenly erupted from the spot in the foliage where the 'special bison' had disappeared. '*OOOWWW-G-G-GRRR-OOO-WWW-LLL!!!*'

The leaves parted and the most terrifying of beasts, a-super-monster-tyrannosaurus, leapt into view with a huge-and-rapidly-growing pink bump sticking out of the top of its head. It was clearly intent on doing serious damage to the cause of its torment, and upon spotting what it perceived to be its 'attackers', it gave a gut-wrenching and horrifying blast of a roar.

'*GE-ERR-RRR-OOO-WWW-LLL!!!*'

Then, with a fierce '*LA-A-A … CHOMP-DA-GNOSH-GNASH!*', it lunged at Wishi who quickly took to the air, leaving Ovi and Gusto as the beast's only two remaining 'attackers'.

Ovi, meanwhile, had instinctively started digging a hole in the dust and was already half-buried. Gusto, on the other hand, was torn. Should he run this way or that? He'd already pointed with his finger and taken several strides in each direction, and was busy re-pointing and switching direction again, when the super-monster-tyrannosaurus made its move.

With another even louder roar, the enraged beast lunged forward and its powerful jaws clenched tight around Gusto's girth. It then lifted its head and proceeded to shake its 'prey' ferociously from side to side in order to finish it off.

'*WH-WH-WH-OOO-OOO-OOO-SH-SH-SH!!!*'

Hopi flew sideways through the narrow gap down the side of the great waterfall with Elli and Zatt holding tight to his horns. Once they were safely through, he levelled off and after a few '*Fah-whoosh-pa-pa-dah-lommopp*'s the cacophonous roar of the falls was far away enough for them to speak.

'Well done Hopi,' said Zatt, leaning forward to stroke Hopi's ear. 'You did that perfectly; I hardly felt a splash!'

'Thank you for your kind compliment my dear Zatt; very much appreciated,' came Hopi's voice from beneath. 'Now that we are free of the cavern, are you sure you two don't want me to simply head for home?'

Elli and Zatt looked at each other and nodded resolute nods.

‘We said we would go “up” Hopi;’ said Zatt, ‘so “up” it is; not “home”, not yet anyway!’

‘“Up” is the way a moon would go,’ said Elli. ‘and therefore, the way Al would have gone too. It’s our best bet if we’re ever to see the others again.’

‘You never know, Hopi,’ added Zatt. ‘We may come across this “Cen Taur” whoever he is, and he might be able to help us.’

‘Are you absolutely sure now? This is your last chance to change your mind. Are you certain you wouldn’t prefer to go “down”? As I said earlier, “down” is much easier; far less far to fall and all that.’

‘We’re strapped in tight and can’t fall off,’ said Zatt. ‘so, feel free to take us “up” as high as you like Hopi!’

‘But first,’ added Elli, ‘at least take us “up” over the top of this waterfall so we can see where this blasted ‘monster-water’ is coming from!’

‘Righty-ho then; “up” it jolly well is! *Hold on tight!*’

Hopi stretched his wings out wide and ‘*Fah-whoosh-pa-pa-dah-lommopp*’-ed as hard as he could. Up-up-up they went, ever upward and upward; all the while against a backdrop of the cascade. Eventually, after what seemed an age, they rose above the giant falls and the roar of the water began to recede.

‘Hopi?’ said Zatt, starting to shiver.

‘Yes Zatt?’

‘I feel very strange all of a sudden.’

‘In what way?’

‘It feels as if my bones are trying to get out of my body.’

‘Oh, that’s nothing to worry about Sis,’ interrupted Elli, adopting his ‘scientific’ tone. ‘The same thing happened to me and Ovi when we were last in God’s Crown. I think it might be something to do with the ambient temperature coefficient being sub-optimal at high altitude working in combination with various meteorological factors such as the wind. I’m feeling it too as it happens; look at what my bones are doing to my hands.’

Elli lifted up his hand; it was bright blue and trembling so much it was all a-blur. Zatt carefully examined it with clinical ‘scientific’ curiosity; then she lifted up her own hand and it was exactly the same.

'Well, I never!' she exclaimed. 'What a fascinating phenomenon! We really ought to give it a name Elli—oh I know, how about "cold"?'

'"Cold" eh? Hmmm, that rhymes with another word I've been toying with in connection with "money"; "gold".'

Elli proceeded to mouth "cold" and "gold" a few times, trying them out as potential scientific terms. As he did so, Zatt leaned forward and shouted once more into Hopi's ear.

'Hopi! Do you think you could stop flapping your wings for a while so we can see what's down below us?'

'Yes, of course my dear Zatt; my pleasure!'

Hopi ceased '*Fah-whoosh-pa-pa-dah-lommopp*'-ing and settled into a gentle glide. The two siblings shared a 'scientific' smile then leaned outwards to look down; the sight that met their eyes made their jaws drop, rendering them utterly, as well as 'scientifically', speechless.

Below them was the most awesome vista to be seen anywhere on Proto-Earth. From their high vantage point they could see the whole of God's Crown spread out beneath them; and it was huge! They instantly realised the reason for its rather odd name for it was, indeed, 'crown-shaped' with countless glistening white peaks loosely forming a ginormous circle that stretched almost to the horizon in every direction. Moreover, at the heart of the mountain range (which they were rapidly approaching) was a distinct 'inner circle' of extra-double-tall peaks that appeared to be clustered round a giant hole of some kind. As they drew near, however, they realised the 'hole' was, in fact, no such thing; it was actually a vast circular lake. The deepest of blues, it constantly twinkled like the stars up above. Just then, Elli spotted something and pointed at the far side of the lake.

'What's going on down there?' he said. 'It looks as if something rather odd is happening.'

Zatt and Hopi both looked where Elli was pointing and sure enough something peculiar was occurring. At several points around the lake's rim, clouds were gathering amongst the 'inner peaks' and merging together before heading out over the lake. As they merged, they were changing from being bright and fluffy small white clouds into great big horrid dark and menacing ones.

Once they were over the lake, they were then lingering for a few moments to release a deluge of rain as if they were somehow "topping it up". After they'd "emptied" themselves, they were then breaking up into smaller white fluffy clouds again which flitted away back to where they had come from.

'How interesting,' said Hopi after observing the curious scene for a while. 'If I didn't know better, I'd say those clouds were somehow being herded together from all across the sky.'

'That's not the only thing that's "interesting" Hopi.' Zatt pointed to their rear. 'If you look behind us, I've just spotted a couple of 'old friends' of ours and it would seem they are closely related: our waterfall and that "river"-thingy!'

Hopi veered round to head where Zatt was pointing. There before them was a gap between two of the 'inner peaks' which looked as if it had been straightened and flattened; and sure enough, flowing over the broad flat 'lip' was, indeed, the great waterfall. As Hopi cleared the crest of the falls, they could also see that Zatt was right; far, far below snaking away from the bottom of the falls was the unmistakeable fast-moving body of water that had caused them so many problems.

'Er, Hopi?' Elli's voice suddenly sounded fragile and a more than a little brittle.

'Yes, Elli?'

'It's a bit t-t-too "cold" up here for m-my liking. Do you th-th-think we c-c-c-could— '

'I beg your pardon? I didn't quite catch that Elli.'

'Take us down quick Hopi! Elli's bones have stopped moving. I think it maybe-be-be-be-becau— '

Hopi looked up with both eyes. Elli and Zatt had turned bright blue and were frozen solid like statues.

'Hmmm. I suppose it is a tad chilly up here. Come to think of it, it *is* getting rather late and we *are* in need of a jolly good rest. I think this might be an opportune juncture for me to find somewhere nice and cosy – all snug, safe and warm – to spend the night.'

'Cor, that – *puff* – was a stroke of – *puff* – luck – *wheeze* – Gusto!'

'Oi shoild soiy soi – *poiff* – Woill doine Goistoi!'

'Well – *puff-burp* – little buddy and much-bigger-than-before-buddy – *puff* – I guess shaking me about like that – *burp-puff-belp* – kinda shook it out of me.'

The three of them had stopped running from the super-monster-tyrannosaurus in order to catch their breath. Wishi had chosen to run rather than fly because his wings were tired. The reaction of the huge beast to Gusto's huge fart had been similar to that of the crocogator, but less severe. It had instantly spat Gusto out and crawled back into the undergrowth, gagging and rubbing the sore bump on its head … and that had been the last they'd seen of it.

'Those farts of yours sure are – *puff* – coming in useful – *wheeze* – Gusto – *puff-puff-wheeze* – one way or another.'

'Yois, thoiy oire oilmoist – *whoize* – ois poiwoirfoill ois noivoirsoirois broith.'

'You know something – *puff-belp* – little and great big buddies, you're abso – *burp* – lutely right there. In fact – *belch-puff-burp* – when I get back to Zatt I'm going to— '

'*GRRR-RRR-OOO-OOO-OOO-WWW-LLL!!!*'

The super-monster-tyrannosaurus suddenly leapt from a bluff and landed immediately in front of them, its wide glaring eyes full of red lightning streaks (the after-effect of inhaling 'Gusto-gas'). It was back with a vengeance, and this time it not only had a sore head, it also had a dicky tummy.

'*LA-A-A … CHOMP-DA-GNOSH-GNASH!*'

Gusto instantly pointed where to go and ran away, leaving Ovi on his own to face the enraged beast.

'*QUICK!*' Ovi shouted up to Wishi who was hovering a safe distance from the tyrannosaurus's lunging jaws. '*FETCH ME A STICK!*'

(A little-known fact about tyrannosauruses is they are the direct ancestors of dogs. Some palaeontologists beg to differ on this, but as far as I'm concerned, the proof is irrefutable. The name's a bit of a giveaway for a start—Tyrannosaurus *REX*; and then there's the key trait they both share … a blind and mindless obsession with chasing sticks which was just as well-known in Ovi's time as it is today.)

'*Roightoiy-hoi! Woit thoire; Oi'll boi roight boick!*'

Wishi hurriedly rushed off into the trees to find one.

'GRRR-RRR-OOO-OOO-OOO-WWW-LLL!!! – burp!'

The bad-tummy-tyrannosaurus kept lunging at Ovi who, in turn, kept scrambling up the boulder then slipping back down again; and each time it lunged its drool-laden incisors 'gnosh-gnashed' closer and closer. Suddenly, Ovi lost his grip entirely and he slid dangerously close to the snapping jaws. Luckily, at that point, Wishi returned.

'Oi coin't foind oine!'

'What do you mean, you can't find one Wishi!? There are—OOOPS!' He had to lift his legs to dodge another lunge. *'There are trees and bushes everywhere!'*

'Yois, loits oif trios oind boishes, boit noi stoicks!'

'LA-A-A ... CHOMP-DA-GNOSH-GNASH ... GNOSH!!!'

'Oi hoive oin oidoia Oivoi!'

'LA-A-A ... CHOMP-DA-GNOSH-GNASH!!! – belch!'

'What? *Quick-quick!* What?'

'Whoiy doin't yoi troiy thoi 'Goim Goim' soing oin oit?'

'The Gum Gum song? On a super-monster-tyrannosaurus? *Are you mad Wishi?'*

'Oit's woirth oi troiy!'

'LA-A-A ... CHOMP-DA-GNOSH-GNASH!!! – burp!'

Ovi managed to grab hold of a creeper and scramble up to the top of the boulder where he was just beyond the beast's reach. As soon as he was on his feet, he span round and squared-up to the raging belly-ache-er.

'Gum Gum
Garah Gum
Gar Gum Guttle
Gyrannosaurus.

Serrum Dittle
Tattle Tittle
Gar Gum Gittle Giiiiiiiiiiiiiiiiii .....

Speak Tyrannosaurus!'

The super-monster-tyrannosaurus was either not listening or not appreciative of good poetry. Instead of breaking into human speech, it roared its loudest roar yet then charged at Ovi's boulder, making it wobble which knocked Ovi over. Once again, he almost slipped into the beast's gaping jaws, but once again he managed to grab hold of the creeper and, instead, found himself dangling within a whisker of the razor-sharp chompers.

'*LA-A-A … CHOMP …* '

'*Troiy thoi* '*Goim Goim*' *soing oigoin Oivoi!*'

'G-G-Good id-d-dea W-W-Wishi! Here g-g-goes … '

'—G-G-Gum Gum—'
'*GNOSH-GNASH!*'
'—Garah G-G-Gum—'
'*LA-A-A ... CHOMP-DA*—burp—*GNASH* ... '
'—Gar Gum G-G-G-G-Guttle—'
'*GNOSH*—belch—*GNASH!!!*'
'—G-G – *um-m-m-m* – '

'*LA-A-A … CHOMP-DA …* Vell, vell, vell; bist du just saying-k "Um"?'

'*Er* – yes … why?'

'Vell, das ist meine Name.'

The super-monster-tyrannosaurus smiled. (I should point out, Dear Reader, that tyrannosauruses back then spoke Human with a really ridiculous, over-the-top and naff German accent!)

'What did you say?' Ovi quickly clambered back up to the top of the boulder to address the huge beast who had calmed down completely and was nonchalantly picking his teeth with one of his claws. 'Are you telling me your name is "Um"?'

'Yah, das ist korrectlich. Meine familienname ist "Um"; aber mein voller Name ist "Poob Um".'

'"Poo Bum"?' repeated Ovi.

'*Nein-nein-nein!* Nicht "Poo Bum"! "Poob … Um"' Poob looked distinctly irritated and started tapping his foot. 'Gottit?'

'"Poob Um"' repeated Ovi. 'Right, gottit!' He struggled to keep a straight face and had to turn away to smother a giggle. Pulling himself together, he turned to Poob once more. 'Nice to meet you Poob. My n-n-name— ' He had to bite his lip to fight back laughter. 'M-m-my name is— '

'*HOI! Hoi hoi!*'

Wishi's sudden outburst caused Ovi to splutter into full-blown raucous guffaws of laughter. He laughed so much he fell off the boulder and collapsed into a heap, clasping his sides.

'*Ha-ha-ha! … Haa-aaa-ha-hah!*'

'*Hoi-hoi-hoi! … Hoi-hoi, hoi-hoi!*'

'Hey little buddy; what's happening?' Gusto's voice came from somewhere nearby.

'*Hah-ha-ha!* Hey Gusto, you can come out now! *Hah-ha-ha!* Come and meet our new friend … P-P-Poob.'

As Gusto emerged from behind the boulder, Ovi decided to attempt some introductions.

'*Hah-ha-ha!* Sorry about this Poob. *Hah-ha-ha!* Kindly allow me to – *ha-ha-ha* – allow me to introduce ourselves. *Ha-aaa-ha-ha-ha-ha!* My name is – *ha-ha-ha* – my name is "Ovi". Up there is "Wishi" – *ha-ha-ha* – and this here – *ha-ha-ha* – this here is "Gusto".'

'Nice to meet you Poob big buddy.'

'Noice toi moit yoi Poib.'

'Vell, hallo zu allen. Nice to meet you Vischi, Offi und Gusto.'

'*Hah-hah-ha!* Tell them your full name Poob.'

'Yah, natürlich. Mein voller Name ist "Poob Um".'

'"Poo – *belp* – Bum"?'

'"Poi Boim"?'

'*Nein-nein-nein-nein-nein!* Nicht "Poi Boim"! Nicht "Poo – *belp* – Bum"! "*POOB … UM*"*!*' The super-monster-tyrannosaurus looked more than a little annoyed and started tapping his feet again. '"Poob … Um" ist meine Name!'

Now it was Gusto's turn to laugh. His laugh started in the depths of his belly, rumbled up his throat and erupted forth with an accompanying loud '*burp-belch*'. For a while, his '*Hah* – belch – *ha*'s combined with Ovi's '*hah-ha-ha*'s and Wishi's '*hoi-hoi-hoi*'s to make a cacophony of laughter, leaving Poob to stare awkwardly about, looking irritably this way and that whilst waiting for their hysterics to subside.

Ovi was the first to pull himself together.

'S-s-sorry about that P-P-Poob.' He sniggered. 'We don't mean to be rude or anything. It's just that—well, you do have a very funny name. You must get people laughing at your name all the time.'

Poob fixed Ovi with a firm stare.

'*Nein!* Das ist da first time it hass effer happened! Vas ist vrong-k mit meine Name anyvay? Ich bin alvays thinking-k it vas a rahzah gut Name meine Eltern, M und D, gave me.'

'Wait a minute. Did you just say your parents were "M" and "D"?'

'Yah, meine Mutter var "M" und mein Vater var "D".'

'*HA-AAA-HA-HA!*' Ovi laughed his loudest laugh yet, causing Gusto and Wishi (who were both rolling on their backs) to look up with 'what's-funny-now?' expressions. '*Ha-ha-ha!* Hey you two; can you guess what Poob's parents were called?'

Unable to speak, they both shook their heads.

'His mother was "M" making her full name "M—Um"; and his father – *wait for it* – his father was "D" making his full name – *ha-ha-ha* – "D—Um"!'

The dawn up high in the peaks and pinnacles of God's Crown was incredibly bright and stunningly beautiful. The dark star-spangled blackness of the night sky slowly gave way to an array of iridescent blues, soon to be joined by a bunch of purples and pinks, followed by a gang of oranges and reds, hotly pursued by a mob of greens bringing with them a whole horde of yellows-mixed-with-golds-blended-with-silvers. The resulting cacophony of colours then vied with each other to put on the most dazzling of displays.

The previous afternoon after Elli and Zatt had frozen solid, Hopi had dived down in amongst the peaks and pinnacles looking for somewhere suitable to rest. Just as the last vestiges of daylight were fading, he'd finally spotted something near the top of a peak. Perched in a cleft between two pinnacles was an old deserted nest made of sticks, held firm with rocks and stones and lined with a plump abundance of nice warm feathers. Keeping a wary eye out for its regular inhabitant, Hopi had carefully nestled his two passengers safely into the feather bedding and found himself a comfortable perch nearby. As he'd drifted into sleep, the idea had flitted through his mind like a white fluffy cloud that the nest might belong to a poltroon, but he'd quickly dismissed the notion realising it was far too well-made and easily accessible. Moments later, all three exhausted members of the Tax-Taker-Backer-Gang had been snoring their way into the deepest of slumbers.

When Zatt awoke she immediately spotted her brother silhouetted against the dawn sky with its myriad of colours; but when she looked for Hopi, there was no sign of him anywhere.

'*Yaa-aaa-wwn!* Where's Hopi?' she said as she stretched her arms and arose from the comfort of her warm feather bed.

'Hmmm?' said Elli distractedly. He was standing on a ledge with his "bow" in hand surveying their surroundings, and his attention had been drawn to a cluster of fast-approaching, and very eye-catching, clouds. Their fluffy tops were ablaze with the colours of the sunrise while their flat bottoms glistened gold and silver as they reflected the sun's rays. At the heart of the cluster was a large purple cloud much bigger than the rest, and all the others appeared to be following it in a huddle.

'Elli! Are you listening to me?' said Zatt, looking around at the contents of the nest. 'I asked where Hopi was.'

Transfixed and mesmerised by the ever-shifting colours of the clouds, Elli didn't answer at first; and when he eventually did speak his voice had a dreamlike faraway quality.

'Oh, he's gone off exploring to see "what's what" apparently ... ' Elli gave his "bow" a single forlorn '*pluck*' that sounded pitifully out-of-tune. ' ... whatever *that* is!'

Zatt looked up just as a ray of dawn sunlight caught her brother's features and saw his melancholy expression.

'I'm sure they're both just fine,' she said gently. 'If I know Ovi and Gusto, they're probably tucking into a really nice breakfast right now.'

Elli smiled.

'Yeah, you're right Sis; Ovi *never* misses a meal!'

They both fell quiet and for a while Elli continued to watch the approaching clouds while Zatt became engrossed with the various bits of discarded bric-à-brac she'd found scattered about the floor of the nest.

'*AHA!*' she suddenly cried out, breaking the silence and distracting Elli from his cloud-watching. 'That goes in there … and *that* has to go-o-o … *there!*'

Curious to see what Zatt was up to, Elli turned round to find she had pulled out some straight sticks from the nest and was busy working on them, mumbling to herself as she did so.

'No, no, no, that has to go *there* and *that* go-ooo-oes … *there! YES—that's got it!*'

'What's that you're making Sis?'

Zatt had just inserted a pointed – and very sharp – piece of flint into one end of a stick and was busy fixing some bits of feather to the other. She had already completed a few similar sticks and they were laying in a clutch on her lap.

'I've decided to call them "arrows",' she declared, 'and I think they will prove to be one of life's little essentials.'

'"Arrows" eh?' Elli put down his bow and picked one up. 'What are they for?'

'They're for cleaning out your ears.'

'Oh, that'll come in handy Sis. I hate it when you wake up in the morning and a poltroon has mistaken your hair for its nest overnight—*yuck!*'

'Precisely! Well, all you need do now is take an "arrow", poke the sharp end in your ear and use it to dig out all that mess. Then, when it's all out, you flip the arrow round and use the feathers to brush it off your shoulders. Go on, give it a go.'

Elli worked the pointed stone deep into his ear then twiddled the stick like a drill***. It worked perfectly. A great spume of waxy-poo-ey flakes filled the air before settling on his shoulder. The feathers then came in really handy as a means of brushing it all off. Elli smiled a 'well-done-Sis-another-triumph' smile and handed the "arrow" back. He then returned to his ledge and was surprised to notice how much closer the clouds were; in fact, they were now almost directly overhead.

(****WARNING:* Do *NOT* try this at home! Obviously, Dear Reader, it would be extremely foolish to try such a thing! It's important to remember that Elli and Zatt were proto-humans and as such were made of much more basic primitive and tough stuff than us modern people. Plus, they were also *achingly* and *epochingly* more stupid!)

Suddenly, Elli heard something.

'*Shhh Zatt; listen!* I can hear a strange noise.'

The sounds of feathers, stones and long pointy sticks being fiddled with suddenly ceased.

'Thanks Sis. Can you hear that?'

Elli strained to listen. The word "metallic" didn't exist then; if it had, he would have made good use of it. He took Zatt's silence to mean she was also straining to listen. There it was again; a sharp staccato '*tippy-tappy*' sound.

'Surely, you can hear that!' He turned to face his sister. 'What do you think— '

Zatt wasn't there; she'd completely vanished.

Far down below in the bottom of the canyon, the dawn was a much more dingy affair. There were no brilliant displays of colour; instead, the bleak blackness of the night slowly became slightly less bleak until it wasn't black at all – more a light grey mixed with ashy-rocky-type colours, mingled with fuzzy murk.

Unbeknown to Ovi, Gusto and Wishi, way up high above them at that very moment, Zatt was being astonishingly accurate in her comments; for they had found a rather convenient and yummy source of food, a huge breakfast-berry bush; and they were, indeed, enjoying a hearty breakfast with Ovi tucking in to all the juicy-fruity-looking berries and Gusto concentrating on the more blob- or splatter-shaped ones. Even Poob and Wishi were in luck because some of the bush's berries were shaped like ragged chunks of raw meat.

Once they had all eaten their fill, Ovi, Gusto and Wishi sat down with Poob and all three fixed him with a 'We-have-something-important-to-say' stare.

'There's something we would like to tell you about us Poob,' said Ovi, suddenly looking earnest (almost as earnest as when he was out maggot-collecting), 'something very im—no, very, *very* important.'

'*Hoo-ooo-ooo!* Das is sehr interesting-k,' said Poob, raising a tyrannosaurus eyebrow (yes, they *did* have them!) 'Pleasing-k du telling-k Mich. Going-k for it!'

'The thing is Poob, we – that's Wishi, Gusto and me – we're all members of a "gang".'

'Eine "Gang-k"?'

'No, a "gang",' repeated Ovi.

'"Going" noit "going-k",' added Wishi.

'Yah-yah, es ist vass ich sage, eine "*Gang-k*", Yah?'

'A-a-aaa-nyway,' Ovi gave Poob a strange look before continuing, 'the thing is Poob, we're on a mission to— '

'Das ist sehr interessant zatt you should say zatt, bekause ich too bin on eine "Mission".'

Ovi, Wishi and Gusto all looked at each other then back at Poob.

'*Really? / Roilloi? / Rea*– belp – *lly?*'

'What's your "mission" then Poob?' asked Ovi.

'Ich muss finden alle die fehlenden Tyrannosauren— vass ist das; ach yah! "missing-k tyrannosauruses".'

'"All of the tyrannosauruses are missing" you say?'

Poob nodded, but Ovi looked doubtful.

'But that can't be true. Only the other day, Wishi's cousin, Hopi, trod on one just as he was entering The Great Ug's Palace.'

'Yah, yah, Ich weiß, Ich weiß, I know, I know! *Das var mich!* Zatt "Freund" off yours ought to vatch his schtep! I vas trying-k to get some off you humans zu helping-k Mich mit zatt Dummkopf der Taxman, der *verdammte* Taxman!'

'*Whoa, whoa* – burp – *whoa!* Wait up there big chomper buddy,' cried Gusto. 'Did you just say what I – *belp* – thought you said?'

'Well, well, well; isn't that something?' said Ovi. 'It turns out we're actually on very similar missions!'

'You mean he's also trying to get his – *burp* – tax back little buddy?'

'In a way, yes. He's trying to get all his fellow tyrannosauruses back, because you-know-who took them!'

'Whoi's thoit?'

'The "Taxman" of course Wishi! Who do you think?'

'*WOIW!*'

'So your gang-k ist hunting-k down ziss Taxman as vell, eh? Vass hass he been taking-k off yours?'

'What has he *not* taken more like Poob? He's taken so much stuff from us my sister actually made a "list"!'

'Vass ist your schwester's Name?'

'"Zatt".'

'Vass?'

'"Zatt"!'

'Yah, du saidst zatt, aber Vass ist "zatt"?'

Ovi gave Poob another strange look.

'It doesn't matter what he – *burp* – took from us big chomper buddy. The point is, whatever he – *belp* – took, we in the Tax-Taker-Backer-Gang aim to take it *aa-aaa-all* back! *Yeah! You betta betcha!*'

'In zatt kase I vish to join ziss "gang-k" off yours. Ich auch vant to be eine Tee-Rex-Teeker-Beecker-er!'

Ovi, Gusto and Wishi briefly shared sideways glances (an exchange accomplished all the more speedily by virtue of Wishi's independent eyes) then all four cheered.

'*Hooray! / Hoi-roiy! / Hoo* – burp – *ray! / Hurra-aaah!*'

'You are duly welcome as a member of our gang-k—I mean "gang", Poob Um!' declared a jubilant Ovi, producing a round of bananas for them to celebrate. 'Congratulations on becoming a Tee-Rex-Taker-Backer!'

They all consumed their bananas with relish, swallowing them together in one big simultaneous '*gulp!*' Ovi then struck a valiant pose, thrusting his big round belly proudly to the fore and raising his empty banana skin high.

'Now let us sally forth … an inseparable troupe of taker-backers … united in our cause … a true brotherhood … in an unbreakable bond!'

The others followed suit and raised their banana skins high.

'*Hoi-roiy! / Hoo* – belp – *ray! / Hurra-aaah!*'

'*We're jolly well gonna go and find that Taxman!*'

'*Hoi-roiy! / You* – burp – *betcha-aaa!*'

'*Yah! Yah! Hurra-aaah!*'

'*And take back that which is rightfully ours!*'

'*Hoi-roiy! / Hoo* – belch-burp – *ray!*'

'*Hurra-aaah! Das ist Wunderbar-rrr!*' Poob lowered his banana skin. 'How are we going-k to do zatt zen? Vass bis wir doing-k first?'

Their jubilation juddered to a sudden halt (rather like a tyrannosaurus losing sight of its stick), and their wild euphoria evaporated as they realised they didn't have a plan. A '*flobbity-blobbob*' sound made them all look down; Ovi's belly had drooped.

Ovi looked at his fellow gang members one-by-one. Hopi looked decidedly glum, Poob looked even glummer and Gusto was so glum he couldn't even manage a belp.

'A-a-a-any ideas anyone; any *at all* on where to start looking for this blasted Taxman?'

'*Oi knoiw! Oi've joist roimoimboired soimethoing!*'

Wishi suddenly started jumping up and down excitedly.

'Oil goive Hoipoi oind moi oi cloiue joist boifoire hoi spoittoid thoi Bloi Moin.'

'Really?'

'Yois, roilloi!'

'*Er* – do you think you could possibly translate little buddy? I can't understand a – *burp* – word big buddy is saying.'

'Yah, yah; Mich auch! Vischi, mein freund, du sprichts mit eine zehr schtrong ak-scent-lich.'

'He said,' explained Ovi, 'that Al gave him and Hopi a clue where to look for the Taxman just before he went off after the – *um* – the – *gulp* – B-B-Blue M-M-Moon.' He couldn't stop himself from shuddering as he recalled recent events.

'Yois, thoit's roight. Whoit hoi soid wois … *Oik-hoim* …

' … "You'll find Cen up-up-up, high-high-high—high-as-the-sky; and Mino down-down-down, low-low-low—down-low-below, don'cha know . . . high and low . . . high and low . . . a bit like meee-eee . . . *weee-eee-eee!*"'

Ovi, Poob and Gusto looked at each other in amazement before returning their gaze to Wishi.

'Do that again Wishi.'

'Yeah, what did – *burp* – Al say big buddy?'

'Ploise loistoin coirfoilloiy. Hoi soid … *Oik-hoim!* …

' … "You'll find Cen up-up-up, high-high-high—high-as-the-sky; and Mino down-down-down, low-low-low—down-low-below, don’cha know . . . high and low . . . high and low . . . a bit like meee-eee . . . *weee-eee-eee!*’’’

‘How come when you sound like Al you don’t have a nevasaurus accent Wishi?’ asked Ovi.

‘Oi doin’t knoiw. Oi joist doin’t.’ Wishi shrugged his shoulders. ‘Oinoiwoiy, ois woi’re doiwn loiw noir thoi boittoim oiv thoi mointoins, Oi thoink woi noid toi goi loikoing foir Moinoi.’

‘Let me see if I’ve got this right,’ said Ovi. ‘We might be able to get some help in our mission to find the Taxman if we go up high or down low; and if we want to go “down” – which I agree is the – *um* – the more practical option – the person we should be searching for is called “Moi-noi”—I mean “Mi-no”?’

The other gang members all nodded solemnly as, each in their own way, they digested Hopi’s new intelligence. Gusto lifted his head to say something but then thought better of it and farted a long-protracted fart instead. Just as the final fartlettes of the fart were petering out, Poob sat up with his eyebrows (yes, they *did* have them!) raised.

‘*Ach, yah!* Ick bin knowing-k ziss “Mino”! Er ist living-k down deep ass Vischi ist saying-k, sehr deep beneath zie ground unter dem berg—*er* – mountain, in eine—how-you-say, eine “Labyrinth”!’

Chapter Seven

Life on the wing

'Ah, good. You're finally coming round,' said a silky-smooth and rather sophisticated-sounding voice. 'Probably best if you sit up dear boy.'

Elli opened his eyes and tried to leap to his feet, but he was instantly blinded by a brilliant bright light and a wave of dizziness prevented him from doing any leaping.

'Wh-where – *cough* – am I?' he said in a croaky voice, 'and – *cough-cough* – where's Zatt?'

'You're on Cloud Nine my dear boy, and your sister is fine; she's actually quite busy as we speak doing a spot of work for me in Utopia. Before she left she asked me to give you this.'

Elli's eyes finally came into focus and there before him, completely bathed in white light, was a huge figure almost as big as Al from head to tail; except, this was no reptilian snake-like being with dangerous teeth and fierce-looking talons. Instead, this "creature" (Elli wasn't sure if it was a beast or a person) had the head, arms and torso of a large, chiselled-featured and very handsome man complete with the legs and body of a fine white charger of a horse. (What Elli wasn't to know, of course, Dear Reader, was that the person-part of the creature bore a striking resemblance to both George Clooney *and* Brad Pitt.) The man-creature also had an elegant pair of huge luxuriantly plumaged white wings neatly furled along his flanks.

The George-Brad lookalike was leaning forward offering Elli his bow. As Elli reached up to take it, he spotted the hooves of the horse-part were moving restlessly as if he was keen to be doing something; and as they moved, they made the '*tippy-tappy*' sound he'd heard back in the nest.

'Thank you – *um* – Sir.' Elli graciously took his bow and used it to stand up.

'Would you care for some ambrosia … or some nectar perhaps?' said the creature kindly in a George-sort-of-a-way.

Two darling little oochie-coo babies with rosy cheeks and flowing locks of hair fluttered their delicate-looking white fluffy wings and descended from nearby tufts of cloud to offer Elli some sustenance from giant clamshells. Elli helped himself to a morsel from one shell and dunked his finger in the golden syrup of the other which he then licked. Instantaneously, his body felt very alive and his mind fully alert.

'Tell, me something – *er* – Sir. Am I right in thinking I'm on one of the clouds that I was watching?'

'Very go-ooo-od Elli.' The creature smiled a cocky Brad-like smile.

'You obviously know my name.' Elli smiled back. 'Would you mind if I take a guess at yours?'

The creature smiled an even larger smile, more George than Brad.

'Why, of course you can dear boy. I can see you have that same twinkle in your eye as your sister does; that same glint of curiosity and inventiveness.'

'You're one of the Taur brothers, aren't you? Am I right?'

The creature looked nonchalantly and non-committally at its fingernails with a brooding Braddish air.

'You may well be right there dear boy; it rather depends on which brother you have in mind.'

'I think you are Cen … Cen Taur?'

The creature's smile turned into a gorgeously-groovy George grin, and as it did so Elli was impressed by how regular and sparkly-white his teeth were.

'The one and only dear boy; yes indeed, you got it in one. I am he of whom you speak and it gives me great pleasure to declare that, henceforth, I shall be at your service should you need any assistance in your labours.'

'"My labours"?' queried Elli. 'What do you mean exactly?'

Striking a Brad pose, Cen gestured to indicate their surroundings.

'We've already established we're in a cloud, haven't we dear boy?'

Elli looked around. Apart from himself and Cen all he could see about him were soft and fluffy wisps of white cloud gently billowing in delicate little wafts and swirls.

'Yes, we – *um* – we're most definitely in a cloud, yes.'

'Well?'

'"Well?" what?'

'What's the obvious thing a land-based human should be concerned about should he-or-she, find him-or-herself "up-up-up in the clouds and … ever so … ever so high"?'

Elli looked at Cen blankly and shrugged.

'You must be more groggy from that bump on your head than you look young Elli.'

'Sorry Cen. You're going to have to spell it out for me.'

Cen smiled a seductively-suave George smile before suddenly producing a straw boater hat and a silver-tipped cane, and bursting into a song and dance routine. The sound of a full orchestra filled the air with a lilting melody and catchy rhythm; as his four hooves started tap dancing in parallel pairs.

'When you're up, up, up — up high in the air …
tap – de-tap-tap!
It's no use just trying to be — debonair …
tap – de-tap-tap, tap-tap-tap
like Fred Astaire …
tap-de-tap-tap – de—TAP!
Because, for solid ground …
tap-de-tap
your feet will be pining …
tap-de-tap
Unless your cloud has …
tap-de-tap-tap – de-tap-tap, tap-tap-tap
a sil …
ver …
LINING!!!
tap-de-tap-tap – tap – de-TAP-TAP-TAP!'

The routine finished as abruptly as it had begun. The music stopped, Cen tossed the boater and cane to one side and he resumed looking non-committally at his fingernails in a wistful Brad-type way. Elli was utterly bemused, and for several long moments he simply opened and closed his mouth mindlessly like a poltroon trying to remember how to eat.

'Who's – *um* – who's Fred Astaire?' he eventually managed to utter.

'Never you mind dear boy. There are some things that transcend even the mythological world.'

Cen stopped scrutinising his nails and fixed Elli with an extremely serious 'now-listen-very-carefully' stare.

'The point is Elli that the only thing keeping you up here is the silver lining on Cloud Nine; the silver lining I personally coated on using my own hands and hooves; the silver lining that makes this a *very* special cloud indeed; and the same silver lining you bumped your head against when you jumped with surprise upon discovering Zatt had disappeared.' Cen gave the cloud beneath his feet a quick '*tap-de-tap-tap*' with his forelegs. 'Is that all crystalline tippety-top clear dear boy?'

'*Er* – yes, yes of course Cen.'

'Go-ooo-od.' Cen smiled, and this time his smile was less George-ey and more Braddish. 'In that case, shall we get back to the pressing question of your "labours"?'

'By all means Cen; glad to.' Elli smiled back, but his smile was masking a sudden sinking feeling.

'Splendid! Now let's crack on; we're losing far too much precious time here. In the same way that Zatt is helping out with Utopia, I want *you* dear boy to paint the lining on Shangri-La.'

'You mean you want me to work on another cloud and give it its silver lining?'

'Precisely dear boy. Got it in one.'

'But, if it hasn't got a silver lining, won't I fall through it and – *um* – plummet downwards to – *gulp* – to down there?'

'I say, well done that man! Yes, of course you will fall; you will fall to a most horrible and gruesome, nasty and noisy, death my dear boy which is *precisely* why you need these.'

Cen rummaged beneath his wing and, with a flourish, produced a pair of white winged-slipper birds.

Elli paused in his '*sploshing*' of silver paint to look furtively over his shoulder and see if Cherub was watching. (It turned out that the Cen's two cutie-pie rosy-cheeked babykin little helpers with dimples and wings were called "Cherub" and "Seraph".) Cherub had obviously been assigned to watch over him as on

Shangri-La; and he assumed Seraph was keeping a close eye on Zatt in much the same way over on Utopia.

Elli smiled and gave a little wave. This prompted Cherub to purse his darling little butterfly lips into a smile, flutter his awww-diddums-doodums eyelashes and curl his inky-dinky-pinky-poo fingers to give the cutest of baby-like waves back. Forcing his own smile to its extremes in reply, Elli returned to his task of dipping his otter-beaver-donkey tail into the bison skull full of molten silver he'd been given and '*sploshing*' more of it onto the wisps of cloud beneath his feet. As he '*sploshed*', he carefully, line-by-line, started to recite the Gum Gum chant quietly under his breath.

'Gum Gum
Garah Gum … '
(pause)
'Gar Gum Guttle … '
(pause)
'*Ginged-slipper bird!*'
(pause)
'Serrum Dittle
Tattle— '

'Fhhhuh-huh-huh-huhmmm?'

Elli glanced up to see Cherub hovering immediately above his head with his dinky-doodum ickle wings all a-flutter. For a moment he thought the irritating little cutie had overheard him chanting, but then he realised he was merely taking a closer look at his work. Elli forced another smile which caused Cherub to giggle as if he'd been tickled.

'F-f-f-huh-huh. Ha-ha-huh-fna-hunnah-hmmm.'

Cherub gave his cutest facial expression yet, flapped his delicate fluffy little wings and fluttered back up to where he was hovering before.

'Tattle Tittle … '
(pause)
'Gar Gum Gittle Giiiiiiiiiiiiiiiiiii … '

Elli chanced another cautious glance upward; Cherub was playing with his own toes—not a care in the world.

'Speak winged-slipper bird!'

'*Whoa there!* You shouldn't be speaking to us,' protested the bird on Elli's left foot in a faint-but-piercing pipsqueak-ey voice.

'*Shhh!*' Elli looked anxiously up at Cherub.

'*Whoops—steady!* No, you really shouldn't,' added the one on his right foot in equally shrill tones. 'We're beneath you.'

'*Shhh!* He'll hear you,' hissed Elli with alarm.

Cherub looked up with a mildly suspicious expression on his 'cutie-pie' features. Elli smiled and waved at him, then conspicuously '*sploshed*' a bit more molten silver. Seemingly satisfied, Cherub looked away again.

'*Phew!* That was close. *Whoa-who-whoa!*' said the left bird with obvious relief. 'Anyway, I'm Flip— '

' —and I'm Flop,' added the right one.

'Pleased to meet you both. I'm Elli. You're honestly not beneath me, *really* you aren't! All creatures are equal in this world. In fact, I think— '

'No-no-no Mister Elli,' interrupted Flop. 'Not "beneath you" in *that* way—*whoa! left a bit, hold it there*—we're beneath you as in holding you up in the air and preventing you from a certain horrible nasty— '

'A-aaa-anyway!' Elli cut in quick. 'Can you please tell me what on earth is going on here? Why has Cen got me and Zatt giving these clouds with funny names silver linings like this? Oh, and where is he by the way?'

'He's gone off again on his Cloud Nine Mister Elli!' explained Flop, or was it Flip? (Elli thought it was most likely Flop, but he didn't want Cherub to spot him looking down to check, so he couldn't be certain.) 'He's always—*whoa, steady*—out and about, rustling the clouds and rounding them up.'

'He herds them like that to ensure the Crown Lake—*whoops, steady-y-y*—is always kept full to the brim,' said Flip (possibly). 'But don't ask us why. We have no idea why.'

'What you have to appreciate Mister Elli … ' said one.

' … is that we only know part of the story,' continued the other.

'You need to understand Mister Elli,' said the first one, 'that we are but mere bit-part players in a whopping great big magnum opus of a play.'

'We are far too insignificant to know more than—*whoops!*—the tiny part of the much bigger picture that we need to know,' added the other.

'So, you see Mister Elli,' continued the one who was most probably Flop, 'I'm afraid we can't tell you the full story. All we know is—*whoa, steady*—he's got eight of these to do for the Big Boss— '

' —And they've got to be finished by the end of the epoch—*whay-hay, wotchit!* —otherwise—' said the other.

' —they won't be ready for "The Off"!' interjected one or the other.

'Who's this "Big Boss"?' whispered a very confused Elli, chancing yet another anxious look up at Cherub. 'And what's "The Off"?'

Flip and Flop looked at each other then back up at Elli.

'We said we only know part of the story,' they both replied in unison.

Elli scrutinised Cherub carefully. He appeared content hovering where he was and playing with his toes; so Elli finally chanced a look down.

'This "Big Boss" fella; does he also go by the name of "Taxman" by any chance?' he asked.

'*Wow!*' exclaimed Flip. 'How did you know that?'

'*Yeah!* That's amazing that is—*whooo-ooo-oops!*—you knowing his real name like that Mister Elli,' said Flop.

'If "Taxman" was his name, why didn't you call him that?' Elli looked from Flip to Flop then back to Flip again. 'Why refer to him as "Big Boss"?'

'We were just trying to *describe* him for you!' Flip was clearly offended.

'*Yeah!*' added an obviously equally offended Flop. '"Taxman" doesn't actually mean anything—*whoa, right a bit, hold it there*—doesn't actually tell you anything about him. Whereas "Big Boss" gives you a real feel for—*whoa-whoa, steady-y-y*—who he is or what he stands for. We were only trying to be helpful. Honestly, some people!'

'All right, all right! I didn't mean to upset you.' Elli could sense the two little birds' indignation through his feet. 'I'm very grateful for the information—thank you, and I'm pleased we've established we're talking about the Taxman; *and* that he is at the heart of all this. I just need a moment to process everything you've told me.'

Elli paused for a much-needed think as he desperately tried to gather his thoughts. While he thought – and '*sploshed*' – Flip and Flop kept station, flapping their wings in unison thereby enabling Elli to hover over whatever part of the cloud he was coating in silver.

'There's one bit of what you've told me that doesn't quite add up,' he said after a while. 'You say we have until "the end of the epoch" to get ready for "The Off" whatever that is; but Cen seems to be in quite a hurry to get these clouds linings done. Surely, if he's got till the end of the epoch, he can take all the time he needs?'

'Not really—*whoa*— ' replied Flip.

'In fact—*wotchit! left a bit, steady-y-y*—I'd say it's the opposite of that,' added Flop, 'especially as—*whoops!*—the epoch ends the day after tomorrow.'

Chapter Eight

The Labyrinth

'Hold on, everyone! I think I've just found another passageway.'

'*Tha-donk!*' '*Ow!*'

'Yah! Ich auch "*Ow!*"'

'That was my head!'

'Und, das var mein Zahn—how-you-saying-k, tooth!'

'Please explain to me one more time Poob.' Ovi picked himself up from stumbling into Poob's gaping jaws and almost impaling himself on one of the super-monster-tyrannosaurus's razor-sharp incisors in the dark—*yet again.* 'Why exactly is it that you have to do this upside down?'

'Vell, das ist mutch easssier fur mich valking auf diese ceiling-k. Die floor auf diese Labyrinth ist mutch glatter—how-you-saying-k, smoother; less bumping-ks on mein Kopf.'

'What did he – *burp* – say little buddy?'

'He prefers to walk on the ceiling, because the floor is less bumpy for his head.'

'Pooir Poib! Oit coin't boi oisoiy foir oi soipoir-moinstoir-toiroinnoisoirous toi goit oiroind oin oi Loiboiyrointh.'

'Never mind "poor Poob", he's fine. Which way do you think we should go now Wishi?'

'Loift.'

'Left?'

'Yois.'

'Right; Gusto! Poob! We need to— '

'Noi! Oi soid "Loift!"'

'Yes, I know you said "left" Wishi.'

Ovi rolled his eyes and gave an exasperated look which was a completely and utterly pointless thing to do, because no one could see a thing in the pitch dark of the Labyrinth, and that especially applied to sardonic facial expressions.

'It's all right everyone, I was right after all— '

'Noi-noi-noi! *Loift!* Oi soid "loift" "loift"!'

'I was *just* about to say that, if you give me a chance Wishi. Right everyone; we have to turn righ—I mean, *left* here.'

'Righty-ho little – *burp* – buddy; off we – *belch* – go!'

The sound of footsteps could be heard disappearing into the distance … to the right.

'No Gusto! Come back towards my voice. I *said* "*left*"!'

The sound of footsteps could be heard returning.

'Oh, this is futile! Are we ever going to find our way out of this blasted blummin' Labyrinth!?'

'How long do you reckon we've – *burp-belp-belch* – been down here little buddy?'

'Oh, I don't know Gusto. My belly has missed more meals than it can remember; and as for poor Wishi, if we— '

'*SHHH*-belp-*SHHH!* Did you – *burp* – hear that?'

They obeyed Gusto's order and went quiet. All they could hear at first was the odd belly rumble; then, somewhere not too far away, there was a distinct shuffling noise.

'Hey there little buddies and big chomper buddy. How many of you are – *burp* – currently on the move?'

'I'm standing still,' said Ovi.

'Soi oim Oi,' came Wishi's somewhat diminished voice in reply.

'Yah-yah; Mich auch. Ich bin resting-k.'

'So – *belch* – if I'm standing still and you're all – *burp* – standing still; what's – *belch-pardon* – making that – *belp* – strange sound?'

The shuffling sounded again and this time it was discernibly closer.

'Are you sure you're not moving Gusto?' Ovi lowered his voice to a faint whisper.

'Nope little buddy. Them there noises sure – *burp* – ain't mine!'

They fell silent once more and listened. The shuffling noises sounded once more this time closer, uncomfortably closer. One of them began to whimper and one of the others went '*shush!*' (because it was dark, I'm not certain who did which). Then, all of a sudden, the Labyrinth was filled with a loud high-pitched noise which seemed to be coming from every direction and continued for quite a while until it eventually tapered off.

'TOOT-TOOT! *POO-OOO-OOHW-POO-OOHW!* TOOT-TOOT-TOOT! *POO-OOO-OOHW-POO-OOO-OOHW!* PRRR-RRR-AAA-AAA-aaa-aaa-aaa-aaa-aap'

When the strange sound ended, the shuffling resumed; drawing ever closer and closer; and as it closed in, they also began to hear low murmuring sounds …

… hauntingly low murmuring sounds …

… the kind of low murmuring sounds guaranteed to send shivers down any creature's spine; especially creatures that are in a strange place in the dark with no real knowledge of where they are or what nasties – noisy or otherwise – might be lurking.

'It's no use Wishi,' hissed Ovi in the quietest possible whisper, 'you're going to have to open your eyes.'

They had originally thought when they first entered the dark and dingy depths of the Labyrinth that it was going to be easy to find their way by using Wishi's light beam eyes; but they'd learnt very quickly to use them sparingly, because they seriously sapped his strength and whenever he used them, he visibly shrank. Now, however, with this mysterious 'shuffler' almost upon them, they had no choice. Wishi opened his eyes and two bright yellow searchlight beams immediately shot out into the darkness to reveal … *nothing!*

Wishi quickly scoured their surroundings. One beam shone upon Poob who was upside down with his feet on the ceiling and head on the floor; the other lit up Gusto with Ovi hiding behind him. He then shone both beams back down the passageway which was still completely empty. The light from the beams suddenly started to fade. Ovi looked down and saw Wishi shrinking again—alarmingly fast.

'Oh dear Wishi, you'd better close your— ' Ovi was cut short by Gusto taking a sharp intake of breath and just for once it wasn't as a prelude to a belch. About two tyrannosaurus lengths away in the rapidly-dwindling beam of light they all clearly saw a peculiar-looking creature carrying a large conch shell shuffle across the passage in front of them in a rather odd manner (by "odd", Dear Reader, what I really mean is "backwards").

With his head now well below Ovi's knees, Wishi had no choice but to close his eyes; the light was extinguished and darkness returned.

'What in swamp blazes was *that!?*' exclaimed Ovi.

'Don't – *burp* – ask me little buddy. I was too busy watching its strange moves to – *belch* – notice what it looked like.'

'Oind Oi wois tooi boisoiy boimoing toi— '

'Ach, yah! Ich veiß das, das var how-you-say der Große Poltroon.'

'"The Great Poltroon"? It can't be! I thought there was no such thing and the Great Poltroon was just a joke.'

'Listen mein Freund, Ich bin knowing-k einen Poltroon venn ich sehe einen Poltroon. Vir Tyrannosauren ist eating-k zem, remember!'

'Yeah, I suppose you're right; but what makes you so certain that one was the "Great" one?'

'Vell, size für ein Schtarter; Er var ass big-k ass du Offi oder Gusto! Und dan war allzo die un-k-mistakeable, inesskape-able fak-t zatt Er var sehr sehr rückwärts how-you-say ffferry ffferry back-vart!'

'He's right there little buddy. Whatever it was, it certainly looked pretty – *burp* – backward to me.'

A bright light suddenly lit the passageway and there, right before them, holding a flaming torch in one hand and the conch shell in the other, was the creature. As Ovi and the others looked on in stunned disbelief, the creature then put the conch shell to its mouth … and sucked.

'TOOT-TOOT! *POO-OOO-OOHW!* TOOT-TOOT-TOOT!-PRRR-RRR-AAA-AAA-aaa-aaa-aaa-aaa-aap'

'Wh-what's your n-n-name?' asked Ovi after the noise had faded.

The creature didn't reply. Instead, it put the conch down, produced a blackened torch stump and stared at it. Suddenly, it burst into flame, followed immediately by the creature blowing it alight.

'Quoick Oivoi! Troiy thoi 'Goim Goim' soing oin oit!' came a tiny Wishi voice from somewhere down below.

'The Gum Gum song? Do you think it'll work Wishi?'

Ovi looked down at Wishi (who nodded) then back at the creature who was just standing completely motionless, holding its flaming torches. 'Right, here goes …

Gum Gum
Garah Gum
Gar Gum Guttle … Goltroon
Serrum Dittle
Tattle Tittle
Gar Gum Gittle Giiiiiiiiiiiiiiiiiii—*Speak Poltroon!*'

The creature did nothing; it just stared at them … and blinked … kind of backwardly.

'Ach das var nicht gut Offi. Du bist getting-k hiss name mistaken-k. Et var der "*Große* Poltroon", nicht nur "Poltroon"!'

Ovi gave Poob a quick sideways look and a nod; then he once again fixed his gaze upon the creature.

'Right, we'll try it again then, shall we? … Gum Gu— '

He froze mid-"Gum" because he suddenly noticed that the two burning torches were both getting visibly longer. It was as if they were 'growing' in the flames rather than being burnt away by them.

'What's up little buddy?'

'Do those torches look—well, a bit odd to you Gusto?'

'No! They look just fine to me – *burp* – little buddy. In fact, they light up my life!'

Somewhere beneath its beak, the creature gave a slight smile. Now it was Gusto's turn to receive a brief sideways look from Ovi. He then cleared his throat and started again.

'Gum Gum
Garah Gum
Gar Gum Guttle … Great Goltroon
Serrum Dittle
Tattle Tittle
Gar Gum Gittle Giiiiiiiiiiiiiiiiiii—*Speak Great Poltroon!*'

They all looked intensely at the creature and again it simply stared back at them and blinked … twice … backwards.

'Moiboiy yoi shoild troiy soiyoing oit boikwoirds Oivoi!'

'Saying what backwards Wishi? Do you mean the Gum Gum song?'

'Yois, oif coirse Oi moin thoi 'Goim Goim' soing! Whoit oithoir— '

'All right, all right Wishi, save your strength; we might need it later.'

Ovi took a moment to run the song through in his mind backwards and then returned his attention to the creature who had remained remarkably still, barely moving at all apart from the occasional backward blink.

'*Ahem* … here goes …

Mug Mug
Harag Mug
Rag Mug Elttug … Noortlog
Murres Elttid
Elttat Elttit
Rag Mug Elttig iiiiiiiiiiiiiiiiiiig … *Kaeps Taerg Noortlop!*'

'Right, then,' said Ovi. 'Now, please tell us your name.'

'oxO,' said the creature in a high squeaky voice that was at once both 'mechanical' and 'organical'.

'"Oxo"?' repeated Ovi.

The creature dropped its head and then lifted it up again in a rather peculiar 'reverse' nod which Ovi instinctively, and automatically, mirrored.

'*Don't nod!*' shouted Oxo who ceased to nod himself, before giving Ovi an odd sideways smile.

'Oops, sorry!' Ovi grabbed his head to keep it still. 'It's nice to meet you Oxo. I'd like to introduce myself as well as my friends here. *Ahem!* I'm Ovi and— '

'*Yo, banana boy!*' blurted Oxo, shifting his smile from one side of his beak to the other.

Ovi looked round and gave the others an 'is-it-me-or-is-this-getting-a-bit-weird?' look, before returning to face Oxo with a broad smile. Oxo stared back at him and shifted his smile back to the other side of his beak.

'Aa-aaa-anyway, moving on … ' Ovi held his arm out downwards to indicate Wishi. 'Down here; this is Wishi.'

'*Ploised toi moit yoi Oixoi!*'

Wishi stepped forward and bowed. Owing to his recent beamage depletion he was now barely the size of a pygmy-poltroon. Oxo did a reverse bow and took a couple of steps backward in order to look more closely at Wishi.

'Was it a rat I saw?'

Wishi bristled.

'Oi boig yoir poirdoin!'

Ovi briskly lifted his arm upward to indicate Poob.

'Aa-aaa-and over here Oxo we have— '

'*Step on no pets!*'

'Vass?'

'*Go deliver a dare vile dog!*'

'*Vass! Vass!* Vass ist ziss-ziss Poltroon just saying-k?' Poob became agitated and growled under his breath (just like a dog). Oxo took a few steps forward in fear at the sight of Poob's rather formidable bared teeth.

'*Dammit I'm Mad! Dammit I'm Mad! Dammit I'm Mad!*'

'Vass ist ziss Dummkopf Poltroon *now* saying-k?'

'Easy, Poob,' Ovi turned to face his reptilian fellow gang member. 'Have you thought he might be as frightened of us as we are of him, especially as one of us normally *eats* poltroons.'

'Yah-Yah! Das ist korrekt-lich; und Ich habe großer Hunger!'

'*Poob!* It's not polite to eat someone just because you don't understand what they're saying.'

Poob looked past Ovi to give Oxo a fierce 'I've-got-my-eye-on-you-take-this-as-a-warning' look, and growled a long dog-like growl.

Before returning his attention to Oxo, Ovi needed a moment to revitalise his warm smile of greeting.

'The thing is Oxo, we've somehow managed to get ourselves a bit, well "lost" here in this Labyrinth.' His smile fully restored, Ovi span round. 'And we're hoping you— '

Oxo had disappeared. In the space where he'd been standing there were just the two burning torches rolling on the floor. Suddenly the conch shell sounded above their heads (apart from Poob's, of course; the sound was *below* his).

'TOOT-TOOT-TOOT! *POO-OOO-OOHW!* TOOT! PRRR-RRR-AAA- AAA-aaa-aaa-aaa-aaa-aap'

They all looked up (except Poob who looked down); and there was Oxo with the conch pressed hard against his mouth, flying away from them backwards.

'TOOT-TOOT! *POO-OOO-OOHW!* TOOT! PRRR-RRR-AAA- AAA-aaa-aaa-aaa-aaa-aap'

'*Palf! Palf! Palf!*' went his wings as he picked up speed, followed by two shorter 'TOOT-TOOT! PRRR-AAA-aaa-aaa-aap's.

'*Wait! Come back Oxo! We haven't got to know you properly yet,*' cried Ovi.

'*Palf! Palf! Palf! POO-OOO-OOHW!* TOOT-TOOT! PRRR- PRRR-AAA-aaa-aaa-aap'

'*Quick!*' Ovi grabbed one of the flaming torches and indicated to Gusto that he should do the same. 'We mustn't lose him! He's the best chance we've got of getting out of here!'

They gave chase down a long passageway that seemed to go on forever.

Oxo was in front of them, flying backwards.

'*Palf! Palf! Palf! POO-OOO-OOHW!* TOOT-TOOT! PRRR- PRRR-AAA-aaa-aaa-aap'

Ovi and Gusto followed about three tyrannosaurus lengths behind, brandishing the torches which flickered and flared as they ran. Behind them came Poob, his large hind legs pounding the ceiling and bounding over the odd boulder sticking out. Finally, bringing up the rear and rapidly getting left behind came Wishi running as fast as he could, preferring not to fly because, like his light beam eyes, using his wings severely depleted his body size.

Several things then happened in quick succession. First, the passageway suddenly opened out into a large underground chamber with a very high ceiling. Both torches then died with a '*fizzle*' just as Ovi and Gusto entered the chamber. At that point, Poob emerged from the tunnel and, with nothing for his feet to run on, came to a sudden halt. Then, from behind Poob they could all hear the staccato 'pitter-patter' of Wishi's feet approaching fast.

'Puff-puff – *STOP WISHI!*'

'Wheeze – *LOOK OUT, LITTLE* – burp – *BUDDY!*'

'*HALT VISHI—VISHI HALT!*'

Their cries were too late.

'pitter-patter-pitter-patter—*THA-DONK!*'

'Oiwww!' came a very nasally, as well as tiny, cry from somewhere behind Poob's massive bulk. *'Thoit hoirt!'*

'Das ist strange-lich. Ich bin nacht feeling-k ein Ding-k.'

'Are you – *wheeze* – all right Wishi?'

'Oi thoink – *poiff* – oine oif moi hoirns ois boint.'

Ovi and Gusto shared an 'ooops-I-hope-he's-fine' look (even though they couldn't see each other in the darkness) while they both wheezed and puffed to catch their breath.

'What are we – *puff-burp* – going to do now little buddy?'

'I dunno Gusto. I know – *wheeze* – Oxo was a bit odd; but – *puff, puff* – we sure could do with – *puff* – finding him again – *wheeze*— '

'You're right there – *puff* – little – *burp* – buddy; or at least some more of his – *puff-belp* – torches – *puff* – they light up my life like a burning flame! *Yii-iii-ha-aaa-aah!*'

'Actually, do you know what – *puff* – I could really do with right now – *puff* – Gusto?'

'No, what's that little buddy?'

'Some bananas – *puff* – and some nice juicy fruit of some kind. I'm parched as well as starving!'

'No lemon, no melon!'

'Who said that? Was that you Oxo?'

The dark void suddenly filled with light and there on a ledge above their heads was Oxo reverse-blowing another of his torches alight.

'Yo, banana boy!'

'GRRR-RRR-OOO-OOO-WWW-LLL!!!'

Without warning, Poob lunged past Ovi and Gusto and went for Oxo with his formidable ferocious-looking teeth.

'LA-CHOMP-DA-GNOSH! LA-CHOMP-DA-GNOSH-GNASH!'

'*POOB!* What do you think you're doing?'

'Sorry Offi; aber Ich habe großen Hunger. Est var how-you-say—Insting-k-t.'

They all looked up at Oxo. His wings were outstretched against the wall braced for impact, his eyes were staring wide with fear and he was visibly shaking all over with knocking knees and beak all a-chatter.

'Oh, now look what you've done Poob!' Ovi stood between the ravenous giant reptile and his prey. 'Sorry about that Oxo. We just— '

'*Dammit I'm Mad! Dammit I'm Mad! Dammit I'm Mad!*'

'Well, I can understand you feeling that way Oxo. I think— '

'*No sir; away! A papaya war is on!* Won't I panic in a pit now?' With that, Oxo extinguished his torch by sucking inwards which plunged the Labyrinth's chamber back into darkness; then they heard him fly off again.

'*Palf! Palf! Palf!* TOOT-TOOT-TOOT! *POO-OOO-OOO-OOHW!-POO-OOO-OOHW!* PRRR- AAA-aaa-aaa-aap'

Ovi span round and fixed Poob with a fierce glare that Poob was lucky not to witness in the dark.

'*POOB!* That's *twice* you've frightened him off! Will you *please* stop doing that?'

There was no answer. The chamber had suddenly become not only completely dark again, but also apparently Poob-less.

'Poob? Are you there Poob?'

'Sounds like we've lost big chomper buddy too – *burp* – little buddy.'

'*POOB? … POOB? ... WHERE ARE YOU POOB?*'

Apart from the odd belly rumble, the Labyrinth chamber was totally quiet.

'Do you know where Poob is Wishi?'

There was no answer; the silence was absolutely devoid of anything resembling a reply whatsoever of either a Poob-ish or a Wishi-esque nature. Ovi and Gusto were now, it would appear, completely on their own.

'*WISHI? … WISHI?*'

'This just keeps getting better and better little – *burp* – buddy. Tell me – *belp* – are we still a "gang" – *burp-belch* – if it's just the two of us?'

'This is serious Gusto. I'm not sure who's in greater trouble me or my belly. Are you sure you haven't got some food—W*ait a moment!* Why didn't I think of that earlier? Of course … '

The darkness was briefly filled with some frantic grunts and rummaging noises, rapidly followed by some deep, and very contented, chewing sounds.

'What have you got there little buddy?'

'Never you mind!'

'Aw – *burp* – pleasc give me a chew little buddy.'

'*No!* Go and get your own emergency lizard!'

The Labyrinth suddenly filled with light once more, and standing directly in front of Ovi was Oxo with one of his torches freshly blown-alight. Immediately behind him, almost hidden in the shadows, was what looked like an entrance to one of the Labyrinth's passages framed with glistening white crystals.

'*MMMMM! MMMMM!*' He reached up to grab the lizard from Ovi's grasp, but Ovi snatched it away and hid it behind his back.

'Oh, hello again Oxo! So, you like dried lizard, do you?'

'*MMMMM!*' Oxo backward nodded.

'Well, you can have this dried lizard— '

Oxo started jumping down and up with delight, while back-clapping his flipper-like wings.

' —But only if you give us some help.'

Oxo stopped jumping and looked quizzically at Ovi.

'Do you want to help us?'

Oxo backward nodded.

'Well, firstly, we need some food … '

Oxo backward nodded again.

'And then we need your help to get out of here … '

Oxo backward nodded again.

'And there's one more thing … '

Oxo hesitated … then backward nodded again.

'It'd be a really big help to us if you could point us in the direction of someone called "Mi-no Taur".'

Oxo back-scratched his head, then backward nodded again. Ovi looked across at Gusto and gave him a 'well-that-was-easy' look.

'Right then Oxo. How about starting off with some of that food?'

Oxo backward nodded and held out his hand for the dried lizard.

'*MMMMM!*'

Ovi reluctantly produced it from behind his back … then hesitated.

'A deal is – *burp* – a deal little buddy.'

'Oh, all right. Here you are Oxo. Go on, take it.'

The moment Ovi held out the dainty morsel-sized half-chewed lizard, Oxo back-snatched it from his grasp, shouting '*Go hang a salami; I'm a lasagna hog!*' and leapt backwards into the 'crystal-framed' passage beside him.

'*CHOMP!*'

A combination of hunger and darkness had caused Poob to revert to a basic form of reptilian behaviour; he had slipped into a dormant torpor, silently waiting in stealth for something edible to 'pop in' his mouth. The moment Oxo entered Poob's jaws, they had automatically slammed tight.

'*Esaelp t'nod mrah em, esaelp!*' Oxo's voice suddenly sounded both faint and close by; and it had an ominous echoey quality.

'*OXO!* Are you where I think you are?'

'*Sey, ma I! Esaelp t'nod mrah em, esaelp!*'

'*Poob!* Whatever you do, do *not* gnosh-gnash. We need him alive!'

'*Grrr-rrr-rrrowling-k!*'

'Don't chew and don't move Poob! We need to know exactly where you – and he – are.'

'*Oivoi, Oivoi, Oivoi!*'

Wishi suddenly returned (by coincidence he had also briefly slipped into a dormant-reptilian state); and his thin little voice sounded from somewhere near Ovi's feet.

'*Oi knoiw hoiw woi coin goit hoim oit oigoin, oiloive!*'

'How Wishi – *how?*'

'*Quoick! Thoire's noi toime toi loise. Goive moi yoir hoind!*'

'My hand? What do you want my hand for? It's completely empty – no bananas, no juicy-chewy lizards; in fact, nothing edible whatso— '

'*Joist DOI oit Oivoi—NOIW!!!*'

'A-aaa-all righty; if you put it like that Wishi. *There* you go … right, you have hold of my hand; now what are you—oh, I see, you're putting my hand very deliberately in a specific place … on what feels like solid rock but which *could* be some kind of reptilian skin … right, just so; I see … now what Wishi?'

'Toickle!'

'"Toickle"?'

'Yois!'

'Right you are. Here goes … '

The darkness was filled with a rasping sound.

'Nothing's happening Wishi.'

'Doin't stoip! Oit'll woirk soin. Doin't foirgoit Oi knoiw moi foilloiw roiptoiles boittoir thoin yoi.'

The rasping sound re-doubled in earnest. All of a sudden, there was a loud '*splutter*' accompanied by a very Germanic giggle. The rasping then became frenetic.

'Pfff-fff … p-p-pfff-fff … *HA HA HA! SCHTOP! SCHTOP!*'

There then followed the unmistakeable and very distinctive sound of a great poltroon being released from the jaws of a laughing tyrannosaurus.

'*Aha! Gotcha little buddy!*'

Light suddenly returned to reveal Gusto holding firmly in his grip a wriggling Oxo who, in turn, held a freshly lit torch in one hand and the dried lizard in the other. He had barely finished blowing the torch alight when Ovi dashed forward and snatched both objects from Oxo's grasp.

'Right Oxo my lad, we've got you! And this time we're— '

Ovi was interrupted by a long and extremely loud inward wheeze followed by an outburst of raucous hysterical Germanic-tyrannosaurial laughter.

Ovi held the torch over toward Poob who was rolling on his back and clasping his sides with eyes streaming tears of mirth. They then had to wait patiently for the outburst to subside before resuming their conversation.

'Aa-aaa-anyway, as I was saying – *ahem* – this time Oxo we're not giving you the slightest chance to escape until you've given us all the help we need. And you're certainly not getting your hands on this— ' He brandished the dried lizard. ' —until *we* get *our* teeth into some decent grub. Is that clear?'

Oxo looked at his captors, including Poob who was now back on his feet and almost back to normal with just the odd giggle spasm.

'*Esaelp t'nod mrah em, esaelp!*'

Ovi gave Gusto a 'what-did-he-just-say?' look, who passed it on to Poob, who in turn looked around for Wishi in order to share it with him.

'*Um* – what was that again Oxo?'

'*Esaelp t'nod mrah em, esaelp!*'

'What did he – *burp* – say?'

'*Oi've goit oit! Oi've goit oit! Doin't foirgoit—hoi's spoikoing boickwoirds. Hoi's soiyoing "Ploise doin't hoirm moi, ploise!"*'

'Sorry little buddy – *burp* – what did you just say?'

'Er ist saying-k "Pleasing-k not to— '

'*Stop! Stop!* Hold it right there!'

Ovi stepped forward centre stage, waving his arms frantically for all dialogue to cease.

'I think it best if I do the translations from now on. We can't have a tyrannosaurus interpreting a nevasaurus interpreting a poltroon; that's far too confusing!' He nodded to indicate you, Dear Reader. 'Think of our audience, for goodness' sake!'

'Yah-yah. Das is Korrekt-lich. Pleasing-k du karrying-k on Offi.'

Ovi moved over to Oxo who was once again trembling with fear.

'Is it true that you are indeed speaking backwards Oxo?'

Oxo did one of his backward nods.

'Sey.'

'So, what you just said was in fact "Please don't harm me, please."?'

'Sey.'

'Well, what was all that other stuff about pets and rats and bananas and papaya wars and salamis and lasagne hogs?'

'Yeht erew drawkcab sgniht I wenk d'uoy dnatsrednu.'

Ovi shook his head and gave Gusto a 'did-you-happen-to-understand-that?' look to which Gusto replied with a firm 'don't-ask-me-little-buddy-you-said-you-were-*burp*-doing-the-translations' stare in reply.

'Would you mind repeating that Oxo?'

'Ylniatrec.'

‘Knaht ouy—I mean, thank you.’

‘I dais “Yeht … erew … drawkcab … sgniht … ’

‘“They … were … backward … things”?’

‘*Doog! Doog!* Enod llew! “Yeht erew drawkcab sgniht … I wenk … d’uoy dnatsrednu.” Tiddog?’

As Ovi ran through the sentence in his head, his face did some strange contortions which made Wishi and Gusto snigger.

‘“They were backward things … I –that means “you” … knew … you’d—that means “we’d” … understand”?’

‘*Sey! Sey! Sey!*’ Oxo jumped down and up with glee and back-clapped his flipper-wings.

‘“They were backward things you knew we’d understand”.’

‘*YAROOH! Ouy tiddig!*’

‘OK, I think I’ve got this. Let’s see … “Yo, banana boy!” backward is “Yob … ananab … oy!”—no, wait “Yo, banana boy!” and “No lemon, no melon” backwards is “No lemon, no melon”!’

‘*Sey-sey! Sey-sey! Uoy tiddog! Uoy tiddog!*’

‘Ri-iii-ight! Well that’s cleared a few things up then.’ Ovi fixed Oxo with the fiercest ‘now-let’s-get-down-to-business’ stare he could muster. ‘Now, can you please help us with finding some food and a way out of here—*oh*, as well as taking us to this Mi-no Taur?’

‘S’taht ysae.’

‘Oh really?’

Ovi turned to the others and translated.

‘He say’s “that’s easy”.’

‘We know! / *Woi knoiw!* / Vie k-nowing-k-st!’

‘Fi s’ti doof uoy tnaw … s’ti dniheb eht rooD.’

‘“If – it’s – food – yo—“we” – want – it’s – behind – the – “Door”?’

‘*Sey-sey!* Fi s’ti a yaw tuo uoy tnaw … s’ti dniheb eht rooD.’

‘“If it’s – a – way – out – we want – it’s behind – the “Door”?’

‘*Sey-sey!* Dna fi s’ti oniM uoy tnaw— ’

‘Don’t tell me, let me guess … is Mino behind the “Door” too?’

'*Sey, eh si!* S'taht gnizama! Woh did uoy wonk?'

Ovi turned to address the others.

'Well, it looks as if things down here in the Labyrinth are really quite simple after all. Apparently, everything we need is behind the "Door".'

Slowly, all the members of the Tax-Taker-Backer-Gang turned their gazes toward Oxo.

'What's a "Door"? / *Whoit's oi "Doir"?* / Vas ist eine "Tür" —I mean "Door"?'

Chapter Nine

The Taur brothers at work

'Zatt says she's finished doing Utopia and is popping over to Cloud Nine for a little tête-à-tête with Cen-i-poos before moving on to Nirvana. She also said, "If you've finished with Shangri-La, why don't you join us before making a start on Paradise. Cen-i-poos and I would love to see you."'

'She said what?' hissed Elli, struggling to stifle his anger and frustration. 'Say that again!'

Dingle gulped. Along with Flip and Flop, he and Dangle were only humble winged-slipper birds and weren't cut out for Machiavellian intrigues and machinations.

'*Um* – which bit do you want me to say again Mister Elli?'

'Oh, never mind; I've got the gist of it.'

Elli looked over his shoulder and waved at Cherub who giggled and gave a cute little ickle wave back.

'Look here Dangle— '

'It's – *er* – it's Dingle actually.'

'Sorry—Dingle! Look here Dingle; I need you and your fellow – *um* – 'birds' to help me. I must find a way to escape from this-this slavish drudgery and go to rescue my sister Zatt, especially now that she has—well, you know … '

'Now that Zatt has what Mister Elli?' asked Dingle.

'Oh, you know.'

'I don't, honest.'

'Now that she's "turned" so-to-speak. Oh, you know what I mean.'

'Sorry, I don't Mister Elli. Do you Flip?'

'*Whoa, steady!*—No, sorry.'

'How about you Flop?'

'*Easy, easy, left a bit!*—Nope me, neither.'

'Come on chaps! Surely it is obvious … '

Elli quickly did a spot of conspicuous silver '*sploshing*' to disguise the fact from Cherub that he was deeply engrossed in conversation with three peculiar-looking white birds, two of which he was 'wearing'.

'Zatt's been "compromised" and seriously distracted from our mission— '

'What mission is that then Mister Elli?' asked Dingle.

'To find the Taxman and take back the tax he's taken, of course!'

'That sounds more like a "quest" to me. What do you think, Fl— '

'Look, never mind that now!' Elli briefly glanced at Dingle before returning his gaze to Cherub and continuing his plotting. 'I need you chaps to help me find a way to snap Zatt out of the spell that Cen has cast on her with his charms. I've got to find a way to get her off these blasted clouds so that she and I can resume our search for our fellow gang members. Then, once the Tax-Taker-Backer Gang has reformed, we can go after the Taxman and try to get some of the tax back that he— '

'*Er* – sorry to interrupt Mister Elli, but what exactly is it that you need us to snap?'

Elli glanced back at Dingle who was looking very confused.

'That was a bit too much information wasn't it?'

Dingle nodded.

'Let's keep it simple, shall we?'

Dingle nodded enthusiastically.

'The main point is really quite simple; I need to get Zatt out of here and you chaps are the only ones who can help me.'

'*Heave!*' Ovi put his shoulder to the "Door" and pushed as hard as he could.

'*Ho!*' cried Gusto, also pushing hard with his hands.

Once again, the "Door" didn't budge and, once again, Gusto pounded it in frustration with his clenched fists.

'*BO-BOOM!*'

'*Heave!*'

'*Ho!*'

'*BO-BOOM!*'

'*Heave!*'

'*Ho!*'

'BO—BOOM-M-MMM!'

'Moffing-k assside pleassse dort!'

The thunderous rumble of a charging tyrannosaurus forced Ovi and Gusto to jump well out of the way.

'BA—DOING!!!'

Poob hit the "Door" at full speed with the top of his head … and bounced off. The "Door" shook and made a loud rattling sound, but failed to budge *yet again.*

'It's no use,' said Ovi 'It's never going to op— '

Suddenly, through the "Door" they heard the sound of very heavy footsteps approaching accompanied by a loud booming voice.

''Ooo's that a-bangin' on the blummin' door?'

The great slab of thick heavy granite flew open inwards, crushing Ovi and Gusto behind it.

'There's not supposed to be any-blummin'-one in 'ere. This side is all finished and ready to go!'

The "Door"'s frame was completely filled by a giant figure looming large and dark. It was the figure of a huge man, except it wasn't a "man" as such, because it had an Ox's head and horns.

'Dammit I'm Mad! Dammit I'm Mad! Dammit I'm Mad!'

Oxo stepped forward in shock then took-off backward, frantically back-flapping his wings '*palf, palf, palf*'.

'Oh no you blummin' don't!'

The figure lunged forward and grabbed Oxo by the tail, causing him to drop his conch shell which smashed on the rocks at the figure's feet.

'So, 'ooo do we 'ave 'ere?'

'Oi coin smoill foid – Oi moist hoive soime!'

The tiny figure of Wishi – now barely the size of a *baby* pygmy-poltroon – made a dash to pass between the figure's legs; but the creature was too fast for him and scooped him up in his other hand.

'And 'ooo in blazes are you little fella?'

'Pleasing-k du putsz diese Freunds off meine *down-k!*'

'Well, well; well. Well, I never! A talkin' tyrannosaurus no less. Why aren't you with the others?'

'Yah! Das ist eine interessant qvesstion! Ich auch vant zu knowing-k dies ding-k! Vo sind die anderen Tyrannosauren? Ich vill— '

'*Shut up you!* I can't understand a blummin' word you're a-sayin'!'

The creature moved into the flickering light of Ovi, Gusto and Oxo's dropped torches. Its bloodshot bull's eyes were full of rage and it had a large silver ring through its nose that glistened fire-red. It pulled Oxo closer for scrutiny, making him shake uncontrollably.

'What about you with the funny beak? What 'ave you got to say for yourself?'

'*E-e-esaelp t-t-t'nod m-m-mrah em, e-e-esaelp!*'

'Nope! Can't understand a word of that either. Complete gibberish as far as I'm concerned.'

He lifted Wishi up close to the tip of his steaming nostrils and stared at him intently; his great bloodshot eyeballs glaring wide.

'And what about you? Got anythin' to say?'

'*Oi'm Woishoi oind Oi'm woith thoi Toix-Toikoir-Boikoir-Going; oind woi're troiyoing toi foind thoi Toixmoin, boit boifoire thoit Oi doispoiroiteloiy noid soim foid boicoise Oi'm foidoing oiwoiy foist. Oif Oi—* '

The creature snorted.

'*Nope!* Can't even 'ear you; let alone understand a blummin' word you're a-sayin'!'

He called back over his shoulder.

'*Oy! You! … Yes, you!* Come over 'ere! We've got a tyrannosaurus 'ere 'ooo 'asn't got a control stick.' He eyed Poob once more then added. 'You'd better bring your whip too; 'eee's a biggun and 'eee's proper lively!'

'Fff-hhhex-fff-kkkyyyuse fff-mmm-hhheee,' came a muffled cry from behind the door.

''Ooo's that?'

'Fff-ca-mmmn hyou pfffl-hhh-eeeze fff-ledd-us hfhfn-out?!'

The creature peered round the side of the door.

'Well, I never! There's more of 'em round 'ere!'

Having his hands full of Oxo and Wishi, he nudged the door back with one of his horns and both Ovi and Gusto fell to the floor each looking—well, a bit flattened.

At that moment a rather large flightless bird with an extremely long neck came into view. It was an ostrich-emu-lator (curiously, not related to modern day ostriches or emus in any way; it just happened to have those words in its name). It's extraordinarily long neck, which was bright yellow in colour with gold and orange flecks and streaks down the side, was in fact so long it made up over three quarters of its body, making its relatively small dark blue pot-belly of a torso with its bright red flappers of flightless wings and equally red duck-like feet look like an appendage. In its beak it carried a stick and in its duck-feet-talons it carried a whip made from a specially selected, and very rare, whipper vine. The moment Poob saw the stick he was 'hooked'.

'*Ach yah!* Jetzt vass comst? Vass ist zatt ich sehe befor mich?'

The ostrich-emu-lator waved the stick to and fro from side to side and Poob's head followed completely entranced and oblivious to all else.

'Ich bin vanting-k diese ting-k. *Gro-ooo-owl!* Ich muss habe diese ting-k. *Gro-ooo-owl-l-ling-k!*'

'Oh, 'eee's a blummin' wild one all right,' said the ox-headed creature. 'You're definitely gonna need that there a-whip!'

The ostrich-emu-lator didn't hesitate. In one blindingly fast, and obviously much-practised, move it leapt on Poob's head and extended its neck so that its stick was dangling directly in front of his nose. Poob was immediately transfixed. It was as if the stick was all that mattered in the whole wide world, and the only thing he was interested in doing – indeed, *capable* of doing – was follow it slavishly. The ostrich-emu-lator then did a couple of routine tests; moving the stick from one side to the other which Poob dutifully followed, panting like an eager puppy and wagging his tail. Satisfied that all was as it should be, Poob's 'rider' then used the thick end of the whip to '*thwack*' Poob hard on the neck like a modern-day jockey on a racehorse.

'Come along there little doggie,' it cried in a rasping dry voice which sounded 'pinched' because it was speaking with a stick in its beak, '*Git along! HUP! HUP-HUP!*'

Without hesitation, Poob stepped up to the open "Door".

'Where to Boss?' asked the ostrich-emu-lator in its grating dry tone.

'Australia, of course! You know it needs another 'alf a mountain of red before "The Off" tomorrow. It's a good thing 'eee turned up when 'eee did. 'Eee's nice n'big, and 'eee should shift plenty before moonrise. *Now, get a-crackin'!*'

'Yes Boss!'

The ostrich-emu-lator made some clicking noises in its throat and gave Poob a couple of harsh '*thwacks*'.

'Git along there little doggie! You heard the Boss. We've gotta get some red on the move to Australia. *YI-III-III-HA-AAA! HUP-HUP-HUP!*'

Poob did what he was told and trotted happily – and mindlessly – off down the passageway.

Satisfied that Poob was taken care of, the ox-headed creature turned and glared menacingly at Ovi and Gusto.

'Now then – 'ooo the 'ell are you two?'

'Me?—I mean, us Sir?''

''Ooo else might I be a-talkin' too?'

'Yes, of course. *Ha ha ha!* Silly me. W-w-well, I-I-I'm Ovi and this is G-G-Gusto Sir. Can I – *gulp* – ask Sir; are you by any chance— '

'Blummin 'eck. Finally, I can 'ear and understand what one of you is a-sayin'! Now what was that you were askin'? Am I what?'

'A-a-are you c-called "M-M-Mino" by any chance Sir?'

'What if I am?'

'Well – *er* – if you are Mino Sir – *gulp* – we have it on the authority of a friend of ours that you m-m-might be able to help us with our qu-quest.'

''Ooo is this "friend" of yours and what kind of a quest?'

'*"Oil"!*'

'What did you say little'un? "Oil"?'

'*Shhhh Wishi! Ha ha ha!* – *gulp* – What he means Sir is "Aloysius Meredith Plantagenet Fortesque-Smyth Fitz-Dragon" or "Al" for short is our friend. And our quest is to find the – *um* – the "Taxman". The thing is Sir, our friend "Al" *Ha ha ha!* well, he thought you might be able to help us find this – *um* – "Taxman" you see. Do you – *er* – know him at all sort-of-thing maybe – *um* – Sir?'

'Do I know 'ooo? Al or the Taxman?'

'Well – *um* – either I – *gulp* – I suppose.'

'Oind coin Oi hoive soime foid ploise? Oi'm foidoing foist hoire!'

There followed an uneasy silence as the creature slowly eyed his captives as if getting the measure of them; his hot bull's breath hissing gently as he breathed with little wisps of steam coming from each of his wildly-flared nostrils. If Ovi had been feeling nervous, the creature's manner now made him feel distinctly on edge as well as extremely uncomfortable.

'So, you're friends of this "Al" eh?'

'Y-y-yes Sir.'

'And, you're a-lookin' for someone called the "Taxman" you say?'

'Why, yes Sir.'

'Yep – *burp* – pardon!'

'Yois.'

The creature suddenly beamed a broad smile.

'Well, why didn't you blummin' say so earlier? Come inside Master Ovi, Master Gusto; and we'll 'ave a proper chat.'

The creature stepped aside and indicated that they should proceed through the open doorway.

'Well, thanks – *belp* – big strange buddy! Great stuff *yeah!* Now we're – *burp* – really rockin'!'

Gusto stepped forward and made his way through the doorway.

'Why – *um* – thank you Sir; very kind of you Sir.'

Ovi nervously followed closely behind Gusto as they walked past the giant creature's huge legs.

'So – *um* – are you in fact he who Al called "Mino" so-to-speak may I ask sort of thing Sir?' he enquired as casually as he could, trying to sound relaxed and nonchalant.

'Hmmm? Oh, yes, yes, I am 'eee of 'ooom you mention. Pleased to meet you I'm sure Master Ovi. Mino Taur at your service.'

'Oh, by the way – *er* – what's happening to our friend Poob the tyrannosaurus you – *um* – "dealt with" a moment or two ago may I ask Mister Taur?'

''Eee's a-makin' hisself useful, that's what your friend the tyrannosaurus is a-doin'; and that, Master Ovi and Master Gusto, is what you two will be a-doin' very shortly too— '

'DA-BANG!!!'

Ovi and Gusto almost jumped out of their skins as Mino slammed the "Door" behind them hard.

'GUARDS!'

Ovi and Gusto were suddenly whisked off their feet by some netting made from creepers that had been lying on the floor and hauled mercilessly up into the air. Mino took one more look at Oxo then tossed him in the netting too, bundling all three gang members into a ball.

Through the netting, the threesome looked on helplessly as a stick-obsessed tyrannosaurus slavishly obeyed the orders of its ostrich-emu-lator controller and lunged forward to grab their creeper netting in its chomping jaws.

'Right, that's that blummin' distraction dealt with. Let's get this lot over to 'In-The-Nest' and toss 'em in—oh, and throw this little tyke in too.' Peering between the creepers, Ovi caught sight of Mino handing something to the controller which had to be Wishi. 'Now move along *sharp!* We ain't a-got much time!'

'*Ha ha ha!* Oh, you are so *wonderfully* funny my silly Cen-i-poos!' Zatt giggled coyly and dipped her finger daintily in the nectar. 'Who would have thought that starfish like to dance in moonbeams?'

Elli had joined Zatt and Cen on Cloud Nine. They were reclining leisurely on the silver lining and helping themselves to some of the nectar and ambrosia that had been placed before them in giant clamshells. Cen's horse-half was at rest with his legs curled up beneath him and his wings neatly furled. Cherub and Seraph were once again in attendance, hovering above their heads a respectful distance away on a fluffy cushion of cloud.

'I'm glad you enjoy such 'tantalising' tales my dear Zatt.' Cen smiled a boyish George-type smile. 'But now, I'm afraid you two really ought to be making a start on Nirvana and Paradise. Time *is* getting rather short you know.'

'Oh, must we Cen-i-poos *dah-hhh*-ling? Can't we have just *one* more story, please, please, pretty-*ple-eee-ease!*'

Zatt was too busy fluttering her eyelashes to notice the slight look of annoyance that flashed across Cen's face … but Elli spotted it.

'I – *er* – I think Cen's right Sis. We ought to get cracking. We— '

'Oh, don't be such a spoilsport!' Zatt rounded on her brother. 'What's the rush?'

'We have a very important deadline to meet … ' Elli glared at Cen who narrowed his eyes in a suspicious Brad-like manner. ' … don't we Cen?'

'"Deadline"? What deadline?' Zatt switched her gaze back to Cen who quickly reverted to the warm boyish George-type expression with a teeth-glistening grin. 'What's he talking about Cen, my-super-strong-soldier-with-the-shoulders?'

Before Cen could answer, Elli continued.

'We have to get all eight clouds finished in time and ready for … '

Elli deliberately paused for dramatic effect to see what would happen to Cen's expression if Zatt looked away. His plan worked perfectly. As soon as Zatt's head was turned, Cen gave Elli a really fierce narrow-eyed 'baddie' stare which both George and Brad would have been proud of.

'He knows what I'm talking about,' continued Elli. 'Go on, ask him.'

Zatt turned back to face Cen who tried to switch back to his charming George persona but didn't quite make it in time which made him look awkward with a hint of Vladimir Putin.

'Go on Cen … tell her.' Elli smiled.

Zatt glanced at her brother then quickly back at Cen who'd started to give Elli another 'baddie' glare but had to hurriedly abandon it.

'Are you all right Cen-i-poos?'

'Eh? Oh yes; I'm fine my dear.' Cen shook his head. 'Just having a spot of trouble with the old facial expressions today, that's all. Anyway, Elli is quite right, we do have to get all eight clouds done on time, and that time my dear *is* very soon.'

'All right you two, I've had enough of this!' Zatt stood up and positioned herself so that she could look at them both at once. 'What's all this about?'

'Well Sis, I've been reliably informed that the entire "fleet" of clouds has to be ready for the start of a "new epoch". Am I right Cen?'

Cen glowered fiercely at Elli in his 'baddie' guise this time with a distinct added touch of 'vampire' which Zatt saw for herself, making her gasp with surprise.

'Yes, Elli my dear boy, you are correct; all eight of our herding clouds *do* indeed need to be ready in time for the end of the epoch, one for each "continent". Heaven, Elysium, Arcadia, Xanadu, Shangri-La and Utopia are all done. That just leaves Nirvana and Paradise to do and as we speak they are both still awaiting completion … *by you two!* You are also correct about our current epoch – this *boring* old even more *boring* old, old ever so *oo-ooo-old* and—did I say "boring"? – "continent-less", or "pre-continental", if you prefer – epoch *does* indeed come to an end tomorrow which is *why-yyy-yyy* … ' Cen fixed Elli and Zatt with a withering 'blood-thirsty-monster' glare, causing them both to start trembling. 'I *need* you two insignificant and ugly little *humans* to … ' he suddenly stamped his front hooves on the silver lining, reared on his hind legs, un-furled his great wings and loomed threateningly over them, '*GET BACK TO WORK!*'

Zatt shrieked and Elli sprang to his feet.

'*Quick Sis—put these on!*' He produced Flip and Flop as well as Dingle and Dangle from behind his back where he'd been hiding them and handed a pair to Zatt. '*Let's get out of here!*'

Cen burst into guffaws of hollow mocking laughter.

'*HA-AAA HA HA HA-AAA!* Oh, come now you two; you don't *honestly* think you can escape from me in *those!* I mean—*really? HA-AAA HA HA HA!*' Cen laughed again, this time with a look of amusement-mixed-with-annoyance that only top-of-the-shop actors like George and Brad can really pull off. '*Per-lease* do not tell me you are *serious!*'

'*You bet we're serious Cen!*' shouted Elli shouted from the edge of the silver lining. 'Go and find someone else to do your dirty work!'

'And to think that for a while there … ' Zatt looked back over her shoulder at Cen, her eyes full of tears. 'I had you down as one of the good guys!'

Cen ceased laughing and his expression suddenly became grim. He turned angrily toward Cherub and Seraph and bellowed.

'Will you two please stop "hanging about" idly up there and make yourselves useful for once! Get down here like *RIGHT NOW* and *GRAB THEM QUICK* for goodness' sake! Whatever you do, do *NOT* let them get away! If they should somehow, heaven forbid, manage to escape, you can guess who'll be finishing off the last two clouds!'

Seraph and Cherub looked at each other … and blinked. For the briefest of moments their ickle-dimple-dumpling rosie-cheeked features looked shocked at what was happening and their darling little eyes grew wide with astonishment. But then their eyes continued growing wider … and wider … and their faces also grew larger and larger, as did the rest of their cutie-cuddly ickle baby-like bodies. Their wings also grew; their roly-poly dimpled arms and legs straightened and their wiggly-tinkly fingers and toes turned into talons and claws. As they turned to face their prey their cute little butterfly mouths sprang open to reveal razor-sharp grills of head-chomping-off teeth.

'*Come on Sis; let's go!*'

Elli waited, poised ready to jump, while Zatt slipped on her winged-slipper birds.

'*Whoa! Hold up there!*' came a shrill urgent voice from beneath his feet. 'Wait Mister Elli; we're not— '

'We can't wait! We need to get going—*NOW!*'

Elli looked back over his shoulder. The creatures that had until very recently been the ultra-cuddly Cherub and Seraph were diving towards them—*fast!*

'Ready Sis?'

Zatt nodded.

'*One – tooth – ree—JUMP!*'

The pair of them leapt off the edge of the silver lining hand in hand. As they leapt Cen made a lunge for them, but he missed. Elli was just about to turn around in mid-air and thumb his nose at the mixed-up multiple-personalitied mythological creature when things suddenly went horribly wrong. His left leg went in one direction and his right leg went in other. He and Zatt barely managed to exchange quick 'oops-that-doesn't-look-good' glances before her legs did the same.

'We tried to warn you—*whoops!*—Elli,' cried the frantic little voice. 'You've muddled us up! I've never worked with—*wey-hey look-out!*—Dangle before.'

Elli's legs suddenly crossed, uncrossed then crossed again completely out of sync. Zatt's were no better; her left leg shot up to her head at the same time as her right leg went round in circles. And all the while the Seraph and Cherub 'creatures' bore down on them with their razor-sharp teeth chomping and drooling.

'It's no use,' cried Zatt as her left leg did a zig-zag behind her back and her right leg did a forward double-twist before attempting a backward somersault. 'We need to swap them and do it right now!'

'But we'll plummet to the ground like stones!'

The creatures were almost upon them claws outstretched and teeth chomping.

'*Just do it Elli!*'

They barely managed to remove the muddled-up birds from their feet in time. Cherub and Seraph made a snatch for their prey but only succeeded in grabbing air in their talons. Looking down to see what had gone wrong, they saw Zatt and Elli falling away from them as Elli had predicted—like stones.

'*Don't just stare at them like a pair of gormless idiots!*' shouted an enraged Cen. '*Go after them you fools!*'

Cherub and Seraph obviously didn't like being called "gormless idiots" and "fools" any more than they fancied the prospects of getting their hands dirty. They shared a look of grim determination, furled their now-eagle-like wings … and dived teeth first.

'*Chomp! Chomp! Chomp!*'

'Hurry up Elli,' cried Zatt, looking up and seeing their hunters gaining on them. 'Swap me Flop for Dingle.'

'No-no-no, I've got Flip not Flop! You need to give me Flop and keep Dingle!'

'What do you mean I've got Flop? I thought you had Flop?'

'Look, here's Dangle.' Elli glanced upwards; the hunters were almost upon them. 'Give me Flop—*quick!*'

'*Chomp! Chomp! Chomp!*'

'Hello you two! Fancy meeting up like this in mid-air so-to-speak.'

Hopi suddenly appeared immediately beside Elli and Zatt, matching their downward speed in a controlled dive.

'*Hopi; is that you?*' cried Elli and Zatt together.

'Well, it certainly was me the last time I checked.'

'*Where have you been?*' shouted Elli. '*What have you been doing?*'

'I can't help thinking this might not be an opportune moment for an exchange of news, Elli … ' Hopi nodded up at the approaching hunters, their teeth now audibly close.

'*Chomp! Chomp! Chomp!*'

'I strongly recommend you avail yourselves of my portage and together we make a collective extrication from this rather unfortunate predicament; otherwise we— '

'*Oh, for goodness' sake you two*' cried Zatt. '*Let's get out of here!*'

Hopi positioned his head directly beneath the pair of plummeting siblings. Using the extra reach of his bow, Elli was able to hook onto one of Hopi's horns then haul himself and Zatt 'on board'. As soon as they were seated, Hopi gave a double '*fah-whoosh-pa-pa-dah-lommopp!*' to build-up speed.

'*Hold on tight, you two!*' he cried then suddenly banked to the right.

Once again, the chomping Cherub and Seraph were left grasping at empty space; but this time they wasted no time on exchanging looks of grim determination. They instantly set about chasing after Hopi who was heading for some large dark clouds that were about to deposit their rain-loads into the Crown Lake.

As the chase unfurled beneath him, looking on from way up high, gliding smoothly on his impressive outstretched wings, sun glinting on his impeccable George-Brad chiselled features, summer breeze rakishly tousling his lusty well-groomed locks … the devilishly handsome Cen Taur smiled.

Far down below, his brother Mino Taur was much too busy with last minute preparations to do any smiling. He had every single tyrannosaurus in the world under his command and was using their raw brute strength to shift large amounts of moon rock through the myriad of tunnels that formed the Labyrinth which linked, and permeated, all eight proto-continents: Asia, Africa, Europe, America-North, America-South, Antarctica, Australia and East Anglia. (Incidentally, Dear Reader, even today many people still question why there isn't a West Anglia? "Surely," they say, "if there's an East Anglia there must be a West Anglia somewhere?" Speaking as an ex-East Anglian, I prefer not to comment.)

In terms of our story, as things stood Asia, Africa, Europe and both the Americas were all completely done and ready for "The Off". They had all needed an awful lot of moon rock inserted in order to address their severe imbalances of red, green and silver; but that was now complete and no more work was required. Antarctica was almost ready and was just waiting for a tad more green. Australia, however, still needed half a mountain's worth of red; and that's where Mino's attention (and therefore most of the tyrannosaurus activity) was concentrated. (Interestingly, East Anglia had been deemed perfect in terms of its rock-blend and hadn't needed any implants whatsoever.)

The eight proto-continents were currently one single land mass called simply "The World". At the epicentre of The World was the massive mega-mountain known as God's Crown and at its heart was the inner-ring of peaks that held the huge body of fresh water called "Crown Lake" which Cen was busily topping up with his herding clouds. Directly beneath the lake was a vast cavernous space called "Crown Cavern" where all the labyrinth's tunnels stemmed from. Lying between the huge body of water and the vast space was a thin 'membrane' of rock which was in effect the bottom of the lake on one side and the roof of the cavern on the other.

Down in Crown Cavern one end of the great chamber was where the moons were kept, or rather what remained of them. Where the beautiful, proud and magnificent Green Moon had once stood there was now a mere scattering of loose green boulders. The superb, brilliant, shiny and splendid Silver Moon was almost completely spent with barely enough left in molten form for Cen to finish off lining his herding clouds. The once grand and majestic Red Moon on the other hand was still just about recognisable as a moon with part of its curvature still intact. It leaned awkwardly and precariously against the wall of the cavern in a fragile hollowed-out "C" tapering to a thin point at its apex; a mournful reminder of its once fully-rounded moon-shaped self. About its base was where the tyrannosauruses were now currently working; and it was only a matter of time before the last residue of its "moon-ness" would be gone and lost forever, leaving behind a meagre pile of red-rock-rubble.

At the other end of Crown Cavern was a recreation area for the tyrannosauruses, where they could go for some well-earned rest and refreshment. In the middle of this area was a special installation known as "In-The-Nest". This took the form of an enormous 'nest-shaped-structure' made of masses of up-rooted trees 'knitted together' in a giant seemingly-impenetrable circle into which all kinds of organic material (rotting vegetation, dead fish and giant insects as well as other dead creatures, even the odd poltroon who looked dead but was only sleeping) was constantly being thrown and left to mulch into a revoltingly-smelly fodder which oozed out from beneath the nest structure for the tyrannosauruses to 'graze' upon.

As it happens, Mino's tyrannosauruses weren't the only creatures to be found feeding on the foul stinking fodder produced "In-The-Nest".

The original inhabitants of the caves and passages of Crown Cavern had been a relatively ordinary and harmless breed of wide-eyed nocturnal cat. When the mining had first started the cats had scurried away from the sudden influx of light (provided by thousands upon thousands of lit torches which, incidentally, is where Oxo got his seemingly limitless supply of burnt-out stubs) and they'd hidden up in the cavern's deepest darkest recesses too frightened to emerge. But eventually, driven by hunger, they had crept furtively up to the giant nest-like structure which had very quickly started to give off mulchy-foodie-type smells and which proved tantalising and irresistible to a nocturnal cat. A few brave individuals had then wriggled their way through the tangle of 'knitted trees' to cautiously taste the fodder held within and had been pleasantly surprised at its epicurean qualities. Word had quickly spread and the rest of the cats had poured in … and tucked in. (Ironically, it turned out that these cats actually liked eating the same things as tyrannosauruses which will of course, come as no surprise to modern day pet owners who have both dogs and cats.) 'Tasting' had rapidly escalated to 'gorging' and overnight the cats decided to permanently swap their cold dark and dank recesses for this nice warm 'nest' with its on-tap ready-prepared food supply; and had stayed there ever since. In an incredibly short period of time they had evolved into a new species of cat … the "fat-cat".

When the 'infestation' of corpulent nocturnal cats had first become apparent, Mino had initially tried to remove them, but he'd quickly realised they posed no threat. Indeed, it turned out that fat-cats actually helped in the 'mulch-to-fodder' process by killing-off any living creature that had been accidentally (or otherwise) tossed into 'In-The-Nest', thereby speeding up its conversion into tyrannosaurus fodder. So, things had eventually settled into an unspoken 'arrangement' whereby 'In-The-Nest' was the preserve of the fat-cats on the understanding that they ensured a steady supply of fodder for the tyrannosauruses.

("What about the ostrich-emu-lators?" I hear you ask. "What did they eat?" I am afraid, Dear Reader, that is still a mystery to this very day.)

'*You don't frighten us Mino! Wherever you're taking us and whatever you're planning to do with us; you can't frighten us, NO WAY MINO!*' Ovi shouted defiantly at the top of his voice. '*We're not frightened of anything, are we Gusto?*'

'*Too right* – burp – *little buddy! It takes more than being caught in a net and held captive to* – belp – *faze the Tax-Taker-Backer-Gang!*'

'*Did you hear that Mino?*'

'*Quiet in the bundle!*'

'*Dammit I'm Mad. Dammit I'm Mad. Dammit I'm Mad. E-e-esaelp t-t-t'nod m-m-mrah em, e-e-esaelp!*'

Ovi managed to wriggle his head round beneath Gusto's leg and peer out through the netting. Immediately in front of them was an absolutely huge nest-shaped structure; and as they got nearer, he could see that it wasn't comprised of mere sticks like a normal nest; it was actually made up of entire trees of all shapes and sizes; and by "entire trees" I do mean the 'entire' tree: trunk, branches *and* roots!

'Whatever that place is Mino, we're not frightened of it! Oh no, not us! It'll take more than some tangled mass of up-rooted trees to frighten us, won't it Gusto?'

'Yeah, man! We – burp – *tear up trees for fun!'*

'No, we don't,' hissed Ovi.

'I know that and you – *belp* – know that,' hissed Gusto back, 'but he – *burp* – don't!'

'I see,' whispered Ovi before resuming his defiant shouting. '*Yeah, me included Mino! I often tear a tree up when it gets in my way! I'm not frightened by all those trees in a tangle – NO WAY!'*

'I said quiet in the bundle! I won't be a-warnin' you again!'

'Dammit I'm Mad. Dammit I'm Mad. Dammit I'm Mad. E-e-esaelp t-t-t'nod m-m-mrah em, e-e-esaelp!'

'Aw, please – *burp* – shut up strange little – *belp* – buddy!'

'Yes Oxo, we want Mino to—*PFFFWHOOORRR! WHAT'S THAT STINK?'*

They had just gotten within smelling range of the 'In-The-Nest'. Ovi wriggled again and managed to peep out from under Gusto's bottom. Through the netting he could see a gap in the tangle of up-rooted trees where a great pile of some horrible browny-green sludge appeared to be oozing out. Around its base a large number of tyrannosauruses were grazing. The turnover was quite fast, and as he watched Ovi realised it was because the ostrich-emu-lators couldn't stand the smell. He could see them taking a deep breath, then manoeuvring their beast of burden up to the goo-mound and allowing it to stay there until their faces went blue, then they quickly whipped their steeds away again.

'I hope whatever you're intending to do with us doesn't involve that horrible stuff Mino!'

'Oh, but it does HAH, HAH, HA-AAA! *it most certainly blummin' does!'*

'Well, we're not frightened of a bit of smelly-pooey-goo, are we Gusto?'

'No we sure ain't – burp – *little buddy! The more smelly and* – belp – *goo-ey the better for a Tax-Taker-Backer!'*

Gusto lowered his voice.

'Actually little buddy – *burp* – I quite like that smell; it reminds me – *belch-pardon* – of home.'

They suddenly came to a halt. Ovi looked up and saw the giant tangle of torn-up trees towering high above them.

'*RIGHT! TOSS 'EM IN!*'

'*WAIT! WAIT! WAIT!*' cried Ovi, realising that the "'em" in "Toss 'em in!" was in all likelihood a reference to himself and his companions. '*Right Mino, I'm warning you! The Tax-Taker-Backer-Gang will take a very dim view of things, if you toss us in there!*'

'Are you sure you want 'em chucked in Boss? We don't want no trouble from no gangs or nuffin',' said the ostrich-emulator controlling the tyrannosaurus carrying their netting.

''Eee's just mouthin' off coz 'eee's frightened that's all. Now chuck 'em in—an' be quick about it!'

'*Frightened? Us?* Ha ha hah! *We're not frightened, are we Gusto?*'

'*Nope, nada and* – burp – *no-siree little buddy!*'

'*Dammit I'm Mad. E-e-esaelp t-t-t'nod—* '

'Will you please shush Oxo!'

'*Well, yous little guys should be a-frightened! There's nothin' for yous in there … apart from certain death!*'

'Hah! *We in the Tax-Taker-Backer-Gang laugh at certain death, don't we Gusto?* Ha ha hah! Ha ha hah!'

'*Too right little buddy!* Ha ha hah! Ha ha – *burp* – hah!'

'On "go". Are you ready?'

'Yes Boss.'

'*Ha ha hah! Ha ha hah!*'

'*Ha ha hah! Ha ha* – burp – *hah!*'

'*Dammit I'm Mad!*'

'Shhh! *Ha ha hah! Ha ha hah!*'

'*GO!*'

The tyrannosaurus holding their bundle started to spin on one leg and as it did so the bundle began to twirl.

'Ha ha hah! *You can twirl us round as much as you like Mino! Twirling doesn't frighten us!* Ha ha hah!'

'Hey little buddy – *burp* – this is real fun! *Ha ha* – burp – *hah!*'

'*Dammit I'm Mad!*'

'Shhh Oxo! *Ha ha hah! Ha ha hah!*'

On the third twirl the tyrannosaurus let go and the bundle flew high up into the air.'

'All right now I'm frightened. *AAA-III-YAAA-AAA!!!*'

'Yup me too. *HEE-EEE-EL* – burp – *P!*'

'Yllautca, I leef hcum retteb won er'ew gniylf.'

'Oh, will you please shut up Oxo! *AAA-III-YAAA-AAA!!!*'

While he was screaming, Ovi could see Mino below watching the bundle to make sure it cleared the tangle of trees. Then, just as it soared over the topmost branches and lingered in the air before its descent down the other side, he saw him turn away and march off toward the Red Moon.

'*AAA-III-YAAA-AAA!!!*'

'*HEE-EEE-EL* – burp – *P!*'

'*SPLA-DUNK!*'

Luckily, they landed on something soft which broke their fall; unluckily, the soft something was also very goo-ey and extremely smelly. While they were disentangling themselves, Ovi began to retch; the combination of his air sickness plus the awful stench proving too much for his poor belly.

'Oh – *retch* – dear! What a – *retch* – awful place! What is – *retch* – that foul smell – *retch-retch* – it really reeks in here!'

Gusto was the first to his feet. He took in a deep breath, stretched his arms out … and smiled.

'*Ahhh!* Man, I really – *burp* – dig it here! Such – *belp* – bracing air!'

'I t'nac llems a gniht. Tub neht I t'nod evah a eson.'

Oxo reached under his wing and produced a couple of baby yellowy-green marrots (the predecessor of both the marrow and carrots) and back-handed them to Ovi.

'Ereh, yrt eseht.'

He back-gestured that Ovi should put them up his nose. Ovi did as suggested and in an instant positively beamed.

'Why, that's great! Thanks Oxo; I owe you— '

'*Tha-donk!*'

A small object hit him on the head and bounced off into the nearby goo.

'*Splat!*'

It was Wishi who by now was barely the size of a tiny little mouse-shrew-dinkety-dumble (which was later to evolve into four species; two of which sadly died out). The ostrich-emulator had only just remembered to throw him into 'In-The-Nest'.

'Foid! Foid! Oit loist, soime foid!'

Wishi didn't bother to pick himself up. He simply turned over where he lay and started tucking in.

'*Wishi!* Thank goodness you're back with us; I thought we'd lost you.'

'Yeah, little tiny buddy, we – *burp*— '

'*Shush!*' hissed Ovi. '*What's that strange sound?*'

Gusto cocked his head to one side, straining to hear; as did Oxo, backwards. At first all they could make out was the contented '*munch-munch-munch*' of Wishi settling in for a good old hearty gnosh. Then they all heard it. Almost imperceptible to begin with, but then rapidly becoming louder and surrounding them on all sides, was the unmistakeable sound of creatures "purring" … and lots of them.

'*WHOOSH! SWISH-SH-SH-SWO-OOO-OSH! WA-WA-WHO-OOO-SHH!*'

'*NOOO-OOO! LOOK OUT!*'

'*WA-WA-WA—WHOOSH-WHOOSH!*'

'*HELP! AHHH!*'

'*WHOO-OOO-WHOOSH!—WA-WA-WHOOSH!!!*'

'*Great-Sun-in-the-Sky! AIYAAA-AHH!*'

Hopi, Elli and Zatt were now in amongst the clouds and flying blind. Every so often a rocky bluff or a jagged pinnacle would suddenly appear in front of them, forcing Hopi to swerve; and each time it happened it was really, really scary.

'Um – *d-d-don't you th-th-think we ought to land s-s-soon Hopi?*' Elli's eyes were wide with fear.

'*WA-WA-WHO-OOO-OOO-OSH! SWISH-SH-SH—SWOOSH!*'

'*He's right, Hopi! We really ought to—AHHH!—we really ought to—AIY-AAA-AHH! —s-s-stop s-s-soon Hopi!*' cried Zatt between screams.

'*Be patient my friends!*' Hopi's reassuring tones could just about be heard in the rushing wind. '*We're almost there!*'

'*Where are you taking us Hopi?*'

'*The place I'm heading for is—whoa-AAAAH!*'

'*WA—WHOOSH! WA-WA-WHO-OOO-OSH!*'

'*Phew! That was close! Are you both all right?*'

Hopi had narrowly managed to avoid a massive lump of mountain by doing a backward loop-de-loop.

'*Hellooo!* Are you both all right up there?'

'Er – *yes … yes, we're b-b-both f-f-fine,*' stammered Elli. '*C-c-can we p-p-please—* '

'*We're there! Hold tight!*'

Hopi banked sharp left and headed straight for a huge overhang which had suddenly appeared before them. Then, just as Elli and Zatt thought they were about to go '*splatt!*' into the mountainside, Hopi banked hard right and tucked down beneath it. On the other side of the bluff a large cave entrance opened up before them and Hopi spread his wings to glide in for landing, aiming for a prominent ledge. With one final '*fah-whoosh-pa-pa-dah-lommopp*', they were safely down and Hopi lowered his head so that a rather shaky Elli and Zatt could disembark.

Their feet were barely on the rock floor, however, when the cascading clouds that masked the cavern entrance suddenly exploded with two loud '*Puff!*'s as Cherub and Seraph punched their way through.

'*OH, NO!*' cried Zatt. '*They're here—they've found us!*'

Fortunately, the two hunters were in such hot pursuit, they overshot Hopi's ledge and rushed past at top speed, flying deep into the cavern.

'*Chomp! Chomp! Chomp! Chomp! Chomp! Chomp!*'

But then, as Elli and Zatt looked on in horror, they skidded to a halt in mid-air, executed a quick turn and started heading back toward them—teeth-grills bared and chomping-a-frenzy.

'*QUICK! RUN!*' Zatt turned on her heels and made to sprint off.

'*NO! STOP!*' Elli grabbed her just in time, then pointed downwards.

Immediately beneath them was a sheer drop which fell away sharply and continued as far as they could see until it was obscured by clouds far, far below. They were just exchanging desperate 'phew-that-was-close-what-are-we-going-to-do-now-though?' glances when a loud familiar voice came from outside of the overhang and echoed throughout the cave.

'*Cherub? Seraph? Come out from there at once! It's no use hiding, I know you're in there!*'

The two ex-cuddly creatures stopped in mid-chase – and mid-chomp – to hover barely a tyrannosaurus length from Hopi's head and look at each other, nonplussed.

'*Come on you two! I know you're in there! We've wasted enough time on this silly pursuit. There's some silver lining that needs doing urgently. It's time for you to get your claws dirty.*'

Cherub and Seraph looked at each other then down at their prey and then back at each other again. They then began to gesticulate in protest as if to say "Look, they're right here; we were just about to catch them; we only needed a couple more moments. Just a few more chomps!"

'*Will you two please do as you are told and come out of there at once! You've had your chance. Now it's time to get some serious work done. The chase is over!*'

Reluctantly, Cherub and Seraph sulkily shrugged their shoulders, forlornly flapped their wings and grudgingly headed back out of the cavern into the folds of white mist. As they disappeared from view, Elli, Zatt and Hopi could clearly hear Cen's voice receding into the distance.

'*I can see you need more practice at chasing prey. When this bit of business is over, I'll hand you over to my brother Mino. He'll lick you into shape. Of that, you can have no fear.* Hah—ha-ha-ha-ha! Hah—ha-ha-ha-ha!'

Realising they were finally safe, a relieved Elli and Zatt looked around at their new surroundings. They were on the lip of a great natural cleft in the side of God's Crown which extended deep into the body of the giant mountain and disappeared out of sight. The opening where they were standing was well-hidden by the massive outcrop of rock they'd just flown under.

'Pretty impressive, isn't it?' said Hopi. 'I discovered it while I was exploring and checking out "what's what". It's a— '

'Excuse me.'

A squeaky high-pitched voice made all three Tax-Taker-Backers jump. They turned around and saw Flip, Flop, Dingle and Dangle hovering in a cluster behind them, their little wings frantically a-flutter.

'Can we go now please Mister Elli?'

'*Um* – yes, I think so, but I'm not sure. Wait a moment, let me check.'

Elli turned to Hopi.

'We – *er* – we won't be doing any more hovering in the air or flying about on our own or anything like that from now on, will we Hopi?'

'Yes, that is correct Elli. You and Zatt will be well and truly 'grounded' from now on.'

Elli turned back to the white winged-slipper birds and smiled.

'You're welcome to go, but before you do, I'd like to thank you for all your support – *um* – down under, beneath me—though not, of course, *beneath* me, in another way, so-to-speak.'

'Yeah, that goes for me too,' added Zatt. 'It was great fun guys—thanks!'

'Try not to get us muddled up next time, eh?'

'No, of course not Flip.'

'*Um* – I'm Dingle actually.'

'Oops, sorry Dingle!' Zatt giggled. 'If you're Dingle, then *you* must be Dangle.'

'Nope, I'm Flop … or am I? Hold on a moment I might be Dingle thinking about it.'

'What do you mean, you might be Dingle? Of course, you're not Dingle! We just established he's Dingle—hold up, did he just say "Dingle" or "Dangle"?'

'*Aaa-aaa-anyway!*'

Elli could see Zatt getting in a tangle as she desperately tried to follow the little birds' 'logic' and decided it was time to move things along.

'You'll have to excuse us Dingle, Dangle, Flip and Flop. We have to get cracking and resume our quest, especially with all this "epoch"-stuff about to happen.'

'Of course. We understand Mister Elli. Come along lads – *let's go!*'

With that the winged-slipper birds took off and fluttered their way back towards the mists and the outcrop. As they exited, they could still be heard bickering.

'*I'm* Dingle, I tell you! And *you're* Flop!'

'*No, I am not!* You're Flop! Just you wait till I tell Gizmo and Gadget that you keep getting me confused with someone else.'

'Well, if you tell Gizmo and Gadget you're not Flop, I'll tell Knick and Knack that *I'm* Dangle.'

'You wouldn't dare!'

'Excuse me. Sorry to interrupt, but if he's Dangle, who am I?'

… and so on and so forth.

'Well, my friends,' said Hopi, turning to face Elli and Zatt with a broad smile. 'It would seem we have rather a lot of catching up to do.'

'Yes, we certainly do,' said Elli, 'but right now there isn't time; we need to get a move on.'

'Oh? Why's that?'

Hopi looked from Elli to Zatt who nodded a sideways 'it's-best-if-I-let-him-explain-things' nod, so he looked back at Elli.

'The thing is Hopi,' said Elli, 'we've discovered that something called an "epoch" is about to end – or start? – any moment now, and we really need to find the others double-quick before it's too late.'

'"Too late"? Too late for what?'

'Eh? Ah, good question Hopi! What a very, very … *very* good question that is! Isn't that a good question Zatt?'

Zatt nodded emphatically.

Elli gave her a 'do-you-want-to-take-it-from-here?' look to which Zatt replied with a 'no-you're-doing-fine-please-go-on' one in reply.

'To be honest Hopi, I don't know what "what" is, but what I *do* know is that, whatever it is, that "what" is very *very* important!'

'I see-eee! Do you happen to know why we mustn't be *late* for whatever it is per chance?'

'*We-eee-ell*, I know it's got something to do with those clouds we were on – they're called called "herding clouds" by the way; and each one has a name like "Utopia" or "Shangri-La" – anyway, they are all getting silver linings in preparation for this new epoch-thingy—oh, and then there are others things called “continents”; and-and—oh, there’s *so* much more; too much to tell! What I mean is Hopi … What I’m trying to say is … ’ Elli took an extra deep breath. ‘ … this is *Big Stuff!*’

‘He’s definitely right about that Hopi!’

Zatt decided it was time to help her brother out.

‘The point is there are big things happening around here and they’re happening fast which means that right now we need to be moving fast too!’ She pointed upward. ‘So far we’ve been “*up*”, done “up” and seen what is going on up there.’ She pointed downward. ‘What we need to do, and in super-quick time, is go “*down*” in order to find out whatever is going on down below … and we need to do so *now!*’

‘Well in that case my friends it’s a jolly good thing I’ve already completed a preliminary exploration of this subterranean feature.’ He nodded to indicate the deep dark recesses at the rear of the giant cave which appeared to lead toward the very heart of God’s Crown. ‘Rather fortuitously methinks, I discovered that if we head that way, we will find ourselves in an elaborate network of tunnels and passageways that is not only prodigious in its extent; it is also primarily and in the main of a decidedly precipitative declivity.’

Chapter Ten

The Taxman stirs the plot

It was difficult to see things clearly because 'In-The-Nest' was so dark, and to the newly-entrapped gang members what little they could see looked downright dangerous and threatening. All around them creature-shaped shadows were moving. Far up above, the distant walls of Crown Cavern were brightly lit by burning torches that were constantly being replenished by a special unit of tyrannosauruses. However, only faint flickers of their light made it through the dense tangle of up-rooted trees to 'dot' the floor with the occasional faint dapple; and it was in between these pale patches that the ever-shifting shadows weaved and flitted … and 'purred'.

'Wh-wh-what's that over there?'

Ovi pointed a trembling finger to where he thought he'd seen a pair of luminescent greenish blobs blink.

'I can't see a – *burp* – thing little buddy.'

'*Look!* There it is again over there.'

Ovi pointed in a different direction.

Gusto looked where Ovi was pointing and sure enough there right in front of them a pair of glowing green lights were winking alternately one at a time. At the same time not far away, another pair – also a radiant green – started blinking.

'*Kool!*'

Ovi and Gusto span round to look where Oxo was back-pointing and there was another pair of blinking green eyes … and another.

'*Oivoi, Goistoi* – gulp-swallow – *whoit's thoit oivoir thoire!*'

Wishi (who was already almost as tall as Oxo) paused mid-munch to point in yet another direction. There were now green lights blinking and winking everywhere they looked … they were completely surrounded.

'We urgently need some light—*like right now!*' cried Ovi. 'Wishi, we need you to use your eyes. Oxo, do you have any more of your— '

Before he could finish his sentence, Hopi's powerful searchlight beams shone forth and Oxo blew alight two of his flaming torches.

'*MIII-III-AAA-OOO-WWW! Too br-r-r-r-right! Too br-r-r-r-right! Yuck! Yuck!* All or-r-r-r-range, yellow and r-r-r-r-r-ed. *Tur-r-r-r-r-r-n it off! Tur-r-r-r-r-r-n it off!*'

The Tax-Taker-Backers were completely surrounded by very large cats about twice the size of Ovi or Gusto. Caught out by the sudden burst of light, they had all reared up on their short stubby hind legs and were trying to shade their eyes with their front paws. They all had puffy round faces with eyes as big as clam shells and long, long whiskers; and every single one of them without exception had a big wibbly-wobbly pot belly that made Ovi's look like a novice. Strangely, although they were all purple-ish in ncolour, they each had their own unique shade, ranging from lilac to violet, puce to mauve.

'*Oh, I bet you'd like that!*' cried Ovi defiantly (which isn't easy with a baby marrot up each nostril). '*Then you'd pounce on us in the dark! We're not stupid, are we guys?*'

'*Noi, woi're noit!*'

'*Sey, er'ew ton!*'

'*Whatever you say little buddy* – burp – *we're with you all the way!*'

'Too much hhh-hhhor-r-r-r-r-r-ibble light! *MIII-III-AAA-OOO-WWW!* Too much or-r-r-r-range, yellow and r-r-r-r-r-ed,' repeated the first of the cats to speak who was a whiter shade of pale purple than the others. '*Tur-r-r-r-r-r-n it off! Tur-r-r-r-r-n it off!* Please, please, pr-r-r-r-r-r-etty please!'

'How come you can speak human?' Ovi looked puzzled. 'I haven't recited the Gum Gum Song yet.'

'Of cour-r-r-r-r-se we can speak human. *Miii-iii-aaa-ooo-www!* We speak purrr-r-r-r-r-r-fect Purrr-r-r-r-r-r-sian!'

'*Miii-iii-aaa-ooo-www!*' said another of the cats who was a rather pleasant plum colour. 'Purrr-r-r-r-r-r-fect Parrr-r-r-r-r-r-*i-i-i-i-i*-sian don't you mean?'

'*MIII-III-AAA-OOO-WWW-III-AAA-OOO-WWW-III-AAA-OOO-WWW!*' A third one pushed the plummy one aside and leaned forward. It was a pucey-lilac in tone. 'We don't speak

Purrr-r-r-r-r-sian or Parrr-r-r-r-r-*i-i-i*-sian. We speak Purrr-r-r-r-r-fect Purrr-r-r-r-r-*SUA*-sion!'

To emphasise "Purrr-r-r-r-r-*SUA*-sion", it unleashed its claws and took a wild slash at Hopi's light beams.

'Poissst!'

Wishi gave Ovi a surreptitious kick. Ovi glanced round and saw Wishi was shrinking again. At that moment, Oxo took matters into his own hands and made several threatening steps backward toward the cat that had just slashed at Wishi's beam, back-waving his torches.

'Senile felines! … Stack cats! … Draw, O coward!'

'OXO!'

Ovi just managed to grab hold of Oxo and drag him back to their huddle before the cats reacted. As one, they dropped onto their paws and started to circle their prey, moving slinkily and slowly; some circling one way, others circling the other, and all of them edging closer and closer. The 'purring' then ceased and was replaced by that other sound which cats throughout the ages have always made when riled; a harsh sibilant nerve-jangling '*HISS-SSS-SSS—SSS-SSS*'.

'Now look what you've done Oxo!'

'Yeah, thanks a – *burp* – bunch little backward – *belp* – buddy!'

'Oi'm goi-oing toi hoive toi cloise moi oiyes soin Oivoi! Doi soimethoing, quoick oir woi're doine foir!'

'Hold back! Hold fast!
Why, whatever's the crime?
Some poor folk need saving
And, as ever …
I'm just in time!'

A large hollowed-out aubergine-plum-eggplant-pear fruit (about the same shape and size as one of those spherical fibreglass chairs so popular with baddies in 1960s movies which were excellent for swivelling round and dramatically revealing their identity) slowly lowered itself from on high to hang suspended in the no-mans-land area between the cats and the Tax-Taker-Backers. While it was descending, the cats ceased their prowling and came to a halt. They also stopped their hissing and reverted instead to a soft gentle purr.

'Why Mar-r-r-r-r-ster. *Miii-iii-aaa-ooo-www!* How nice of you to join our-r-r-r-r little soir-r-r-r-r-rée; verr-r-r-r-r-ry br-r-r-r-r-ight brr-r-r-r-r-rown, verr-r-r-r-r-ry br-r-r-r-r-ight brr-r-r-r-r-rown, indeed. What arrr-r-r-r-re you doing herrr-r-r-r-re?' said the lead cat, the one who was a whiter shade of pale purple.

As the giant chair-shaped hollowed-out fruit swivelled round, Ovi and Gusto both gasped with surprise. There right before them, sitting cross-legged and sucking on a nice big juicy peach-apricot-nectarine-orange-vanilla-twist-lime-and-soda … was Granddad.

'S-s-s-c-c-crape-rumble—rattle-drumble—clunk-a-chunk!'

'*Stop! Shush!* I think I can hear something ahead,' hissed Elli in the darkness. 'I can see something too! Look down there. What's that in the distance?'

'It's some kind of light,' said Zatt, straining hard to see down the long passageway. 'What do you think that is Hopi?'

'I'd say it was one of your human fires Zatt,' said a much-diminished Hopi now barely the size of a tyrannosaurus, 'except it appears to be on the move.'

'Rattle-rattle s-s-s-c-c-crape-drumble-roar!'

'There's that noise again!' said Elli, sounding more than a little anxious.

'Whatever it is,' said Zatt, 'it's getting closer.'

'Rumble-rumble—s-s-scrape-rattle-roar!'

'It's getting *very* closer Sis! Hopi, why don't you shine your beams down the tunnel? Then we can— '

'*No, don't Hopi!*' cried Zatt. 'If you shine your beams, whoever, or whatever, it is will know we're here!'

'Drumble-drumble, scrape-roar—rattle-rattle, s-s-s-c-ccrape-s-s-s-crape, drumble-drumble—clunkety-clunk-donk!'

'Whatever it is,' cried Elli, '*it's coming straight for us!*'

'Drumble-drumble-drumble—roar—s-s-s-c-c-c-c-crape-drumble-dunk-clacklety-clonk!'

'*Hey, you two!*' Zatt had to shout to be heard. '*There's a gap in the wall just here! Move over to the side—quick!*'

'DRUMBLE-DRUMBLE—S-S-S-C-C-CRAPE—S-S-S-S-C-C-CRAPE-ROOO-AAAR!!!'

The recess Zatt had found was barely big enough for the three Tax-Taker-Backers and they just got out of the way in time to avoid being crushed. A huge lump of rock – so large it filled the entire tunnel – ground and grated its way past them almost scraping their noses as it forced its way forward. As soon as it had passed, the tunnel was filled with the bright glow of flaming torchlight; and the '*roaring-scraping-drumbling*' came to a sudden halt.

The three Tax-Taker-Backers froze. Although the bright orange light of the flickering torches lit them up, it also provided them with a disguise, blending them into the shapes and shadows of roughly hewn rock, making them look like frozen monotone ochre-coloured hieroglyphs.

'Why 'ave we stopped?' asked an ostrich-emu-lator.

'Did you 'ear somefing-k?' said another.

'O'course I didn't 'ear nuffing-k. You can't 'ear a fing-k over all this blummin' a-scraping-k.'

(In case you're wondering, Dear Reader, constant exposure to Mino as well as the odd speaking tyrannosaurus had had the unfortunate effect of giving ostrich-emu-lators a rather odd cockney-Germanic twinge to their already bizarre accents.)

'*Git along there!* We aint got no time to go a-wasting-k. We've got to get this green to Antarctica. It's the last load. After this we're a-done. Now, git along there little doggie. *Hup! Hup!*'

'*YIII-III-HA-AAA!* Let's git a-going-k little doggie. *YII-III-HA-AAA!*'

Remaining completely still in their recess, Elli, Zatt and Hopi looked on wide-eyed in amazement as a team of two tyrannosauruses held side-by-side in a yoke prepared to resume pushing a huge lump of green rock along the tunnel. Upon their heads sat their ostrich-emu-lator controllers who had their extra-long necks stretched out in front with sticks in their beaks which the tyrannosauruses were totally fixated upon. Obeying their controllers' orders, they placed their shoulders against the giant slab of rock and heaved in unison. The rock was reluctant to budge at first so they re-doubled their efforts and gave it an extra hard shove.

'SSS-S-SCRAPE-DRUMBLE-DRUMBLE—R-R-R-ROAR!!!'

They were off again and the last consignment of Green Moon rock resumed its journey to its new home in Antarctica. (When I say "last", Dear Reader, what I *should* say is "the *first* of the last" because this was not the *entire* consignment by any means; far from it! One massive chunk of Green Moon rock does not actually "an entire consignment" make. This was in fact the first of *many* such '*sub*-consignments' on the move that day bound for Antarctica. Indeed, no sooner had the torches carried by the two ostrich-emu-lators receded into the distance when back at the other end of the tunnel the next one appeared.)

'Rumble-drumble, s-s-s-c-c-crape-rattle-roar!'

'There's another one coming. We're trapped!' cried Elli as he realised what was happening. 'We can't go forward and we can't go back. What are we going to do?'

'Calm down Elli; we need to think,' said Zatt while her brother looked anxiously back and forth between boulder-departing to boulder-approaching.

'What are we going to do Zatt? What are we going to do?' He was so nervous he was hopping up and down, first one foot, then the other.

'Look, will you please calm down Elli—and think!'

'I am thinking,' – *hop-hop* – 'I *am* thinking!'

'Drumble-drumble, rattle-rattle, scrape-roar—clatter-de-clunk—d-d-drumble-drumble!'

'Oh dear, what are we going to *do* Sis?' – *hop-hop-hop* – 'What *are* we going to *do?*'

'Wait, wait. I'm thinking … '

Elli gave up watching the departing boulder in order to concentrate his efforts on the approaching one. As the massive lump of rock bore down upon them with its flashing flickers of light round the edges, he stopped hopping and started jumping with both feet instead.

'Hmmm … let's see-eee-eee … we can't go that way,' Zatt pointed at the departing pair of tyrannosauruses, 'because if we do, they'll see us running behind them— '

'Yes-yes!' – *jump-jump* – 'And?'

‘ … and we can’t go that way,’ she pointed to the rapidly approaching lump of rock, ‘because if we do, we’ll get flattened and— ’

‘Yes-yes, good thinking Sis; yes-yes!’ – *jump-jump-jump* – ‘*And?*’

‘Drumble-drumble-drumble—roar—s-s-s-c-ccrape-drumble!’

‘*Ahem!* Excuse me; I’m sorry to interrupt, but can either of you— ’ Hopi tried to speak but Zatt waved him quiet.

‘We could try hiding in the gap again but it’s very risky; we just got lucky last time. All of which means, as far as I can tell there’s only one thing we *can* do … ’

‘Yes-yes-yes Sis!’ – *jump-jump* – ‘Thank goodness you’ve come up with an idea in the nick of time!’ – *jump* – ‘What is it?’

‘*PANIC!*’

Zatt joined Elli in jumping frantically up and down, and pointing madly at the approaching giant boulder of green rock.

‘*AK-HEM!*’ Hopi had to give an extremely loud cough in order to distract their attention. ‘Can either of you feel what I can feel—a rather refreshing cool breeze blowing up your bottoms?’

Elli and Zatt both ceased jumping, looked at each other then dashed over to where Hopi was standing in the recess.

‘Really?’

‘Where?’

‘*DRUMBLE-DRUMBLE—S-S-S-C-C-CRAPE—ROOO-AAAR!!!*’

‘*Quick Hopi!* Shine your light beam round behind you.’

Hopi did as requested and twisted his neck round so that the two yellow beams emanating from his eyes could illuminate the area behind him. All they could see, however, was a narrow strip of tunnel floor that appeared to be comprised of nothing but solid rock plus an awful lot of Hopi’s rear end.

‘You probably imagined it Hopi; but I’d better take a closer look just in case there is something there.’ Zatt squeezed her way past Hopi’s broad bottom. ‘Maybe what you felt was—*AAA-AAA-AHH-HHH!!!*’

She disappeared downwards.

‘*SCRAPE-DRUMBLE-ROOO-AAAR!!!*’

'*ZATT!*' Elli squeezed through after her.

'*No Elli! Don't!*' shouted Hopi in alarm.

'*ZATT!* Where are yo—*AAA-AHH-HHH!*'

The tunnel suddenly filled with the light of flaming torches and the '*scrape-rumble-drumbling*' came to an abrupt halt. Spotting movement, an ostrich-emu-lator raised its torch and turned to peer at Hopi who was still bent backwards examining the tunnel floor to his rear.

'*OY!* 'Ooo goes there? What's your game?'

'Elli? Zatt? Is that— '

Hopi span round and found himself eyeball to eyeball with a rather strange long-necked bird plus a particularly vicious-looking tyrannosaurus which was baring its teeth in a snarling growl. Normally, of course, Hopi would have brushed aside such lesser creatures with ease, but he hadn't eaten for a while and he'd been doing quite a bit of flying recently, all of which had somewhat 'depleted' his stature.

'*Ah* … Hello there!' Hopi smiled. 'Lovely day, isn't it?'

Caught off guard the ostrich-emu-lator replied cordially.

'Yeah, not bad actually. It's warmed up nicely since this morning-k. In fact, I was only saying-k to my companion just now—*'ere 'old up!* What's a-'appening-k 'ere?'

Suddenly, Elli and Zatt's screams sounded from the hole in the floor; already distant and fading fast.

'*AAA-AAA-aii-iii!*'

'*HELP MMM-MMM-EEE-EEE!*'

'You'll have to excuse me, my dear chap … ' Hopi glanced round behind him to check the proximity of the hole he'd just spotted. ' … I really must be going.' He took a big step backward and disappeared.

'*'ERE! 'OLD UP!*'

'*WEEE-EEE-EEE-EEE-EEE-EEE-EEE-EEE-EEE-EEE-EEE-EEE!!! Oh, this is fun Elli! WEEE-EEE-EEE-EEE-EEE-EEE-EEE-EEE-EEE-EEE-EEE-EEE!!!*'

'*HOH-HOOO-OOH-HO-HO-HOOO-OOO-OOH! YES-YES-YEE-EES!!! You can say that again Sis! HOH-HOOO-OOH! HO-HO-HOOO-OOO-OOH! YES-YES-YEE-EES-SSS!!!*'

Hopi's wildly erratic light beams kept catching fleeting glimpses of Zatt and Elli as the three Tax-Taker-Backers slid at top speed down the highly polished surface of the chute they'd fallen into. Suddenly, they found themselves together swirling round and round a huge hollow bowl shape.

'*WHO-OOO—Ha-aaa-ha-ha-ha-OOH-HOY-YYY!*' Zatt squealed in between fits of laughter as she spun down towards a big opening at the bottom of the bowl.

'*WHA-HA-HA-AAY—HA-HA-HAYYY!*' shouted Elli, following closely behind. Then, without any warning—

'*Tha-dollop-pa-domp!*'

Zatt shot through the opening and landed on a platform of some kind that was covered with an extra-thick pile of sea sponges.

'*Pa-lommop-pa-domp!*'

Elli landed right next to her.

'*Ha-ha-hah!* What about *that* Elli! Wasn't that fun!'

'*WOW!* I could do that all over again, couldn't you Sis?'

'*Ha-ha!* Yes, I most certainly could!'

Still giggling, they bounced their way across the platform on their bottoms and got off. Once on the ground they looked around and realised they were at the back of a very large cave. Not far away they could see some daylight emanating from around a corner suggesting a possible way out.

'Where do you think we are Elli?'

'*Hmm* … Do you know something Sis, this all looks a bit familiar! I have a strange feeling I've— '

'*LOOK-OUT BELOW!*'

Hopi shot through the large round opening head first and landed on the sponges behind them with a loud '*DA-BOING!!!*'

'Well, I never! I say, I say, I say; well, I never … '

'Wasn't that fun?' said Elli as they watched Hopi trying to retain a dignified manner whilst bouncing up and down upon the sponge landing pad. 'Did you enjoy that Hopi?'

'*Um* – yes, yes, yes, indeed. I do think that rather brief and – *ahem* – diverting 'diversion' was – *um* – most agreeable, or – *er* – "fun", as you quite rightly said. Though, I hasten to add that I am greatly relieved to see neither of you came to any harm in our – *er* – "fall"-so-to-speak.'

Elli left Zatt to wait for Hopi and set off around the corner to explore the main part of the cave.

'That was quite a sticky situation we were in up there, wasn't it Hopi?' she said as Hopi clambered clumsily down from the platform. 'Did you know that "hole"-thingy was there?'

'*Er* – no-no-no, finding that was not down to any perspicacity on my part. It was purely a propitious fortuity; a happenstance that— '

Zatt placed her hands firmly on her hips and fixed the 'depleted-in-stature' nevasaurus with a withering stare.

'Are you trying to say we were "lucky" by any chance?'

'*Um* – yes, precisely, spot-on, "lucky". Yes very, "lucky" indee— '

'*Come on you two!*' Elli's voice came from around the corner and he sounded excited. '*Take a look at this!*'

Zatt and Hopi continued their bickering as they hurried after him.

'I do wish you wouldn't keep using such big words Hopi when there are perfectly good smaller ones that are easier to underst—*Oo-ooo-oh!*'

'I must say young Zatt, I'm disappointed in your lack of appreciation for scientific discourse. Discursive vocabulary, I'll have you know, gives us the verbal tools we need to—*Ahh-hhh!*'

They both came to a sudden halt and their mouths fell open in awe. There before them was a vast open cavern packed full of brilliant sparkling crystals. Everywhere they looked they could see crystalline structures shining and glistening with every colour imaginable as they reflected the sunlight from the cave's entrance. There were huge floor-to-ceiling columns interspersed with stalagmites and stalactites. In between were spurs jutting out at odd angles plus outcrops and bluffs of all shapes and sizes. Just then, Elli appeared from behind a spur.

'I *have* been here before!' he declared, plucking his bow. 'This is the cave where Ovi and I found God's lunchbox.'

'Oh, wow!' said Zatt. 'Really?'

'Where exactly did you find – *ahem* – the comestibles?' said Hopi. 'Can you remember?'

'Yes, they were over there.' Elli pointed to a raised platform over to one side … it was completely bare and empty.

'*Shhh you two!* Keep absolutely still and don't say a thing,' said Zatt, speaking in a hushed tone with a finger to her mouth. 'Can you hear that?'

All three of them held their breath and listened intently.

'What are we listening for?' whispered Elli after a pause.

'I'm afraid I can't hear anything,' muttered Hopi, pricking up both of his giant ears.

'Listen very, *very* carefully,' murmured Zatt quietly. 'Isn't that the most beautiful sound you've ever heard?'

They all listened again. Zatt was right; the vast echoey cavernous chamber was intricately and exquisitely infused with faint tinkling sounds; a dainty, little '*plop*' here and a fine soft '*tinkety-tinkle-dillop-drip*' there. For a long while the three of them remained utterly transfixed, savouring the wondrous scenery surrounding them and enjoying the peaceful tranquillity that the delicate sounds induced.

'*tinkety-tinkle-plippety-plop … tinkle-ploppety-plop … drip-tinkly-dillop-drip … dopple-ploppety-plipperty-plop … tinkety-tinkle-ploppety-plop*'

Then, all of a sudden—

'*clatter ... clatter ... clatter ... clatter ... CLUNK ... DONK!*'

'What was that?' said Elli.

'*Shhh! Listen!*' hissed Zatt.

'*plippety-plip-plip-plip ... tinkety-tinkle —plip-plop ... drippety-dimple-dipple-plip-plop ... tinkety-dinkle—dillop-dip-dop*'

'*clatter ... clatter ... clatter ... clatter ... CLUNK ... DONK!*'

'There it is again,' moaned Zatt. 'What *is* that awful noise? It's spoiling the lovely peacefulness?'

'Whatever it is, it's coming from outside,' said Elli. 'Come on, let's go and see what's making it.'

They carefully made their way through the cave with Hopi taking extra care not to break any of the crystals with his ears or his tail. And, all the while, the irritating sound coming from outside continued.

'*clatter ... clatter ... clatter ... clatter ... CLUNK ... DONK!*'

Eventually, they passed between two giant pillars of crystal and emerged out into the open where the sound became even louder.

'*clatter ... clatter ... clatter ... clatter ... CLUNK ... DONK!*'

Once outside, they paused to take in the incredible view that presented itself. A broad expanse of golden sand extended into the far distance where it appeared to merge with a line of gently undulating shimmering blue and white … the "Sea".

But all that was mere backdrop, because dominating the vista before them was a large symmetrical structure as tall as a modern-day suburban house … and indeed, that is precisely what it was—a red brick, two-story, detached, suburban home with a front door and porch, bay windows, two chimney stacks and a side garage. (You and I, Dear Reader, would have recognised it in an instant, but to Elli, Zatt and Hopi, of course, it was just a funny-shaped large 'box-type-thing'.)

'clatter ... clatter ... clatter ... clatter ... CLUNK ... DONK!'

There was the annoying sound again, coming from the other side of the big box-type-thing. Elli put his finger to his lips to 'shhh' the others quiet then led them round the strange object, tip-toeing quietly. As they passed down its side, Zatt scrutinised the large structure closely, peering at its walls and windows. She then huffed and muttered out loud to herself.

'If that was mine, I'd have to do something about those curtains.'

'What did you say?' Elli turned to face her.

'I dunno. It was just something that popped into my mind. I wonder what a "curtain" might be?'

'It's a close cousin of a "veil" actually,' said Hopi, 'similar in function to a "mask" or a "cloak" or indeed anything used to disguise things … or hide them.'

'I see,' said Elli, giving Zatt a wink. 'In which case Sis, maybe all is about to be "un-veiled"?'

They pressed on and had almost reached the rear of the house when, suddenly, they heard a man's voice chanting.

'This baby-bison went to market' … '*clatter*'
'This baby-bison stayed at home' … '*clatter*'
'This baby-bison had roast hyena' … '*clatter*'
'This baby-bison had none' … '*clatter*'
'And this baby-bison went "*wee-wee-wee*" all the way home' …
'*CLUNK ... DONK!*'

Slowly, they edged their way round the 'house's corner and were amazed at what they saw. Stretching from the rear of the 'box-type-thing' in a dead straight line out towards the far-off "Sea" was a huge 'groove' or 'ditch' dug deep into the sand. It was as deep as Hopi was tall (Hopi at his full height that is; not the severely-depleted Hopi who was with them now) and a similar width to the river they'd encountered many days earlier. The floor of the giant 'ditch' was a bed of pebbles that had been exposed and they were all glistening in the sunlight. Some of the spoil from the excavations was piled up behind the 'house' and standing at the base of the pile was a large man with his back to them. All they could see of him was a wild mane of dark spiky hair that covered his entire body apart from his lower legs, and he was wearing a shiny metallic hat. As they watched, they saw him bend down to select a handful of pebbles from the spoil and then start tossing them onto some piles by his side.

'This baby-bison went to market' … '*clatter*'
'This baby-bison stayed at home' … '*clatter*'
'This baby-bison had roast hyena' … '*clatter*'
'This baby-bison had none' … '*clatter*'
'And this baby-bison went "*wee-wee-wee*" all the way home' …
'*CLUNK … DONK!*'

The man tossed the first few pebbles onto one of four heaps: a pile of big blues, a pile of small blues, a pile of longs and a pile of knobblies. However, when it came to the fifth pebble, he threw it up high in the air and, with the flourish of a showman, whipped off his hat to catch it – '*CLUNK!*' before flinging it hard onto a fifth heap immediately beside him; a pile of perfectly-round silvers and golds – '*DONK!*'. With a further showman's flourish, he then placed the hat back on his head and began to select another handful of pebbles. Elli recognised the hat immediately; it was the water urn – the "thingummy" – he and Ovi had found in the cave the previous year along with Nourishment and Savourscent.

'This baby-bison went to market' … '*clatter*'
'This baby-bison stayed at home' … '*clatter*'
'This baby-bison had roast hyena' … '*clatter*'

'Excuse me Mister?'

It was Elli who spoke.

The man span round in surprise. His face was all hair and beard and didn't appear to have a mouth, but he did have two great staring eyes with a penetrating gaze and a dinky little pink button of a nose.

'Now, that was *NOT* funny, *not* funny at all! You can't go creeping up on people like that! Goodness me; you gave me a dreadful fright!'

'Sorry about that Mister,' said Elli. 'We didn't mean to— '

'"Sorry"? What's the use in saying "sorry"?'

The man shook his head vigorously from side to side, then stared hard at the ground and started deliberating with intense concentration.

'I'm afraid "sorry" just isn't good enough, oh no … oh, no-no-no, that won't do, it just *will* not do! There's only one thing for it … ' He looked up decisively. 'I shall have to make a *law* against that!'

Elli and Zatt glanced at each other and mouthed "law"?'

'Now, what shall I call it, this new law? Oh, I know … "creeping up on people without due care and attention". Yes, that's right, that's correct, true and just; forthright and firm-yet-fair as well as wholly legitimate and easily enforceable; all done and dusted so-to-speak; nice, nice – *nice!*' He smiled to himself. 'Furthermore, hitherto and whitherto, it shall come into force with immediate effect, henceforth, thenceforth and whenceforth; hereafter, thereafter and whereafter, from this moment onward and so on and so forth. There you go; that's your new law—*nnn-noo-ooo-oww-www … OBEY IT!*'

Elli looked questioningly at the others. Zatt gave a firm 'don't-ask-me-what-he's-on-about' shrug of her shoulders while Hopi gave him an equally unequivocal 'nope-no-good-asking-me-either' look. Zatt then gave Elli a sharp nudge, spurring him to step forward.

'Right – *er* – hello there. I don't suppose you remember, but we've – *um* – we've actually met before. You're the Taxman, aren't you?'

The Taxman narrowed his eyes then opened them wide again and nodded.

'Well, the thing is – *um* – Mister Taxman,' continued Elli, 'we – that's my friends and I here – we are half of the Tax-Taker-Backer-Gang; and we're here to— '

'*Hmmm!* The "Tax-Taker-Backer-Gang" eh?' repeated the Taxman. 'So, presumably, that means the three of you are … "Tax-Taker-Backers"?'

'Yes, we are; and we're here to— '

'Pleased to make your acquaintance, I'm sure,' said the Taxman. 'I'm most grateful to you.'

'"Grateful"?' said Zatt, stepping up beside Elli. 'What do you mean "grateful"?'

'Why, for your kind offer of support, of course, as "backers" of my tax-taking.' The Taxman's wide questioning eyes moved slowly from Elli to Zatt. 'At least, I *presume* that is what a "Tax-Taker-Backer" does?'

'No-no-no, you've got that all wrong,' said Elli. 'What we mean by "Tax-Taker-Backer" is— '

'Did you say we've met before?' interrupted the Taxman, once more peering intently at Elli.

'Yes, yes we have. My name is Elli and you took one of my inventions if you recall, m-m-my – *um* – my "money".'

'You? The inventor of money? *No way-y-yyy!*'

Elli blushed, looked bashful and nodded.

The Taxman's cold glaring stare suddenly thawed; somewhere beneath his profuse beard they could sense a smile had broken out.

'Aa-aaa-ah yes, I *do* remember. You and your wonderful "money" were in a wadi. There were two of you I seem to recall. You were with some other chappie who was rather chub—*er*, overwei—*oh*, how can I say this without being rude? Extra-well-stocked, more than comfortable within himself; you know what I mean, amply-proportioned; fuller-figured, overly— '

'If you're talking about our Ovi,' interrupted Zatt. "I think the word you're looking for is "fat".'

The Taxman's attention switched to Zatt; he walked up to her, took her hand and bent forward to kiss it.

'I don't think I've had the pleasure.'

'I'm Zatt, Elli's sister.'

The Taxman released her hand and bowed a courteous bow.

'The Taxman … at your service … Zatt.'

'You're not at all what I was expecting Mister Taxman.'

'And what, exactly *were* you expecting my dear Zatt?'

'Oh, I don't know. A monster of some kind perhaps; you know, something big and dark, casting a long shadow or making menacing rumbly noises—but definitely not you! You don't look like a "monster" at all.'

'Well Zatt, I'm sorry to disappoint you.' The Taxman smiled politely. 'Now, if you'll excuse me, your brother and I have some – *um* – some "business" to discuss.'

He put his arm round Elli and led him away.

'So, Elli—*er*, may I call you "Elli" Elli?'

'*Um* – yes, but— '

'Goo-ooo-ood. Now then Elli my friend—*er*, is it okay if I call you "my friend" Elli?'

'Your "friend"? Well, I'm not sure about that. You see the thing is Mister Taxman we've come all this way to— '

'Do you know what really pleases me, Elli, about us being "friends" like this? Well, I don't mind telling you, Elli, I think this "money" idea of yours is a real winner; it's the future, Elli; I'm absolutely certain!'

'"The future" you say?'

'Oh ye-eee-esss, most definitely! And what's more if you and I – us two "friends" – put our heads together, I think we can really go places with it— '

'You do—I mean, can we?'

'Most certainly; yesseroo-ooo indoo-ooo-dy-deedy! Ah, money, money, money; it's such wonderful stuff, isn't it? Rich like milk and honey; and it makes you feel sunny just like a bunny having a runny. Hey, come to think of it—it might even be *funny!* Tell me Elli, how did you come by such a glorious concept, such an ingenious idea?'

'Well, it's quite simple really. I— '

'*EKK-KKK-SSS-SSS-KKK-YYY-YYY-OOO-OOO-OOZ-ZZZ ME-EEE!*' Zatt's voice filled the air.

The Taxman paused and looked back over his shoulder with a rather annoyed 'can't-you-see-I'm-busy?' expression.

'Yes, Zatt? What is it?'

'We have come all this way Mister Taxman because we want to talk to you about *THIS!*'

She thrust her list in the air.

'And what, exactly, in God's good grace, is that?'

The Taxman's arm dropped from Elli's shoulders and he slowly turned round to face her.

'It's a "*list*" that's what it is; and it clearly itemises all the – *um* – well, the "items" you took from us, the very same items that we are here— '

'*No-no-no!*'

'What do you mean "no-no-no"? *Yes-yes-yes*, we fully intend— '

'No-no-no, what exactly is *that* you are waving? That-that "stuff"?'

'As I said, it's a "list", a list of all the— '

'Anyone can make a "list" madam. I've made loads in my time, but never on stuff like that!'

The Taxman walked up to Zatt, took the list from her hand and examined it very closely.

'What is this stuff and where did you get it from?'

'It's one of my inventions; I call it "paper". Look, the material the list is made of is not important. We're here about the items that are contained *on* the list and represented *within* it, not the actual physical list itself. We— '

'"Paper" eh? *I like it!* In fact, I like it a *lot!* Hold on a sec folks, I'm having an idea here. What if … what if we could make "money" out of "paper"—wouldn't that be something! Imagine that … paper money. Now, that really would be funny! What's this "paper" of yours made of by the way Zatt?'

'Well, it's a special mix of leaves and bark and snake skins mashed into a pulp and eaten then regurgitated by a—look, *stop distracting me!*'

Zatt snatched the list back from the Taxman and started reading from it.

'There's so much here … vines and creepers … lush jungle undergrowth … a load of choice hyena cuts … tortoises … bladders of dog puke … the list goes on. *This* is what we want to talk to you about, *not* blasted paper!'

'*Hmmm*, let me see … vines … creepers … lush jungle undergrowth … hyena joints … tortoises … ' pondered the Taxman. '*Yep!* That all sounds like perfectly legitimate tax takeage to me.'

'What do you mean "perfectly legitimate tax takeage"?' exclaimed Elli. 'Please explain how we are supposed to travel through the jungle without creepers? What are we supposed to eat when we're hungry; and how are we supposed to cook it? You took most of our fire too, remember?'

'Did I? *Flaming heck!* Well, what if I did? It was perfectly legitimate tax takeage, all of it! I mean, how am I supposed to go on levying taxes, and completing the arduous task of collecting them, without a means of transport … and decent eating?'

'Hold on just a moment; let me get this straight.' Zatt looked puzzled. 'Are you saying you need to take tax from us in order to pay for the costs you incur in taking the tax from us?'

'Well – *er* – in the first instance, yes! But then there's the rest of it of course.'

'"The rest of it"?'

'Why yes, the tax I need for my Big Plans! I need to levy *loads* of tax in order to pay for all of them – *tonnes* of it, oodles-upon-*oodles* of it – in fact, I need to collect more tax now than all the tax that has ever been levied befo— '

'What "Big Plans"? interrupted Zatt.

'*A-HA!* That would be telling!'

The Taxman turned and started to walk back toward the 'house'.

'*A-HA-AAA!* That's why we're asking!'

Zatt dashed forward and grabbed the Taxman by the shoulder to stop him walking away which caused him to freeze and visibly 'bristle'.

'Look Zatt … Elli … I don't mean to be rude but … '

The Taxman tugged his shoulder free with a jerk then span round to glare at them angrily.

'*Who do you people think you are!?* You can't just *rock up* here and start demanding answers! I'm not *answerable* to you, and in any case, I haven't got the time; I need to be finalising preparations for "The Off".'

Elli glanced at Zatt who was looking 'pent-up' like a geyser about to blow and decided it might be better if he did the talking.

'Look Mister Taxman, we haven't just "rocked up" here; we – that's us and the rest of our gang – we have crossed a huge "river" to get here; we've also flown over the World's tallest mountain, been behind the most gigantic-est of waterfalls; we've even flown up high, high into the clouds before falling down a long, long slippery hole. It hasn't exactly been the easiest or most enjoyable of trips—well, apart from the last bit.'

'So, after being through all that— ' fumed Zatt. 'I think we *may* just have "earnt" ourselves a few answers!'

'Well, put like that, I ... ' The Taxman paused and gave them both a strange look. He began to say something, but then hesitated and said something different instead. 'Look, tell you what; why don't you go through your list again and I'll explain why I needed it.'

'All righty!' Zatt consulted her blotch of paper. 'Let's see—*ah*, yes, here we go ... an incomplete set of cloud-catcher straps ... half a cooking fire— ' Zatt glanced at the Taxman and saw he was nodding while she spoke. ' ... half a jungle's worth of succulent vegetation ... a stash of melons, some with maggots ... a year's supply of hyena ... a collection of poltroon eggs ... a complete set of water bladders full of dog puke—I mean, why do you need all this food?' She looked up at the Taxman who was still nodding. 'Well?'

'Yes, I recognise those things. It's all down below and accounted for. Much of it is in 'In-The-Nest' where the fat-cats have mulched it into fodder for the tyrannosauruses. Go on.'

Zatt gave Elli an exasperated 'did-you-understand-any-of-that?' look to which he gave an equally bewildered 'not-a-word!' shrug of his shoulders; then, suddenly, he thought of something else.

'What about the foundations of my "wall" Taxman? Why did you take those?'

'Those large flat stones holding up that pile of rocks just outside your cave's entrance?'

'Yes.'

'Oh, I just took those away to see what would happen. Did anything happen, by the way?'

'*Er* – like, *yee-ees!* The "wall" fell down then the rocks rolled into our cooking pit and put out what was left of our fire … *thank you!*' Elli looked up to the sky in vexation. 'Oh, I've just remembered—*Granddad!* You took Granddad for goodness' sake. Why on earth did you take him?'

'I liked him. I thought he would fit in here, and I was right. He and Og have done wonders down below. You are in for a big surprise when— '

'*AK-HEM!*'

Hopi coughed loudly to command attention.

Elli, Zatt and the Taxman turned to face him.

'You have all omitted to mention one thing that is very important to me and my cousin Wishi.'

The Taxman suddenly looked grave and started nodding slowly as if he knew what Hopi was about to say.

'There is one very serious item on Zatt's "list", a very serious item indeed; one that is a matter of life and death to us nevasauruses; our— '

'We took it while you were both sleeping.'

Hopi and the Taxman glared at each other intently. Elli and Zatt could only look on helplessly as they engaged in a silent battle of wills. After a long silence, Hopi eventually spoke.

'"We"?'

'Yes, me and – *um* – Herman.' The Taxman coughed to clear his throat before elaborating; as he did so the three gang members exchanged quizzical looks and mouthed "Herman?" '*Ahem* – We had no choice, Herman and I. We had so much to do, so much to accomplish and in so little time. Herman has his brute strength, yes; but we knew his strength alone was not going to be sufficient. We needed to recruit an "army" of tyrannosaurus and we needed to do it fast. There was only one way we could do it and that meant we had to … well, you know.'

'Yes, I *do* know!' said Hopi darkly. 'You decided to steal all of poor Wishi's breath and half of mine. Why only half of mine, incidentally?'

'We were intending to take it all but a nearby poltroon suddenly fell out of its nest and landed in the middle of a tickling tree, so we left double-quick before it started laughing and woke you up. As it turned out we had taken more than enough. That nevasaurus breath of yours is pretty strong stuff! Herman was easily able to herd up the tyrannosauruses we needed. In fact, it was Herman who— '

'*Enough! Enough! I can't bear it any longer!*' shrieked Zatt. 'Who is this "Herman" you keep mentioning?'

'Why, my dear Zatt— '

The Taxman smiled a wry smile.

' —you're standing on him!'

(It occurs to me at this point, Dear Reader, that you might benefit from an explanatory note of some kind. You may recall that in our earlier adventure Elli and Ovi were aided in the final stage of their quest to find God's lunchbox by a small hermit crab which later went on to devour the actual box itself after Elli and Ovi had taken away its contents, Nourishment and Savourscent. This resulted in the crab growing into a gargantuan beast of enormous—nay monstrous proportions. This is the creature we are about to encounter once more. (How or why it acquired the name "Herman" I am not quite sure; though being a child of the 1960s, I have an inkling.) Its shell has also grown considerably and evolved into one of those 'archetypes' that are often found in nature (like the hexagon); the very same archetype as it happens that we humans were to latch onto many epochs later, enabling it to manifest in many of our dwellings as "the two-story suburban home". Interestingly, a distant relative of the hermit crab, the wild-party crab, would later evolve an extreme hatred of anything resembling a nice safe n'cosy suburban home and go on to develop a natural inclination to completely ruin them. I mention this fact purely as a point of interest, Dear Reader; it has absolutely no bearing whatsoever on Elli, Hopi and Zatt's current predicament.)

'*Oh, Herrr-rrr-man!*' cried the Taxman. '*Herrr-rrr-rrr-maa-aaa-ann-nnn! We have visitors!*'

'*SSS-SSS-SPLA-AAA-DOP!*'

A huge mucus-covered sand-speckled eye about the size of a bison suddenly burst out of the sand between Zatt and the Taxman and started waving slowly to-and-fro at the end of a long stalk. It was so unexpected, all three Tax-Taker-Backers jumped with surprise and Zatt emitted a loud shriek. The eye surveyed its surroundings and quickly noticed Hopi protecting Zatt as well as Elli standing a few steps away with his bow slung across his back. The moment it realised strangers were present—

'SSS-SPLA-DOLLOP-PPP!'

—a second eye burst from the sand behind Zatt and Hopi, making the Tax-Taker-Backers jump again. While both giant eyes were blinking to remove specks of sand the Taxman continued.

'Oh, please don't be shy Herman! Our visitors have come an awful long way to see us; so, come along now; *show yourself!*' He leaned forward and whispered to Zatt and Hopi in a hushed-but-helpful manner. 'You might want to move; I suggest you go over there.' He pointed to a patch of sand between a pair of sand-covered rocks.

Hopi and Zatt had barely moved across to where the Taxman had indicated, when—

'RRR-RUSTLE-HISS-SCRAPE-CRACKLE-RUMBLE ... BLA-AAA-AST!!!'

—the entire beach exploded. Sand spewed upward, outward and every-way-ward, and pebbles shot out from the maelstrom in random directions like cannonballs, forcing Elli, Zatt and Hopi – even the Taxman – to duck and dodge to avoid them. Through the sandstorm they could clearly see the large box-like structure that you and I would call a 'house' rise up into the air. Then, as suddenly as it had begun, the turmoil and chaos ceased; the sand settled and standing there before them the size of three full-sized Hopi's, blocking all else from view was a giant crab called Herman.

'Herman; this is the Tax-Taker-Backer-Gang—oh, I beg your pardon, this is *half* of the Tax-Taker-Backer-Gang. They've come to pay us a visit. Isn't that nice of them Herman?'

Herman didn't speak. Instead he made giant-crab-like crackling noises that always ended in a long hollow whistle-type-sound which could best be described as a protracted '*Wh-o-o-o-o-o-oh!*' Each crackle mixed with a '*Wh-o-o-o-o-o-oh!*' was unique and the listener was left to infer its meaning from its intonation. It was at this point in the proceedings that Elli, Zatt and Hopi heard Herman make a crackling '*Wh-o-o-o-o-o-oh!*' for the very first time; and this particular crackly '*Wh-o-o-o-o-o-oh!*' undeniably meant "Pleased to meet you Tax-Taker-Backer-Gang. How nice of you to come all this way and pay us a visit."

'Now, I want you to listen carefully Herman … '

The Taxman walked up to the huge creature and stood immediately before him. In front of the towering beast he looked like a tiny mouse-shrew-dinkety-dumble standing in front of a large crocogator with extra legs … *several* extra legs.

'Are you listening carefully?'

'*Wh-o-o-o-o-o-oh!*' ("Of course, Master.")

'I want you to take these two "guests" of ours— ' he nodded to indicate Zatt and Hopi, ' —down to 'In-The-Nest'; understood?'

'*Wh-o-o-o-o-o-oh!*' ('Understood Master.')

'Leave this guest— ' he nodded to indicate Elli, ' —here with me; understood?'

'*Whoa! Hold on!*' exclaimed Elli, suddenly looking alarmed. 'What are you doing?'

'*Wh-o-o-o-o-o-oh!*' ('Understood Master.')

Before anyone could do anything, the sand on either side of Hopi and Zatt erupted and a giant claw snapped shut around them, clamping both of them tight. It turned out the pair of sand-covered rocks were nothing of the sort – they were, in fact, the two halves of a giant pincer that Herman was resting after a long spell of digging.

'*HEY-Y-Y!*' shouted Elli as Zatt screamed. '*You moved Sis and Hopi over there deliberately Taxman! That was a trap!*'

Elli dashed forward, but the instant he did so the sand in front of him erupted and Herman's other claw burst into view, blocking him off and pushing him away.

'*HELP US ELLI! DO SOMETHING QUICK!*'

Zatt and Hopi were now firmly in Herman's grip—unable to escape.

'*LET THEM GO YOU MONSTER!*' cried Elli.

'Take them down below Herman and hurry back. We need to complete the channel before "The Off" at noon.'

Having given his orders, the Taxman turned his back on the Tax-Taker-Backers and returned his attention to sorting the pile of spoil.

'*Wh-o-o-o-o-o-o-o-o-o-oh!*' ('Right! You're coming with me.')

Herman set off sideways giant-crab-style at remarkable speed, heading for the nearby headland, clearly following a well-practised path. He was far too fast for Elli to give chase but this didn't stop him from trying. Elli ran and ran, leaping over rocks like a hurdler and splashing though pools. He continued to run after the giant crustacean, desperately crying out "*ZA-AAA-TT!*" and "*HOPI-I-III!*" long after they'd disappeared from view and Zatt's shrill cries had faded into the distance.

Eventually, overcome by his exhaustion, Elli fell to his knees, gasping for breath. After a few moments he stood up, still panting and wheezing, and slowly made his way back to the Taxman. As he crossed the wild open expanse of beach, wading through rockpools, tripping over seaweed and clambering over boulders, he muttered to himself.

'I wonder what else you have got in store for us Mister Taxman? Whatever it is, you haven't beaten us yet. It takes more than giant monster crabs, strange birds with long necks carrying sticks and an "army" of tyrannosauruses – whatever that is – to beat the Tax-Taker-Backer-Gang.'

'*Aaa-all-lll-lll—right! Is everybody ready?*' cried Ovi, rubbing his hands excitedly.

'*Yois!*'

'*Sey!*'

'*Sure am little buddy!*'

'*Oh yes, we'r-r-r-r-r-re r-r-r-r-r-eally r-r-r-r-r-eady! Let's r-r-r-r-r-ock'n'-r-r-r-r-oll!*'

'*Gr-r-r-r-r-eat! Start putting those claws and paws together people for the latest ... the hottest ... the most exciting and no doubt the very best poem ever ... from the one and only ... the truly unique ... the superlicious-duperlicious poetess-de-luxe! Our very own ... O-O-O-OOO-GGG!*'

The instant Wishi's spotlight beam shone upon Og the wild outburst of applause was deafening. She was clothed head-to-toe entirely in leaves, including a dramatic leaf-plume hat; and she was holding two extra-large leaf-fans across her front while fluttering her specially-made-up leafy eyelashes.

The applause eventually died down and gave way to a hushed silence of eager anticipation.

'What is your new poem called Og?' asked Ovi-the-compere.

'It's called "Things you can do in the Treetops" and I'm dedicating it to-ooo-ooo … ' The crowd drew a collective sharp intake of breath. The excitement in the air was palpable and would have been called "electric" had that particular adjective been available. ' … *HAWKINS!*'

Wishi's other spotlight found Hawkins in the crowd of fat-cats. He was pale mauve in colour and the light caught him turning dark blue with embarrassment which spurred a fresh outburst of whoops and cheers.

'*I hope you're ready for this Hawkins,*' shouted Ovi. '*Coz we most certainly ARE!*'

Clapping enthusiastically, Ovi stepped backward out of the spotlight and exited stage-left. (Oxo later revealed that Ovi's back-stepping was his favourite part of the show.)

'*WELL, AAA-AAA-ALL-LLL-LLL—RIGHT!*'

Og's loud cry signalled she was ready and the crowd fell silent. She struck a dramatic poetic pose, peering out over the top of her leaf fans and looked eye-flutteringly about the gathering.

'*HERE WE GO PEOPLE … "THINGS YOU CAN DO … IN THE TREETOPS!"* … '

She began tapping her feet to set up a rhythm and the audience immediately started clapping along.

'*We-e-e-he-he-he-eee-ell-lll …*
you can go "*POP!*" … in the treetops
And, you can go "*BOP!*" … in the treetops
You can even go "*TOP!*" in the treetops …
… and shout "*DO-WOP-A-SHOP-SHOP!!!*" … '

'EVERYBODY NOW!'

She waved her leaf-fans to indicate they should join in.

'What canya do in the treetops?'

'GO "POP!"'

'What else canya do in the treetops?'

'GO "BOP!"'

'And what ELSE canya do in the treetops?'

'GO "DO-WOP-A-SHOP-SHOP!!!"'

'ONE MORE TIME?'

'YEAH!'

'WELL, *AAA-AALL-LL-LL RIGHT! What canya do in the treetops?'*

'GO "POP!"'

'What ELSE canya— '

'KER—ASH! CRACKLE-KRICKERTY-KRICK-CRACK—BOOM! KER—LATTER!!!'

The 'poetry recital' was brought to an abrupt halt by Herman smashing his way through the tangle of uprooted trees to enter 'In-The-Nest'. The sudden burst of light from the outer cavern's welter of torches just caught the tails of the departing fat-cats as they scurried for the shadows, leaving the members of the Tax-Taker-Backer-Gang plus Granddad and Og alone to face the giant monster-sized crustacean. As soon as Herman came to rest, Og marched up to him waving a clenched fist in fierce indignation.

'HERMAN!' she yelled at the top of her voice. *'YOU JUST* COMPLETELY *RUINED MY RECITAL!'*

'Wh-o-o-o-oh!' ('Sorry Og.')

'I was just finishing off "Things you can do in the Treetops" – it was going down extremely well by the way – and I was about to move on to my next number; though I hadn't quite made up my mind whether it was going to be "Things you can do in the Jungle" "More things you can do in the Treetops" or "Things you can't do in the Treetops". Anyway, the point is Herman, you can't just— '

'*Aaa-aaa-anyway* my dear … ' Granddad hurriedly dashed over to Og and grabbed her by the shoulders.

'Methinks it might be better if we *can-n-n-n* …
warmly welcome our friend … Her-*man-n-n-n!*'

He raised his voice in greeting.

'*Hail, Herman!*'

'*Wh-o-o-o-o-o-o-o-o-o-o-oh!*' ('Oh, hello there old timer. Nice to see you again.')

'For what happy reason do we deserve this honour …
… that you should visit us in this manner?'

'*Wh-o-o-o-o-o-o-o-o-o-o-o-o-oh!*' ('The Taxman told me to bring you these.')

With an attempt at panache and a hint of a swagger (crab-style of course), Herman dramatically produced his large pincer-claw from behind his back and held it out for all to see.

'*ZATT!*' Ovi leapt to his feet. '*IS THAT YOU?*'

'*Holy* – burp – *polony! IT'S ZATT!!!*' Gusto also leapt to his feet and ran forward. '*How in* – belp – *blazes did you get here* – belch-pardon – *dearest?*'

'*OVI? GUSTO?*' cried Zatt. '*Oh, thank goodness! And is that you Granddad?*'

'Tsss-sss-ssp, ihsiW!' Oxo turned and back-hissed into Wishi's ear, whispering quietly so as not to attract the attention of the most humongously gigantic creature he'd ever seen with giant viscious-looking snapping pincer-claws. 'Ohw si ttaZ?'

'Zoitt oiz Goistoi's woife oind Oivoi's soistoir; ooih, oind Groinddoid's doightoir,' explained a fully-restored Wishi, who, if truth be told, had rather overdone the restorative eating and was now the size of—well, a very large nevasaurus.

Wishi then stood up from where he'd been squatting to greet Herman. As he turned and rose to his feet, he suddenly found himself eye-to-eye with a much smaller Hopi.

'*Wishi?*'

'*Hoipoi?*'

Wishi was about to cry out with joy when Hopi gave him the very fiercest of 'don't-say-or-do-anything' glares – a glare so powerful it would have forced a poltroon to lay one of its spikey eggs. As it happened, Hopi didn't need to bother with his glare because before Wishi could say anything, Granddad took centre stage.

'Oh, such excitement, such happiness, Herman.
You really are where it's at!
You make us cry with tears of joy, that's for certain.
Now, please release my Zatt!'

'*Wh-o-o-o-o-o-o-o-o-oh!*' ('Of course, old timer; my pleasure.')

Herman gently lowered his giant pincer-claw to the ground and released his 'catch'. Zatt was immediately engulfed in a big reunion embrace. Hopi, however, didn't bother with any hugs; instead, he nabbed Wishi, bustled him hastily to one side and proceeded to whisper feverishly in his cousin's ear. After a few moments, Granddad looked back up at Herman from his family huddle and gave him a big 'thank you' wave.

'Our thanks to you my friend
for making us all so happy
For bringing us our beloved Zatt
And, for *not* being, well, you know … "snappy"!'

'*Wh-o-o-o-o-o-o-o-o-o-o-oh!*' ('My pleasure old timer. Ah well, I'd best be going.') Herman smiled a broad crab-like smile, then turned and began pushing aside a couple of trees in order to make his exit from 'In-The-Nest'. '*Wh-o-o-o-o-o-o-o-o-o-o-o-o-o-oh!*' ('I've got so much work on "up top"; you lot wouldn't believe what the boss wants me to— ')

'NOT SO FAST … HERMAN!!!'
'NOIT SOI FOIST … HOIRMOIN!!!'

The combined booming voices of the two nevasauruses filled the entire Crown Cavern … and caused Herman to halt in mid-tree-push.

Slowly, both eyes of the monster-sized crustacean twisted round on their stalks to stare at his adversaries; and then very deliberately, leg-by-leg, the rest of his body followed. As he swivelled to face Hopi and Wishi, he snapped his two great pincer-claws, readying them for action.

'*Wh-o-o-o-o-o-o-o-o-o-o-o-o-o-oh!*' ('I aint a-lookin' for no trouble with you pair of strangers.')

'We're no strangers to you Herman; we've met before remember? You know who we are … and you also know what we want back!'

Hopi stepped aside to let the much bigger Wishi move to the fore, and as he did so the eyelids on Herman's eyes-on-stalks narrowed.

'*Wh-o-o-o-o-o-o-o-o-o-o-o-o-o-oh!*' ('I'm a-givin' you one last chance to step aside strangers.')

Hopi and Wishi looked at each other, then slowly turned back to face Herman.

'Let's do this!'

'Loi's doi thois!'

The two nevasauruses spread their wings and leapt into the air—then they both zoomed at Herman. Wishi zeroed-in on his larger giant-pincer-claw while Hopi went for the smaller-but-still-very-big one. Their plan, such as it was, was to ensure Herman was unable to snap at them while they wrestled him to the ground.

At first, it looked as if their plan was working. Both of his giant-pincer-claws were firmly held shut by the tight grip of the two nevasauruses and, at the same time, their combined weight appeared to be wearing him down as, one-by-one, each of his legs started to buckle.

But then, Herman fought back and with a vengeance. With one extra-forceful lunge, Hopi was sent flying through the air into the mulch pile which meant Herman's smaller claw was free to attack Wishi. It took several snaps for him to catch hold of the wriggling and writhing nevasaurus, but eventually he managed it and caught him by the tail. Wishi tried to hang on with all his might, but Herman was too strong. Wishi's grip began to slip and the giant-pincer-claw started to flex.

Meanwhile, Hopi had picked himself up and was sparring round Herman's feet, looking for an opening and a chance to re-join the fray.

'It's all right – *burp* – big buddy! Leave this to – *belch* – me!'

Gusto strode past Hopi, stood before Herman and shouted upward.

'*OY YOU!* – burp – *BIGGEST BUDDY YET!* – belch-pardon – *PUT HIM DOWN!* – belp – *RIGHT THIS INSTANT!*'

'*Wh-o-o-o-o-o-oh!*' ('Who are you?')

'*Never mind who I am; just* – belp – *do as I say … or else!*'

'*Wh-o-o-o-oh!*' ('Or else what?')

'*You'll* – burp – *get it!*'

'*Wh-o-o-o-o-o-oh!*' ('Get what, exactly?')

'*Right* – belch-pardon – *you've had your warning!*'

Gusto turned to Hopi who was still side-step-sparring and throwing imaginary punches in readiness to spar.

'Hopi, big buddy, when I give you the – *belch* – word, I want you to lift me up and get my – *belp* – bottom as close to his – *burp* – breathing hole as you can.'

Hopi stopped jab-dancing, looked down at Gusto's bottom then up at Herman's breathing hole.

'Roger that Gusto! Wilco and standby!'

Herman could sense that whoever this strange human was, he certainly meant business. Very slowly, he did just as Gusto said and lowered his giant-pincer-claw to the ground to allow his attacker to go free. But this wasn't a true surrender, it was really a cunning ruse on Herman's part (something quite rare for a crustacean, even a humungously huge one, especially in those days).

The instant Wishi was out of the way, Herman leered forward and let rip with a full blast of one-and-a-half-strength nevasaurus breath. The overpoweringly pungent and rancid air filled the 'In-The-Nest', smothering every living thing within range, including the other Tax-Taker-Backer-Gang members.

Hopi and Wishi were, of course, immune to their own breath and neither batted an eyelid. Luckily, most of the other gang members had marrots up their noses (including Zatt who'd just been given some by Ovi), and all they had to do was hold their breath while the odious gas enveloped them. Oxo, however, being unable to put marrots up his beak, fainted on the spot with a feeble 'Dammit I'm-m-m-mmm-m-m … '

That just left Gusto who, up to that point, hadn't felt the need to use a marrot.

The others looked on in amazement as the full force of the blast went straight up each one of his nostrils … and yet he remained standing.

His eyes *did* water, forcing him to close them; and he *did* wobble a little; but to the wonder and astonishment of all present (apart from Oxo, of course) he did not collapse or faint. Instead, he opened his mouth wide and took in an even deeper breath of the rank and toxic gas which he appeared to savour. By now, everyone, including Herman, was utterly transfixed as Gusto simply stood motionless, chewing – and apparently enjoying – the deadly noxious gas that was coursing through his system.

'Are you – *ahem* – are you all right my love?'

Zatt stepped forward looking concerned.

At that moment, Gusto opened his eyes. They were a bright luminescent green with scarlet and yellow streaks.

'Never – *burp* – felt better! Man, that nevasaurus hunting gas sure takes some – *burp* – chewing!'

He turned to Hopi.

'Right big buddy – *belp* – are we ready?'

'Yes, I think I can declare with a reasonable degree of confidence, if not full-blown assurance, that we are, indeed, as you rightly say … "ready"!'

'Well then – *belch-pardon* – what are we waiting for big buddy? Let's show even bigger – *burp* – buddy here why Life really is – *belp* – a Gas!'

'*YES-SIREE!* You got it Gusto!'

Hopi un-furled his wings, gave the biggest '*fah-whoosh-pa-pa-dah-lommopp*' he could muster and took to the air. He then swooped down, grabbed Gusto in his talons and flew up towards Herman's breathing hole.

Weaving this way and that, the two Tax-Taker-Backers managed to dodge Herman's pincer claws as they 'snipped' and 'snapped' from either side. The moment they were clear of the giant claws, Gusto twisted round so that his bottom was aiming straight ahead. Hopi then made a sweeping pass across the centre of Herman's face. Just as Gusto's bottom was lined-up directly in front of the giant crab's gaping mandibles, he let rip with an absolutely monumental fart of gigantic proportions. It was not only the most toxic fart he'd ever produced (a direct product of eating prodigious amounts of tyrannosaurus mulch), it was also the loudest fart ever made by any living creature … *EVER!*

'FFF-P-P-PRA-AAA-RRR-R-RRP-FFF-F-F-F!!!'

The full blast of Gusto's fart went straight down Herman's gizzard and deep into his innards. His gigantic body instantly juddered and froze; then, very quickly, it began to tremble. At the same time, he started changing colour from the normal mix of creams, yellows and oranges that are the markings of a healthy hermit crab to an ever-shifting constantly blending kaleidoscope of rancid reds and putrid purples interspersed with blotches of bile-green and puke-puce.

'*Wh-o-o-o-o-o-o-o-o-o-o-o-o-oh!*' ('Oh dear. I don't feel too good.') the giant monster crab 'Wh-o-o-o'd' in a tiny high-pitched crackle; and then … down he tumbled.

'*YEE-EEE-HAH!!! WE DID IT BIG* – belp – *BUDDY!*'

Gusto cheered and cheered as the enormous crustacean's legs splayed out at all angles and his two great eyes on stalks, now glazed in a putrid purple mist, fell to the floor where they lolled in an ooze of fodder-mulch.

'*YEE-HAA! YEE* – burp – *HAAA-AAA!!!*'

As soon as Hopi and Gusto landed, Zatt ran up to her husband and give him a huge 'I'm-so-proud-of-you' hug. A crowd then gathered and started to applaud. The fat-cats purred appreciatively, and the others, including Granddad, Og and the rest of the Tax-Taker-Backer's present, began cheering and shouting "*whoops!*" of delight.

Hopi and Wishi shared in the celebrations for a few moments, but then quietly slipped away to return to the knocked-out Herman in order to … finally … at long, long last … engage in a spot of actual "Tax-Taker-Back-ing".

'Thanks for helping me with stashing those money-pebbles away in a safe place Elli. As I always say "It's not enough to simply *have* money; you've also gotta know where you've put it."'

The Taxman smiled and slapped Elli on the shoulder, then he led Elli over to a large rocky outcrop just outside the entrance to the Crystal Cave for a well-earned rest. There they sat down together side-by-side and took a moment to enjoy the view, looking out over the open sand to the white-crested blue line of the "Sea" in the distance.

'Right then young Elli,' said the Taxman once they were rested. 'Do you fancy another go at "gobbledygook-ing"?'

'Oh, go on then. Why not?'

'Right; are you ready?'

'Ready.'

'*Ahem!* Now, listen very carefully … ' The Taxman held Elli's gaze and spoke very slowly and deliberately, emphasising each and every individual word. '"This – pebble – is – worth – ten – times – more – than – all – the – other – pebbles – because … dot-dot-dot … "'

Elli nodded sombrely then took in a deep breath.

'Right, here goes … ' Elli had to concentrate harder than he'd ever done before. '"This – pebble – is – worth – ten – times – more – than – all – the – other – pebbles – becau-au-au-ause … *ahem* … a gobbledygook can often gobbledygook another gobbledygook, particularly when a gobbledygook is overly and unduly gobbledygook'd; and, as everybody knows, an over-gobbledygook'd gobbledegook always out-gobbledygooks an under-gobbledygook'd gobbledygook, especially when you pay with an ups-a-daisy." *There!* How's that?'

'Not bad, not bad. I'm not sure about the "pay with an ups-a-daisy" at the end. Finishing on a "gobbledygook" would have given the sentence much more clarity, more gravitas, more authority. Let's do that bit again shall we?'

'Righty-ho. How about this … *A-a-ahem!* … "an over-gobbledygook'd gobbledegook always out-gobbledygooks an under-gobbledygook'd gobbledygook, especially when you—*er* – especially when you gobbledygook it with a gobbledygook"?'

'*Excellent, excellent*—much better! We don't want to be reminding people that they have to "pay" for things, do we Elli? We need to keep that to ourselves.' The Taxman nudged Elli in the ribs. '*Ha-ha-ha!*'

'*Ha-ha-ha!* Gosh, I *am* learning a lot from you Mister Taxman.'

They lapsed into silence and the pair of them once more looked out at the view while they awaited Herman's return. Elli was surprised to see that in the brief time they'd spent stashing "money-pebbles" the "Sea" had moved much closer and now covered half the beach. He also saw that a long tongue of water was rapidly filling the trench that Herman had dug and was almost up to where the giant monster crustacean had been resting under his 'house'. He suddenly noticed that the Taxman kept looking up at the sky then back at the approaching waves as if gauging something. At that moment, without glancing at Elli, the Taxman spoke.

'It won't be long now you know.'

'No-no, I – *er* – I don't suppose it will – *um* – whatever "it" is.'

'I'm talking about the Sun reaching its zenith … its "high noon".'

'Oh, right. I thought you might be referring to—*oh,* I dunno, a "change of epoch" or something like that.'

The Taxman turned to face him.

'How did you know about that?'

'Oh, it was just something that someone somewhere mentioned recently … can't remember who or where exactly.'

'Well, whoever mentioned it was right. Yes, there is that happening too … '

The Taxman tailed off and returned his gaze to the scenery before them, though he kept giving Elli sly looks out of the corner of his eye.

'Can I ask you something?' asked Elli after another long pause.

'Yes, of course Elli. What do you want to know?'

'It seems quite a coincidence, you being based in the very same cave that God kept his lunchbox in. Do you – *um* – do you know him at all? Have you ever met him?'

'How do you know God is a "him" Elli? "He" might be a "her".'

'Oh right, I hadn't thought of that. Well, in that case, do you know "her" then?'

'Or an "it" or a "them" or a "something else entirely"?'

'*Ha-ha-ha!* Well he must be something—*I mean* "she"—*I mean "it"—oh,* you've gone and got me all confused now! Oh, I know … have you ever met Gobbledygook?'

'God is most certainly *NOT* gobbledygook!'

The Taxman span round to glare at Elli who swiftly returned his attention seaward.

'Oh, right.'

'"God? Gobbledygook?" Perish the thought! No, I've never met God; and no, I don't know where God lives. *Nobody* knows where God lives OK? I hope that satisfies your curiosity young Elli.'

'Oh yes; yes, it certainly does; thank you.'

They lapsed once more into silence as they both stared down the beach on the lookout for Herman. It was the Taxman who eventually broke the awkwardness. He gave Elli a fleeting sideways glance then leaned across and spoke in a hushed conspiratorial voice like a spy divulging a secret.

'Although nobody knows for certain where God lives,' he said out of the side of his mouth. 'There are … rumours.'

'Really?' Elli kept staring straight ahead. 'What kind of rumours?'

The Taxman looked about to check no one was listening then continued speaking in a secretive tones.

'Some say there are three worlds Elli, and that God made all three. They say the first, Dearth, was barren and far too dry, mostly desert; so, God decided to make the second, Earth, which turned out fine. It was luscious with plenty of water, it had food a-plenty, life abounded all over the place and so on—*but there was something missing!*'

'Really? What was that?'

'God wasn't actually sure. All God knew was it lacked something, needed something more, something extra, to make it perfect. So, God made yet another world, and finally everything in this third world *was* perfect. Like Earth, there was plenty to eat and drink, and no-one had anything to grumble about; but in addition to all that, everyone everybody was happy and could do whatever they wanted; there were no laws to break or rules to get cross over.'

'Well, that all sounds very nice.' Elli continued staring straight ahead with his eyes fixed on the distant horizon. 'What's it called by the way, this extra-special and really happy third world where God lives?'

'"Mirth".'

'Ah, right. Do you happen to know where this "Mirth"-place is or how to get there?'

'No, I don't young Elli, sadly I don't; but that's the reason I'm here Elli; here in this very cave where God left the lunchbox … I'm – *um* – well, I guess I'm looking for clues.'

'You mean— '

'Yes Elli, I'm trying to find Mirth. I'm *determined* to get to Mirth one way or another.'

'But what if Mirth is nothing more than a mere rumour? I mean there might not be three worlds. There might just be one world … this one. This might be Mirth *and* Earth *and* Dearth all mixed up together. You might already be there—I mean, here.'

The Taxman slowly turned round to stare at Elli and was about to say something when he suddenly got distracted.

'Oh, looky-look who's here … '

He leapt to his feet and pointed. Elli followed where he was pointing and, sure enough, there was Herman making his way back. He was staggering front-to-back (which is how crabs stagger, given that they normally walk sideways) and looking more than a little worse for wear, as well as being a rather worrying shade of green with lots of purple blotches.

'Well, well, well,' said the Taxman as he strode out to meet the enormous crustacean. 'So, you've finally decided to come back and finish your work, have you?'

'*Wh-o-o-o-o-o-o-o-o-o-o-o-o-oh!*' ('Please don't shout Boss. I don't feel too good.')

'Where on Mir—*I mean*, Earth have you been? And what on Mir—*Earth* has happened to you?'

'*Wh-o-o-o-o-o-o-o-o-oh!*' ('It's better if you don't ask Boss.') '*Wh-o-o-o-o-o-o-o-o-o-o-o-oh!*' ('Come on; let's get this trench finished.')

Herman got stuck in just in time. The trench needed about ten more scoops with his giant pincer-claw to reach the entrance of the Crystal Cave; and already each fresh scoop was immediately filling with water as soon as it was dug. Elli and the Taxman stood side-by-side as they watched a still-very-groggy Herman going about his work, with the Taxman in particular showing a keen interest.

'*Um* – Taxman?' ventured Elli after the third scoop.

'Hmmm?'

'Can I ask you another question?'

'As long as it's not about God, yes.'

'Heaven's no! *Ha-ha-ha!* No no no! I think we – *um* – we "bottomed that one out" so-to-speak. I – *um* – I was just wondering – *um* … '

'Yes?'

'Well, the thing is, I've been thinking—you know, "mulling things over" so-to-speak and – *um* … '

'Ye- eee-ess?'

'What I mean is … the thing I'd like to know is … well, I've been meaning to ask you for a while now – *um* … '

'Look Elli, I'm a very busy man! *Will you please get on with it!* What *IS* your question?'

'There's no need to shout.'

'I apologise. You're right; I shouldn't have shouted.'

'No, you were right to shout; there *is* a need to shout— '

'There is?'

'Yes, there is because I really, *really* need to know— '

Elli span round to face the Taxman.

'*WHAT IN SWAMP-FUME BLAZES IS GOING ON AROUND HERE?*'

The Taxman turned to face him.

'I thought you'd never ask.'

'Well, I didn't want to appear rude.'

'Don't worry, you didn't. Now, what exactly do you want to know?'

'Well, for starters, why is Herman busy digging this huge trench, *especially* when he's not feeling too well poor thing? I mean to say Mister Taxman; what's the rush?'

'That's an easy one Elli. The ditch is going to channel the seawater into the cave precisely when we need it, when the tide is at its highest. We must have a good high tide if the water is going to build sufficient pressure to force the break-up of the

Earth's mantle. It will take sub-hydrostatic compression of a magnitude never seen before to engineer the kind of tectonic strain necessary for the successful commencement of inter-continental fracture and shift.'

'Oh … right.'

Elli turned away and, for a fleeting moment, he allowed his face to express the utter mind-boggling incomprehension and confusion that he was experiencing.

'*Stop pulling faces!* I saw that!' snapped the Taxman.

'Sorry, I won't do it again.'

Elli regained control of his features, then forced himself to formulate a question from the raging turmoil going on inside his head.

'Would you please explain to me once more in simple basic terms why you are channelling a lot of seawater into this lovely beautiful and peaceful cave – the cave where God left his lunch box?'

The Taxman smiled.

'At last, a proper question! Now we're really getting somewhere. I mean to say, I haven't got all day you know!'

'Sorry. I-I-I just want to understand— '

'The thing is Elli this Crystal Cave that we have here isn't just a pretty cave.'

'Isn't it?'

'No, it isn't. It's also a very useful cave as it happens.'

'Is it?'

'*Ho, yesseroo*; it most certainly is; *ho, yes indeed!* It is a key access point into a vast system of underground tunnels that extend right throughout God's Crown.'

'I'm not entirely surprised to hear that. Hopi mentioned there were a lot of tunnels.'

'There's much more than "a lot" of tunnels Elli. The whole of God's Crown is riddled with them like a honeycomb; all made by our "friend" here.' The Taxman nodded to indicate Herman. 'You see, the rock is still very young and fresh which means it's very easy to dig.'

'But, why make Herman do all that digging? What do you need so many tunnels for?'

'We call it the "Labyrinth" by the way. The network of tunnels is so labyrinthine in its vastness, we decided to call it "The Labyrinth".'

'Right. So – *um* – what is this "Labyrinth" for exactly?'

'*Ha!* This is the clever part. I'm particularly proud of this bit.' The Taxman chuckled to himself. 'You see, the thing is Elli, the Labyrinth serves more than one purpose. It actually serves two purposes.'

'Does it really?'

'Ho yes, it most certainly does! Up until now it has been used by my friend Mino who— '

'Mino Taur?'

'Yes. Do you know him?'

'No, but I've heard of him. Please go on.'

'Well, old Mino has been helping out with loading the continents. You see— '

'Excuse me, but what are "continents"?'

'I was just about to explain.'

'Oh right, sorry; please go on.'

'I will. Now then, where was I? Ah, yes— '

'Don't let me interrupt you.'

'But you just did.'

'When?'

'Just then.'

'Did I?'

'Yes, you did. When you said "Don't let me interrupt you".'

'Did I say that?'

'Yes, you did.'

'Sorry.'

'Anyway. As I was saying— '

'It won't happen again.'

The Taxman gave Elli a fierce 'will-you-please-stop-interrupting-you're-making-me-lose-my-flow' glance, to which Elli replied with an 'I-know-I-don't-mean-to-it's-just-that-this-is-the-crux-of-the-matter-and-that's-making-me-kinda-nervous' expression.

'Now, as I was saying ... ' The Taxman hesitated to see if Elli was going to interrupt again; and Elli nodded for him to continue. 'There are, in fact, eight continents: America-North, America-South, Europe, Asia, Africa, Australia, Antarctica and East Anglia. As we speak, they are all joined together as one land mass, one huge "super continent" you might say— '

Elli tried to interrupt, but a swift 'look' from the Taxman quickly silenced him. As the Taxman continued, Elli mouthed to one side 'Why isn't there a West Anglia?' just to get it out of his system; then he snapped back to giving the Taxman his full attention.

'Along with his "army" of tamed tyrannosauruses, Mino has been making use of the Labyrinth to distribute the different types of moon rock which I – *um* – "obtained" a while back, and share it out amongst the proto-continents, so that when they divide and move apart there will be plenty of each rock type for the people on each continent to utilise.' The Taxman paused. 'That was rather a lot of information. I'll stop there in case you have any questions.'

'Nope, you're fine so far, thanks. We saw some of the tyrannosaurus in action moving rock down one of your tunnels just before we fell down a chute into the back of the cave, so I'm following you so far—no problem.'

'You fell down "a chute" into the back of the cave?'

'Yes, it was great fun.'

'So, *that's* how you found me. You used my "escape chute". Herman made that by dropping loads of pebbles down a natural crevasse. I told you the rock is still very young and soft. It only took about four scoop-fulls and the chute was all finished, nice and smooth and shiny – and yes, why not "fun" indeed.'

'I'd quite like another go on that sometime.'

'Why not? Why not, indeed? I'm sure that could be arranged.'

'Really? That's great! Thank you.'

'Shall I go on?'

'Yes, yes, please do. You – *um* – said something about the Labyrinth having two uses?'

'Did I? Ah, yes; you're right, I did. Well, the moon rock is all in place now, or so I believe, at least; a little bird told me.'

'Oh, which one? Was it Flip or Flop by any chance?'

'No, it was Knack, actually … or was it Dingle? Does it matter?'

'Not really. It's just that I met Flip and Flop, *and* Dingle and Dangle as it happens, when we were with Cen.'

'You know Cen?'

'Yes.'

'Cen Taur?'

'Yes. Mino's brother, I believe.'

'The very same.'

'We met him when we were flying over God's Crown. Spent a bit of time with him and his – *um* – helpers, Seraph and Cherub. We helped him put some silver lining on a couple of his herding clouds.'

The Taxman looked quizzically at Elli.

'You spent time with Cen Taur?'

'Yep.'

'And you put silver lining on a couple of his herding clouds?'

'Yep.'

'I see. So, that's how you know the winged-slipper birds. I suppose, that's also where you heard something about the new epoch.'

'Yep.'

'Did Cen also tell you what the herding clouds are actually for, and what the new epoch involves?'

'Nope. We – *um* – we had to leave in a bit of a hurry before he had a chance to tell us any of that, unfortunately.'

'I see. Well, in that case, perhaps you'd like me to "fill-in the gaps" so-to-speak?'

'Oh, yes, that would be great! But – *um* – do you think you could be a bit quicker please? Sorry to hurry you, but I'm feeling rather peckish.'

'Maybe I should have sent you down to 'In-The-Nest' with your companions? There's plenty to eat down there.'

'No, you're all right thanks. Thanks anyway.'

'My pleasure.'

The Taxman paused to check on Herman. Seeing there were only a couple more scoops needed, he took a deep breath and readied himself to speak quickly. This needed to be brief.

'You see my dear Elli … It's all really about trade.'

'Excuse me?'

'"Trade"? You know what "trade" is, don't you Elli?'

'You mean like when I give you something and you give me something back?'

'*We-eee-ell*, almost, but not quite; I mean when one party gives something to another party *for money* and we, that's you and I my dear Elli, us "friends", us "fellow fiscal foxes" … *wee-eee TAX IT!*'

'Hold on a moment. Let me get this straight. You're saying that your purpose in all this, in Herman doing all this work, all this digging, in moving moon rock about, in herding clouds … is purely to get more *tax?*'

'Yup!'

'Through "trade"?'

'Yup! Got it in one!'

'So that you can find Mirth?'

'Ultimately, yes; but that's just a final goal, a dream if you like. The main idea, the real purpose of all this is to get trade going. Proper serious trade. Int*ra*-continental trade in the first instance; and eventually the Big One … int*er*-continental trade.'

'But I still don't get it. What does Herman's trench have to do with "int*ra*-" or "int*er*-continental" trade?'

'Listen carefully, this is the clever bit.'

Once again, the Taxman checked no-one was listening; then winked at Elli, tapped his nose and leaned forward to speak in even more 'hushed-and-conspiratorial' tones than before.

'I worked out long ago that people will only start to engage in real proper – "*taxable*" – trade when there's water to cross.'

'Water?' Elli looked bemused. 'How does that work exactly?'

'Look. If I live right next to you and one of us wants to give the other something, we can just reach out and do it, right?'

'Yes, nice and easy—right.'

'Now, imagine we live far away from each other with a wide stretch of water between us. If we want to give things to each other, one of us going to have to build something to take them across the water, let's call it a "boat" for now. Do you follow me?'

'I think I can see where this is going.'

'Go on.'

'Well, if I have to go to all the trouble of inventing and building a "boat"; after I've built it, I'm going to want to fill it with more stuff – other stuff, different stuff – to trade with you in in order to make the whole thing worth my while.'

'Spoken like a true entrepreneur! Young Mister Elli, I am proud of you!'

'Spoken like a "what"?'

'Never mind. The point is, we've got to start putting some water between people so that they start inventing and building things called "boats"; and that's where— '

'You know when we, the Tax-Taker-Backer-Gang, first started out, we came across a broad expanse of water. Hopi called it a "river". I'd never seen one before. We sure could have done with a "boat" that day.'

'You've crossed a river too Elli?'

'Yep.'

'Great Blazing Sun in The Sky, you've been around boy! I'm learning to like you Elli. That river you crossed was my first, a prototype if you will. I only set it up a short while ago to see if it would work.'

Elli slapped his forehead.

'*That* must be why we never came across it on our earlier travels!'

'Did you enjoy crossing it Elli? Did it make you want to "trade"?'

'Well I never thought of it like that … but come to think of it … yes, yes, in a way, I suppose it did.'

'*There you go! I knew I was right!*' The Taxman leapt up on a rock and danced a little jig. '*I was right! I was right! I was right!*'

Elli smiled. He'd never seen anyone look so happy before; or for that matter so "right".

'Think of it Elli, very soon each of the eight continents will have its own river system and will then have a basis for trade. That'll be the start of the new epoch Elli; let's call it the "Int*ra*-Continental Epoch"!'

'Gosh.'

'And there's more?'

'I don't think I can take any more in.'

'Try.'

'Oh, all right, go on then; give it a go.'

'Good lad! Not only will all eight continents soon have their own river systems Elli, they will also be separated by ever-expanding expanses of water called "seas". Then, after an epoch or two, the seas will be so wide they'll be known as "oceans". Remember Elli, the more water to cross, the bigger the "boats"! Eventually, in the fullness of time, we'll have the ultimate trade, the mother-lode of all trade, "int*er*-continental trade"! Now, if *that* is not truly "*taxable*" trade, I do not know what is!'

Elli was dumbstruck. He was shocked at what the Taxman had told him and even more shocked that he'd actually understood it.

'This is Big Stuff, I mean seriously Big Stuff Taxman.'

'I know.'

'Which continent are we on right now out of interest?'

'We're somewhere between America-North and Europe. We'll know for sure once the Crown Lake collapses and God's Crown breaks apart.'

'"Crown Lake"? You mean that huge lake up on top of the mountain; the one Cen is constantly filling with water from his herding clouds?'

'That very one.'

'Wait a minute! If that lake "collapses", won't it fill all the tunnels and passages in the mountains? Won't it flood the Labyrinth?'

'*Yup!* That's the plan Elli. That's the Labyrinth's second purpose; it's how the rivers all get started.'

'But what about my friends and all the creatures in those tunnels?'

'What about them?'

'Well, you *have* warned them all to get out, I hope … '

The Taxman tried to say something but hesitated.

'You *have* warned them,' pressed Elli, '*haven't you?*'

'Oh, that's a mere detail Elli. Focus on the Big Plan here, the Big Picture. Don't worry about your friends Elli; they'll be fine.'

Elli leaned forward so that he and the Taxman were close-up face-to-face, then forcibly shook his head.

'*Oh, no they won't!*'

Feeling more than a little threatened by Elli's sudden, new-found 'proximity', the Taxman was momentarily forced to close his eyes while nodding a 'yes'-nod with extra-firm assertiveness.

'I can assure you Elli, that if I *say* they will be fine, they *will* be. I wouldn't *allow* any harm to come to them. I mean, surely you believe that; why would I allow that? In any case, they wouldn't dare put themselves in any danger. They haven't got my permiss—' He opened his eyes. 'Where did he go?'

The Taxman looked around. Elli was frantically running as fast as he could towards Herman who, having just finished his work, was settling down in the foaming waves and beginning to withdraw into his 'house' for a well-earned rest.

'*Where are you going?*' called out the Taxman, cupping his hands to his mouth.

'*To warn the others!*' cried Elli over his shoulder. '*And I'm taking Herman! Don't try to stop me!*'

'*Don't be a fool Elli! Stay here where it's safe!*'

Elli came to a halt with waves lapping around his knees.

'*Do you know something Taxman?*' he shouted. '*I'm beginning to ask myself if you being in the world is actually making it a better place—* '

'*And? What is your answer?*'

'*You're a very clever man Taxman … But right now, the world needs you about as much as it needs another great poltroon!*'

Elli splashed his way towards Herman, shouting as he went.

'*Get up Herman! We've got some really important work to do!*'

'*Wh-o-o-o-o-o-oh!*' ('What is it now?') '*Wh-o-o-o-o-o-o-o-oh!*' ('It's been a long day!')

Herman begrudgingly lifted himself back up onto his tired legs. As he did so, Elli clambered up onto the roof of his house-shaped shell.

'*Take me to all the others Herman; and make it quick!*'

Watching Elli and Herman set off, the Taxman pulled a face and clenched his fists with exasperation.

'Details, details, *blasted* details! Those confounded pesky details—*I hate 'em! I hate 'em! I hate 'em!*' Then, slowly, his expression softened, becoming less 'up-tight and angry' and more 'lost and lonely'. 'Off you go young Elli, and take care. I like you, you learn fast. You might even have learnt enough to save yourself as well as all your friends … *good luck!*'

He looked at the waves splashing about the entrance to the Crystal Cave, and a wry smile returned to his features. The channel was working perfectly; soon the seawater would reach the threshold of the Labyrinth toward the cave's rear. Satisfied all was going according to plan, he headed out along a long thin spur of rock that stuck out into the sea. When he reached the end, he turned and looked back up the mountainside. He knew that the Sun was at its zenith when it reached the top-most pinnacle of God's Crown which he could now see high overhead directly above the cave's entrance.

At that moment, the Sun appeared, closing in on that very pinnacle. Suddenly, from way up upon high, he heard the slightest of '*dink*'s as it clipped the tip of the mountain.

'*Oh, now look what you've done! You've only gone and dinked it!*' came a tiny distant voice from somewhere inside the Sun's disc.

'*Blasted God's Crown! Why does it have to be so blasted high? Oy, you down there; can you see if we've dinked it? Has it left a mark?*'

'*No, not a scratch! You're all right!*' yelled the Taxman.

'*Thanks mate!*'

The Sun moved on past the pinnacle, and as it did so the Taxman rubbed his hands in eager anticipation.

'Right then,' he said gleefully to himself. 'Time to get this new epoch under way!'

As he made his way back toward the cave, he was pleased to see that the bases of the columns at the entrance were almost submerged. Picking up his stride, he put his fingers to his mouth and gave a shrill whistle.

From the depths of the inner recesses of the cave's ceiling, a pair of white winged-slipper birds appeared and fluttered out towards him.

'The time has come my fine feathered friends; our moment – the moment we have been waiting for – is finally upon us. History—*no*, not just mere History—*Destiny* beckons!'

He waved his arms in the air with a dramatic flourish.

'*Go forth little birds! Be on your way!* Go play your part; Foretellers of Fortune, Prophesiers of Profit, Soothsayers of-of—*oh*, just *go* and deliver the all-important message that kick starts the whole thing!'

'Right, so we're to tell – *um* – was it Cen? – *um* – that – *er* – what was it again exactly?'

'Look, we've rehearsed this countless times. One of you needs to go and tell Cen that it is time for "The Off"; and the other needs to deliver the same message to Mino—gottit?'

'Ah yes, yes; I think that's clear. So, Knack goes to Cen and tells him to go to Mino while I stay here and tell the time.'

'*No-no-no*, you—you're Knick I presume?'

'Yes, I am—*or, hold on!* Am I Tish?'

'It doesn't matter who you are or which of you goes where. The important thing is that *one* of you – it could be Knick or Knack or Tish if you prefer – as long as *one* of you actually *goes* to Cen *right now* and tells him it is time for "The Off"; and the other one— '

'Right, that'll be me then.'

'Eh?'

'I've just remembered, I'm Tosh actually. What *am* I like!'

'I don't care who you blasted well are, as long as you go – *right now* – and give Cen the blasted message.'

'Wouldn't it be better if we both went? That way we can help each other out if we get confused.'

'*Look!* I want you to listen very carefully. One of you needs to go, right this very instant, to Mino—*no,* to Cen to—*DOH!* Give me a minute; I'll gather my thoughts and start again.'

The Taxman looked exasperatedly upward to the heavens and mumbled to himself through gritted teeth.

'The quicker we get some real trade started the better. Maybe then someone somewhere will develop proper decent long-distance communications.'

(I think we'll leave the Taxman there for now, staring exasperatedly upward. Suffice to say the beginning of the new epoch was "subject to delay owing to technical problems".)

Chapter Eleven

Once in a Blue Moon

By coincidence, the Taxman wasn't the only one looking upward at the heavens. Far, far below, a large drip of water landed on the tip of Mino's enormous bull-like nose, causing him to look up. The moment he did so, a second drop '*plopped*' into his fierce blood-veined eye followed by another … and another.

'*OY!* 'Ooo's blummin' ploppin'?'

'There's a leak in the roof Boss, right up there at the top, look,' said a nearby ostrich-emu-lator.

'But it can't be; we ain't been given the blummin' off yet! *OY YOU!*'

'Yes Boss?' said another ostrich-emu-lator.

'Run up to the top of the Red Moon double-quick and check that blummin' roof out will ya? We don't want it springin' a blummin'leak before we're ready.'

Meanwhile, inside 'In-The-Nest', Zatt was cleaning out one of the fat cat's ears, using one of the "arrows" she and Og had made earlier.

'Will you *please* keep *still* Hawkins? And stop that annoying purring.'

'Oh, but my dear-r-r-r-r-r Zatt, you have no idea how pur-r-r-r-r-fect that feels. It's r-r-r-r-really gr-r-r-r-r-eee-eeen.'

'There, you're done. Now off you go. *Next!*'

As Hawkins moved slinkily off, Frobisher and Grenville started arguing and jostling each other.

'Cur-r-r-r-r-se you Gr-r-r-r-r-r-r-r-r-r-enville! It's me next you r-r-r-r-r-rascal!'

'Who ar-r-r-r-r-e you calling a r-r-r-r-r-scal, Fr-r-r-r-r-r-obisher-r-r-r-r? R-r-r-r-r-etr-r-r-r-r-act that at once you-you-you r-r-r-r-r-rapscallion!'

'Kindly unhand me, sir-r-r-r-r, o-r-r-r-r-r I'll be for-r-r-r-r-r-ced to r-r-r-r-eso-r-r-r-r-t to for-r-r-r-r-ce!'

'*Boys! Boys!*' Zatt turned to Og who was helping her with the fat cats. '*Honestly!* You would've thought being cats that they'd be much better groomed. I'm really surprised at how dirty their ears are.'

'I know Zatt, you are *so* right. They've really let themselves go since they had it easy, the greedy things! Eat, eat, eat! That's all they do all day, and nothing else! No preening, no washing; why, they don't even bother to scratch an itch!'

'*R-r-r-r-r-ight!* That does it Fr-r-r-r-r-obisher-r-r-r-r! You have ser-r-r-r-r-riously offended my honour-r-r-r-r-r Sir-r-r-r-r. I demand r-r-r-r-r-recompense!'

'Where did you get their names from by the way. "Drake" "Raleigh" "Hawkins" and such like?'

'Oh, it was your father's idea; he came up with them. Goodness knows where he got them from; something to do with "taming the wild sea". I love him to bits the silly old fool, but he does have some strange— '

'*KA-BOOM!!! KER-ACK-CK-CK!!! CRACKLE-CRINKLE-CRUNCH!!!*'

Og was interrupted by the barrier of up-rooted trees being torn apart and Mino bursting in.

'*All right, where is it? Where is the blummin' thing?*'

Granddad leapt to his feet and bravely placed himself before Mino, blocking his path.

'Oh, woe, oh woe, oh thrice woe
More woe, and woe again.
What brings you bursting in Mino,
invading our domain?'

'Stand aside old man! I aint a-wantin' no harm to come to you. I need that beak—*and I need it fast!*'

'What do you mean by "that beak"?' Og ran over to Granddad. 'We have no idea *what* you are talking about!'

'*Ooooo-eeehpp … tro-o-o-o-ons!*'

'*Shush, all of you!*' ordered Mino. 'What's that noise?'

'*Ooooo-eeehpp … tro-o-o-o-ons!*'

Just then Granddad's dangling purple chair slowly turned around to reveal a still-knocked-out Oxo. He had been placed there to sleep off the effects of the nevasaurus breath; and as he came into view, they could all hear his backward snoring amplified by the chair's acoustics.

'*Ooooo-eeehpp … tro-o-o-o-ons!*'

'Ah, *there* it is!' Mino lunged forward and snatched the sleeping great poltroon.

'*Leave him be, you bully!*' cried Zatt, standing up and dropping the arrows from her lap. Mino glanced at Zatt and 'harrumphed' then left as noisily as he'd arrived, forcing his way through the tangle of uprooted trees. Once outside, they heard him barking his orders.

''Ere you are! Now, go n'use this to put a bung in that 'ole up there. Quick, quick, snap to it! The rest of you better start preparin' to evacuate. We'll be gettin' "The Off" any moment now and believe me, you lot do *NOT* wanna be down 'ere when that there ceilin' goes.'

'Hello Cen.'

'Oh, hello there.' Cen smiled as the little white slipper-bird settled and perched on his outstretched hand. It was a nice, warm George-type smile with just a hint of Brad. 'I think I know why you're here and what you have to tell me.'

'Do you?' The little bird looked pleasantly surprised. 'Then, why don't *you* tell *me?*'

'Well, that might get a little "complicated" don't you think? I mean, we don't want to get ourselves confused now, do we? *Ha-ha-ha!*'

'*Ha-ha-ha* … as if!'

'So, tell me; what is this message you've been sent to deliver?'

'Oh right; well, now let me see … the Taxman has sent me to tell you, Cen, that Mino's off—*no, no,* that's not right! Hold on a moment; ah yes, what's the time?—*no,* that's not it, oh— '

'If I could just interject here?'

'Certainly.'

'Could it possibly be that the Taxman has sent you to tell me it is time for "The Off" perhaps? Just a suggestion.'

The little bird mulled over Cen's proposal, mumbling the odd "hmmm, let me see" and "ah, yes!" to itself … then looked back at Cen.

'What did you say?'

'Look, let's keep this simple, shall we?'

'*Great!* I am all for that; most certainly. *Ho yes!*'

'*Right!* Now listen carefully. Was it the Taxman who sent you?'

'*Er* – yes, it was.'

'And was it me, Cen, who he sent you to?'

'*Er-rrr* – yes, it was.'

'Are you sure it wasn't Mino?' The little bird started to yes-nod, but quickly switched to a no-shake, then paused and blinked. 'Never mind, that was probably a spurious question.' Cen furrowed his brow. 'Right, here's the clincher Knack— '

'It's – *er* – Tish actually.'

'Sorry Tish— '

'No, it's not; *what am I like?* I'm Dangle.'

Cen turned to one side and said quietly to himself. 'I *must* remember not to bring their names into it.' He then refreshed his smile and turned back to the little bird. 'Anyway – *er* – Dangle, here's the clincher … Did the Taxman say it was time for "The Off"?'

'*Er-rrr* … oh, *um-mmm* … '

'"The Off"? Did he mention "The Off" at all? Or did he say "it's on" or something like that?'

'*Er* – "off" you say? – *um-m-m-mmm* – "on" you say? Hmmm, let me see … Do you know something? I think he did; yes, yes *he did!* I'm sure he did—*of course he did!* How could I get such an important message muddled up? How stupid would that be? *What - am - I - like?*'

'Great! I'm glad we got that straightened out. Well delivered little bird. Thank you for that.'

Cen turned away and prepared to shout some orders.

'Or did he?'

'Excuse me?'

'*Ye-eee-ess, he di-iii-id!* Of course, he did! I'm *sure* he did. It's *on!* "The Off" is definitely … absolutely and certainly … without any doubt whatsoever … "on"!'

Cen gave the bird (who I shall refrain from naming, because even *I'm* confused which one it is) a long hard look which had a lot of George in it and just a smidgeon of Leonardo

DiCaprio (which made for an interesting blend) before finally turning away and issuing his orders.

'*Seraph! Cherub!* Where *are* you? You've got some *work* to do!'

'F-f-f-huh-huh. Huh-fna-huh-hmmm.'

The two little 'darlings' in their 'nice' form appeared from on high to join Cen.

'Ah good, there you are. Right you two; it's time for "The Off"!'

Like a pair of dainty butterflies, Cherub and Seraph fluttered over to a big round rock and positioned themselves ready to commence pushing. (I think I should point out, Dear Reader, that this was all happening on the top of one of the pinnacles overlooking the Crown Lake. By one of those happy coincidences that only ever *really* occurs in fiction, Nature had providently perched a large boulder conveniently near the edge of a dramatic vertical plunge directly down onto an even larger boulder which was also handily placed on the lip of a second ledge to drop directly onto a third even larger boulder, and so on. The cumulative effect of so many conveniently placed boulders plummeting down into the deep blue waters of the lake was guaranteed to be a massive pounding on the bottom of the lake's floor which, you may recall, is also the ceiling of the Great Cavern.) Seraph and Cherub pushed and pushed with their ickle-tiddly wings all a-flutter, but to no avail. They then switched to their 'nasty' guises and pushed again, teeth gritted as well as bared, but still the boulder refused to budge.

'Come on you two,' moaned Cen. 'Put your backs into it!'

Cherub and Seraph tried again and again, in both their 'nasty' and 'nice' guises, but still the boulder remained stubbornly motionless.

'Oh, I've had enough of this! Move aside you two—*move out of the way I say!*'

Muttering 'As mother used to say; if you want a job done properly, do it yourself' and adopting a square-jawed Bruce Willis-type expression with just a soupçon of Jackie Chan (good choice), Cen shoved Cherub and Seraph to one side and positioned himself with his rear flanks facing the boulder.

'Right! Here goes! One new epoch coming *rrr-right up!'*

Mino started kicking the boulder with all his might and, after his third kick, our obstinate boulder finally teetered … then tottered … then toppled … and fell.

'BO-BOOM-BO-BOOM-BOOM! BO-BOOM-BO-BOOM-BOOM-BOO-OOO-OOMMM!!! BOO-OOO-OOO-OOM!!!'

Every living creature in Crown Cavern, both 'In-The-Nest' and elsewhere, looked up. Tyrannosaurus, proto-human, ostrich-emu-lator, fat-cat, nevasaurus and member of the Taur family alike, were all momentarily frozen with fright at the terrifying pounding and beating that suddenly started drumming on the ceiling of the vast cave. The noise wasn't just a noise, it was a gut-wrenching rumble that you could feel in your bones.

'BO-BOOM-BOO-OOO-MMM!!!'

The loudest rumble yet snapped everyone from their momentary shock; and a loud cry went up …

'LOOK!!!'

Fingers, talons, claws and paws all pointed up to the highest point of the cavern roof where Oxo was. His beak was firmly rooted where it had been rammed-in earlier to stop the leak. A pause in the pounding booms created a sudden shocked silence and all eyes watched as a hair-line crack appeared either side of Oxo's limp body then shot out in both directions creating a break-line the entire width of the cavern ceiling. Owing to the unique acoustics of the Crown Cavern, all ears could also hear, for the briefest of moments, Oxo's gentle snores.

'Ooooo-eeehpp … tro-o-o-o-ons!'
'Ooooo-eeehpp … tro-o-o-o-ons!'
'Ooooo-eeehpp … tro-o-o-o-ons!'

Then—

'BO-BOOM-BOOM-DI-BOOM-BOOM-BOOM!!!'

—the rumbling came back with a vengeance.

Panic broke out as everyone in the Crown Cavern (apart from Oxo, of course) started running as fast as they could to escape the terror unfolding above them. The hysteria 'In-The-

Nest' was no less than outside with humans, creatures and cats scattering in every direction; but then, suddenly, over the sound of screams, shrieks and general mayhem—

'KER-ACKLE! CREAK! KER-ICKETY CRUNKLE-CRUNCH!!!'

—the barrier of interlocking up-rooted trees once more burst asunder and Herman forced his way in.

'ZATT! HOPI! GRANDDAD! WHERE ARE YOU?'

Elli's shout could be heard over the ruckus.

'ELLI! IS THAT YOU?' cried Zatt.

'ZATT!!!'

Elli bounded down off Herman's shell like a mountain-goat-on-springs intent upon running towards Zatt for a full-on reunificatory hug. However, he'd barely opened his arms and gotten into his stride when Ovi appeared from behind Herman along with Hopi and Wishi.

'ELLI!' he cried. *'What are you doing here? We thought you were with the Taxman!'*

Elli skidded to a halt and span round to see his lost brother standing behind him.

'OVI!!! IS THAT REALLY YOU? YOU'RE ALIVE!'

Still with his arms outstretched, Elli pivoted on his heels and swivelled from Zatt to Ovi unable to decide who to reunite with first. Just then, Frobisher darted past chased by Grenville. Catching Elli in mid-swivel, Grenville's flowing tail and Elli's extended arms became entangled. This caused Grenville to start spinning round in in circles and Elli to topple over. The out-of-control Grenville then banged into Og, knocking her arrows into the air. Elli's tumble flung him forward into some tree roots where his bow became badly snagged, firm and rigid. He started tugged at the twine to free it and the moment he did so not one, but two of Og's arrows – one dead straight; the other slightly crooked – landed across the bow's twine with their feather ends caught in his fingers. Elli then pulled back hard to free his fingers and in doing so lost his grip.

'TWEE-ANG-GGG!!!'

Both arrows shot up into the air, heading for the far-off ceiling of the cavern. The first arrow – the straight one – flew fast and true straight for Oxo's bottom. It hit home, waking him wide-eyed with a start; however, before he could let out a yell, he first needed to get his beak out of the hole. The very instant he wiggled it free, in what can only be described as a freaky coincidence, the second wonky arrow skewered its wobbly way past his falling body and bunged the hole up again. As he fell away, Oxo exhaled deeply then, finally, gave vent to his sharp bottomly pain.

'*Wwwwwwoooooooeeeeeeyyyyyyy!!!*'

His shriek complete, Oxo then concentrated his efforts on gaining control of his free-fall. By frantically back-flapping his wings, he managed make his way safely to the ground. He was just about to land beside his old friends (plus a new friend he didn't recognise) when, with one final gigantic ground-jarring—

'*BO-BOOM-BOOM-MMM!!!*'

—the terrifying rumbling suddenly stopped.

Once again, Crown Cavern filled with an expectant hush and everybody looked up. The crooked arrow that had replaced Oxo's beak was vibrating extremely violently as if some terrible force was about to be unleashed which, of course … it was.

Suddenly, the arrow shot out of the hole, and a powerful jet of water spurted into the chamber with a great rush of spray, filling the vast cavernous space with a giant rainbow that formed a complete circle. The cries of wonder at the marvellous effect were quickly replaced with shouts of fear and anguish as through the mist everyone could clearly see more cracks rapidly opening up and spreading. Within moments the cavern's ceiling became a mass of jagged lines and irregular shapes like the baked mud in a dried-out wadi. Then—

'*KER-RRR-ACK-CK-CK-CK!!!*'

—the entire ceiling gave way.

Complete and utter pandemonium broke out, along with absolute hubbub and total hullabaloo. Realising he needed to act fast if he was to save everybody, Elli raced back to Herman shouting at the top of his voice.

'*HEY! HERMAN! CAN I USE YOUR TALKING TUBE?*'

'*Wh-o-o-oh!*' ('Of course.')

'THAT'S GREAT! THANKS!'

'Wh-o-o-o-o-o-o-o-o-o-o-o-o-o-o-o-o-o-o-oh!' ('I hope you noticed Master Elli that I said "of course" just then rather than the longer "of course *Master*" in order to be brief and save time.')

'GOOD THINKING HERMAN!'

'Wh-o-o-o-o-o-o-o-o-o-o-o-o-o-o-o-o-o-o-o-o-oh!' ('I thought that might help in this situation what with it being a bit of an emergency, especially for those creatures without their own shelter like me.')

'Very true. Now if you— '

'Wh-o-o-o-o-o-o-o-o-o-o-o-o-oh!' ('Oh, and no ability to breath under water like me.')

'Yes, thanks, Herm— '

'Wh-o-o-o-o-o-o-o-o-o-o-o-o-o-oh!' ('Creatures like tyrannosauruses or ostrich-emu-lators, for example; or— ')

'LOOK! WILL YOU PLEASE JUST PICK ME UP AND HOLD ME TO YOUR TALKING TUBE, LIKE—RIGHT NOW!'

The wall, or perhaps I should say "ceiling", of water was already half way down the chamber and falling fast. Despite Herman's nifty lift straight to his talking tube, Elli barely had a few brief moments in to relay his life-saving instructions.

'Wh-o-o-o-o-o-o-o-o-o-oh.' ('Testing, testing. Can you all hear me?')

A collective cry of *'Get on with it!'* filled the rapidly diminishing subterranean cavity as the raging water reached the top row of torches and snuffed them all out.

'Wh-o-o-o-o-o-o-o-o-o-o-o-o-o-o-o-o-oh.' ('Right, listen carefully! I recently developed a handy technique that will help you survive under water.')

'What is it? Tell us quick!'

'Wh-o-o-o-o-oh.' ('Are you ready?')

'Of course, we're ready! Now, get on with it!'

'Wh-o-o-o-o-o-o-o-oh.' ('Right; the trick is ... take a deep breath and hold it as long as possible.')

'We already knew that! Now we've run out of time thank you very much! Here we go ... one ... tooth ... ree ... '

The descending mass of water hit everything all at once with tremendous unstoppable force.

'In-The-Nest' was washed away in an instant, ostrich-emu-lators were separated from their tyrannosauruses and even giant beasts like nevasauruses, Mino and Herman were plucked from where they stood to be plunged, pounded and pummelled as well as twirled, swirled and whirled.

Every single living creature in the Crown Cavern was caught in the raging churn as the all-conquering water engulfed absolutely everything … and blended it.

Luckily for everyone caught in the 'blender', the rocks that had smashed through the lake floor were still young and soft which meant they had pretty much dissolved by the time the water reached them. Even *more* luckily for everybody, the great churn didn't actually last that long. The mountain's labyrinthine network of tunnels acted like a giant sponge and rapidly soaked up the water rather like a dry sponge. By the time it was on its third swirl round the vast chamber, the raging torrent started to recede down into the earth's depths. As it departed, it left behind its captured creatures, depositing them here and there about the cavern's walls on various ledges, bluffs and promontories.

Eventually, the final white-crested wave of the deluge completed one last circuit of the cavern floor before disappearing into the Labyrinth with a dainty swirl and an extremely loud '*GURGLE-PLOP!*'

For a long moment afterwards, the vast hollow space was completely silent and still. Then gradually, throughout Crown Cavern, dazed creatures began to stir; but just as they were getting back on their feet, they found they had two new problems to contend with. Firstly, a fierce wind started to blow which meant they had to brace themselves in order not to be blown over. It was actually a powerful back-draft of air that was being drawn into the Labyrinth to fill the vacuum left behind by the rapidly departing water. Secondly, they also had to shield their eyes to block out the blazing sunlight that was now pouring in through the gaping hole in the cavern's roof, allowing the Sun's brilliant bright rays to reach places that had never seen daylight before.

Suddenly, the back-draft ceased and the entire cavernous hollow once again fell eerily silent.

Somewhere way up high in the sky among the peaks and pinnacles of God's Crown, something was causing the dazzling daylight to shimmer. Still groggy and disorientated, everybody in looked upward. By squinting and shielding their eyes, they were able to make out that far up above their heads in the vast open space that was now the very heart of the mountain, a wondrous sight could be seen.

There, hovering in the centre of the great hollow and framed by scintillating sparkles of sunlight, was a magnificent mythological creature. It was difficult to make out its form and features precisely because spray was still falling throughout the cavern creating an iridescent array of ever-changing ever-blending rainbows. It appeared to have the graceful body of a great white horse with enormous white wings that were gently beating up and down; and its face was almost invisible, being shrouded in a voluptuous white mane.

'Mino? Cen? Are you both all right? It's your mother, GG Mystery. Can you hear me?'

A rich and velvety woman's voice – very feminine yet at the same time very strong – suddenly resonated throughout the vast cavernous space.

'I'm here Ma!'

'Cen? Thank goodness you're safe and well. Now, where's your brother? Mino! Mino!'

'I can 'ear you Ma! I'm all right. Don't go getting a-flustered. What blummin' 'appened just then?'

'A new epoch is starting boys; it's time for us to leave.'

The great creature began beating its wings faster and very quickly it rose up toward the far-off pinnacles and peaks.

'Oy, Cen! Cen, I'm dahn 'ere! Come and give us a lift up, will ya?'

'I can see you Mino. Here I come.'

All the living creatures in Crown Cavern looked on in wonder as a much smaller winged creature swooped down out of the dazzling bright haze and plucked Mino from the ledge where he was standing. In a move that was surprisingly nimble for a someone who was half-bull, Mino leapt up onto his brother's back and took hold of his flowing white mane.

'*Thanks a blummin' bunch Silver Toes!*'

'*Don't mention it Silver Nose. MA! WE'RE COMING!*'

'*WE'RE RIGHT BEHIND YOU MA!*'

With just a few flaps of his broad powerful wings Cen ascended out of the vast hollow space and the Taur brothers departed. The instant they left, the back-draft returned, snapping everyone from their trance.

Throughout the now immense hollow interior of God's Crown, the same scene was then played out countless times with many variations, but essentially all following the same script: tyrannosaurus looks around, asking itself such questions as: 'Where am I?' 'What is this place?' and 'How did I get here?' plus 'Why was I being swirled around in a giant whirlpool just then?'; tyrannosaurus then notices an ostrich-emu-lator nearby, coughing, spluttering and stretching its neck; ostrich-emu-lator spots tyrannosaurus looking at them funny and desperately looks around for a stick; ostrich-emu-lator then realises they've lost their stick and begins to panic; tyrannosaurus, as if waking from a dream, has distinct recollection of ostrich-emu-lator using a stick to give orders and mete out punishment; tyrannosaurus gets angry and starts to growl at ostrich-emu-lator; ostrich-emu-lator nervously edges away attempting sickly grin; tyrannosaurus gets riled by grin and roars back; ostrich-emu-lator gives in to full-blown panic and legs it; tyrannosaurus gives chase, shouting things like '*Grrr-rrowling-k!* Kommen sie backen hier zurück!' or '*Grrrowling-k!* Ich wanting-k ein Wort mit ziss damn Bird!'

Thus, it was that soon after the great deluge and churn, the whole of the Crown Cavern erupted into one huge scene of chaos and mayhem as hundreds and hundreds of tyrannosauruses started pursuing a similar number of ostrich-emu-lators hither and thither, up bluffs of rock, over piles of debris and through puddles of sludge, slime and goo.

For a while, things looked pretty grim for the ostrich-emu-lators, but they were actually quite clever and resourceful creatures and they quickly realised they stood a much better chance of not being chomped and gnoshed if they ran into the various tunnels where there was not only the real possibility of being able to lose their pursuers under the cloak of darkness, there was also a good chance the tyrannosauruses would knock themselves out on the irregular ceilings.

The Taxman witnessed all these developments from the topmost pinnacle on God's Crown – the one that the Sun had snagged itself on earlier; and it was from this high vantage point that he waved 'goodbye' to the Taur family.

('How in swamp-fume blazes did he manage to get up there so quickly?' I hear you ask, Dear Reader. Well, I'll tell you. After eventually managing to send his despatches to Cen and Mino, he'd then made his way to the sponge platform at the rear of the cave where Elli, Zatt and Hopi had landed after their ride down the chute. There, he'd put on a leather strap with loads of full water bladders tied to it and had squeezed himself into the chute's opening. Then, as the seawater had risen, a pocket of air had built up in the cavity behind him ever increasing in pressure until, suddenly, with a loud '*POP!*' he shot up the chute like an escaping champagne cork, emerging in a burst of bubbles right next to the base of the upmost pinnacle where he had an observation platform. So quick had been his accent up through the innards of the mountain, he'd actually reached his vantage point in time to see the avalanche of boulders tumble into Crown Lake. He'd then seen with his own eyes the vast lake lurch like a jarred bowl of water before plunging down into the Crown Cavern below.)

Content that all was going according to plan inside the hollowed-out mountain, he was about to re-position himself so that he could concentrate on 'external' matters when something caught his eye deep in the heart of the vast sunlit cavern. An odd-looking tiny grey-beige object appeared to be fluttering up away from all the turmoil and heading in his direction.

'What on Mir—*er,* Earth is that?'

The Taxman's face filled with curiosity as he watched the object flitting awkwardly to-and-fro in a haphazard zigzag sort of movement. It took a while, but eventually, after making painfully slow progress, the unidentified flying object drew close enough for him tell it was a flying creature of some kind and furthermore … it was flying backwards. Then, as it drew ever closer, he could hear that it was repeatedly saying something as it flew.

'Dammit I'm Mad! Dammit I'm Mad! Dammit I'm Mad!'

'*Ahoy there!*' cried the Taxman. 'I see you've managed to escape from all the turmoil down below.'

'*Dammit I'm*—ohw era ouy?'

'Eh? I beg your pardon. What was that you said?'

'I dais "ohw era ouy?"'

'Oh, I get it. You're speaking backwards.'

'Sey, s'taht thgir. Llew enod, llew dettops. Ym eman si oxO. Er'uoy ton eht namxaT yb yna ecnahc, era uoy?'

'I ma deedni taht nosrep oxO.'

'*Wow!* Ev'I reven tem enoyna esle ohw nac kaeps sdrawkcab.'

(Being a fluent speaker of gobbledygook, it should come as no surprise, Dear Reader, to discover that the Taxman was proficient in backward-speak. He could also talk perfectly good upside-down and inside-out as it happens, but thankfully, neither has a part to play in our story.)

'Woh dab si ti nwod ereht? Era ereht ynam – *mu* – "seitlausac"?'

'S'ti mehyam nwod ereht! I tog tuo sa noos sa I dluoc.'

'Did uoy – *mu* – I t'nod esoppus uoy wonk rehtehw illE dna sih sdneirf era yako?'

'Eht tsal I was fo illE, eh saw ylevarb gniyrt ot evas enoyreve. I hsiw I ev'dluoc deyats ot pleh mih, tub ti saw oot suoregnad. I wenk I dah ot teg yawa, esiwrehto I dluow evah emoc ot emos mrah … *ooh-oob!*' Oxo started to back-cry. ' … *Ooh-oob!*'

'Ho, t'nod yrc oxO. M'I erus s'eh … M'I erus er'yeht … *Ooh-oob! Ooh-oob!*'

The Taxman started to back-sob too. The two of them clung on to each other and cried their hearts out at the thought of what was happening down below, each one sobbing wretchedly, interspersed with the odd howl and occasional deep, deep sigh – though, in Oxo's case this was all done backwards, obviously. Then, suddenly, the Taxman pulled himself together.

'*Oxo!*'

' —*Ooh-oob*. Sey?'

'We're not going to leave them to their fate!'

'Er'ew ton?'

'We most certainly are not. In fact, I forbid it!'

'Tahw era ew gniog ot od?'

'Not "we" Oxo—*"YOU"!* I've got much more important things to do.'

'Fi uoy kniht m'I gniog kcab nwod ereht, uoy nac kniht niaga ynnoS. *Dammit I'm Mad!*'

The Taxman grabbed Oxo by the shoulders and turned him to face the outside of the mountain range. Just at that moment, there was a loud '*rumble*' and immediately beneath them a huge jet of water burst out from a crevasse, sending forth a great spume which cascaded down the mountainside.

'See that?'

'Sey.'

'That's the Amazon.'

'S'tahw "eht nozamA"?'

'That will become the greatest river system in America-South.'

Just then, with a loud '*crack*' followed by a giant '*roar*', another giant spume erupted far over to their right.

'*THAR SHE BLOWS!* There's the Mississippi! That's America-North up and running.'

'S'tahw "eht ippississiM"?'

Before the Taxman could answer, an even louder '*crack*' could be heard from the far side of God's Crown.

'That'll be the Nile. Africa's off.'

Another '*crack*' sounded from the far side and this time the spume could be seen between two pinnacles.

'I think that's probably the Rhine or possibly the Danube? Europe's joining the party.'

Over to their left yet another erupted.

'The Yangtze I think, or perhaps the Yellow. *HELLO-OOO ASIA!*'

By now, there were so many spumes erupting, it was as if the whole of God's Crown was springing leaks.

'What do you think Oxo?'

'*LOOC!*'

'They're my new "rivers" being born Oxo. Each continent will soon have its own unique river system. Pretty soon, people won't be able to go anywhere except by a "boat", whatever one of those is.'

'*Hooooo!*'

The Taxman twisted Oxo back to face him.

'You want Elli and all the others to be part of that exciting future, don't you Oxo?'

'Sey.'

'You can now see why I'm needed here, can't you Oxo?'

'*Mmmuuu*, sey. I esoppus os.'

'*Great!* Does that mean you'll do it?'

'Sey-sey. ll'I od ti … *re – mu* – od tahw yltcaxe?'

The Taxman put his fingers to his lips and gave three short whistles. From somewhere down below, six white birds flying in pair formation started fluttering up towards them. He turned back to Oxo.

'How many of them—sorry, woh ynam snamuh era ereht taht deen gniucser, yltcaxe, eht xaT-rekaT-rekcaB-gnaG dna rieht sdneirf?'

'*Mu* – tel em ees … xis snamuh – dna owt sesuruasaven.'

'Nevasauruses have wings, don't they? They can fly for themselves, can't they?'

'Sey, er'uoy thgir—yrros, siht si lla gnineppah a tib oot tsaf rof em.'

'Don't worry, you're doing fine. Sounds like six ought to do it'

The Taxman turned and gave three more whistles. Immediately, three more pairs of white winged-slipper birds appeared, heading upward behind the others. As soon as all twelve birds were assembled, the Taxman addressed them.

'All present and correct?'

'*Yes, Sir!* Certainly "present" Sir, but – *um* – '

'*Right!* Now listen carefully chaps. I need you to go on an urgent mission and we don't have much time.' He indicated Oxo. 'This here is Oxo. He's going to be your squadron leader.'

'Olleh spahc!'

'Beggin' your pardon, Sir. What did he just say?'

'Don't worry about understanding what he says; just follow his lead. Got that?'

'Yes, Sir.'

'Now, unfortunately, some very good friends of ours—that's me and Oxo here—are caught up in the – *er* – the "events" occurring down there ... ' he paused to indicate the deep hollow and the vast cavern far down below, ' ... and we want you chaps to go down there and—well, do what only you can do ... what you guys do best.'

'And, what is that, Sir?'

'He means go and pick up some humans stupid!'

'Oh, right! No problem, Sir; got you now, Sir.'

(I should point out that the winged-slipper birds had been so embarrassed by their recent clumsy performances they had been practising their drills. As a result, they were much more disciplined; indeed, most of them now even remembered their names ... well, some of the time.)

'Right then. Oxo?'

'Sey, riS?'

'Era uoy ydaer ot od siht?'

'Sey ... *riS!*'

'Then be off with you one and all! *And jolly good luck!*'

The winged-slipper birds drew up in formation behind a hovering Oxo who, of course, was facing them.

'*Neht thgir! S'tel og spahc!*'

'Pardon?'

'He said "Let's go",' shouted the Taxman.

'Oh right. *Lead on Oxo!*'

Oxo completed two '*palf*'s then paused in order to make a stirring speech. Unfortunately, the false start caused the two winged-slipper birds bringing up the rear to bump into the ones in front. Undeterred, Oxo delivered his carefully selected words of inspiration with real passion.

'Are we not drawn onward, we few, drawn onward to new era?'

'Blimey! I understood that.'

With that the Oxo-led 'rescue squadron' set forth.

Down below, things were not going too well for the long-necked ostrich-emu-lators. They had barely led their pursuers into the tunnels when the howling wind, which had hitherto masked their retreating footsteps with its noise, suddenly dropped. As a result, the tyrannosauruses were able to hear the '*slap slap slap*' of their pattering feet and began to close in on them.

But then, a just few moments later, things changed again, causing everyone to pause in mid-chase, both hunter and hunted alike.

A new wind started to blow but in the opposite direction. Instead of a back-draft being sucked *into* the Labyrinth, an even more powerful hurricane was now blasting its way *out*. More worryingly, the reason why the wind had returned was because the water was coming back. (Technically speaking, Dear Reader, it wasn't the same water; this was the seawater from the Crystal Cave, but the ostrich-emu-lators and tyrannosauruses weren't to know that. All they knew was that the tunnels were suddenly resounding with the roar of an approaching torrent; and it was time to get out – *fast!*)

The Taxman had actually been uncannily accurate in both his reasoning and his planning. The fresh water of the Great Lake had rushed down into the deepest parts of the Labyrinth (thereby creating the aquifers that were now feeding the newly-created rivers) just as the seawater reached the threshold at the rear of the Crystal Cave where it could pour into the Labyrinth's upper levels. It was this inward gush of seawater that was now chasing both the ostrich-emu-lators and tyrannosauruses back towards the vast cavernous hollow of the Crown Cavern.

Meanwhile, back in the cavern, Hopi and Wishi – ridden by Gusto and Granddad respectively – were frantically flying broad circuits of the vast hollow space in a desperate search for their fellow Tax-Taker-Backers. As they flew, they were constantly calling out for the others.

'*ELL-LLI-III!*'

'*LITTLE* – belp – *BUDDY-YYY!*'

'*OI-III – VOI-III!*'

'*ZA-AAA-TTT! Dainty* – belch-pardon – *of my life!*'

'*OI-IIIG!*'

'Og, Og, my dear sweet Og! Please let me see you through this fog!'

'OXO!'

'LITTLE BACKWARD – burp – *BUDDY!'*

'ELLI, ELLI, YOUR FEET AREN'T SMELLY!'

… and so on.

Suddenly, from somewhere way up high, above where Hopi and Wishi were doing their circuits, a faint voice could be heard calling out.

'HELP! Help me – please! Will somebody please come and help me? HELP!'

Hopi, Wishi, Gusto and Granddad all looked up and saw Og dangling from the top of the C-shaped crescent of the Red Moon. The flimsy hollowed-out remains of the moon were just about standing, though they had clearly taken quite a battering in the churn and were now looking rather fragile and rickety with bits of red rock crumbling here and there that *'pattered'* on the ground in showers of dust and stones. Right at the very tip of the crescent, Og was holding on by her fingertips. Somehow, the churn must have deposited her there; and it was obvious to all looking up from below that the fragile point of rock she was hanging from was about to give way at any moment.

'Please help me! Will someone please help me!'

'HOLD ON TIGHT OG! WE'ER – burp – *COMING!'*

'OG! OG! OG! DON'T LET GO!
WE'RE ON OUR WAY, DON'CHA KNOW!'

Hopi and Wishi needed no further bidding. They both did a treble-*'fah-whoosh-pa-pa-dah-lommopp'* and accelerated upwards as fast as they could.

At that very same instant, flying in formation high up above, Oxo and his 'rescue squadron' also spotted Og's plight far beneath them.

'Nac uoy lla ees tahw I ees spahc?'

'What did he say?'

'Never mind that! Look down there lads! There's a human in serious trouble!'

'*Thgir!* I tnaw kcinK dna kcanK ot leep ffo dna eucser reh. *Tittog?*'

'"Tittog?" Sir?'

'Sey, "Tittog". Lliw uoy esaelp netsil ylluferac dna od sa I yas? Thgir! I tnaw kcinK dna kcanK ot leep ffo dna eucser reh. Tittog?'

'Look lads; I've got an idea. That poor human can't wait for us to work out whatever he's saying. I'll keep him talking while you two, Knick and Knack, go and see what you can do.'

'*Righty-ho!*'

With that, Knick and Knack peeled off from the rest of the squadron and accelerated downwards towards Og.

'*S'taht taerg!* Uoy did yltcaxe tahw I detnaw uoy ot od. Won I tnaw pilF dna polF ot og dna tsissa kcinK dna kcanK.'

'Tell you what boys. I think Knick and Knack might need a bit of help with that one. Flip and Flop, are you up for it?'

'*You bet Dingle!*'

'It's Dangle actually.'

'Does it matter?'

'Not a jot.'

'Toodle-pip then. Come on Flop; *let's go!*'

A second pair separated from the squadron and dived double-fast toward the stricken Og.

'*Llew enod spahc! S'taht eht tirips!* Knaht ssendoog uoy nac dnatsrednu gnihtyreve m'I gniyas.'

'Now then Boss; you were saying?'

There was no time to lose. Creaking and cracking loudly, the tip of the Red Moon's fragile crescent was about to snap-off at any moment; and to make matters worse, Og was losing her grip.

'*He-eee-elp! Help! I can't hold on much longer!*'

Og looked down at the terrifying drop beneath her, then back up at the narrow point of red rock.

'*Help me someone! The rock's about to break and it's a very long way down!*'

'Hold on Og!
Hold on tight!
We're almost there!
You'll soon be all right!'

'Granddad? Is that you?'

'*Hey!* You up there! Stop wiggling your feet; we can't get into position!'

Og looked down again and saw two winged-slipper birds attempting to manoeuvre themselves onto her feet.

'*Oy!* Who are you?' she cried. 'What do you think you are doing?'

'Never mind that; it's too confusing, and we don't have much time. Now, do you want saving or what?'

'*Hey!* Move out of the way – *burp* – little buddies! We're here to rescue our friend.'

'*Here!* Who do you think you are, bossing our friends around like that? They're only trying to help.'

Two more slipper-shaped white birds (Flip and Flop) joined the scene just as Hopi and Wishi took up position either side of Og.

'*Ahem!*' Hopi coughed politely. 'I'm not sure why you are here my dear fellows, but we – that's my cousin here and I – would be most terribly grateful if you could possibly move to one side while we and our friends attempt to rescue this young lady from what you can readily see is a most infelicitous predicament, wouldn't we Wishi?'

'Yois, woi moist coirtoinloiy woild!'

'What did he just say?'

'I dunno; he's got a very strong accent.'

'No, not him. The other one!'

'*KERRR-RRR-UMBLE!*'

'*Look!* Will you all please stop bickering!' cried Og. 'I just need someone – it doesn't matter who – to save me—*fast!*'

'Who's bickering? I'm not bickering. Are you bickering Flip?'

'Nope, I'm not Flop.'

'All I'm saying is,' said Knick (or possibly Knack), 'we were here to save her first; now … *shove off!*'

'Look, little – *burp* – buddy, I know you mean well, but— '

'*Ahem!* I think you'll find we *were*, in fact – *um* – bickering just then, that is if you take "bickering" to mean "to engage in a petulant, or peevish, argument which has no direct bearing on the matter in hand." What do you think Wishi?'

'Woill, Oi'm gloid yoi oisked moi thoit— '

'*KERRR-RRR-ACK!*'

The tip of the crumbling moon rock gave way and with a tiny little shriek Og slipped from view. All eight of her 'rescuers' looked down and watched as she plummeted away from them.

'Anyway, my point is … ' continued Hopi, ' … that we—*hold on*, I've lost my gist.'

'*GREAT FLASHES OF LIGHTNING!*' Granddad suddenly realised what was happening. '*THIS IS MOST FRIGHTENING!*'

With that, he leapt off Wishi's head and dived after Og headfirst.

Far down below, Og was thinking fast. Despite being thrown around in the churn, she was still wearing her leaf-plume hat and leaf-plume tail. She deftly managed to unfasten them and started using them as wings which instantly had the effect of slowing her descent. This enabled Granddad to catch up and hurtle past calling out …

'Fear not dear Og; I'm a-coming to get you!
After all you've done for me; it's the least I could do!'

'*Granddad! Wait!*'

Now it was Og's turn to dive. She folded her wings by her side and plunged downward headfirst. As soon as she caught up with Granddad, she grabbed him tight, wrapped her arms around him, pulled him close and …

… for the briefest of moments their eyes met—

—but, then they both realised they were falling fast and the ground was rushing towards them.

'O woe, my blessed luck; to find true love like this;
just one brief warm embrace; and not enough time for a kiss.'

With a loving glance, Granddad released himself from Og's arms and resumed his fall. As he fell away, he signalled that she should start flapping again in order to save herself.

'Elli; we need to find some water to wash you down … *you stink!*'

The words were barely out of Ovi's mouth when, from out of nowhere, a rogue wave of water washed over the two brothers with a large '*SPLASH-SH-SH!*'

'Well, that was a bit of lu— '

A tyrannosaurus suddenly rounded a nearby corner and rushed past at full speed.

'*GETTEN SIE OUT OFF HIER! RAUS! RAUS!*'

A frenetic '*patter, patter, patter*' then sounded and two ostrich-emu-lators appeared round the same corner, running at full pelt. As they rushed past Elli one of them knocked him over.

'*Hey!* Do you— '

'*Run for your life!*' it shouted, '*Run for your life!*'

Curious as to what might be causing such panic, Ovi fought against the now hurricane-force wind and peered around the corner. There, thundering towards them, was a terrifyingly angry wall of water topped with fierce-looking white-crested waves.

'*Quick Elli! We've got to free Zatt! The water's coming back fast—and lots of it!*'

With the wind billowing hard against their backs, the two brothers rushed over to the tangle of sticks, roots and foliage and tried desperately to pull Zatt free. Her head and shoulders were just emerging when the wall of wild water appeared from round the corner of the rocky bluff beside them.

'*Quick, boys – qui-iii-ick!*' she shrieked, her voice full of fear. '*It's almost upon us!*'

'*HALT, I SAY!*'

A rich, deep and resonant voice reverberated throughout the entire Crown Cavern; it sounded both terrifying and reassuringly familiar.

'*YOU WILL HALT AT ONCE, I SAY—YOU WAVES OF "THE SEA"!!!*'

All over the Crown Cavern the raging waters appeared to hesitate—but only for an instant. Then, onward they churned and gushed, roaring and rampaging—intent on devouring all.

'YOU WILL DO AS I SAY, FOR I BRING WITH ME ... THE TIDE!!!'

Elli and Ovi looked up, and so did Zatt. Over in the centre of the vast cavernous hollow Granddad, Og and Gusto also looked up along with Hopi and Wishi. Elsewhere, the winged-slipper birds looked up alongside Oxo (who was somehow looking up backward) and throughout the Crown Cavern, thousands of tyrannosauruses and ostrich-emu-lators were looking upward too.

There, descending from the bright sunlit sky high up above, was Al in all his majestic mythological glory; his great wings '*fah-whoosh-pah-lomp*'-ing and his neck fully extended, frills and fronds aflame with iridescence. As he called out his commands, the acoustics of the enormous hollow space amplified his words for all to hear.

'AND NOT JUST ANY OLD TIDE; OH NO! ... THE "BLUE TIDE" DON'CHA KNOW!'

Just then, from between the pinnacles of God's Crown far, far up above their heads, the edge of a gigantic blue disc came into view ... the Blue Moon. The moment the great celestial body appeared, the raging waters began to calm down. Then, as more and more of the moon became visible, the waves ceased to '*roar*', '*crash*' and '*pound*'. Instead, they became quelled and subdued, ever less wild, more and more tame, until they were little more than ripples hardly making any noise at all; just the occasional gentle '*lap ... lap ... lap*'.

'NOW LISTEN CAREFULLY ONE AND ALL! THE BLUE MOON AND I WILL NOT BE WITH YOU LONG, BUT YOU SHOULD HAVE ENOUGH TIME TO CLIMB TO SAFETY. BEFORE THE GREAT CHURN RESUMES, YOU NEED TO MAKE IT TO THE LEDGE AROUND THE PERIMETER OF THE CAVERN THAT IS THE REMAINS OF

THE FLOOR OF THE CROWN LAKE. THERE, YOU WILL BE BEYOND THE REACH OF THE CHURN'S RAGING WATER ... NOW HURRY!!!'

Across the whole of the Crown Cavern no one moved. Every living creature was spellbound and dumbstruck, and stood utterly motionless with its mouth agape, completely transfixed.

'I DID SAY "HURRY" DON'CHA KNOW!'

The spell was broken and a mad scramble began.

Some tyrannosauruses tried to clamber over each other; and others got tangled with ostrich-emu-lators as they frantically attempted to scale the slime-covered rocks. Here and there some of the birds formed gangs and started bullying their way up. In one or two more-enlightened instances an ostrich-emu-lator and a tyrannosaurus teamed up, the former doing the navigating and the latter the climbing. One way or another, every living creature starting doing what Al had ordered and scrambled upward, heading for what was left of the Crown Lake's floor. And all the while, the light in the cavern grew darker and darker – and ever more blue – as the massive disc of the Blue Moon slowly filled the open canopy of sky far up above.

In the fading light, Elli and Ovi were finding it harder and harder to free Zatt from the tangle of twigs and other debris that she was ensnared in.

'Oh, come on you two; we're running out of time,' she cried in desperation. 'Look, will you please free up my hands? Then I can— '

'Not wishing to be rude Mister Elli, Sir; but if you want those twigs moved fast, you'd be better off letting us experts do it. We're the best there is when it comes to urgent twig-moving.'

Elli and Ovi looked round and there before them was a small flock of white winged-slipper birds.

'Wh-Wh-Who are you?' stammered Ovi.

'Oh Ovi, allow me to introduce you,' said Elli. 'This is— '

'*Er* – 'scuse me interrupting, Sir, but there's no time for introductions. Now if you would kindly move aside.'

Elli and Ovi did as requested, allowing the birds to set about their task. They moved blindingly fast and for a fleeting moment all that could be seen was a white blur of activity; but then, as suddenly as it had started, the activity ceased and there – standing before them with Elli's bow in one hand and a clutch of arrows in the other – was Zatt.

'Thanks boys,' she said with a broad smile. 'Now, would it be too much to ask, if we were to request a ride?'

'That's what we're here for, Ma'am.'

'Is that you Dingle? I thought that was you tickling my toes, you naughty little bird!'

The little bird blushed.

'Where would you like to go, Ma'am?'

Zatt looked at the others and they all shared a 'that's-obvious' nod.

'Take us up to Al.'

Chapter Twelve

Doing the Continental

'Come on everyone; help me try to find Poob.' Ovi carefully stepped closer to the edge in order to scan the panoramic – and spectacular – view spread before them. 'He must be down there somewhere.'

With the exception of Poob, the whole of the Tax-Taker-Backer-Gang were assembled on an outcrop of rock overlooking the vast cavernous space that the 'roof-less' Crown Cavern had become. Elli, Ovi, Zatt, Gusto, Granddad and Og were in a cluster near the lip of the outcrop with Al, Hopi and Wishi perched on a ridge behind them. The winged-slipper birds were all clustered on a small ledge further up along with Oxo.

Al and the other creatures were staring upward at the Blue Moon which had completely blocked out the canopy of sky over God's Crown. As a result, the whole of the cavern was now bathed in an ethereal dream-like blue glow that gently sparkled with a purple mist whenever anyone or anything moved through it. Entranced and captivated by the mystical light, they were all frozen like statues carved from blue rock and coloured in shades of blue sepia. The humans, on the other hand, were busy looking downward, monitoring events below. From their vantage point, they could clearly see the many thousands of tyrannosauruses and ostrich-emu-lators desperately clambering to reach the safety of the ledge that was the remnants of the floor of the lake (or the ceiling of the cavern, if you prefer). They were all doing as Al has instructed, climbing as fast as they could in order to avoid the soon-to-be-churning-again seawater that was temporarily quelled by the "Blue Tide".

'What are we supposed to be looking for?' asked Zatt. 'Does he have any distinguishing characteristics this "Poob Um"?'

'Let me see,' said Ovi. 'Well, he's a super-monster-tyrannosaurus, of course, not just your everyday tyrannosaurus-next-door. What else? Ah, yes, he's mad about chasing sticks, and – *um* – anything else … ' Ovi scratched his belly to stimulate more thought. 'Oh yes, I know! He once told me he loves "ballroom dancing" – whatever that is!'

Elli tutted and sighed a sardonic sigh.

'That doesn't exactly give us a lot to go on does it Ovi? What you're saying is we're looking for an average ordinary-looking 'Mister Normal' super-monster-tyrannosaurus.' He gesticulated with exaggerated irony to indicate the countless tyrannosauruses (including hundreds of 'super-monster' ones) they could see below then. 'I hate to say it, but there are quite a few of those to choose from!'

'Has anyone spotted any of the fat-cats?' Og was wringing her hands and sounded anxious. 'Any sign of Frobisher or Hawkins, or-or Drake or Nelson, or-or-or any of them at all!'

'Hold up everyone! – *belp-pfffart-scuse-me* – I think I've spotted something!' Gusto pointed to what looked like a mud island in the area where 'In-The-Nest' had been. 'Is that – *burp* – Herman I can see down there?'

They all looked where he was pointing and there in the midst of the slimy goo they could see the outline of a big box-type thing upon the goo-covered mound of fodder-mulch.

At that moment, the curtains on Herman's house-shell twitched then opened wide, and a big cat-shaped face peered out. In the background behind the face, lit-up by the flickering flames of a burning fire, various 'ample-portioned' cat-shapes could be seen moving about.

'Well, well, how about that; it looks like some folk are nice and cosy!' Zatt put her arm round Og's shoulder. 'You can stop worrying Og. I think the cats are—*WOW!!!*'

A ray of golden sunlight, shimmering in a cascade of rainbows, suddenly burst into the cavern like a spotlight being turned on; it was rapidly followed by another, and then another. The Blue Moon was beginning to move away which meant the tranquil quiet waters of the Blue Tide were about to rediscover their 'wild side'; and throughout the cavern, shrieks of panic could be heard from those yet to reach the ledge.

The shrieks snapped Al out of his reverie and, with an urgent look of concern, he extended his long neck over the edge of the outcrop to scour the scene below. After a few moments' scrutiny of the situation he appeared to be reassured that all the creatures were going to make it to safety in time, at which point he turned round to address the others.

'*Well, my friends, my very special friends …* ' He smiled a broad smile and his frills oscillated in waves down either side of his neck; first gold, followed by red, then yellow and, finally, a rich ocean blue. 'The Music of the Spheres is calling, don'cha know; I'm afraid it is time for the Blue Moon and I to go.'

'"*GO"!*' exclaimed the Tax-Taker-Backers in one voice (apart from a "*GOI!*" and an "*OG!*").

'B-B-But you can't go Al, at least not yet!' pleaded Elli. 'We have no idea what's about to happen here; we still need your help!'

'Yes, indeed, that certainly is very true,' said Granddad, looking serious. 'And, let's not forget we still have unfinished business with "you-know-who".'

'Who's that?' murmured one of the winged-slipper birds only to be 'shushed' quiet by one of the others.

'*Ah yes, the Taxman.*' Al narrowed his eyes as Elli stepped forward to stand directly in front of him.

'You need to understand Al; this Taxman is completely mad, in fact he's madder than mad, he's *CRAZY* mad; there's no telling what he might do next. Did you know it was him behind all this mayhem? For example, after he stole your moons, did you know he persuaded Mino Taur to help him break them down so their rock could be "distributed" throughout the Labyrinth; which he also created by the way! And did you know he got Cen Taur to overfill the Crown Lake till it burst? I mean, if that isn't complete and utter madness, I don't know what is! *AND* he hasn't finished yet—*HO-OHH NO!* There's more madness to come—*much more!* Did you know he now plans to create things called "continents", whatever they are? And-and-and then there's some business about "*intra-*" and "*inter-*continental trade; and what else?—oh yes, he's totally obsessed with finding somewhere called "Mirth" and— '

Al suddenly lowered his head to look Elli directly in the eye. The unexpected move made him jump.

'*We had a meeting.*'

'"We"? Who's "we"?'

'The Council of Mythological Creatures, that's "we"— er – *who.'*

'Oh, I see.'

'And, at our meeting we decided he can have his "continents" and his "trade", both "intra-" and "inter-continental", and all the rest of it. In fact, one or two of my fellow mythological creatures were really rather keen on the whole thing.'

'Really?'

'Yes. I think a couple of them have their eye on those herding clouds Cen Taur has come up with; quite fancy the idea of taking on a pet continent and making sure it has plenty of rain, don'cha know. You two did a jolly good job there, by the way. All that silver lining you sploshed on; you both did a much better job than those wretched servants of his.'

A sudden gust of wind distracted everyone and drew their attention back to events below. The water was beginning to look rough again and the odd white-crested wave was starting to lash at the rocks on the cavern floor. Luckily, apart from Herman who was nice and snug in the goo, no creature was in harm's way as the last straggler had just scrambled onto the ledge.

'*ALOYSIUS MEREDITH PLANTAGENET FORTESQUE-SMYTH FITZ ... DRAGON!*' Zatt stepped forward to stand beside Elli and gave Al one of her fiercest looks. 'You simply cannot – you must not – leave us here like this! We need your help and in so many ways! How will we get out of here? What's going to happen next with all this water? Will there be another of these so-called "tides" to control it long enough for us to get out of this horrible smelly cavern and away from this blasted mountain?'

'Fear not my dear Zatt! I'm sure a way out will become clear to you. And you have no need to worry about the waters which, ultimately, are your friend not your enemy. By the way, the Yellow Moon has kindly agreed to tame them and act as Regulator of the Tides. It is a far gentler moon than the Blue Moon, don'cha know; and a much, much more reliable one. The Blue Moon is far too unpredictable; a loveable rogue of a moon; a true "rover". Why, this time tomorrow ... ' he looked wistfully up at his cherished celestial body; only a thin slither of its blue-

ness was now visible in the sky above their heads. ' … *I could be anywhere!*'

With a powerful '*fah-whoosh-pah-lomp!*' Al took off. His wing-beats rapidly faded as he soared upward, chasing after his beloved Blue Moon. Then, suddenly—

—both he and the moon were gone.

For a long lingering moment, the Tax-Taker-Backers and their associates stood in awe-struck silence, staring at the spot where his silhouette had disappeared from view. But then, some renewed shrieks of alarm sounded, snapping them out of their collective daze and drawing their attention back to events down below. The moment they looked downward, they gasped with surprise. The cavern was once again full of raging seawater with wild crashing-cresting waves and the water level was rising – *very fast!*

While the Tax-Taker-Backers had been looking upward, the Blue Tide had finally waned, allowing the seawater to rush into the cavern from the numerous caves and tunnels of the Labyrinth. Very quickly, the entire cavern floor along what remained of the mound of fodder as well as the last vestiges of the captive moons had been totally engulfed; and Herman was nowhere to be seen.

As they watched, the rampaging waters continued their relentless rise ever higher and higher. The giant waves grew in strength and started pounding the cavern walls hard with loud resonant '*BOOM!*'s, each one causing the entire mountain to shudder.

All of a sudden, the whole of God's Crown shook with a mighty judder. It was such a powerful tremor; all of the Tax-Taker-Backer-Gang lost their balance and wobbled. Fortunately, the humans all managed to grab hold of each other and prevent themselves from falling. Hopi and Wishi did topple over but, luckily, toward each other, so they didn't fall. The little birds all took to the air, but Oxo was confused and momentarily forgot how to fly. He swayed fro-and-to before tumbling, heels-under-head, several tyrannosaurus lengths up the mountainside – backward.

Deep, deep down far below God's Crown, immensely powerful forces were at work. When the lower reaches of the Labyrinth had filled with the fresh water from the Crown Lake, they had placed the foundations of the great mountain under enormous strain. Now, the added weight of the seawater rapidly filling the upper layers was becoming too much for the soft honeycombed rock of the young Earth's mantle to bear. Something somewhere had to give and just as the winged-slipper birds were helping Oxo back on his feet … it did.

'*KER-RRR-RRRACK!!!*'

A jagged crack appeared up the side of the cavern wall, not far from the Tax-Taker-Backer-Gang.

'*Quick everybody!*' shouted Elli. '*Let's fly!*'

Gusto and Ovi leapt onto Hopi's head, Granddad and Og scrambled onto Wishi's while Elli and Zatt hurriedly – but not so hurriedly that they got them muddled up – donned their pairs of winged-slipper birds. As they were doing this—

'*B-BANG-CRACK!!!*'

Two more full-length sky-to-floor cracks appeared on the far side of the cavern wall, then—

'*KER-RRR-RACK-BANG!!! CRACK-KERR-RRR-RACK-ACK-ACK!!!*'

Several more cracks opened up, too many to count; just before—

'*SHHH-WOOO-OOO-SHHH-SHHH! WO-WHOO-OOO-OOSH-SH! SWISH-SH-SH-SH—SWO-OOO-OSH-SH-SH—GURGLE!!!*'

—the seawater disappeared and an eerie silence fell.

The airborne Tax-Taker-Backers quickly assembled in a cluster, hovering in the empty space that had previously been the Crown Lake. Along with all the creatures gathered on the ledge below them, they looked nervously about, listening intently and wondering what was going to happen next.

Down below, in the hidden depths of the Labyrinth, the odd faint '*gurgle*' could be heard along with the occasional '*splash*'. Then, from somewhere deeper than the deepest depths of the mountain, a faint "grumble" sounded, which quickly grew to a "growl" … then rapidly amplified into—

'RUMBLE-RUMBLE-RUMBLE-RUMBLE-RUMBLE-RUMBLE-RUMBLE … ROAR!!!'

—as God's Crown broke apart!

Where the first crack had been, the mountainside was torn asunder and a gaping fissure opened up, allowing blinding bright shards of sunlight to pierce their way through.

Then—

'RUMBLE-RUMBLE-RUMBLE-RUMBLE-RUMBLE-RUMBLE … RRR-ROAR-RRR!!!'

—another fracture opened up; this one much bigger than the first. Then—

'RUMBLE-RUMBLE-RUMBLE …

ROAR!!!'

—another jagged fissure appeared; followed quickly by—

'RUMBLE-RUMBLE-RUMBLE-RUMBLE-RUMBLE … ROAR!!!'

—yet another.

God's Crown was now no longer "*A*" mountain; instead, it had become several separate ones; or, as the Taxman might say … several separate and completely independent "continents".

The Tax-Taker-Backer-Gang and the rest of the creatures in the Crown Cavern stared about them in wonder as beams of warm soothing afternoon sunshine began to flood the vast open space. The Sun's rays brought with them some very welcome warmth; so much so, some of the ostrich-emu-lators decided to enjoy a spot of sun-bathing. They were just getting settled into a reclining pose when, suddenly, from somewhere near to where the most recent fissure had just opened up (it was actually the break between America-North and Europe)—

'AYY-YYY-EEE-EEE-EEE!!!' A shrill feminine shriek rang out. *'Ich bin slipping-k! Somebody helping-k mich, bitte! Schnell! Schnell!'*

A female tyrannosaurus had lost her footing and slipped off the ledge. She was desperately trying to hold on with her front claws, but they were beginning to lose grip. Her body was dangling in mid-air over a gaping chasm; a fathomless void that disappeared downward into the darkest depths.

'Let's get down there *quick!*' shouted Elli; and the Tax-Taker-Backers dived towards her.

While they were diving, a monster-tyrannosaurus who'd been standing nearby the stricken female, flopped forward onto his belly and reached out to grab hold of her. It was Poob.

'*Hier! Taking-k hold off mich—SCHNELL! Ich vill pulling-k Sie up!*'

The female was too scared to let go. She looked up at him with eyes full of fear.

'*Ich kann nicht! Ich kann nicht!*' she squealed.

Poob crawled forward until the bulk of his own body was well over the lip of the precipice, and stretched out his front claw as far as he could.

'*Yah-yah, Sie kann! SIE KANN!*'

'*She can now!*'

All of a sudden, a whole squadron of winged-slipper birds fluttered around the female's body and grabbed hold of her.

'*Steady boys! Left a bit!*'

Poob's front claw was right beside hers. She took courage from his fiercely intent 'trust me' gaze, closed her eyes and let go. He clasped her tight and their claws entwined in a firm grip. She opened her eyes and saw the look of relief on his face. He was just about to say something when—

'RUMBLE-RUMBLE-RUMBLE-RUMBLE-RUMBLE-RUMBLE ... ROAR!!!'

—elsewhere in the great cavern a new fissure opened up, causing the whole mountain to jolt.

Poob's look of relief instantly turned to one of panic as he too started to slide forward.

'Hold steady boys! Hold steady!'

Stones and shards of rock 'skittered' away from beneath Poob and fell past the female into the darkness below. In a reflex action, Poob kicked out with his rear legs trying in vain to gain a fresh grip—but to no avail.

'AYY-YYY-EEE—EEE-EEE!'

The female screamed as she felt Poob's bodyweight slip.

'Oh, no you don't my friend!'

Hopi grabbed hold of Poob's left leg while Wishi grasped his right, and both nevasauruses started pulling backward with all their might.

'Hold on tight Poob! We'll soon have you both up!'

'Keep pulling-k! Keep pulling-k! Harder! HARDER! Ich kann nicht holding-k on mutch länger!'

With his other front claw now free, Poob managed to stretch forward and grab the female's other front claw. She was now dangling free from the ledge with her life now, literally, in Poob's grasp.

Unfortunately, the transfer of her weight added tremendously to the strain on Wishi and Hopi and the two nevasauruses shared a look of alarm as they both felt their feet starting to slip. The female felt the slippage too and screamed again.

'AY-YYY-EEE-EEE!'

'Pull her up boys! Up-up-up as hard as you can!'

'RUMBLE—RUMBLE-RUMBLE—ROAR!!!'

Somewhere over on the far side of God's Crown America-South broke away from Africa. The resulting lurch caused Hopi to lose his footing. He stumbled forward and went straight over the edge, with Gusto and Ovi still on his head.

'AYY-YYY-YYY—EEE-EEE!'

For a brief moment, Wishi managed to hold firm. His grip on Poob's leg was good, as was Poob's grip on the female's front claws; but then, the combined weight of so many 'danglers' proved too much for him and he couldn't hold on any longer.

The whole ‘string’ of creatures; female-tyrannosaurus-plus-winged-slipper-birds, Poob, Hopi-plus-Gusto-and-Ovi, and Wishi-plus-Granddad-and-Og, slipped off the precipice and tumbled into the void.

‘AYY-YYY-EEE—EEE-EEE-EEE!’

A giant shadow suddenly engulfed them accompanied by a loud rumbling sound—the drumming of multiple extremely heavy feet.

‘SNAP!’

Something caught hold of Wishi’s tail and gripped it tight. Wishi looked back over his shoulder—

—it was Herman’s giant pincer-claw.

Of course, there was always a possibility, if not a probability, that the female tyrannosaurus and her ‘rescuer’ would forge a close bond after sharing such a terrifying ordeal, but when Poob discovered her name was “Tumt” their fate was sealed.

The whole of the Tax-Taker-Backer-Gang thought it highly amusing that Tumt was about to become “Tumt Um”, apart from Oxo who couldn’t see what was funny at first; but then after a couple of days he finally twigged, and when he did he couldn’t stop back-laughing … very loudly.

(A great poltroon’s back-laugh, incidentally, sounds very strange; especially in the middle of the night which was when Oxo suddenly got the joke. The sound woke Elli, Zatt and Ovi with a start and they each had nightmares for days afterwards; Gusto, on the other hand, couldn’t get enough of the weird sound and from that day forth kept telling Oxo funny stories whenever they met.)

After a few days’ well-earned rest, the Tax-Taker-Backer-Gang were ready to hunt down the Taxman and finally confront him with a view to doing some serious taking-back of tax. Because he was the last member of the gang to actually see the Taxman, they began their search by retracing Oxo’s steps (which, as you can imagine, Oxo found excruciatingly difficult). They eventually found the Taxman exactly where Oxo had last seen him high up in his vantage point on the highest pinnacle of God’s Crown, sitting comfortably in what had previously been

Granddad's globe-chair, surveying the "New World Order" he'd created in a state of heightened excitement and unbridled glee.

In fact, he was so deliriously happy with the outcome of events, he not only agreed to pay back all the "tax" he'd taken according to Zatt's "list" *twice-over*, he also said they were welcome to have as many goes on his "escape chute" as they wanted. Happily accepting his offer, they spent two whole days enjoying themselves (it would have been one day, but they kept having to wait for Oxo to use the chute backwards). Once they'd finished having fun, the Taxman gave them a lecture on how "trade" needed to develop; and he strongly suggested that Elli and Zatt make a start on "boat" designs as soon as they got home, especially if they wanted to "get ahead in the game".

It was at this point they discovered they actually lived somewhere on a continent called "Africa" and they had several of the newly-formed rivers to cross in order to get back home, including a really big one called the "Nile". In readiness for this, Zatt and Hopi decided to prepare a stock of Gusto's special 'fart-fuel' dainties which delayed their departure by a couple of days.

Eventually, however, the preparations were all complete; the Tax-Taker-Backer-Gang were ready to make their way back home and the moment had finally arrived for everyone to say "goodbye".

They all assembled in the Crystal Cave where Elli and Ovi had discovered God's lunchbox, and which the Taxman had used as the conduit for filling God's Crown with seawater. To be precise, they actually congregated in the African half of the cave, because it had been split in two by the fissure separating Africa from America-South.

From Africa's newly-formed Atlantic Shore, the other 'half' of the cave – a kind of "mirror image" – was still visible across the baby Atlantic Ocean. Interestingly, America-South was still close enough for them to see that the tyrannosauruses had begun using their half of the sparkling cavern as a kind of ballroom. Rather annoyingly, however, it was already too far away for them to tell what dance they were performing. It looked a bit like a Samba, but it could have easily been a Paso Doble.

Back in their 'half-cave', the Taxman had taken to using a rather striking feature that looked like a giant multi-coloured crystalline chair as his "throne". There was a broad flat area of orange-coloured crystal in front of the "throne" which was ideal for the "throne-sitter" to greet visitors or receive an audience; and it was upon this that everybody gathered.

The first to depart were the white winged-slipper birds and Oxo. During the preceding few days, despite being mostly unable to understand each other, at a deep level they'd 'clicked'; and, as a result, the squadron of little birds and their leader were now inseparable. Indeed, it was in response to a suggestion of his that they'd unanimously decided to head for East Anglia.

(Little were they to know that, once there, they were destined to meet a very ancient, intelligent, wise and talented old sage of a tyrannosaurus called Morris Da Vinci who was not only the very first creature to conceive of the motor car as a form of transport, he was also the inventor of a rustic style of dancing which can still be enjoyed there to this very day. You might be interested to know, Dear Reader, that amongst his countless incredible achievements, it was he who actually created the myth of a lost world called "West Anglia"; a land steeped in intrigue, mystery and an awful lot of confusion. Indeed, their meeting with him was to lead to a whole separate adventure of its own which, sadly, is for another day.)

'Right then you lot,' said the Taxman, standing before his "throne" and barking his orders in a crisp militaristic voice. 'Winged-slipper birds … *FAA-AAA-ALL IN!*'

The entire squadron of twelve birds fluttered out of a nearby breakfast berry tree where Oxo had trained them to roost and assembled in their pairs, hovering to attention. Oxo hovered to one side—also to attention, but backward.

'Reppils-degniw sdrib lla nellaf ni, *riS!*'

'Right you are Sergeant. I think we'd best check they're all present and correct? We don't want you leaving anyone behind now, do we?'

'Yletulosba ton, *riS!* I kniht ll'uoy dnif er'yeht lla "tneserp", riS; tub ton ylirassecen "tcerroc" … *ah ah ah!*'

'Siht si on gnihgual rettam, tnaegreS.'

'Yrros, riS. *Meha!*'

'Right then … Flip and Flop?'

'*Yessir!*'

'pilF dna polF era ereh, *riS!*'

'Go-ooo-ood. … Dingle and Dangle?'

'*Yessir!*'

'elgniD dna elgnaD era ereh, *riS!*'

'Pssst, listen-up chaps!' Flip whispered loud enough for the others to hear. 'We can't have Oxo saying "Tish" and "Tosh" backwards; this is a children's story for goodness' sake!'

'What's wrong with "Tosh" backwards?'

'Not "Tosh" you idiot! "Tosh" isn't a rude word. It's "Tish" that's the problem; when you say it backwards it sounds like "sh—"'

'*Shhhhh!*'

'Jolly good! Now, who's next? Ah yes … Knick and Knack?'

'*Yessir!* – We've got to stop him somehow!'

'How?'

'kcinK dna kcanK era ereh, *riS!*'

'Excellent Sergeant, excellent … Gizmo and Gadget?'

'*Yessir!* What are we going to do? What are we going to do?'

'omziG dna tegdaG era ereh, *riS!*'

'He's going to say it! He's going to say it! I know he is!'

'Excellent … ' The Taxman paused to survey their ranks and the entire squadron held its collective breath. 'I can see for myself that Tish and Tosh are here Sergeant, so I won't bother to call their names out.'

'*Phew!* For a moment there I thought Oxo was going to say "sh—"'

'*Shhhhh!*'

'T'nera uoy gniog ot tuohs rieht seman tuo, riS?'

'There's no need Oxo. I can see they're here.'

'*Um* – excuse me, Sir?'

Two birds at the back put their beaks up to ask a question.

'Yes?'

'What about us, Sir? You haven't called out our names.'

'You're Flip and Flop, aren't you?'

'No, Sir.'

'We're Flip and Flop, Sir,' said another pair.

'Who are you two then?'

'Dunno, Sir.'

The Taxman paused and did a double-take followed by a quick bit of silent counting.

'Oxo?'

'*riS?*'

'I do believe I've found the reason why these birds are always getting their names confused.'

'Yllaer, riS? S'yhw taht, riS?'

'You're two names short! Either that or you're two birds too many.'

The birds looked at each other and blinked. One or two started double-checking, counting heads and running through names under their breath. Oxo too muttered a list of their names backward.

'*He's right!*'

'*Cor blimey!*'

'And all this time I thought it was us getting confused.'

'Who'da thought it?'

'*Well, I never!*'

'Od uoy wonk gnihtemos, riS? I od eveileb er'uoy thgir!'

'Well, of course, I'm right; I'm always right; I'm the Taxman! Now then … *aaa-ak-hem!*' With an overly-dramatic flourish, he pointed over to the very far side of the now fully-fragmented God's Crown. 'It is time for you to set forth on your journey and fulfil your destiny little birds. There's still sufficient daylight for you to cross four continents before dark. You have my permission—nay, *I order you* to go and seek your fate and hopefully your fortune too in … *EAST ANGLIA!*'

'*Yarooh! ailgnA tsaE, ereh ew emoc!*' Oxo clapped his flappers in jubilation, but he'd forgotten he was hovering and fell to the ground. He quickly picked himself up, took to the air again and addressed his squadron. 'Thgir neht, uoy ylgu tol! Ouy draeh eht naM! Teg ydear ot—*yeh*, uoy ereht txen ot hsoT. hs— '

'Yessir?'

'*Pots gnilggig!*'

'Sorry, Sir.'

'*MEHA—ydaer sevlesruoy spahc!*' Oxo back-braced himself. 'Yb eht sreppalf … *kci-iii-iuq—PALF!*'

In perfect formation, the Oxo-led squadron set off on their epic cross-continental journey to East Anglia and the many wonders that lay in store for them there. As they headed out across the baby Atlantic, the others could clearly hear them bickering about the two missing names they still needed.

'I have an idea chaps. What do you think of "Splish" and "Splosh"?'

'Nah, they're a bit sissy. Let's have something a bit tougher for a change. How about "Rumble" and "Roar"?'

'Oh, I know; here's a good one ... "Gunpowder", "Treason" and "Plot".'

'That's three; we only need two.'

'Oh, right. I hadn't thought of that; although it might be handy to have a spare.'

The rest of the Tax-Taker-Backer-Gang continued watching Oxo's squadron until they disappeared round an outcrop of rock on America-South. As the last flicker of their white wings faded from view, Zatt, Elli, Granddad and Og had to wipe tears from their eyes, Ovi felt the need to blow his nose, Hopi and Wishi drooped their ears and horns, Poob and Tumt shared a 'this-is-a-really-sad-moment' look and squeezed each other's front claws; and Gusto let-go a forlorn fart which sounded like a bagpipe playing a dirge.

The Moment of Departure was finally upon them. The remaining gang members moved forward and took up position before the Taxman's "throne"; Hopi, Wishi, Poob and Tumt stood in a row at the back with Granddad, Og, Elli, Ovi, Gusto and Zatt in front of them. Elli and Zatt then stepped forward to deliver their prepared "farewell" speeches.

Zatt was just about to speak when the Taxman clapped his hands together loudly and stood up.

'*Right!* That's that then!' He leapt off his throne and began walking away, rubbing his hands eagerly like someone keen to be getting on with something. '*Oh, Her-rrr-ma-aaa-an!*'

'*Hold on a moment Taxman!*' exclaimed Elli. 'I thought it was *us* who was doing the leaving?'

'*You're* not supposed to leave,' protested Zatt. '*We are!* I've prepared a big speech and everything.'

The Taxman didn't bother to turn round; instead he called back over his shoulder.

'You lot can do whatever you like. You've had my permission to leave for several days now. As for me; I'm off. *Oh, Her-rrr-rrr-ma-aaa-an!*'

With a huge '*SPLASH*' and a loud '*SWOO-OOO-OSH!*', Herman emerged from the baby Atlantic where he'd been resting.

'Ah, there you are Herman. Are you ready?'

'*Wh-o-o-o-o-o-o-o-o-oh!*' ('As ready as you are Boss.') '*Wh-o-o-o-o-o-o-o-o-oh!*' ('Where are we going, incidentally?')

The Taxman led Herman away. He was walking so fast; his voice was already becoming faint.

'What do you know of "intergalactic travel" Herman?'

'*Wh-o-o-o-o-o-o-o-o-oh!*' ('Not a lot, I'm afraid Boss') '*Wh-o-o-o-o-o-o-o-o-o-o-o-o-o-o-o-o-o-oh!*' ('I think you're going to have to enlighten me.')

'*Whoa! Whoa! Hold it! Hold it! Hold it!*'

Leaving the others behind, Elli ran after the Taxman who paused and turned to look back at him with a fierce 'what-is-it?-can't-you-see-I'm-busy?' glare.

'You can't just, well – *er* – "*GO*" like that Taxman!'

'Why not? I can do what I like. I'm the Taxman.'

The Taxman's eyes narrowed.

'You are, of course, welcome to join me Elli … or Zatt? … or Ovi? … or any of you? I can guarantee it'll be a blast!'

Elli hesitated. He stared at the Taxman and blinked. Then he looked back at Ovi and the others.

'Just think of it Elli; you and me and Herman here; developing trade routes, new sources of tax … making lots and lots, and *lots*, of "money"!'

'Elli?'

Zatt took a step toward her brother and held out her hand.

'Where are you going Elli?'

Ovi also moved forward to stand by Zatt's side.

Elli hesitated and looked back over his shoulder; then he took a few more steps toward the Taxman.

'You know something Taxman? I think I just might— '

At that moment, Ovi's belly gave a low rumble which was followed by two short-but-very-loud farts from Gusto.

'You know Mister Taxman … I think I just might— '

Elli looked round once more at his assembled family and friends, then returned his gaze to the Taxman.

' —give it a miss this time. I'm going to stay here where I belong … but thanks anyway for the offer.'

'*YEAH!*' cried Gusto. '*Right on* – burp – *little buddy!*'

Decision made, Elli ran back to his family.

The Taxman scoffed led Herman away.

'As I was saying, Herman. I think it's time we looked to the stars for more revenue.'

'*Wh-o-o-o-oh!*' ('Really?') '*Wh-o-o-o-o-o-o-o-o-o-oh!*' ('How will we go about doing that, Boss?')

'Let's head for the other side of Africa—you know, where that river the Nile is. I have an idea for a stairway to the stars that I want you to build for me. It's called a "pyramid".'

'*Wh-o-o-o-o-o-o-o-o-oh!*' ('Right you are Boss.')

Just then, Herman's shell wobbled and some faint voices could be heard from deep within.

'Cur-r-r-r-r-se you Dr-r-r-r-r-ake! You'r-r-r-r-r-re hogging the fi-r-r-r-r-re place again.' 'Yeah, move over-r-r-r-r, will'ya! Me and Gr-r-r-r-r-enville ar-r-r-r-r-e fr-r-r-r-r-eezing!'

'*WH-O-O-O-O-O-O-OH!*' ('Quiet in the house!')

Elli, Ovi and Zatt exchanged 'what-are-we-waiting-for?' glances.

'Come on everybody,' cried Elli. '*Let's go home!*'

Within moments the Tax-Taker-Backer-Gang were on their way. Granddad and Og were snuggled-up on Hopi's head while Zatt and Gusto were together on Wishi's; Elli was riding on Poob's head and Ovi was on Tumt's. They had barely gotten going when Elli suddenly thought of something. He moved Poob over beside Hopi, cupped his hand to his mouth and shouted at the top of his voice up to his father and 'soon-to-be' mum-in-law.

'*HEY DAD! OG! Can you hear me?*'

Granddad and Og appeared over the side of Hopi's head, peering down at Elli with questioning expressions.

'*I've just thought of something!*' he shouted. '*When we get back home, how are you going to explain things to The Great Ug? He still thinks Og is one of his wives!*'

Granddad smiled at Og then called out his reply.

'Have no fear my son—no, never, never, never!
For I always know how to handle ... Clever Trevor!'

'Oh Ted, you can be so wonderful sometimes!' Og playfully tweaked his cheek. 'I used to say to myself, "Like father, like son", but now I know what I *should* be saying is, "Like son ... *love* father"!'

The first thing Elli and Zatt did when they got home was start work on their "boat" designs. Zatt made a fresh batch of paper and dried tyrannosaurus poo sticks which gave them the tools they needed, and within days they had both finished their plans. Elli had come up with a "rowing boat" idea, including: a pointed prow, a rudder for steering, two long wooden oars and a pair of rowlocks, futtocks and a bilge; whereas Zatt had arrived at a fundamentally different concept which she'd dubbed a "ship" complete with a bridge, poop deck, propellers and a funnel.

The two drawings placed side by side would, of course, be instantly recognisable to any modern-day reader. However, as the two 'inventors' lowered their paper blotches to view their respective model prototypes "in action" it quickly became clear that a lot more work was still needed.

Ovi and Gusto were both in the wadi and neither was making much progress, apart from getting *very* wet. Ovi had the "boat" strapped to his back with the pointed prow over his head as if he was wearing a cloak with a hood. He was using the oars like supports and was attempting to cross the wadi by walking. On the positive side, the rudder *was* in the water, but instead of helping him steer, it kept catching the oars, causing him to fall flat on his face with a '*Splosh!*'

Meanwhile, Gusto was also 'wearing' his "ship", but upside-down, because he'd gotten his head stuck in the funnel. As a result, he couldn't see where he was going and was forever tripping over Ovi's "boat".

THE END

POSTSCRIPT

It occurred to me, Dear Reader, that you may be interested to know how things went after God's Crown broke asunder and became fragmented into eight separate "continents".

The new 'world order' initially created problems for the tyrannosauruses, especially the newly formed "oceans" because, unlike their descendants (modern-day dogs), they couldn't swim. This meant that the separate groups of tyrannosauruses on each 'continent' developed different cultural habits, particularly when it came to ballroom dancing. In both Europe and America-North, for instance, the main dance to emerge was a blend of the Foxtrot and the Fandango; whereas in Africa and Asia, by far the most popular dance was one more akin to the Rhumba with just a hint of Punk. (Something often omitted from modern-day histories of the dance, incidentally, is that for a whole epoch a land bridge survived between America-South and Antarctica, enabling those on the two continents to hold annual Bossa Nova competitions.)

'What about the ostrich-emu-lators?' I hear you ask. 'What became of them?'

Well, Dear Reader, latest research suggests that while the tyrannosauruses were working on their Latin rhythms, these curious creatures began to display the kind of behaviour that would eventually lead to their subsequent evolutionary form. They started using their long, snake-like necks to forage for food while allowing their bodies to take it easy with their feet up, gently tapping to the catchy beat. As their bodies became less and less active, and their long necks took over the chore of foraging for food, it wasn't long (little over an era, in fact) before they lost their bodies entirely. They ceased having "snake-like necks" and were now simply "snakes" instead. Once they were without their legs, of course, they also became totally incapable of any type of dancing which is why still to this very day snakes spend most of their time slithering about looking mopey.

As for the Tax-Taker-Backer-Gang, they all stayed firm friends and made a point of meeting up every once in a while.

This was given extra impetus when, barely a year after the great 'continental divide', Poob and Tumt had their first clutch of babies – twin boys and a girl – and decided to ask their fellow gang members to name them.

The results of the exercise were to put it mildly "mixed"; there was no shortage of suggestions (indeed, there were so many Zatt didn't have enough 'paper' to capture them all); but there was a complete shortage of agreement on which names to choose.

Elli was vehement that "Minim" and "Maxim" for the twins and "Optim" for their sister was the way forward; Zatt felt equally strongly that "Opprobri" and "Pandemoni" were best for the boys with either "Euphoni" or "Harmoni" for the daughter; while Ovi was emphatic that the boys should be called "Y" and "G" with the girl being named "Pl".

Hopi, meanwhile, wouldn't budge from his suggestion that the boys should be "Equilibri" and "Disequilibri" with the name "Continu" for the girl (Wishi, incidentally, pronounced them "Oiquoiloibroi", "Doisoiquoiloibroi" and "Cointoinoi" respectively which, interestingly, Tumt much preferred).

Granddad and Og were both adamant that their suggestions were the best – "Planetari" and "Aquari" for the boys plus "Empori" for the girl. Gusto also felt strongly about his suggestions, but nobody could hear them over the noise of his prolific farting which had been brought on by his gorging of the various dainties on offer.

The arguing became more and more heated until Wishi eventually intervened with a loud 'clackety-clack' of his talons.

"Oi Loike Oixoi's soiggoistioin; Oi thoink thoi goirl should boi coilled "Cois"'

'Ach Nein-nein-nein; Ich bin nicht liking-k diese idea at alle! Ich nicht vant to be calling-k meine daughter "Kiss"!'

'*Noi!* Not "Cois" Poib … roimoimboir oit's Oixoi's oidoi … souy oit boikwoirds!'

'Vass … "Sick"?'

'Oilmoist! Noiw oidd yoir foimoiloiy noime'

'Vass … "Sick – Um"'

'Boikwoirds!'

'Vass … "Mu – Sick"'

Oxo started jumping up-and-down excitedly.

'*Sey-sey-sey!* Ouy tiddog booP! "Cis–Um"!'

Poob glanced at Tumt and they both looked equally flummoxed.

'It's "*Music*" Poob!' cried Elli, having what would epochs later be called a "light-bulb moment". '"Sick – Um" backwards is "Mu-sic"; and I for one think it's that's the best idea we've heard yet!'

Elli picked up his new bow (as a safety measure to prevent any more accidents with "arrows", he'd added a few more strings which, by sheer accident, gave it a rather pleasant range of notes for him to play). He then nodded to Poob who started tapping a catchy rhythm with his front claws on a handy bongo-bush.

'Listen everybody! This is a little number Poob has come up with. What gave you the idea Poob?'

'Ich bin vanting-k something-k zu remember how Tumt und Ich uns zuerst trafen—how-you-say … ' he looked lovingly into Tumt's eyes as she, in turn, picked up the rhythm with a pair of dried breakfast berry fruits which were a precursor of modern-day maracas. ' … our very first effer meeting-k.'

Elli began to strum and announced the name of the song.

'OK everyone; this is called "Concrete and Clay"! Now I want you all to join in on the chorus.'

They were all tapping their feet by now; and Elli was just about to move it up a gear—when Ovi cut in.

'I know what "clay" is Elli—it's "goo"; but what's "concrete"?'

'Oh, you know Ovi; it's that stuff I'm using on my new "super-duper wall"—the one with *a door!*'

Distraction dealt with, the rhythm could really take off. Hopi took over the bongo-bush to allow Poob get the dancing started and Wishi joined-in on a nearby drum-kit tree. Tumt then handed Hopi the maracas which allowed her to join her husband. Following the Ums' lead, Zatt grabbed Gusto and Og grabbed Granddad. Not having anyone to dance with, Ovi was about to slink off sulkily; but just then, his and Elli's wives came down the path doing a conga to the music with all their kids in a line behind, including Zatt's children who were covered in blue feathers and hopping on one leg.

Elli let rip with a fantastic bow solo (he'd secretly been practising); and then—with Poob taking the lead and Ovi, Hopi and Wishi doing the backing vocals … they were off.

You to me
Are sweet as roses in the morning

You to me
Are soft as summer rain at dawn, in love we share
That something rare

The sidewalks in the street
The concrete and the clay beneath my feet
Begins to crumble
But love will never die
Because we'll see the mountains tumble
Before we say goodbye
My love and I will be
In love eternally
That's the way
Mmm, that's the way it's meant to be

All around
I see the purple shades of evening
And on the ground
The shadows fall and once again you're in my arms
So tenderly

The sidewalks in the street
The concrete and the clay beneath my feet
Begins to crumble
But love will never die
Because we'll see the mountains tumble
Before we say goodbye
My love and I will be
In love eternally
That's the way
Mmm, that's the way it's meant to be

Printed in Great Britain
by Amazon